"YOU NEEDN'T GUARD ME."

Josephine wished J.D. wouldn't stand so close to her. She would have taken a few steps backward, but if she did, she'd feel the stab of thorns from a hawthorn bush. "I'm capable of fending off a stolen impropriety."

"Stolen improprieties?" J.D. returned, and she could have sworn he gave her a lopsided smile at her expense.

"You know perfectly well what I mean."

"Yes. I think I do." His face inched closer. Josephine's breath hitched in her throat. "But you're not fast enough to get out of my way should I decide to steal an impropriety from you."

"I wish—"

But he cut off her thought of "I wish you wouldn't say that" with his velvet-warm mouth covering hers in a slow, exploring kiss. Her knees trembling, she felt like a silly girl. She was too mature for this . . . this folly. Too wise to succumb to him. But his lips were more persuasive than she cared to admit. A far-off thought bobbed to the surface of her mind.

It would take more than a bash with a parasol to thwart J.D. McCall.

Worse yet, had she been holding one, she wouldn't have used it.

Praise for
STEF ANN HOLM
and Her Suspense-Filled
Tale of Love
PORTRAITS

"The last chapter gave me a tear-in-the-eye. The epilogue finished me off. Good thing I was alone."
—Merry Cutler, Annie's Book Stop

"My favorite author has come through with another 'keeper' book!"
—Roberta Kochinski, Bobbi's Books

"Can this impossible match ever work? Your heart knows it must in the end. This is a love story, but your mind keeps wanting to sneak a peek to find out how! Stef Ann Holm does it again! WOW!!"
—Mary Joy, Books to Enjoy

"One of the most powerful stories I have read in a long time. I wept and smiled as I read this. Wyatt and Leah deserved a happy end and I stayed up all night to make sure they had it!"
—Sharon Kosick, Annie's Book Stop

"*Portraits* is a warm and wonderful book. Leah and Wyatt stepped right off the page and into my heart! I laughed and I cried and I loved this book."
—Kim Ver Hage, Reading Books

"Stef Ann Holm's depth of character study is simply magnificent. I grew to love the residents of Eternity, Colorado. This is a love story that will make you laugh and make you cry. It deals with emotions, the power of forgiveness and the human spirit. I loved it."
—Suzanne Coleburn, Belles & Beaux of Romance

Books by Stef Ann Holm

Portraits
Crossings
Weeping Angel
Snowbird
King of the Pirates
Liberty Rose
Seasons of Gold
Forget Me Not

Published by POCKET BOOKS

STEF ANN HOLM

FORGET ME NOT

POCKET BOOKS

New York   London   Toronto   Sydney   Tokyo   Singapore

This book is a work of fiction. Names, characters, places and incidents are products of the author's imagination or are used fictitiously. Any resemblance to actual events or locales or persons, living or dead, is entirely coincidental.

An *Original* Publication of POCKET BOOKS

POCKET BOOKS, a division of Simon & Schuster Inc.
1230 Avenue of the Americas, New York, NY 10020

Copyright © 1997 by Stef Ann Holm

ISBN: 0-671-00204-X

First Pocket Books printing May 1997

10 9 8 7 6 5 4 3 2 1

POCKET and colophon are registered trademarks of Simon & Schuster Inc.

Cover art by Kam Mak

Printed in the U.S.A.

For Rose Gonzales,
friend and teacher,
an honest-to-goodness cowgirl
living the true spirit
of the American West

FORGET ME NOT

CHAPTER

→ 1 ←

Everything that Josephine Whittaker owned was packed in the valise at her feet. As she stood on the hard earth platform, watching the Union Pacific No. 35 gain speed out of the ramshackle station, she had the strongest urge to chase after the hissing engine and its cramped string of cars and declare she'd changed her mind. But the notion to flee was a thought too late.

She turned her gaze toward the rutted street empty of a single carriage, not daring to step outside the crudely constructed fence that separated her from the Wyoming Territory town of Sienna. The pungent smell of cow dung permeated the air, and she glanced at a bawling group of the large animals crammed together in a crowded wooden pen next to the depot. Rickety buckboards drove past with rough-hewn men at the reins. A wind-tattered flag hung limply from a pole in front of a saloon called Walkingbars. Though the sun was high and full, the scenery was dull and gray.

The city resembled nothing from the grandiose descriptions she'd read in the Beadle's dime novel. That famed Sienna had elegant red brick hotels—some four stories tall—and boasted numerous fine

1

restaurants, even an opera house touting an extravagant playbill. Arnica Street had been the rendezvous place for Pearl Larimer and Rawhide Abilene, the fated lovers in the Beadle's Issue No. 639, *Rawhide's Wild Tales of Revenge in Sienna*. The couple had stayed at the Line House Hotel and dined at the Bar Grub restaurant, both of which had been—despite their less-than-affluent names—heralded as the finest establishments between San Francisco and Chicago.

From the train station, Josephine could see neither the restaurant nor the hotel, much less a brick building. The structures that greeted her were built out of wood, and not a one over two stories tall. It would seem the book's author had taken some creative liberties.

Josephine worried the decorative collar button at her throat with gloved fingers. The daring prospect of living in the wide-open West she'd read about had given her the strength she'd needed to leave New York. Thus far, she hadn't been disappointed. The train ride—though she'd suffered indignities—had been worth the discomfort as soon as she'd gotten her first glimpse of the Wyoming Territory. As the train had clacked beyond the jagged mountains, the dazzling waterfalls, and the spectacular gorges, chugging headlong into the open terrain, a host of prairie dogs had stood in welcome. Meadowlarks sprang from the newly budding trees, and herds of white-faced cattle had run whenever the train sped by.

Sienna was to be the best of all. A town that lived up to its pretty-sounding name and fictitious allure. This was to have been where she would start over. Where she would secure her first employment position. Though she'd been raised in an affluent family and never had to work a day in her life, she'd made a list of all her attributes on the tablet in her calf pocket book. The checklist was ready and waiting for her to read to the glamorous owner of the Line House, who would be aptly impressed and hire her on the spot. Because Josephine Whittaker was willing to do as none of her female peers had ever done before her: travel to the West and seek her freedom.

Out here, she was no longer an extension of the gilded home that belonged to her husband. She wouldn't have to be under the gaze of watchful servants or have to acknowledge the perpetually renewed stack of cards and invitations on the hall table.

When she'd married, she'd been forced to bury her aspirations of spontaneity and daring beneath her husband's sudden single-mindedness. Being Hugh's wife had sucked her confidence and any hope of fledgling independence away from her. She'd lived with that grim truth for six years as a model of ladylike repression. But that was before she'd drawn a different conclusion from her wedding vows. *Thou shalt not be unfaithful—to thyself.* She realized she had to leave if she wanted to keep her dignity. So with the well-worn and reread copy of the Beadle's novel in her handbag, with its artist's rendition of a charming western city sketched across its cover, she'd decided on Sienna.

Giving the watering-hole town a grimace, Josephine picked up her wicker valise and decided to begin her new life in San Francisco instead.

She made an about-face and walked to the depot house. The door didn't readily open, and she gave it a slight shove with her elbow. The interior was poorly illuminated by a small rectangular window covered with a rotten roller shade. Furnishings were rudimentary. A single corner desk with pigeonholes and only one bench for passengers to sit. She recognized the elderly man who rose to his feet, hooked a pair of spectacles behind his ears, and squinted at her.

"How may I help you, ma'am?"

"You aided me from the train that just came in, but

it seems I've gotten off at the wrong stop. I'd like to purchase another ticket. To San Francisco. What is the departure schedule?"

"Thursdays."

Today was Thursday. Thank goodness she wouldn't have to spend the night here. She set her valise on the bench. "How much is the ticket?"

"Eight dollars."

Josephine nodded but didn't open her purse. She wasn't so ignorant as to keep all her cash in her handbag. She'd read enough of the Beadle's stories to know that ladies' purses and men's wallets were what robbers absconded with during a train holdup. She was thankful she hadn't encountered any. But just the same, she was glad she'd hidden the majority of her money in her silk underdrawers, safely tucked at the bottom of her valise. All she carried in the way of money in her handbag were some small coins so that she could purchase those open-to-suspicion meals served at the whistle-stops.

With her fingers on the luggage clasp, she asked, "What time does the train depart?"

"Two fifty-three," he replied.

Josephine straightened and lifted the lid to her valise at the same time as she faced off with the depot manager. "Two fifty-three? Why, I just disembarked from the two fifty-three train."

"Yes, ma'am. The Number Thirty-five is the connection to San Francisco. It only passes through here once a week."

Josephine lowered her gaze, letting out a shaky breath of disappointment, only to have it solidify in her throat as she stared into the opened valise.

This wasn't her luggage!

There had to be a mistake. She wasn't seeing clearly. Closing her eyes for a few seconds to clear her vision, she reopened them and stared hard at the clothing. The garments still didn't belong to her. In disbelief, she rummaged through the layers of drab

4

cotton ladies' clothes, searching for silk underdrawers that had more than five hundred dollars hidden in them. She could find only muslin pantalets with plain eyelet trim on the hems. A full-blown panic sprang to life in her breast; her heartbeat quickened its rhythm.

"Is there a problem, ma'am?"

Josephine snapped her chin up. "You have to stop the train. My valise has been stolen!"

"McCall, you've got some nerve shoving demands down my throat," Sheriff Charlie Tuttle challenged while tilting on the back legs of his chair after hoisting one booted foot onto the top of his paper-scattered desk.

J.D. McCall paced with agitation in front of the lawman, absently rubbing his fingertips across his unshaven jaw. Pausing to point, he cautioned, "You should be damn glad it's only words I'm shoving down your throat, Tuttle." Absently, he gazed at his raised hand. Its swollen back had two long, deep scratches from busting through bush in search of a cow. Another cut ran the length of his thumb—a heifer had kicked him when he was milking her out after her calf had died. His palm was marked with three deep holes from slivers that he'd picked up trying to remove the bars from the door to the cinder-block shed when he'd been in a hurry to let in an angry cow. J.D. didn't bother to assess his right hand, which was throbbing as if he'd punched a block of rock.

He could use a hot bath, a good meal, and several hours of uninterrupted sleep. But that wasn't to be during calving. His life was organized entirely around the instincts and needs of his cows. Though the majority of cows calved just fine by themselves, on any given day a couple of dozen needed attention. J.D. enlisted the help of every available man he had to keep losses at a minimum. But he was short a pair, no thanks to Tuttle.

"Peavy told me you bagged two of my hands last night," J.D. said, impatient to be on his way. "I want them out."

"I arrested them with just cause." Tuttle gave J.D. a hard-set frown. "Did Peavy tell you that Rio bought himself a new rope, and in order to stretch it he was roping posts and making his horse pull it to get the kinks out? Whether or not it was intentional, the kid lassoed a big-wig cattle buyer up from Texas who was none too happy to find himself sitting on his cheeks in the street right there in front of Walkingbars. I had to throw Rio in the cell for assault and battery."

"Hell, Tuttle," J.D. scoffed. "You didn't have to keep him overnight. I needed Rio first thing this morning to feed and water the horses. That's what I pay him for."

J.D. moved to the door with a barred window that separated the sheriff's front office from the jail cells. Testing the knob, he found it wouldn't turn. "Unlock the damn door."

"Not just yet."

Tuttle seemed dead set on sparring with him, and J.D. wasn't in the mood. His hands ached to grip anything, mostly Tuttle's throat. J.D. cued into the fact that the sheriff was holding out for something. This wasn't the first time he and Tuttle had gone rounds over the incarceration of one of J.D.'s cowboys. "What's it going to cost me?"

The sheriff shrugged without mentioning a dollar amount. "That itinerant cook you hired . . . Mr. Pete Denby." Tuttle steepled his fingertips together, his tone growing fastidious. "He's a mean hombre when he's drunk. He spurred his horse up and down Arnica, popping his pistol while swilling lager. Shattered the front window of the merc and just about scared Zev out of his hide. When I caught up with that cook, he jumped off that piebald of his and took a swing at me." Tuttle punctuated evenly. "I will not be held accountable for the lump on the side of his head. My fist had a mind of its own."

"What's it going to cost me?" J.D. repeated. "With this drought, I've got to be moving cattle in less than a week. I need Denby and Rio."

Flawed as the two men were, J.D. couldn't afford to be without them. His longtime cook, Luis, was killed in an accident with a bull some weeks ago. It had taken that long to get a relief man for the kitchen. Initially, no one answered J.D.'s post on the mercantile's wallboard, as all the good chuck-wagon cooks had been hired out as far back as February. When Pete Denby showed up at the ranch yesterday and claimed he was the best cook that ever threw dishwater under a chuck wagon, J.D. couldn't see any way in disputing that without giving Denby a try. So he'd taken him on, mindless of the reservations he had. Everybody in the outfit had been eating creamed corn on toast and bad Arbuckle's belly wash compliments of Boots, and J.D. had been looking forward to a thick fried steak last night for supper. Only Denby never showed.

As if Denby wasn't his only problem, there was Rio Cibolo, his eighteen-year-old, full-of-guts-and-glory wrangler. Rio was hell-bent on infamy with his rope. The kid could catch anything that moved, and more often than not he practiced on live subjects. J.D. doubted the rope throw was unintentional. Rio liked to get people's dander up and joke about it.

After reaching inside his vest pocket for his wallet, J.D. tossed a bill onto Tuttle's desk. "That ought to cover things."

"You can have the kid, but the cook stays." Tuttle lowered his heel, took the money, and deposited it into a cash box. "Drunk and disorderly, public intoxication, defacing property. That's a loaded offense, and I'm not all that convinced Denby's not wanted elsewhere."

J.D.'s fingers balled into aching fists. "I paid Pete Denby his wages for a month just to hold him!"

"That's your hard luck, McCall. Denby stays for five days until I get a reply from a Cheyenne judge."

Sheriff Tuttle got up, slipped his hand into his trouser pocket, and came up with a small ring of keys. Before he could open the door leading to the cells, the street entrance was filled with a woman who, without any preliminaries, uttered frantically, "I've been robbed!"

J.D. was about to jump all over Tuttle's back when his focus veered toward the feminine voice. The lady looked so out of place framed inside the raw-wood doorjamb, wearing her eastern window-dressing clothes, that J.D. couldn't help staring. It wasn't every day a woman laced up like that came into Sienna. From head to toe, she was decked out in pleats, sashes, laces, flounces, and straw flowers. The colors were springlike, soft shades of rose and a blue likened to the early-blooming forget-me-nots that grew alongside Buffalo Creek.

She wasn't classically beautiful, but her face was pretty enough to keep his gaze lingering. Thick, cinnamon-colored hair was braided behind her ears, the coils twisted and pinned upward beneath a sassy-looking hat sporting dyed plumes. The shape of her mouth was wide, and her cheeks were structured high with a light dusting of cosmetic color. Her eyes were an amber hue, just like the shimmer of bourbon splashed into a sunlit tumbler. She had a pampered figure, the kind that said she wouldn't last five minutes out-of-doors doing anything more than taking a leisurely stroll.

"Robbed?" Tuttle said, the keys jingling in his fingers. "Where?"

"On the train." Her voice held a faint tremor, as though she were in serious trouble.

"The Number Thirty-five? Why didn't old man Vernier come tell me?" The keys were put back in

Tuttle's pocket, and he grabbed a rifle from the rack. "How many gunmen were there, ma'am?"

"None."

Tuttle froze. "But you said you were robbed."

"I was."

"How so?"

She answered quickly and with a note of alarm. "I've gone over the course of events from here back to Laramie, and I think I know what happened. After we left the last tank tower, we came upon a herd of buffalo. The train stopped suddenly so that those gentlemen wishing to shoot could do so. But with the screeching halt, floor luggage slid beneath everyone's seat. In the confusion, someone handed me what I thought to be my valise, only it turns out that it wasn't."

"Then you weren't exactly robbed."

"My valise had five hundred dollars in it. This valise does not." She motioned to the wicker case in her grasp. "For all intents and purposes, I *was* robbed," she insisted. "You have to telegraph the next depot and tell them to search the train for my luggage. A terrible error has been made."

"Ma'am, for the next seventy-five miles the rail stations are nothing but cow pastures without a telegraph office to be had. Could be whoever gets off at one of them has your case. There's no way for me to track down each individual. Folks are too spread out in this country."

A strangled cry broke from her throat. "But my five hundred dollars!"

"The best I can do is wire the first town over, which is Tipton," Tuttle said while replacing the rifle, "and see if we can get this cleared up."

"What am I going to do in the meantime? I have no more than fifty cents to my name . . . no clothes . . . no . . . nothing." She rapidly blinked, clearly on the verge of spilling tears.

J.D. folded his arms across his chest and shifted his

weight. Crying women had their hearts in the wrong place. A true survivor wouldn't be weeping over her situation, she'd be cursing it. J.D. could see that this one was about as helpless as they came. He didn't have a high tolerance for women who had no guts.

"Tuttle, at least unlock Rio so I can get out of here with one man," J.D. said, resigned to the deal.

The woman looked at him for the first time, her eyes widening. He knew he presented a sight. A week-old beard, muck on his Levi's up to his knees, dried blood on the sleeves and edges of his leather duster.

He took her stare for what it was: mortified curiosity. It wasn't the first time he'd been given the up-and-down from some gal. He was taller than most cowboys, and a little too long-legged astride a saddle to be easy on his horses. Most of his punchers were medium-sized; but then again, most of his punchers had come from generations of ranchers. J.D. came from a Mississippi cotton plantation.

"Excuse me a minute, ma'am," Tuttle said, then went to collect Rio.

After the sheriff's departure, a silence dropped on the room as weighted as a bale of hay. The woman turned away, keeping her eyes downcast. If J.D. had been more like some of the good-natured men working for him, he would have offered her his sympathies. But he guessed there were times when he was too much of a son-of-a-bitch, just like Boots.

A moment later, Rio Cibolo appeared, broadly grinning like a jackass coming out of the mess tent after eating a batch of the cook's pumpkin pies. "Hey, boss."

Even at a young age, it was clear Rio was destined to be a lady's man. He was lean, quick, and wiry, with a mane of sun-bleached blond hair, soft mustache, and blue eyes. Though he could be trouble, he was intensely loyal to the outfit and would herd the horses through hell and back and never complain. Knowing this, J.D. never went too hard on him. But that didn't ease the annoyance he was feeling right now.

"You cost me good, kid. I ought to start calling you George again." J.D. rearranged the angle of his low-crowned hat with his bruised hand.

Rio's eyes widened as his gaze shot from J.D. to the woman. "I expect you know how I feel about that."

J.D. did. Rio's real name was George Ikard, but he'd taken to calling himself Rio Cibolo as of winter because he'd claimed a wrangler bound on infamy ought not be saddled with the name George.

"I expect I do," J.D. replied. "Keep your rope off of two-legged animals and stick to them that have four, and I'll forget all about George."

"Sure, boss."

"Tuttle, you tell Denby I'll be back in five days for him." Then J.D. added with caution, "And for your sake, he better damn well be here."

The sheriff waved him off. "Rio, your horse is down at the livery, along with your rope. I catch you swinging that lariat on my streets, you'll be looking through bars again."

Rio disregarded the warning. He was too busy gawking at the lady. Tipping his hat, he offered, "How do, ma'am? Welcome to Sienna."

"Thank you," she replied softly.

"It's not often we're allowed the privilege of such a fine-looking woman in our town," Rio said.

J.D. walked past Rio, went out the door, and called over his shoulder, "If you've got nothing to do but stand around, I reckon you'll be going up the trail to the Shaw outfit to earn your keep."

Every cowboy from here to the territorial borders knew that the Shaw outfit was a tough, gun-toting bunch of drunks. Leaving the sheriff's office, J.D. let Rio ponder that thought.

Seconds later, the kid caught up to J.D., who was walking in a brisk stride. "Now, boss, you have to admit she was as pretty as a thirty-dollar pony."

"I didn't notice."

Rio's deep laughter implied he wasn't fully convinced of that.

"I'm an excellent hostess with impeccable etiquette and a flair for choosing the appropriate table service for the appropriate party. I know how a table should look when presented for breakfast, lunch, and dinner. Also, I'm highly qualified to supervise domestics in a large household." Josephine tried to sound as if she knew what she was doing, but she had no experience seeking employment.

The woman at the hotel counter stared at her as if Josephine were an oddity. A thickset bulldog with a smashed face sat next to the proprietress's skirt. She was certainly not the Adalyn Hart who ran the Line House in *Rawhide's Wild Tales of Revenge in Sienna*. This woman's name was Effie Grass.

Regrouping her rambling thoughts, Josephine hastily went on. "I have an eye for fashion and extensive knowledge in the harmony of colors in dress." Then, to send her point home, she declared, "Rich colors are for brunettes or dark hair; delicate colors are for light hair or blond complexions."

"You don't say?" Effie's blouse and skirt were sparrow brown. A poor match next to her salt-and-pepper coiffure of two braids pinned high on her crown.

At least Josephine had triggered Effie's interest, which had been bouncing back and forth between Josephine and the runny-nosed dog. She plunged on while she had the opening. "I'm a master at archery. I've held the position of Lady Paramount at the Manhattan Archery Club. I won the title in the Columbia round, successfully parlaying twenty-one out of twenty-four arrows in the bull's-eye mark."

"Hmm."

Josephine forced a smile on her lips. She'd gone from "You don't say?" to "Hmm." Not exactly encouraging. Perhaps she should have taken Sheriff Tuttle's offer of five dollars to see her through until he could contact the railroad. But it was a matter of principle for Josephine. For the first time in her life, she was on her own. Despite things being dire, she didn't want to spoil her independence with a handout. She just *had* to get a job in Sienna to tide her over. She was an educated woman with perfect decorum. Somebody would surely find her invaluable . . . at least for a week.

"Honey, that's awfully interesting, but I just can't use you." Reaching down, Effie patted the bulldog's flat head. He licked her hand with his drooling tongue.

Josephine took the defeat by swallowing the lump in her throat. She wasn't skilled at being aggressive. She had never had to be. Everything she'd ever wanted had always come to her because she'd had the money to buy it.

"Thank you just the same," she said quietly.

Josephine exited the Line House hotel's lobby, stepping outside and squinting her eyes against the late-afternoon sun. She'd already tried the Bar Grub eatery; she'd bypassed the livery and the Walkingbars saloon. She was in serious need of a job, but she wasn't cheap. She'd rather take the money from the sheriff before she dressed up like a floozy and served alcoholic refreshments to rowdy men.

Unbidden, the image of that man in the sheriff's office filled her head. He looked tough and hardened by a life on the range that seemed to demand a lot from a cowboy. She'd gleaned that much from the Beadle's. Men out West had to be as strong as leather. He certainly had been. The bulk of his power had been in his torso, where the muscles across his chest filled out the shoulders of his coat. Open to her view was his blue plaid vest and a pistol with a pearl-like handle which rode in a holster belt lashed around his hips. He was a brawny man, given to few words in a lady's company. Just like Rawhide Abilene. When he'd moved, the big spurs on his boots made a sound like tin bells.

Josephine carried on to her final destination: the general store. She looked down as she walked, noticing spears of grass had pushed up through the boardwalk. From the larger cracks, yellow-petaled flowers rose to bloom. In the city, the sidewalks were brick and unaccepting of nature's wildly sewn seeds. Here the slats of sagging wood buffered her heels and, in places, gave a slight bounce to her steps.

If only she hadn't left New York in such a hurry, none of this would have happened. After the Beauchamps' party, she'd hastily packed her valise rather than her heavy Gladstone trunk so that she could get away faster. If only she hadn't decided to travel in coach rather than first class. But she had had to economize her limited funds because she hadn't known what to expect by way of prices out West. In coach, Josephine had had to be in charge of her own luggage—a responsibility she'd never in her life had to contend with.

If Hugh could see her now, he'd have a riotous laugh at her expense. She hadn't come to hate him yet. Perhaps in time she would. For now, she could only look back with bitterness and resentment.

She'd been doomed the moment the ink from her signature had wetted the surface of the legal documents Hugh had gotten his lawyer to draw up. After that day, society had insulted and excluded her. The circles she had traveled in existed only in the margins of charmed little lives. Once she'd become an outcast, social pressures and prejudices had been inflicted on her. She'd suffered disgrace and, ultimately, exile. Which she'd accepted with a greater courage and compassion than her destroyers had flung at her.

It was horrible being talked about. However unfounded the charges against her, they were still charges of reprehensible behavior.

Josephine reached the store's door, where, just above, a placard had been hung and scribed: Zev Klauffman, Mercantilist. The picture window to her left had been boarded up, leaving her to wonder what disaster had befallen the glass. Letting herself inside, she gazed at the interior. The space was narrow with a wide aisle that ran from the front door to a rear exit. On the right side, six cast-iron stoves were lined up in a proud display. Behind them, shelves of spices, remedies, flatirons, kerosene lamps, and books. Opposite were barrels of crackers, barrels of undiscernible contents, boxes of shoes, a rack of hats—both men's and ladies'—shelves of folded clothing mostly of denim, and a tableful of various fabrics.

The aroma of coffee came to her. Her gaze traveled to the shelf, and she saw large manila bags. Arbuckle's was printed in bold letters across the front, beneath which was the picture of a flying angel in a long flowing gray skirt, around her neck a streaming red scarf.

"May I help you, ma'am?"

Josephine looked up at a man dressed in a frock coat with a neat black tie at his shirt collar. A white apron was fastened around his waist, and he held a feather duster.

"Yes, you may." She squared her shoulders for fortitude and went into her memorized list of qualities, trying to sound as impressive as possible. When she was finished, Mr. Klauffman merely looked at her with a wan smile.

"That's something," he said with brows raised. "But unfortunately, I don't have need of a clerk with your . . . background. Frankly, there isn't a single job in the whole town that needs those qualifications."

"Yes . . . I can see that," she mumbled, her hands clasped together so tightly her fingers hurt. Tears stung the back of her eyes, and she fought them. Humiliation seemed to be her shadow these days. She recoiled at the thought of returning to Sheriff Tuttle and asking him for the money. She just couldn't humble herself in such a way.

Josephine felt a wave of dizziness assail her. She faltered.

"Ma'am?" Mr. Klauffman came to her aid, putting his hand on her elbow to steady her. "Are you ill?"

"No . . . I'm just . . ." She was sick at heart. "I didn't eat on the train today. I suppose I'm a little weak."

"By all means, then, sit down." He ushered her to a stool and deposited her in front of the cracker barrel. "Would you like something to eat?"

"No. Just a glass of water, please," she said as she removed her gloves. A shaft of sunlight poured in from the smaller window on the door's right and caught the stones glistening on her fourth finger. Bright dots of reflected light showered the planked floor. Gazing at the ring, she didn't know why she hadn't taken it off in New York.

Zev Klauffman returned with a metal cup filled with water. "Here you are, miss."

She took the glass and sipped the cold water. The liquid cooled the heat on her cheeks. Lowering the glass, she said, "Mr. Klauffman, I'd like to sell you my ring. It's solid gold set with a flawless diamond and six emeralds." She held out her hand for him to inspect the piece of jewelry.

"Why, ma'am, um, Mrs.—"

"No, it's Miss," she quickly corrected. "Miss Josephine Whittaker." Hugh had been so flamboyant in his purchase of the ring, nobody would suspect it was a wedding setting.

"Why, Miss Whittaker, I couldn't possibly buy that."

"I'm not asking for its full value. One hundred dollars would suffice."

"One hundred dollars?" Mr. Klauffman's Adam's apple bobbed. "I couldn't even come close to reselling it for that."

"But it's worth one thousand dollars."

"Miss Whittaker, nobody in Sienna has that kind of money."

Josephine struggled hard against the tears she refused to let fall. "Are you married, Mr. Klauffman?"

"Yes, ma'am."

"Then you could give it to your wife."

"Where in God's green earth would she wear such a ring?"

"That's entirely up to her. You name your price, and it's yours."

Zev Klauffman shook his head. "I couldn't make you a fair offer."

"I understand that."

"The best I could do would be ten dollars. Now, Miss Whittaker, that would be like stealing it from you. I couldn't do that."

She wiggled the ring free and pressed it into his palm. "I'm sure your wife will be exuberant."

Josephine Whittaker left the mercantile ten dollars richer than when she went inside. She had enough money to get a room at the hotel and buy a meal at the Bar Grub. She spent a restless night, too upset to relax yet too physically fatigued to fight sleep. The next morning, she went to see Sheriff Tuttle, who informed her that her valise had not shown up in Tipton. From there, she went to the depot and asked Mr. Vernier if he could please telegraph the Union Pacific and put in a lost claims report for her.

For four days, Josephine paid visits twice daily to Sheriff Tuttle and Mr. Vernier. Each time, she was told her valise had not been returned. On the fifth day, she was nearly out of money.

Discouraged and desperate, on Tuesday she had no choice but to accept that her five hundred dollars and her handsome clothes were gone. The wardrobe in the luggage she'd ended up with was cut a size too small for her. She'd had to wash out her foulard suit once, its grosgrain underblouse and her intimate wear three times. Ironing the spring walking costume with all of its pleats and lapping flounces was impossible for her. She'd paid Effie Grass a whole dollar to press everything.

Earlier in the day, she'd requeried all those establishments she'd gone to before, hoping that one of them had had a change of heart and would give her the opportunity to prove herself. Mr. Vernier still didn't require an assistant at the rail office, nor did Sheriff Tuttle need her archery services. Effie Grass had remained adamant she had no positions available, and so had the postmistress and the man who ran the land office. And nobody at the half-dozen other businesses had had a sudden opening for someone with her talents.

Now, as she stood in front of Walkingbars, she listened to the tinkle of piano music. The saloon had no windows. The concentrated smell of stale liquor and rancid perfume spilled over and under the swinging doors.

A gnarl-toothed old cowboy approached her, spitting a foul juice in the street. "Hey, sugar darlin', come on inside with ol' True. I heared y'all've been lookin' for a job. Billy'll hire you."

"N-no, thank you."

Josephine quickly went on her way. How could she have thought even for a second that she could go inside? But a cold reality had finally set in. She had to have a job. *Any* job to get the money to buy a ticket to San Francisco. As it was, Thursday's train would be pulling out without her, leaving her hopelessly deserted.

Deep in thought, Josephine crossed the street and was almost hit by a fast-moving wagon drawn by a team of horses. Her heartbeat lurched, and her breath felt cut off. She barely got out of the way, turning her head as her pulse continued its dancing and she glanced at the man holding the reins. Her surprised gaze skimmed over his silhouette. She recognized him immediately as the one from Sheriff Tuttle's office the day she arrived in Sienna. His eyes momentarily locked on hers, and he appeared as if he wanted to say something, but she turned away before she could make any sense out of his expression or hear his words.

The rugged man unnerved her. She couldn't be sure why. Perhaps it was because she'd never encountered a man so . . . so larger-than-life off the pages of the dime novels.

Disconcerted, she managed to put the near-accident out of her head as she entered Zev Klauffman's mercantile.

"Miss Whittaker," he greeted in a friendly tone.

"Mr. Klauffman." She felt inside her handbag for the lawn handkerchief she normally kept butterscotch candies in. She'd been out of the treats for days. It was odd how even that little luxury was missed. Laying out the square of white on the counter, she showed Mr. Klauffman a pair of delicate gold-filigree earrings. She'd worn them on the train. "I'd like to sell these, please."

He sadly shook his head. "Now, Miss Whittaker, I just can't buy those from you. It's too much already that you just about gave me that ring. I'd rather give you a few dollars."

"No," she broke in. "I can't accept money from you that way." Lowering her gaze, she chewed the inside of her lip. "If you can't buy the earrings, then I want to work for you. I know what you said before, but perhaps you can reconsider. I could do whatever needs to be done. I'm sure I could manage the feather duster, and I could—"

"Miss Whittaker, I don't get much traffic through here this time of year with all the local boys on cattle drives. I barely have enough to do myself without going stir crazy."

She mutely nodded. "I understand."

But she didn't accept that understanding without

remorse. She milled around the merchandise tables, absently fingering the items while trying to think of what to do next. She was seventy-five miles from nowhere without a single prospect of getting even a few feet out of Sienna.

The bell above the store's door bounced against the jamb.

"Zev," came a man's booming voice. "I hope like hell you kept that notice for a cook I tacked up on the board a few weeks ago. Tuttle put his deputy and Pete Denby on the noon stage for Cheyenne. Goddamn," he swore harshly. "Said Denby had a warrant out on him, if you can believe that."

Josephine lifted her gaze from the sewing notions in the glass counter case.

"Well, J.D., Denby did have that look about him," Mr. Klauffman remarked.

The man called J.D. barely paid Josephine any regard as he stepped around her to stare at an almost bare space of wall behind Mr. Klauffman's counter. A few fliers and handbills were pinned up, and promotional literature for something called barbed wire from Washburn & Moen Co. of Worcester, Massachusetts. Straining to see, Josephine couldn't find any advertising copy about work for a cook.

"Where's my notice?"

Mr. Klauffman replied, "I took it down when you hired Denby."

"Dammit to hell, make up another one." J.D.'s voice was so inflamed and belligerent, Josephine started. "I need to be moving out the day after tomorrow if I want to keep my cattle alive, and I'll be damned if my outfit is eating Boots's slop for the next couple of weeks. I need to hire a cook right now."

Before Josephine could think, she blurted, "I'm a cook."

CHAPTER

→ 2 ←

J.D. McCall pinned Josephine to the spot with his piercing gaze. Up this close, she could see that his eyes were a clair-de-lune color, just like the pale, grayish-blue glaze on the Chinese porcelains she owned. Or, rather, used to own. His deep brown hair was very long—several inches past his wide shoulders—and had some wave to its length. She sensed he wasn't as old as the squint lines at the corners of his eyes and the short-bearded jaw made him appear to be.

"If you're a cook," he said, "I'm a preacher."

"But I am," she insisted. She couldn't lose this opportunity.

"She *is* a cook, J.D.," Mr. Klauffman jumped in. "She told me so." Then he cleared his throat, giving Josephine a hasty glance. "J.D., this is Miss Josephine Whittaker. Miss Whittaker, this is Mr. J.D. McCall."

Mr. McCall's sarcasm didn't fade. "Five days ago you were crying on Tuttle's doorstep. What are you still doing in Sienna?"

She found it surprising that he remembered her. But she wasn't in a big city anymore, where one person blended into the next on the crowded streets. Here, she unintentionally stood out among the meager inhabitants who moved with a slowness she hadn't been able to get used to after years of hustle and bustle.

Josephine didn't think Mr. J.D. McCall would feel sorry for her if he knew the dire truth of her situation, so she twisted it a little. *A lot.* "I've decided to stay for a while. I like it here."

"Your money didn't turn up, huh?"

Against her wishes, she felt her face hotly color. "No."

"You're stranded," he stated bluntly. "But it just so happens you're a cook."

"Yes." Her monotone answers would get her nowhere, but before she could recover enough from his astute declaration and list her attributes, his firm mouth broke into a smile.

To her utter chagrin, he laughed. At her. "I wouldn't have figured you for the type who could fix a meal for eighteen men with big appetites."

She felt as if he were baiting her, trapping her in her ignorance. With a sense of conviction she didn't know she could fake until now, she said in a purposeful tone, "I most definitely can plan a menu for eighteen." Then, to dramatize her declaration, she laid her palm on the top Bible of a stack on the table next to her. "I promise." And that was the God's truth. She could *plan* a menu. In fact, she had planned them for more than eighteen dinner guests. Only she hadn't prepared the meal. But that wasn't what she was attesting to.

"Get your hand off that book," J.D. said dryly. "I don't have any use for religious bull."

Her hand numbly slipped away.

"You don't have the stamina it takes to wrangle grub for men with the ferocious hunger of a wolf. That takes a lot of strength, know-how, and guts."

"I have guts," she prompted, though she was loath to speak a word that conjured the image of entrails rather than fearless daring. She racked her brain for an appropriate line from *Rawhide's Wild Tales of Revenge* she could use in her favor. Under the stress of pressure, she couldn't think swiftly enough.

"You have too much meat on you to tackle the job. I need someone who can lift a ten-pound sack of beans without falling apart at the seams."

His implication was horrifying. She'd never in all her life been told she had large proportions. She, like her lady friends in Manhattan, was considered quite in vogue with her voluptuous figure. It was offensive to be too thin on the bones; she'd never had that problem.

"I find your reference to my personal nature defamatory," she stated plainly, in disbelief that she had the backbone to stand up for herself. But if she didn't, he would think she was spineless, and he wanted someone plucky. "You know nothing of my character. I'm in fine physical form. On my behalf, I would say that I won the Manhattan archery title in the Columbia round after successfully parlaying twenty-one out of twenty-four arrows in the bull's-eye mark."

"I don't need someone to shoot the beef, just cook it."

"I can do so. Quite admirably," she added for good measure.

"You're a woman. And unmarried women on a ranch go against the grain and are nothing but a set of problems."

J.D.'s bluntness nettled. In New York, a future of economic security had required marriage for women. She'd thought—*hoped*—that out here her status wouldn't matter. But apparently conventional necessity knew no boundaries.

Mr. Klauffman remarked, "The Shaw outfit had itself a woman cook some time back."

"True. And that cook's duties weren't limited to the kitchen," J.D. countered dryly.

Josephine took brittle offense. Clenching her teeth,

she swallowed hard, trying not to reveal her outrage. She glared at him with reproachful eyes. "If I were of a mind to do more than cook, I would be at the Walkingbars saloon this very moment." On an impulse, she tacked on, "I was assured Billy would hire me on the spot."

She hoped that by announcing she was wanted elsewhere, he would give her more regard and not let her slip through his fingers.

J.D. McCall grew thoughtful. He stood very still, with his eyes narrowed in on her. The pent-up tension wound in his muscular body was enough to make her run, but she couldn't. He was her last hope.

"J.D., it's her or Boots," Mr. Klauffman said, coming to her aid once more.

From the display on Mr. McCall's face, she thought he was going to tell her to stop pretending to be something she wasn't. But he didn't. In his hard expression there was a flicker of indecisiveness, more than a little resentment, then a shade of resignation, but not without anger—which she couldn't be all that sure was directed on her rather than himself.

"Can you fix fried beef?"

"It's my specialty," she returned without blinking.

"All right, *cookie*. I'll give you the job. Only because there isn't another dough wrangler to be had." He turned toward Mr. Klauffman. "Zev, keep my notice on that board, and send anybody who answers it my way. Miss Whittaker's position is just a temporary one."

Which was exactly what Josephine had in mind. She didn't want to be stuck out at a ranch any more than Mr. J.D. McCall wanted her there.

"My wagon's out front." Spurs jingled as the tall cowboy shifted the position of his boots, transferring his weight from one lean leg to the other. "Load it up with the supplies she'll need. I'll be back in an hour."

Then J.D. McCall strode to the door and was gone

before the danger of the situation finally occurred to Josephine.

"I don't know if I did you a favor, Miss Whittaker, or delivered you to the devil's own," Mr. Klauffman murmured in the ensuing calm. "That J.D. McCall is just like his father. And Boots is a son-of-a . . . gun."

"You needn't worry about me, Mr. Klauffman." But Josephine was worried. She had the eerie feeling of having been pelted by a storm when there had been no gray clouds in the sky.

Despite the store being empty, Mr. Klauffman whispered, "I don't mean to pry, Miss Whittaker, you being a fine lady and all . . . but can you really cook?"

In an equally soft tone, she replied, "No. But I can read."

"Ma'am?"

"Could you loan me one of your cooking books?"

"Miss Whittaker, I most certainly could give one to you. Consider it going toward the ring."

"Thank you, Mr. Klauffman."

"I'll get started on that order."

She nodded, wishing she had a candy to suck on so she could think. Her gaze fell on the jar of round golden treats.

Mr. Klauffman apparently read her mind. "How about I throw in some butterscotch candies for you?"

"That would be nice." She would need them for fortitude.

An hour later, she rigidly stood in front of the general store waiting for Mr. J.D. McCall to return. Everything Josephine Whittaker owned was packed in the valise at her feet: a set of ladies' plain clothing that didn't fit her and a book of cooking recipes she didn't quite understand.

J.D. slid his glance to the woman beside him. After the way she'd gone on at the sheriff's office about her stolen valise, and when she'd talked up her qualifications to handle the cook's job, he figured her for a chatterbox. But she wasn't. She'd been real quiet ever since he picked her up at the mercantile. Maybe she was having doubts, just like him.

Miss Josephine Whittaker sat stiffly, her spine as straight as a branding iron handle. The confining style of her hair didn't allow any tendrils to escape and catch on the breeze. Her feet were crossed at the ankles of scuffed black shoes; her lace-gloved hands with the dirty tips were folded into a tight ball and rested on her lap. As rigid as she was, he could put his forefinger to her shoulder and probably knock her over without any effort.

Damn, but compassion had gotten in the way of his better judgment. Seeing her in the same suit she'd had on that day in Tuttle's office, only now looking worse for the wear, he'd taken pity on her. Under circumstances other than crucial, he never would have hired a woman, much less a lady. But they were in the third year of a desperate drought. The prior summer had been hot and dry, the rivers seemingly boiling mud. Hope for a wet winter had been dashed when they'd received no significant moisture, either by rain or by snow. A month ago, he'd had no choice but to cut his herd down to two-thirds its normal size so as not to damage the fragile land. What grass had sprouted was being grazed to the nub. If he wanted his cattle to survive, he'd have to move them to the spring range as soon as possible and chance that the mountains were lush.

He couldn't wait around for another cook to replace Denby. His stock would be dead by then. So he was just going to have to make do with who he had. Like Zev had said, it was either her or Boots. And the boys had threatened to up and quit if they had to face another plate of creamed corn on toast—though not a one of them spoke up in disfavor of the unpalatable dish, because Boots was likely to do something like spit in the skillet as retaliation.

J.D.'s gaze left Josephine for the rambling road. He

doubted she could cook a decent meal. But she was a female, and he assumed what she didn't know she could pick up on instinct alone. Whatever she put together had to be better than Boots's specialty.

Rather than dwell on Boots, J.D.'s thoughts moved to the surrounding terrain.

He owned twenty-nine thousand acres of range broken here and there by steep ridges and deep gulches. Sagebrush, ponderosa pine, and knotted cedar dotted the land. The McCall Cattle Company was pieced together from dozens of homesteads. As much as it bothered him, he'd profited from the despair of families seduced by their government into buying— homesteading—plots of land too small to support them. When the nesters called it quits, somebody had to buy them out. J.D. made fair offers, and slowly he'd acquired a respectably sized ranch.

When J.D. had come to Wyoming after the Civil War, he'd gone to work for a man named Dillard on Buffalo Creek. J.D. worked his way up from wrangler to foreman, but when Dillard died, he owed J.D. a couple years' back wages. J.D. could have moved on instead of staying those two years, but he'd had a roof over his head and three square meals a day, and he'd at last found something he enjoyed.

After Dillard's death, J.D. took out a lien and got the title to what would become the core parcel of the McCall Cattle Company. Through the years, he bought more cattle and more land, vowing to make himself a success Boots could be proud of. After all, he'd taken a bankrupt ranch and made it financially sound. But Boots had his own views of success, and J.D. should have known better than to try and impress him.

Even though Boots was his father, J.D. had never gotten along with him, and now he didn't even pretend to. Boots was an iron-rod individual, high-handed and presumptuous—the worst of which was always reserved for J.D. Boots was going to have a mouthful to say as soon as J.D. pulled into the yard with Miss Forget-Me-Not. And when the boys got a look at her, J.D. could guarantee she'd have no trouble keeping her wood box filled with fuel as they vied with each other to stand well in her favor. Therein would lie the heart of his problem.

The presence of a woman would more or less handicap the cowboys in their language. Salty tales would be watered down to nothing, and discussions of sexual experiences would have to be corked up tight. The boys would feel obligated to come in for chuck wearing clean pants and shirts. And should a creek be handy, their faces would be shining and their hair slicked down. Hats would have to come off during the meal. All this emphasis on proper appearances would make for poor digestion.

Steering the team up and over a ridge called the Point, J.D. made the descent toward the ranch on a trail scattered with pebbles. Almost everything he could see in the distance he could call home. The bunkhouse, barn, and horse corrals. The shingled roof of the house where he and Boots lived was on the far side of Buffalo Creek. Farther down the creek stood a cabin where One-Eyed Hazel lived. And up behind the house, toward the hogbacks on Sienna Butte, was the shimmering blue patch of the catch pond that provided them with irrigation water. J.D. could track the gurgling flow though a system of ditches Boots and One-Eyed Hazel had dug over the course of three summers.

The horses picked up their feet lightly as J.D. guided them beneath the gateway of three sturdy pine poles—two as vertical posts and the third as the cross pole. A sun-bleached cow skull hung over the gateway, below which was chained on both sides a wooden plank with the ranch's name and brand—an interlocking M and c—burned in the front. The drive was a mile long, with the west pasture to the left. Handsome red cattle with clean, curly-haired white faces and white-lined backs grazed on the spring shoots of grass. The breed had a blockiness to its body, with short bones. J.D. looked forward to a thick slab of well-cooked meat on his plate for supper tonight.

"How do you fry your steaks?" J.D. asked, breaking the silence that had stayed with him and Josephine for the last fifteen miles.

"The usual way," she replied in a voice that seemed faraway.

"I meant thin or thick? Fried quickly or slow?"

Her wide eyes darted nervously to his, and they exchanged a subtle look of apprehension that had nothing to do with their current discussion.

J.D. didn't much trust the staying power of eastern women on the range. His mother had barely lasted a year at the ranch before returning to his grandmother's home in Boston. Women came West for only one reason that J.D. could see. To marry cowboys and cattlemen. And if that husband died or was badly injured, a woman had three choices: she could return to the East, move to town and wash clothes or serve drinks, or take over the spread.

In J.D.'s mother's case, she'd packed up before Boots cashed in his life for a tombstone. J.D. couldn't blame her for leaving. If Boots had died, Eugenia wouldn't have settled into town, and she didn't have the will to run a large spread. J.D. sensed that Josephine Whittaker and his mother shared something in common.

At length, Josephine said, "I haven't quite decided yet which way I'll fix the steaks."

J.D. veered his eyes forward and made no comment. Anything he said was bound to come out wrong.

As he brought the team to a halt at the open barn doors, they were met by a whirlwind of vocal dogs. Several cats of various colors lurked in the background of the dimly lit interior.

Boots sat on a tree stump in front of the comfortable frame house with wide verandas, whittling on a short stick. He rose on stiff legs that quivered until he got the kinks out. His joints were crippled up from too many bad horses and too much bad weather. He couldn't ride anymore, and that made him as nasty as a loco steer. In his frustration, he would sometimes stomp from the house and have Hazel hitch up the buckboard so he could find the boys and cause some sort of trouble.

"Good gawd, who in the hell is that?" Boots bellowed in a voice that sounded like it came from deep within an old mine shaft. He slipped both his knife and the stick into his pocket with a hand that was swollen by years of hard labor and work's mistakes. He adjusted the weather-beaten brim of his hat against the sun, and a shock of steel-gray hair fell over the collar of his buckskin shirt as he approached.

"The cook." J.D.'s spurs clinked on the hard earth as he stepped down from the wagon to the continued bark of Toby. He bent and chucked the dog's ear, giving Boots a minute to digest the news while he lavished attention on Toby, a pitiable-looking dog with white fur freckled with gray and tan spots on his body, black ears, and a jagged white blaze up his nose and between his eyes. Despite his sorry appearance, Toby was the best cow dog he'd ever had.

"Cook?" Boots snapped. Crackling cornflower eyes that saw life like the eyes of a goshawk sized up every inch of Josephine Whittaker. "What happened to Pete Denby?"

J.D. explained as he went around to assist Josephine from the buckboard.

"Good gawd," Boots cursed again. "Why'd y'all go and hire a woman cook? It'll be just like having your mother around."

Ignoring Boots's dry commentary, J.D. turned to Josephine and held out his hand. She didn't readily take it. Her expression was so severely restrained, she must have been waging one hell of a battle for control inside that head of hers. Though he knew she didn't fit in, he was hoping she'd overlook that fact and still be able to fry up something satisfactory for supper.

She slipped her fingers in his, squeezing his hand as she disembarked, as if she needed his strength for support. Once on her feet, she straightened the short coat to her dress and brushed the dirt from her skirt. Boots came forward, Toby trotting alongside with his spotted tail wagging. Josephine took a step backward.

"He doesn't bite," J.D. offered.

"The dog doesn't bite," Boots corrected.

"Just the same," she replied, keeping her distance from both the dog and Boots.

Measuring his words with gravelly precision, Boots asked, "Are y'all afraid of dogs?" He gave Josephine no opportunity to answer before going into a short version of his cat speech. "It's not dogs that give a man grief. It's cats. I don't like cats. They have no loyalty to the hand that feeds them. Neither does a man's son. And I don't like children, either. About as much as I don't like cats."

Boots habitually proclaimed his aversion for children and cats, yet he was forever asking J.D. when he'd give him a grandson, usually while rubbing the thick coat of the yellow tomcat curled up on his lap.

"Did you get my cigars?" Boots's tone was impatient.

"They're in one of the boxes from the merc," J.D. replied.

Rio Cibolo and Gus Peavy sauntered over from the corral, where Ace Flynn and Print Freeland were dehorning and pasting the last of the calves. Upon seeing Josephine, Rio's face lit up in a broad grin.

"Rio, get Hazel to pull the wagon inside the barn," J.D. said, putting a delay on the introductions. "Tell him not to unload anything. It's all going in the chuck wagon tomorrow."

"How do, ma'am?" Rio doffed his felt hat and ran a blood-splattered hand through his mashed-down hair. "Pleasure to see you out here. Boss," he said to J.D., "did you go and get yourself a wife?"

J.D. gave Josephine a sidelong glance to gauge her reaction. She blushed a faint shade of pink that softened her brown eyes. Coyness in a woman wasn't something he liked. Those women who artfully blushed at the tiniest suggestion of coarseness or indelicacy were more often than not spoiled and overindulged. But with Josephine, the embarrassed flush of color on her cheeks looked unpracticed.

"She's the new cookie," J.D. answered. "Miss Josephine Whittaker. I'll save the formal introductions for the table when all you boys are gathered 'round."

Peavy fumbled for his hat's brim, removed the Stetson, and clutched it in his hands. "Welcome, Miss Whittaker. Thank the Lord, we'll be eating good tonight." As soon as he said it, he gave Boots a hasty squint, then nudged Rio to save himself. "You heard the boss. Go get One-Eyed Hazel."

Rio tipped his hat and went to do as he was bid. Peavy continued to stare open-mouthed until J.D. told him to ask Print what the final tally would be for the drive.

Boots's fingers, bent and scarred with nails craggy and jagged, scratched his white-stubbled chin. "Can y'all fix creamed corn on toast?" he asked Josephine. "A good cook can make creamed corn on toast." Then he abruptly changed the subject. "My wife, Eugenia, looks a lot like you. She was no cook. She never lifted her finger for a thing but to ring that gawddamn servant's bell she kept in every room of the house."

Raising her chin a little, Josephine looked Boots right in the eyes—a gesture that even the toughest cowboy sometimes had trouble doing. "Rest assured, I am a cook."

Boots's pale brows arched. "Good gawd, but y'all're a sassy little outfit, aren't you?" Once again, he gave her no room to reply. Boots rarely gave anyone a chance to add their two cents' worth after he'd had his say. "I'm going to see what Seth and Jidge are up to in the shed. I have to be busy or I get picky," he said, more to J.D. than Josephine.

J.D. watched Boots amble off in a walk that was slow and shuffling yet steady and determined. Then J.D. reached in the bed of the wagon and grasped Josephine's valise. "I'll bring your bag into the house and show you where you'll bunk."

She lagged behind, and he looked over his shoulder. She stood like a statue, her eyes dark with concern.

"Bunk?" she asked woodenly. "Am I to share the residence with you?"

"Unless you'd rather bunk up with the hands."

"No."

"Then you're stuck with me and Boots. Come on."

Josephine's first view of the clean, painted home and splashes of spring flowers had left her with an inward sigh of relief. All she'd seen on the ride out had been endless piles of flat cow droppings, swooping birds feeding on a decayed carcass of a rabbit, and animal bones.

As Josephine followed J.D. around the side of the white house, the ugly dog trotted along trying to sneak a sniff of her skirts when she didn't shoo him away fast enough. White bed sheets hung lifeless on a line, and scattered here and there were half-barrels containing purple and yellow crocus, buttery-colored daffodils, and strawberry-red tulips. She wouldn't have expected such a feminine touch and wondered if there was another woman on the premises.

"Mr. McCall, are any of the men married?" she ventured.

"No."

"Who tends the flowers?"

"Our chore boy, Hazel. Though he's no boy. He's older than Boots."

Boots—the man who was disagreeable and surly. He'd spoken with a drawl distinctly southern, but he'd had manners that definitely were not from the Old South. He and Mr. McCall bore a certain resemblance, but if Mr. Klauffman hadn't told her Boots was the father, she might not have known. J.D. McCall, despite his sullen temperament, was easier to bear.

J.D. went up a set of back steps and held the door open for her.

"Toby, stay," he ordered the dog, then fell in behind her.

As she entered the house, her first impression of its hominess came from the kitchen. The room was impressively spacious with a row of eastern-facing windows covered by a plain Swiss muslin. There was a large black stove with a wall pipe—just like the kind Mr. Klauffman sold—a tall cupboard with legs and panels of tin in front that had holes in the shape of stars punched in it, a work counter and basin, numerous shelves with enamel pots and pans, but there was no indoor pump.

"This is the kitchen, in case you didn't know." There was a hint of mockery in his tone that she didn't quite care for.

"Yes, I know," she returned briskly.

He continued on through a narrow doorway, but Josephine lingered a moment, inhaling a deep breath. She could manage this, she told herself, taking in the intimidating cookery and utensils. She *had* to manage this.

Exhaling, she strode after J.D. The room he'd gone into was small with a single window for light. The floors were bare, and the ceiling was exposed wooden beams. Sidled up against the window wall rested a narrow iron bedstead that was unmade; its faded red chintz spread was folded at the foot of a thin mattress. There was no wardrobe, just a shelf and hooks made out of bent horseshoes. A washbasin and towel rack were supplied on the corner stand

J.D. stood back and hooked his thumbs in his gun belt. Josephine swallowed. He intimidated her greatly, but she vowed not to let on that he did.

"Those must be your sheets on the line. I'll have Hazel bring them in."

"That won't be necessary." She didn't want a man named One-Eyed Hazel doing her any favors. He was surely a swarthy fellow, missing teeth as well as an eye. "I can get the sheets."

"Suit yourself."

Josephine backed away from the door so that J.D. could leave. She was in dire need of breathing room. She felt as if someone was tightening her corset until her ribs were fused together.

J.D. went around her, pausing in the doorway to say, "Have supper ready by five."

An ambush of trepidation struck Josephine, and she had to force herself not to read the time on the delicate chatelaine watch pinned to her bodice. "I will." *Five o'clock* . . . How much time did that leave her to rectify errors?

Rather than leave, J.D. lounged against the jamb. Her gaze darted to the window, the ceiling, and the floor until she could no longer avoid looking at him. She couldn't deny he was a striking figure, with his long coat unbuttoned to his calves revealing the slim fit of his denim pants and the soft fabric of his shirt. Not to mention, he was quite tall. In boots and hat, he filled out the height of the frame. She imagined that even in his stockinged feet, his bare head would nearly touch the underside of the doorway.

"You never asked how much the job paid," he drawled, dragging her from her imprudent thoughts.

It was just as well that he had. She was no longer inclined to romantic daydreams that would prove false anyway.

When his question registered, she felt foolish and inept, the full awareness of her inexperience slapping her on her burning cheeks. "I assumed it paid a cook's wage."

"Which is?"

He was abominable. She could say nothing, because she didn't know—and he knew it.

"Thirty dollars a month," J.D. supplied. "Unless somebody comes down the road. Since the duration of your stay is questionable, I'll pay you once a week."

Stoically, she nodded. She'd have to work at least a week and several days more to earn enough to buy a train ticket. She hoped nobody else would show up until then.

"I'll have one of the boys bring you some loin beef for supper." J.D. pushed his hip away from the jamb and straightened. "We'll need fresh meat for the drive anyway. We're leaving the day after tomorrow, so that doesn't give you much time to get the wagon in order."

"I don't need but a few minutes' notice," she replied in an accommodating tone. "I have no special travel requirements that would have to be taken into consideration when arranging the wagon. But just the same, perhaps it would be better if I stayed here. I can't see how much use I would be."

J.D. gave her the first crack of a smile that she could put a label on. It made her uncomfortable. "Do you know what a cattle drive is?"

"Of course I do." But suddenly she wasn't sure. Why was he talking about bringing meat along? The Beadle's No. 478, *Colorado Charlie's Escape and the Young Desperadoes,* had touched briefly on cattle management. Charlie Macready was assigned to go along with a shipment of cattle by rail cars. She'd assumed that Mr. McCall had been referring to taking his cows to the train station. Be that the case, they would be back here in a few hours.

"I'm glad you aren't green. But just the same," he said, using her words and smiling while he spoke them, "I'll tell you how it'll go. I'll be moving out twenty-five hundred head of cattle and fifty-seven cutting horses, with ten cowboys and one wrangler to keep the animals from stampeding. We'll be covering fifty miles to get to the summer range. If we're lucky and don't hit any rough spots, that'll take us five ten-mile days. Boots'll come along. There's no keeping him here. He'll drive the wagon so you don't have to. Rio will cut your firewood, assist with the dishes and the grind coffee. All you have to do is have the grub hot and ready when it's supposed to be."

She tried to keep the waver of alarm from her tone. "I'm to cook out on the open range over a fire."

"You're right, cookie, you aren't green. You know exactly how it goes." With a dip of his head, he parted with, "See you at supper."

Josephine's first reaction to a crisis was to do nothing. There had always been someone available to cope with whatever it was that needed coping with. To do nothing had been part of her childhood training. Only now there was no one, and to do nothing wouldn't suffice. She had to make her own decision about how she was going to handle the cattle drive. So she did what came naturally to her.

She put off making a decision until she had to.

In the meantime, since she had nothing to unpack that could be of any immediate use to her, she wanted to make up her bed and lie down a moment to collect herself before tackling the process of figuring out the evening's menu.

Outside, signs of the weather turning were apparent in the budding greenery. A high sun shone brilliantly from a cloudless sky. The day was beautiful and windless. Josephine wandered toward the clothesline. Removing the sheets from their wooden pins, she gazed around for a basket. There was none. She put the pins in the bedclothes, then bundled them up in her arms.

Several yards behind the clothesline was a small graveyard fenced in by gray pickets. One mound of earth appeared to be freshly turned. Curious, she walked to the slated gate and let herself in. There were several markers, but the newest read:

Sacred to the memory of
Luis Francisco Escalante
Cook and Friend
He was buried by his friends and fellow cowboys on
April 2, 1874.

A bouquet from a slender plant with oblong leaves and light blue flowers with yellow eyes had recently been placed at the base of the cross. Josephine couldn't explain the sudden wave of sadness that passed through her as she quietly stared at the resting place of her predecessor. She wondered how he'd died.

Her gaze roamed to read the other graves in the well-tended tiny plot. Those that intrigued her the most were markers with single names on them. Some female, some masculine.

"Ginger"
May we all meet and have
some good rides again.

It had never occurred to her to bury a pet. Perhaps because she'd never had one. Having not been around them, she wasn't much for dogs and cats, and neither was she fond of domestic animals. The Beadle's volumes she chose to read were more centered on Wild West adventures and romance rather than livestock. Let alone cattle drives. How purely unenlightened J.D. McCall must think her.

Josephine let herself out of the grave orchard, the stiff sheets still wadded in her arms. At the far corner of the yard stood a small corral with a single, reddish cow in it. Seeing her, the cow mooed. She gave the animal a critical inspection from a far distance and came to the conclusion its face wasn't that displeasing to look at. Its eyes were mild in a face that resembled the panda bear's she'd once seen in a world atlas of nature book.

Two cowboys exited a shed that was connected to the corral. They each held a rope; one carried an ax. The cow shuffled but didn't try to run away; it merely stood there working its mouth in circular chewing motions. The taller of the two men threw his rope and caught the cow by its head; the other roped its hind feet, threw it down, and stretched it out. The animal struggled, now mooing with a pitiful sound. The ax was retrieved, and Josephine felt the saliva thicken in her mouth.

Unable to watch any further, she ran back to the house, slammed the kitchen door, and pressed her back against the panel. The sheets fell from her arms as she brought her hands to her face to shield her eyes from the thought of that stupid cow being killed with an ax. She felt a headache coming on. A delicate glass of sherry was needed to calm her nerves. If only there was some sherry to be had.

Stepping over the sheets, she began to rummage through the cupboard and the shelves, searching for the telltale shape of a slender liquor decanter. There was nothing. Not a drop of spirits to be had in the whole room. What kind of cowboys were these, that a little indulgence was not allowed?

Josephine went into her room and slumped down

on the bare mattress. She shouldn't be so upset. She ate beef. As a matter of fact, beef Wellington was one of her favorite dishes. Only she'd never had to see the cow's face before its meat was served up on her china plate with *pâté de foie gras.*

A wave of desolation swept over her as she stared at the cracks in the floorboards. *What am I doing here?*

CHAPTER

→ 3 ←

The answer came simply inside Josephine's head, and in the form of her mother's voice. "One way of finding out whether a risk is worth taking is *not* to take it, and see what you become in the long run." Throughout the imprisoning years of her marriage, Josephine had taken her mother's advice. But she heeded it no longer. That was why she'd given up assorted snobberies, tedium, and fossilized rules of conduct and had ended up in Mr. J.D. McCall's house working for thirty dollars a month.

Thirty dollars. It seemed like a fortune, yet on her twenty-first birthday she'd been worth more than four million dollars.

Grudgingly, Josephine rose, went to her valise, and opened the catch. She removed a deep blue canvas-bound book entitled *The Kitchen Companion and Housekeeper's Own Book.* In smaller print beneath the title it read: *Containing All the Modern and Most Approved Methods in Cookery, Pastry & Confectionery with an Excellent Collection of VALUABLE RECIPES.*

Josephine might not have known the first thing about cooking, but she knew what would *not* be on the menu tonight. Panda-faced cow. She couldn't possibly face the meat, much less touch it or slice it with a butcher's knife.

Thirty minutes later, Josephine stood at the stove, book in hand. She'd taken off the smart jersey to her suit and refastened her gold watch by its pin to the thin fabric of her underblouse. She followed through the instructions for lighting a cooking fire, improvising when she wasn't clear on the exact meaning of the directions. The section on dampers thoroughly confused her. Rather than concern herself over something that she didn't have to worry about until the fire was hot, she skipped that part.

When she was finished, her hands and patches on her pristine cuffs were the color of coal. She hadn't had the foresight to pump water into a bucket before beginning. Helplessly looking about for something to wipe her hands on, she could find nothing. Earlier, she hadn't come across an apron or a towel, so she ransacked what turned out to be a moderately sized larder. Everything she touched got smudged with black dust: the knob, the inside of the door, the shelf, the stack of flour sack towels with faint traces of the brand name still dyed on them.

After wiping off her hands, she remained standing in the modest pantry. She scanned the shelves for the ingredients she would require. There was a barrel of molasses, a half-bag of Arbuckle's coffee, peppercorns, mace, nutmeg, cinnamon, ginger, salt, a tin of baking powder, and flour. Then came the meager supply of canned goods: milk, sardines, tomatoes. But there was an open case of canned corn on the floor, with a full case beneath it. Boots hadn't been kidding about the creamed corn on toast.

Despite the scarcity of staples, milk and tomatoes were exactly what she needed to get started on the soup. Though she couldn't understand why they'd need canned milk on a ranch when there were all those cows to be milked. With a shrug, she juggled five No. 2 cans of tomatoes, the dented tin of baking powder, and a couple cans of milk that were supposed to add up to one quart.

Depositing them on the counter in a heap, she skimmed through the recipe once more. *Heat the tomatoes, add the baking powder, and allow to effervesce.* She wasn't all that sure what *effervesce* meant, but she'd heard of champagne referred to as effervescent. So that must mean to cook the tomatoes until they bubbled up.

She picked up a can and read the label. There were no instructions on how to open it. A dilemma was brewing. She couldn't make tomato soup if she couldn't get the can open. Her headache began to pulse anew at her temples. She put the can down and went into her room to get a butterscotch candy so that she could think better. Once the sweet tidbit was melting against her tongue, she approached the can at a different angle. Perhaps if she gouged it with a knife . . .

With handle in hand, she raised her arm and readied to stab the lid.

"What in the hell are you doing?"

Josephine's arm froze, and the butterscotch in her mouth slid down her throat making a lump in her windpipe. She coughed, her chin coming up with a start as J.D. closed the door behind him. He had to step over her discarded sheets in order to enter the kitchen. His boot tip hit a clothespin, and the wooden peg skittered across the floor and hit her in the shoe.

"What's this?" he asked, looking at the clean bedclothes in a bundle. She'd forgotten all about them. Always before when she'd forgotten about something, her maid had tidied it up before she'd remembered what it was she'd forgotten.

"My sheets," she half whispered, wishing desperately for a glass of water to drink to dislodge the candy from the center of her chest where it had settled. Self-consciously, she lowered her arm and set down the knife.

43

"I can see that." He carried a metal pan with a large, cloth-wrapped piece of meat inside. Splotches of vivid red soiled the linen, making her stomach clench. "What are they doing on the floor?"

Telling him she'd been distraught over witnessing that helpless cow being readied for slaughter would imply her cowardice at the very least. So she fabricated an answer she hoped sounded credible. "I was anxious to begin supper and didn't want to spare a minute to make up the bed."

J.D. put the pan on the counter, then picked up the sheets. His large bootprint was on one of them. "Do you always throw down what you're doing to start something else?"

"Only when I'm inspired."

He went to her room to put the linens on her bed. In his brief absence, she used the flat of her palm to pat herself between the breasts. She felt the candy slip down. Gasping, she forced a cool collectedness on herself. *Don't do anything that will make him suspect you are the fraud that you are.* She had to look busy. Like she knew what she was doing. Proceeding with the cans was out. What else? *What else to do?*

The fire. Check the fire. That was important.

She acted like a seasoned cook when she fiddled with, moved, and adjusted each damper by its knob—though she had no idea if what she was doing was right.

"Are you finding everything you need?" J.D. asked, having drawn up behind her without her hearing him approach. He stood a respectable few feet from her, but he may as well have stood right on her toes for as close as he was watching her.

Unable to meet his eyes, she stared at the can and said, "Yes. I have everything I need."

"Except an opener for those."

She needn't question what "those" he was referring to. Any simpleton could have figured out she had been about to puncture the can open.

He pulled out a drawer beneath the counter and came up with a very lethal-appearing apparatus. It had a wooden handle with a short but very sharp-looking blade and catch on the end. He said nothing about her near venture at puncturing the cans with a knife. Without a word, he grabbed a tomato can and jabbed the blade into the edge. He held the can and turned it, running the blade along the rim. There seemed to be a fair amount of strength needed to operate the opener. She wondered if he'd open everything.

"What are you making?"

Her throat was still sore from that butterscotch going down whole. Coughing slightly, she said, "It's a surprise." And it would be, too, if everything turned out the way it was supposed to.

"Pan-fried steak with tomatoes would be damn welcome."

"Yes, it would." But it wasn't on the menu.

"That's a nice loin I brought you. I prefer my steaks cut thick. We've got plenty."

She gave him a noncommittal response.

J.D. whipped through all the cans in no time, leaving their jagged tin lids on. "What do you need the milk for? The boys don't like it in their coffee."

"That's good to know," was all she replied, not telling him what the milk was for.

Stepping back, his gaze fell on the black powder staining her cuffs. Then his eyes traveled up her arms, the column of her throat, her lips, and lastly her eyes. The way he carried on with his thorough inspection had her flustered inside to distraction. She didn't know where to look, what to look at, or what to say. She'd never felt so exposed in all her life.

"You should have put on something more appropriate," he remarked in a deep voice. "Out here women don't have much call for fancy duds like what you've got."

That was all he'd needed to say to make her cry,

only she refused to let her tears fall. Her poor attempt at opening the cans, her misunderstanding of how the dampers operated, her uncertainty of her abilities, the sheets on the floor, her lost valise, her missing five hundred dollars. She had but to pick one, and she could turn herself loose in a monumental crying spree. Throw in the fact that she had but one spring suit to wear, and her not knowing how to iron it was enough to send her to her room to claim a headache from now until late next week.

The problem with that scenario was J.D. McCall would most likely drag her from her sickbed and demand she fry eighteen thick steaks. She had the strongest urge to feel utterly and completely sorry for herself. But that was no way for a woman of independent means to behave. She had longed for this moment—albeit with a faceless opponent—when she could stand on her own two feet and speak for herself. To make her *own* views clear. People with "guts" didn't snivel. They were courageous and faced their opponents head-on.

"If you recall," she said, keeping her eyes level with his, "my valise was taken from me. This is the only dress I own." As she spoke the well-aimed words, her rapid heartbeat grew deafening in her ears.

If he felt any compassion for her, he certainly didn't exhibit it. "When I carried your case, it felt heavy enough to have clothes inside."

She was appalled that he would make reference to her personal belongings in such a frank manner. Refusing to retreat no matter how embarrassed she was, she said simply, "The clothes in that valise were intended for another type of woman."

"What do you mean?"

The thoughtless cad wanted her to spell it out. "A woman with a different bone structure than myself." On that note, she plopped the contents of a tomato can—lid and all—into a round-bottom pot. Moisture broke out on her palms; her staid barriers were teetering. "Now, if you don't mind, your presence is destroying my creativity."

She turned away from him, then proceeded to dump out the tomatoes from the remaining cans. Their juice splashed her hands. Seconds ticked by. She fished out the lids and stacked them. Perhaps a full minute passed. When she could abide the strain no longer, she looked up.

Mr. McCall was gone. For a big man, he moved quietly. She'd forgotten to thank him for opening the cans. But she consoled herself with the reminder that he'd insulted her mode of dress. When she'd first worn the Dolly Varden cretonne suit last Easter on Fifth Avenue, she'd demonstrated the epitome of refined taste and character. J.D. McCall called her attire "fancy duds." She shouldn't have been so affected by his comment. What did he know about fashion? All she'd seen him wear were denim pants, vests, and cotton shirts.

Josephine pensively stared inside the pot at the tomatoes, then shook herself out of her thoughts to read the recipe. After sprinkling two teaspoons of baking powder over the whole tomatoes, she slid the pot onto the foremost hot plate of the stove.

Afterward, she scanned the ingredients list for cornmeal rolls since she didn't have the necessary time involved to prepare bread.

Exploring the larder's shelves once more, she brought down three stoneware canisters: flour, cornmeal, and sugar. It took her a good fifteen minutes to find the needed utensils. She hadn't been sure what a sifter was, so she'd had to refer to the chapter on kitchen economy. At length, she found the round gadget with the screen on the bottom. She was to sift the dry ingredients.

Ready to begin, she dove a teacup into the flour. A fine dusting of white puffed up. She blinked her lashes to get rid of what was in her eyes. Resuming her measurement of the flour until she had four teacups, she then lifted the crockery lid to the cornmeal.

She needed one pint of cornmeal. Was she supposed to add that to the flour sifter as well? What did *dry ingredients* mean? How many teacups in one pint? She wasn't very good at mathematics. Hugh used to drink his brandy from a pint. She closed her eyes and conjured the size of that pint. Opening them, she dipped the teacup once, twice, three—

"Y'all don't do it like that."

Josephine turned toward the sound of Boots's condemning voice. He stood in the doorway that went to the dining room. "I beg your pardon?"

"Beg my pardon all you want, but y'all aren't going to get it. I'm old, and I don't remember who I've pardoned and who I haven't, so I don't pardon anyone anymore." He shuffled to her and stared down his nose at the mess she was making on the counter. "Y'all don't sift the cornmeal in with the flour."

Trying to save herself, Josephine set about cranking the handle on the sifter, spreading a cloud of white and yellow powder into a bowl. She replied, "Where I come from, we do it this way."

"Where do you come from?"

"New York."

"Good gawd," Boots cried. "Y'all should meet Eugenia."

Josephine's eyes met his. "She's here?"

"No, but you should meet her." Angling a stool next to the counter, Boots sat down and made himself at home. "The infernal woman deserted me."

Josephine could probably guess why, though she gave no more than a second of pondering to the marital problems of Boots McCall. How could she manage to continue with him watching her every move?

"Do you intend to sit there?"

He looked at her as if she were daft; she returned

the open stare. His face was a cobweb of lines, aged and tanned by sun. "I don't intend to, I am." His arm rose, and he pointed with a knobby finger. "Watch what you're doing. Y'all're making a hell of a mess."

She quickly averted her eyes and repositioned the sifter over the bowl instead of the counter where she'd deposited a small pile of the flour mixture—half of which had fallen onto the floor.

With a healthy crank of the sifter that sent flour spraying, Josephine worked herself into a diminutive fit of temper. The McCall men were draining. They had no deportment when it came to a lady's presence. Both freely spoke their minds, not caring a whit for delicacy, and using swear words to boot. Not that she'd never heard an oath or peppered curse. Andrew Tilden, her father, before amassing his fortune, had been an uneducated steamboat captain. His vocabulary had been liberally salted with words not ordinarily heard in polite society. He'd never given a moment over people's reactions to his language, but her mother, Victoria, had. His coarse verbiage had nearly been her ruination.

"I did the cooking before y'all came along. J.D. had no call to hire you. The boys like what I fix."

Josephine detected a hint of jealousy in his grizzled tone. To think, Boots McCall was jealous of her. It was absurd.

"I'll tell y'all right now, them boys don't like anything showy on their plates. None of your ornamental, highfalutin foods that's dressed up with greens. If the good Lord wanted man to eat salad, he would have made him into a cow."

An odious smell came from the stove. A burning, smoky scent that stung her nose. Josephine dropped the sifter to investigate, momentarily putting her opinion of Boots to the side.

Billowing through the seams in the plates, a thick stream of black smoke rose from the stove. Panicking, Josephine opened the dampers that were closed and closed the dampers that were open. Her quick switches didn't make matters any better. She stood back, helplessly staring at the growing cloud of smoke, at a loss over what to do next.

Scooting off his stool with an unexpected spryness, Boots slid open the oven damper, half closed the chimney damper, and fine-tuned the other two. When he was finished, he took up his stool once more.

"Good gawd," he muttered, "you're like to burn the place up."

The hiss of the stove and crackle of burning wood filled the gap of silence between them. At length, Boots further accused, "Y'all don't know a kitchen from a bull's hind end."

Josephine didn't know whether she should be relieved the jig was up or staunchly deny his accusation. She had no opportunity to do either. A bubbling sound—or, rather, an ominous rumble that crackled like thunder—came from the pot. No sooner had she decided that the pot was dangerous and should be examined from a safe distance than the lid shot up and smacked the ceiling, and a blurred expulsion of red blobs erupted like a squished bug.

"Good gawd!" Boots swore as he backed off the chair and scooted toward the back door.

Particles of tomatoes shot through the kitchen, smattering Josephine with hot darts on her thin sleeves as she held her arms out.

"Ouch!" she screamed, leaping backward to the sting of something hitting her in the cheek. She felt the debris fall in her hair, pepper her shirt, her skirt, and her shoes. Red everywhere. Everything was covered with tomato pulp. The open cookbook, the counter, the flour, the bowl, the sifter. It was a disaster. A great, big, disastrous mess.

The meal was ruined.

Having never tried and failed so miserably at something, Josephine hadn't honed her strong or full emotions. She hadn't developed a thick skin. Everything she'd done in her life up to leaving New York had been safe. Secure. For the first time, she had to face the facts. She was a failure.

A failure of a wife.

A failure of a cook.

Once she accepted that, the high dam that had been keeping her innermost feelings from emotional exposure finally burst. She fell into a fit of weeping the likes of which she had never before unleashed.

The boys had assembled at the dining table, with J.D. sitting at the head. All of them had gotten spiffed up to meet the new cook. Those who had been covered with mud and grime, several reeking with blood from a day's work in the corral, had all taken frigid baths in the creek wearing their long johns. Manners were in place. In an unspoken courtesy, not a single revolver was present. Each had hung his gun belt on one of the series of hooks in the front room. Hats weren't necessarily removed unless a lady was present, so there wasn't a hat to be seen. Along with the hardware, the bands of Stetsons were slung over those hooks as well.

J.D. ate with his cowboys. Here, there was no distinction between boss and hired hand. Normally, ranchmen didn't make a formality of a meal. The eating hour was strictly business with no time for idle gossip.

But tonight was different.

The low hum of conversation circulated around the table, as each man was eager to make the acquaintance of Miss Josephine Whittaker and taste a bite of her delectable offerings. They'd been waiting for an interminable ten minutes—a clear breech of etiquette, as one of Luis Escalante's rules was promptness. But nobody had beaten on the triangle at five o'clock to bring them from the bunkhouse, the corral, or wherever they happened to be. Five o'clock came and went without the signal; it was the boys' stomachs rumbling for some good victuals that had sent them seeking the house.

J.D. made a mental note to tell Josephine that she had to use the triangle when calling the boys to the table. He leaned back in his chair, folding his arms across his chest. The smell of something peculiar came from the kitchen. He recognized the aroma of tomatoes, but there was a trace of something else. He could swear it was . . . creamed corn. But that couldn't be. Stretching out his legs, he shrugged off the thought. He'd been eating too much of it to get the smell out of his nose.

After waiting another five minutes, J.D. was just about to get out of his chair and investigate when Boots appeared in the doorway carrying a platter of creamed corn on toast.

"Evening, boys," Boots said proudly, depositing his fare in the center of the table. "Dig on in while it's hot."

They all grumbled, looked at one another, then glared at J.D.

J.D. lifted himself straighter in his chair. "Where's the cookie? And where in the hell are our steaks?"

Boots gave him a brittle smile. "She took to her bed. Had herself a bit of an accident in the kitchen."

J.D.'s eyes narrowed. "What kind of accident?"

"An 'effervesce of tomatoes' is what she called it."

Sliding his chair back, J.D. stood and went for the closed kitchen door.

"I wouldn't go in there if I was you," Boots warned. "She made one hell of a mess."

J.D. turned and shouted, "Then she's got one hell of a mess to clean up before she fries those steaks!"

"She's not frying anything up tonight. Last I seen her, she was on her way to a good drunk."

"Drunk?"

"Said she needed some sherry to calm herself, but I told her Eugenia drank all we had. So I gave her my corn liquor bottle." Boots scraped the legs of his chair out, sat, and began to serve himself. "I suspect y'all'll be taking her back to Sienna tomorrow."

Boots apparently thought he had things cleverly figured out. Get the cook drunk. Then get her fired.

"I ought to take you to Sienna tomorrow and leave you there, you crafty son-of-a-bitch," J.D. blazed, then stalked out of the dining room.

CHAPTER

→4←

Rather than waking to the inviting aroma of coffee brewing, J.D. opened his eyes to the lingering smell of spent wood coming from the banked fireplace in the front room. He lay on his bed, staring through the darkness toward the ceiling. The time was probably in the vicinity of three-thirty. When Luis had been the cook, every morning at precisely three thirty-five, the rich flavor of Arbuckle's wafted through the house and slowly brought J.D. around. He wasn't an instant riser. It took him a good fifteen minutes to wake up enough to get out of bed. On cold mornings, he'd lie back, put his hands behind his head, and think about what needed to be done that day. He'd work up an appetite for Luis's savory sourdough pancakes fried in salt pork drippings with molasses poured on top, and a cup of hot black coffee, strong enough to float an old horseshoe.

For several weeks, J.D. had been getting up and fixing breakfast for the boys. He got too busy around the place to deal with dinner and supper, so Boots had taken on those shifts. J.D. wasn't lame in the kitchen; he just didn't like cooking.

J.D. swung his legs over the side of the bed, then ran his fingers through the stiff growth bristling on his chin. He figured he'd avoided his razor long enough. He dressed in the near dark. After slipping into a fresh pair of Levi's, he slid his arms into a loose-fitting blue flannel shirt that was worn and soft. He grabbed his boots, shoved them on by the mule ears, then fit his pants over the scarred leather.

His tread out of his bedroom was light, despite the rolling walk he'd adapted as a cowboy from wearing the chunk-heeled boots of his profession. Boots's door was closed, and no light shined from within the room. More and more of late, Boots didn't keep regular hours. Sometimes when J.D. would get up to check on a calf or to investigate what the dogs were barking at, he'd find Boots's lamp lit at any hour of the night. J.D. had asked him why he didn't sleep, and Boots had grumbled that his mind was going and he forgot when to go to bed. Boots would be sixty years old in a couple of months. Though he was getting on, J.D. didn't think the old man's mind was going. J.D. sometimes wondered if Boots stayed up late to figure out ways to torment him. For as long as J.D. could remember, he and Boots had never been father and son, much less friends. In spite of that, it seemed to J.D. that he'd been answering to Boots all his life.

J.D. had inherited Boots's bad temper, and the rage that J.D. sometimes felt made him distance himself from people when he was angry. That was why, after last night's exchange with Boots in the dining room, J.D. had left the house rather than confront Josephine. He'd gone for a fast ride on Tequila to burn off some energy. He'd been in such a vile frame of mind, he hadn't been able to trust himself around anyone. He was liable to knock somebody for a loop. And he sure as hell would never hit a woman. Or his father. Though there had been times he'd been damn close to jumping on Boots's back.

They fought often, and were they ever to apologize to each other, they'd have to chip through layers upon layers, years upon years of fighting and walking away, just to get to the root of the problems between them. Both were bull-headed, and J.D. doubted he and Boots would ever have a kind thing to say to each other.

Faint light from a thin wedge of moon lent the front room slight illumination. Rawhide had been pretty much incorporated into everything. It made the woven bottom of the springless bed J.D. slept in and was the cushions and backs of the chairs he and the boys sat in for a spell at night after supper. Cowskin made up the soft rug spread at the stone hearth. Wagon wheels and a sanded plank of wood had been converted to tabletops for card playing. Old horseshoes came in handy for just about anything in the house or the tack room.

J.D. went to the mantel and opened a box of matches. He struck one and lit a kerosene lamp. Turning up the flame, he proceeded toward the kitchen. When he pushed the door inward, he stopped short, lifting his arm to cast light about the room.

"Good gawd," he whispered, then cursed himself for uttering Boots's favorite expletive.

There were tiny pieces of tomato pulp everywhere. Nothing had been cleaned up from Josephine's "effervesce of tomatoes." J.D. hadn't been sure exactly what Boots had been talking about. Now it was all too clear.

Stepping into the kitchen, J.D. put a flame to all the lamps. When the wicks were hissing with a bright glow, he stood back to view the damage. Nothing was free from red stains. Walls, ceiling, stove. The counter where the tomato cans still sat, a bowl of flour, the cornmeal canister, and a bunch of kitchen utensils. At least the meat he'd brought Josephine had been stored. Boots had probably done that. Actually, he'd probably relished doing that while his creamed corn was on to boil.

J.D. went to Josephine's door and knocked.

No answer came.

He knocked again—louder—and waited a few seconds.

Still no response.

Maybe she'd lit out in the middle of the night. But even he didn't think she'd be fool enough to do that. Just the same, he turned the knob and let himself in.

Light from behind him poured into the small room. Josephine slept on the unmade bed. She hadn't made any attempt to do up the sheets. One was sprawled beneath her, and one came up haphazardly to her waist. She was sleeping in her underwear. A frilly white camisole, petticoat, and drawers. She lay on her stomach, one knee bent. Her bare foot, with its well-shaped toes, peeked out from the edge of the sheet.

Proceeding farther, he stepped on something. He picked up a hairpin and straightened, his gaze falling to her once more. She had unbound her hair. He was surprised by the unsettling hint of appreciation slamming him in the chest as he viewed the mass of brown curls falling past her bent elbow. He wouldn't have pegged Josephine Whittaker as the type of woman possessing provocative hair. She was too restrained to be sensual.

Her cheek rested on her pillow; her lips were parted. The creamy expanse at the side of her neck looked soft . . . kissable. Her skin had the look of polished ivory. A pale hand with slender pink nails rested palm down on the pillow, right in front of her nose.

He gave her entire body a raking gaze. She was curvy. Her derriere had a swell to it that would fit nicely in a man's hands. An unwanted attraction toward her tightened his muscles. His skin felt hot even though the air was cool. He was by no means blind to her, but he was puzzled by his body's strong reaction. In a hasty rationale, he reasoned he'd been too long without a woman. Perhaps he should have gone into Sienna and visited Walkingbars with the rest of the cowboys more than he did. If he had, he wouldn't be looking at Josephine the way he was.

Josephine Whittaker came from exactly the same stock as his mother. And Eugenia hadn't been able to make a go of it in the West. Eastern women had no call to be marrying western men. Though Boots and Eugenia had been married in Arcola, Mississippi, Eugenia's heart had never left Boston. He couldn't blame her for going back. At least she hadn't stayed and been a martyr.

Right now, J.D. didn't have the time to think about getting married, and he didn't have the time to be lonesome. Should he ever sit down and really consider what he wanted in a woman, he wouldn't be having Josephine in mind.

J.D. glanced at the washstand, where there was an empty glass and Boots's corn liquor bottle, corked and nearly full. However much Josephine had drunk, it hadn't been a lot.

He went to the bedside and bumped his toe on the leg of the headboard. "Get on up, cookie."

She didn't budge.

"Come on, cookie, it's time to get up."

She muttered. Moaned, actually. A low, throaty sound that brought his gaze back to her face. Her eyes remained closed, but her breathing was no longer the steady rhythm of a deep sleep.

"Wh-what is it . . . Annabel?" she whispered hoarsely. "Is Hugh drunk . . . again?"

J.D. couldn't help wondering who Hugh was. A brother? Fiancé? Whoever he was, it wasn't his concern. Laying his hand on Josephine's shoulder, he gave her a soft shake.

"Cookie, pick it up. It's time to get out of bed."

"Wha . . ." Josephine's eyes fluttered open, her long lashes thick, dark fringes. "What?"

"I said, time to get up." For the hell of it, he gave her bottom a light smack.

She gasped, then rolled onto her back and jerked the sheet beneath her chin. "What are you doing here? It's the middle of the night."

"It's past three-thirty. You should have been up a half hour ago."

"You're crazy." Her eyes were wide. "Get out, or . . . or I shall scream."

"I'm getting out. So are you." Turning, he looked for her clothes. He found them in a wrinkled pile on the floor. Grabbing hold of a fistful of fabric, he tossed the skirt and blouse onto the bed. "Get dressed. You've got a kitchen to clean up."

Even in the dim light, he saw the dejection shimmering in her eyes. "I was going to. When the sun came up."

"Sun'll be up just after you're done." The corn liquor bottle was within reach, and he grabbed it before she got any more brilliant ideas. "Get dressed."

She sat upright, her hair falling over her shoulders. Her gaze fell on the pile of clothing strewn at the foot of the bed, but she didn't say anything about the poor condition they were in. Even he could see the splotches of red over everything.

"Give me a moment," was all she said.

J.D. walked away from her then. Beneath his hardened exterior lay a spark of respect for her. He'd thought for sure she'd feel sorry for herself and tell him she wasn't able to clean up because she was too tired.

Josephine Whittaker was turning out to be a contradiction to his predisposed opinion of her.

Josephine was fully awake now. Her fingers fumbled with the buttons of her blouse. She had the slightest fringes of a headache. Three short sips of Boots McCall's fiery liquor had been all she'd been able to swallow. She'd never been a drinker. Just a social glass of sherry shared with friends, and perhaps a small splash every so often in a moment of emergency. Hugh had done enough indulging for the both of them, so she had never abused liquor.

Now, looking back on the evening, she was ashamed she had resorted to the spirits. She'd taken the coward's way out. Josephine Whittaker had vowed no longer to be spineless the moment she'd boarded the train in Manhattan. She should have attacked the mess with vigor and been done with it before going to bed. But Boots had deflated her to jelly with his jests at her expense.

In the clarity of daylight—well, almost daylight— she was angry. Mostly at herself, a lingering bit at Boots. She'd clean the kitchen. And she'd do a good job, too.

By the time she was as presentable as she could get, the aroma of coffee came from the kitchen. Its pungent scent reminded her that she hadn't eaten the night before. Nor had she eaten much at all since leaving New York. She was used to a fine selection of rich foods and sauces. All she'd been offered thus far on the train and at the Bar Grub restaurant were greasy portions of unidentified platters heavy with meat and thick gravies. If she didn't eat something agreeable in flavor soon, she was going to wither away to nothing. Already the clasp on her skirt seemed to have loosened.

Josephine took a deep, fortifying breath, then left her room feeling as if she could do anything.

J.D. had his broad back to her when she entered the kitchen. He stood at the dry sink, viewing angles of his chin in a mirror hanging by a string from a cupboard knob. A basin of water was before him, and he held a straight razor. He scraped the blade across his neck in an upward motion, then swished off the soap in the water.

She couldn't recall ever seeing Hugh shave himself. His valet had always groomed and dressed him. Impeccably so.

J.D. was very efficient with his movements. Watching him, she felt like an intruder, but she couldn't turn away. An unwelcome spark of excitement at the prospect of seeing what he would look like clean-shaven made her continue to stare. Her senses seemed to flicker into definable emotions. Awareness was at the forefront. It struck a vibrant chord in her; she had never been so aware of a man since she'd met Hugh at a party and he'd charmed nearly every dance from her.

J.D. spied her in the mirror, moving his head a fraction to the left to see her fully. An instant of glaring self-consciousness surfaced within her. Her appearance was beyond dreadful with all the speckles of red staining the fabric of her suit. A hot flush worked its way across her skin.

He picked up a towel from the counter and ran the nap across his jaw and neck, wiping away the lingering traces of white lather. A kettle of water began to sputter and boil on the rear stove plate. Folding the towel in two, he used it to remove the pot by the handle.

"I got you a bucket half full of cold water." He motioned to the wooden receptacle next to the back door. "The lye soap is under the sink. You add some of this hot water to the bucket. Use a brush and a rag, and you'll be able to clean up."

"Yes, sir."

His brows slanted into a frown. "Don't call me that. If you have a mind to call me anything, I answer to J.D. or boss."

The tiny words had slipped out naturally. All her life she'd heard the staff at the Madison Square home address her father as "sir."

"All right," she conceded.

J.D. flung the damp towel over his shoulder and modified the oven damper without any uncertainty. "I'll fix breakfast this morning. Hell, I guess we'll have to let Boots wrangle up dinner since we'll be stocking

61

the wagon. But you're in charge of supper. Steaks. Fried. Not rare, but not burned. You got that?"

"Yes, er, boss."

He stole a sideways look at her before taking the basin out the back door and tossing the dirty water on the ground. With an easy stride, he returned and went about getting the flour from the larder. He'd already wiped off the counter so that he would have a clean work space.

Josephine propelled herself into motion. She took up the bucket where a brush and rag floated on the surface, and then she retrieved the soap. The kettle at the stove was full and heavy, and she struggled to lift it. Without a word, J.D. brushed her hand aside and poured some of the steaming water into the bucket. She stood back, observing him, watching the play of muscles stretch the shirt across his back as he was bent over. She stared at the cuts and scars on his hands, thinking he didn't live an easy life.

The scent of soap on his skin was noticeably pleasant. In Sienna, she'd thought him remotely handsome—in a rugged way. But without the short beard hiding half of his features, he was very attractive. His mouth was fuller than she had guessed. There was a slight cleft in his chin, and if she looked closely, she saw faint dimples at the corners of his mouth. She'd always equated dimples with someone who laughed quite a bit. But J.D. was far too serious. Too brooding.

Crouching down, Josephine dunked the rag in the warm water. Her gaze fell on J.D.'s hair. She'd never known a man who kept his hair so long. She would have thought she'd be put off by its unruly length that went against her social standard of etiquette. But she wasn't. She was rather intrigued by the dark hair that fell softly around his collar. Did it feel as silky as it looked?

J.D. caught her staring at him. She hadn't been

paying attention to where she was squeezing the water, and it sloshed onto the floor. He couldn't have missed her obvious examination—and approval— before returning to what he'd been doing.

Chiding herself, she squared her shoulders and vowed to keep her eyes on her work. She dragged the stool from the corner and strategically placed it in the center of the room so that she could wash the ceiling first.

The time passed quickly, and soon the night's darkness broke as a misty fog blurred the curve of yellow at the horizon. Josephine paused to stare out the window. She'd never seen a western sunrise before. The colors were warm, running from burnt orange to red. At least the Beadle's hadn't lied about that.

She was only three-quarters of the way finished with the kitchen when J.D. brought a pan of biscuits out of the oven. The heavenly scent of browned dough filled the room. He removed a frying pan of something smelling similar to bacon from the stove plate and set it on the sideboard.

"When you've got a meal done," he said, "you walk around to the front porch and ring the triangle. That'll bring the boys in."

Josephine smiled inside. She knew what a triangle was, having read about a character named Vinegar Jim who'd banged a wand inside one.

"I can do that," she replied confidently, then lifted her gaze.

She'd been so set on getting her job done, she hadn't paid J.D. too much mind. Until now. He stood with his legs braced apart, sleeves rolled up. Around his lean waist, a white towel had been tied by thin strings to make an apron of sorts. She'd never envisioned a cowboy as a cook, but J.D. looked like he belonged in a kitchen with his no-nonsense stance and command of the pots and pans.

Tossing the towel he was holding onto the counter, he said, "I'll get the grub on the table while you finish up in here." J.D. grabbed the platter of biscuits in one hand and the frying pan in the other. On his way out, he called over his shoulder, "Take a load off and eat something." He inclined his chin to the counter, then departed through the door.

She went to see what he'd been indicating. It was a napkin-covered plate. Slowly, she lifted a corner of the napkin. Arranged on the plate were two fluffy biscuits and some kind of crispy meat. What drew her attention was the canned peach dead center, making the arrangement symmetrical. Mismatched silverware was laid crosswise at the head of the plate, knife blade pointing out.

Josephine looked up as J.D. returned to the kitchen to get the coffeepot. He was in and out in seconds without making eye contact with her. A host of masculine voices drifted from the dining room as he exited. Her gaze fell on the plate once more.

She couldn't explain why, but she thought J.D.'s breakfast offering was the most thoughtful thing any man had ever done for her.

Rio Cibolo and One-Eyed Hazel rolled the chuck wagon from the shadowy barn out into the blaring sunlight. J.D. examined its wooden outsides with a critical eye. The sight was discouraging. One of the wheels was missing a spoke. At least Hazel could make a replacement. All the hubs squeaked; they needed a good cleaning and greasing.

"It don't seem right getting the wagon out without Luis telling us what to do," Hazel said softly.

One-Eyed Hazel was older than the hills, but he was just as enduring as the land itself. His life was etched on his grizzled face. Years of sun and wind, long winter nights, and hot summer days made a network of lines at the corners of his eyes and thin mouth.

Most of his front teeth were missing, and those that were left were yellow—like the tobacco stains on his fingers. A black patch covered his right eye. A colt had kicked him in the side of his head some nine years back when he'd been breaking horses at the Bar W. The accident had left him blind in that eye.

"Boss'll tell us what to do," Rio stated, pulling a tiny sack of Durham out of his breast pocket. He took a pinch of the cowboy candy, then closed the pouch by pulling on the drawstring with his teeth. "Or is the cookie going to scrub it down and give me 'n' Hazel the orders?"

"She'll be helping us," J.D. replied, laying his hand along one of the wagon's sideboards where the outfit's brand had been burned in the wood.

"Where is she, then?" Rio asked around the lump in his cheek, the tone in his voice anxious.

"She'll be along."

J.D. had left a set of his work clothes on Josephine's bed while she washed the breakfast dishes. The lace-up knit jersey would give her some warmth, and a pair of his blue denim britches would give her the freedom needed to organize the wagon's bed. It had been her lack of complaining about cleaning the kitchen and her holding her head high in a skirt and blouse his mother would have rather burned than wear that had sent him searching through his dresser drawers. He'd thought for sure she'd throw in the towel and say she couldn't get the job done. But she hadn't. The walls were spotless. So were the floor and ceiling.

Josephine appeared through the front door. She'd rolled up the bottoms to the pants and turned up the sleeve cuffs once or twice. The shirt's hem hung out of the britches, giving her the shape of a straight board. There was no body definition to her. No outline of breasts, waist, or hips. Which was just as well with the boys dallying around.

She stepped off the porch, her eyes narrowing to

adjust to the bright sun. She wore her fancy hat—the only thing left of the Miss Forget-Me-Not attire. The wide blue ribbon was tied at an angle beneath her chin, and the brim was all but worthless. He lowered his gaze to her feet. She wore her fine dress shoes.

As she approached, he caught a glimpse of her hands. They were red and chapped. He thought of those soft-looking ivory fingers lying on her pillow this morning when he'd awakened her. A pang of guilt racked him, but he willed it away. There was nothing he could do. He was paying her to do a job that required physical effort and a lot of cleaning.

"Morning, ma'am," Rio said in a sugary voice, tipping the brim of his hat. Then he turned his head away and spat watery juice between his lips.

Rio was the only hand favoring Josephine Whittaker. Hell, Rio favored any woman, so that didn't count. The fact of the matter was, besides Peavy and Boots, nobody had met her yet. The no-show of the steaks J.D. had promised she'd deliver last night was reflected in the morale of the boys this morning. A cattle outfit was only as good as its cook, and for the past three weeks the McCall outfit had been suffering. The cowboys, as loyal as they may be, wouldn't keep on working to the bone for creamed corn on toast.

"Good morning," Josephine replied evenly as she drew up to the wagon. She eyed Hazel with trepidation.

"This here is Rio," J.D. said without preamble, "and that's Hazel. Hazel, this is the new cook, Miss Josephine Whittaker."

Hazel instantly doffed his hat and held onto it in front of him, fidgeting with the brim. "Ma'am." Despite being a big, slack-jawed fellow with a patch over his eye, Hazel had a gentle voice that put people at ease.

"We'll take everything out first, then scour the bed." J.D. laid his hand on the wagon's side and hopped in. He tossed Rio the bows and tarp that went on top. "Air out that canvas sheet," he told him. Then to Hazel, "Hazel, get the boiling water and lye soap."

J.D. could have sworn he heard Josephine stifle a groan.

"You stand over here," he directed her, "and take what I hand you."

Josephine came forward.

The cooking vessels, which had been coated with a layer of grease to prevent rust, had now accumulated an additional coating of winter dust and particles of hay. They'd all have to be washed out with the lye soap and sand to remove the grease, both burned and unburned.

"Make a pile over there," J.D. told her, motioning toward the large kettle of water Hazel had set up earlier. Then he gave her a skillet and pan he thought for sure she'd drop. The cast-iron vessels were heavy, and he could see she was barely able to manage holding on to both of the slippery, lard-covered handles at the same time. But she did. Once at the designated spot, she haphazardly dropped them, then stared at her soiled hands. She examined one of her fingernails with a frown.

J.D. gave her more cookware to stack without a break in between. She must have made the trip a good two dozen times before they'd unloaded it all. She never uttered a single protest.

"Come here, and I'll show you the chuck box," J.D. said as he jumped down from the bed.

Josephine followed him to the back of the wagon, where a high chest had been mounted. Dropping down the tall tailgate, which served as a table, J.D. assessed the compartment. The shelves of the cupboard showed signs of where the rats and mice had wintered.

"Take all the drawers out. They have to be washed, too."

Dutifully, she nodded. She hadn't said much all morning—which suited J.D. fine. He wasn't much of a talker when he was working.

Josephine had no sooner put her hand on one of the knobs and pulled, when she let out a blood-curdling scream that had J.D. palming his Colt.

CHAPTER

⇒ 5 ←

As Josephine sprinted across the yard, J.D.'s yell of "What's wrong?" followed her.

She couldn't answer him. She just kept on running and screaming until she came to the shed door and pressed her back against it. Out of breath, she gasped. The skin on her arms tingled with gooseflesh.

"What the hell is wrong?" J.D. asked, storming down on her. He brandished a big gun. She gulped. Fighting for air, she remained silent.

His gaze scanned the ground from the spot on which she stood to the wagon. Since there was nothing to be seen, he apparently thought the coast was clear; he reholstered his revolver.

Rio called from behind, "What's going on, boss?"

"I don't know," J.D. yelled back, then faced Josephine. "What's going on?"

In between the short, huffy pants that possessed her breath, she managed to get out, "M-m-m-m—"

"Mmm what?"

"M-m-mouse."

"Mouse?"

"There was a m-mouse in the drawer."

The fear of it still pounded through Josephine's veins. Though the offending creature had been so motionless it could have been dead before she'd discovered it, she'd instinctively run for safety. A rodent was a rodent. Dead or alive.

J.D. backed away, his eyes full of disgust. "Hell, cookie," he chided in a tight voice, "if it had been something poisonous, I could see why you'd run."

When he used that tone, she felt restless and irritable. "Maybe you're used to rodents, Mr. McCall, but I'm not."

"You better get used to them, *cookie*. There could be more in that wagon."

His second-in-a-row reference to her as "cookie" had her lifting her chin and boldly meeting his eyes. She'd let the other times slip by because she hadn't wanted to confront him for fear he'd dismiss her. But when he spoke the word in that manner—emphasized and sarcastic—her lips thinned. She responded without thought.

"Kindly refrain from addressing me as a piece of oven-baked dough. I'm neither flat nor round, and at this moment especially I'm not at all sweet. You may engage my services, but that doesn't give you the right to speak down to me. I have been in your position, Mr. McCall, and to my credit I can say that I was always civil and courteous to the staff employed in my household. Call me Miss Whittaker or, if you must, Josephine. But don't call me Cookie."

Stunned by her own outburst, Josephine stood there, mouth agape, waiting for the tongue-lashing that would surely come next. All her life, she'd never talked back for fear her father would take her to task or Hugh would tell her she was being unreasonable.

The longer J.D. stared at her, she realized that nothing was going to happen. No tirades. No chastisement. No berating. Nothing.

"I'll remember that," he said at length. Then, with a long stride, J.D. left. Only when he was gone did she let out her breath. She'd done it. She'd actually spoken her mind and hadn't been punished for it.

Josephine vented a few quick half-gasps that were more like tiny, nervous laughs. "My goodness," she spoke to herself, more in awe by the second.

Uncertain of her next move, Josephine lingered. J.D. had climbed back into the wagon. She had no desire to go near it again until every nook and cranny had been searched. She watched as Hazel added another coffeepot of hot water to the wide-mouthed kettle. The one-eyed man wasn't as frightening as she'd gathered by his appearance alone. His voice had been as soft as down.

As he mixed the soapy water with a wooden paddle, she knew what was to come. The washing. In less than twenty-four hours of gainful employment, she didn't recognize her own hands.

Josephine pushed away from the shed and began rolling her sleeves up a few notches higher. She found that in trousers her walk took on a more casual and less careful step, as she didn't have to worry about tripping over her petticoats. At first, she'd been adamantly opposed to wearing men's clothing—much less J.D. McCall's. But the shirt and pants were clean. They smelled like sunshine and soap. Not lye, but another variety. And they smelled vaguely like the man who owned them. She couldn't put her finger on the source, but it reminded her of leather to a certain degree. And perhaps, too, of tobacco, though not the sickly sweet blend her father smoked in his pipe.

There were, however, tradeoffs to the masculine garb. In denim trousers, the outlines of her legs showed. Though the pants weren't tight, the definition was still there, and it made her feel painfully exposed.

Nearing the kettle, Josephine decided to plunge into the dishes without being told rather than return to the wagon and more mice.

Although less leery about Hazel, Josephine still skirted around him widely to get to the pots and pans. She dumped them one right after the other into the pot, causing a flow of water to run over the rim and spot her French kid shoes.

"What are you doing?"

She barely turned toward the direction of J.D.'s voice. "Washing dishes."

She was glad he didn't take issue with her, though her relief was short-lived when he said, "When you're done with those, you've got all that."

She followed his gaze to Rio Cibolo, who was crouched by the front wheel of the wagon with a bucket of thick black paste. At his back was an immense stack of plates and tin cups, not to mention a mound of knives, forks, and spoons.

Forcing her thoughts at bay, Josephine kept her mind on one pot at a time.

After a while, Hazel drew up to her with a bucket.

"Ma'am, I need some of your water."

She moved her waterlogged hands out of the way, mindful of how she gazed at Hazel. She didn't want to stare into his good eye or overly linger at the patch. The simple fact was, there was no place to look at Hazel's face without potentially insulting him. So she cast her eyes downward and watched his hands.

He had stubby fingers with cracked thumbnails embedded with lines of dirt. A scab covered one knuckle, and blue veins rose distinctly on the backs of his hands as he held on to the bucket's handle.

"Thank you, ma'am."

Hazel hoisted the bucket to J.D., who emptied it on the wagon floor and then called for another. From the corner of her eye, Josephine watched J.D. as he stood tall waiting for Hazel to return with more water. He removed his hat and tunneled his fingers through his thick hair before settling the leather hat back on.

"This is the last I'll be disturbing you, ma'am," Hazel said as he dunked the bucket into the tepid water. Then he climbed into the wagon with J.D. to scrape out the cracks, corners, and nailheads for what she assumed were an accumulation of dirt and grease.

While they did that, Josephine continued to wash. And scour. And scrub.

Periodically, a cowboy would come over and talk to J.D., all the while stealing glimpses of her. One by one they'd come. She lost count after thirteen. Each time, J.D. would send them off with a quick glance in her direction and a shake of his head. She didn't like being on display. She'd run away from that. As a child, she may have enjoyed dressing up in her mother's best finery and playing lady for attention, but now she didn't want to be an ornament.

By the time she plopped the last fork into the rinsing water, she was ready to crawl back into bed for a week. Muscles that had never been abused in such a manner ached—her lower back, her forearms, her legs. Her hands were sore, the skin wrinkled. Her fingernails were an abomination.

Squaring her shoulders to stretch the tension from them, she gazed around at the conglomeration of pots, pans, and skillets in various sizes, the utensils, plates, cups, and silverware—all laid out to dry on the grass beneath the sun. In disbelief, she wiped her hands on a soggy kitchen towel to the amazing thought that she had cleaned every last piece herself. Though the defining emotion was foggy, she almost felt . . . satisfied.

A tinny peal erupted from the porch. Josephine spied Boots at the triangle. Stoop-shouldered, he put a lot of zeal into the banging of the metal. "The banquet awaits, fellers!" he hollered. "Grab 'er now, or I'll throw 'er out!"

Josephine heard J.D. grumble above the noise, "Throw it out . . ."

Her gaze veered to him. He was still standing in the wagon's bed, which was gleaming from the ash and sand he and Hazel had used on the wood. His arm was propped on the end of a mop handle, supporting the mop upright. His firm mouth was curved in an expression bordering on cynical.

J.D. caught her looking, and she felt the need to say something as she folded the towel. "We've finished just in time for lunch."

He rewarded her with a sheepish smile that quickly turned out to be a wolf's in disguise. "Miss Whittaker, we've barely even started."

"I couldn't believe it when I saw her things still in that room this morning," Boots said around a bite of toast.

"Close your trap, Boots," J.D. cautioned, eating while trying not to taste what was in his mouth.

The others at the table kept their heads down and wolfed what was in front of them so they could be quickly on their way back to the corral and the yard.

Boots waved a spoon. "I figured y'all would've sent her packing after last night."

J.D. stabbed the air with his finger in the direction of Boots. "I'd keep her on just to irritate you."

"Good gawd, y'all hate me that much." Boots dove the spoon into a side plop of beans on his plate. "I'm telling Hazel to shoot me in the head when my number is up. I'm going to cheat you out of the chance to watch me turn into a drooling old man."

"You already are an old man."

"But, by gawd, I don't drool!" Boots shouted.

With that, the crew made a fast exodus out the front door.

Shoving his half-eaten plate aside with disgust, J.D. remembered a time when Boots had talked like a southern gentleman. Over the years, his drawl had become a blend of western quips with only lingering traces of the Mississippi dialect present.

J.D. scraped his chair back, stood, then headed for the kitchen. Prior to his trading words with Boots, the daring of Josephine's little "cookie" speech had occupied his mind. He hadn't pegged her for the type to make a man feel like he was a skunk. Not that she had done so vindictively. Hell, he'd had it coming to him, and he knew it. But that didn't make being rubbed like dirty laundry over a washboard any less stinging.

He'd been pushing her. Trying to break her. Trying to prove to himself that she was eastern born and bred and would always be.

For a moment afterward, J.D. had thought to apologize to her, but he lacked the know-how. He was clumsy with words of remorse. He always had been. He spoke his mind without thought, having learned his excessive frankness from Boots.

At least he'd gained some manners from Eugenia, and his strong education came from her insistence that her three sons would excel academically. Rather than sending them to the parish school, his mother hired a private tutor—Mr. Gerald P. Archer, who resided with them and taught lessons to J.D., Lewis, and William.

As J.D. pushed the kitchen door in, he caught Josephine sitting on a stool at the counter, a barely touched plate in front of her and an open book in her hand. He couldn't make out the title because she snapped the soft cover closed and slipped it title-side down on her lap.

Her amber eyes were bright, and shiny tendrils of auburn hair framed her face. Though she had arranged her hair in its previous style of braids and twists, the morning's work over a steaming kettle of water had turned the fine strands at her temples and cheeks into wispy curls.

"You didn't sit at the table for dinner," he said without preamble.

"Boots said the cook eats in the kitchen."

"You weren't the cook for this meal. You could have sat with us."

She fingered the edges of her book. "If it makes you feel any better, I heard most everything that was said."

"You and half the town of Sienna," J.D. replied, testing the heat of the big coffeepot on the back

75

burner. The motion was done more out of habit than actually wanting another cup. For some unexplainable reason, he felt like an intruder in his own kitchen. He needed to do something that made him belong in the room.

The coffeepot checked, his gaze landed on Josephine once more. He was again taken aback by the softness of her features with her hair less severely styled. He had to remind himself that she wasn't his type. He liked a woman who was willowy and strong. One who could handle a gun and help with the stock if the cows broke down a fence on the back forty. His ideal woman was one who could make great pies and still belong to the outdoors and the real work of cattle, horses, and land.

Shaking off his contrary thoughts, J.D. said, "Time to get a move on. We need to load the wagon."

Josephine stood, hugged the book to her breasts, then replied, "Let me get my hat." She returned in a moment, minus the novel, tying the ribbon to her bonnet.

Boots came through the dining room door carrying a load of dirty plates and utensils. He puffed on a fat cigar clamped between his teeth, its smoke creating a cloud that rose to the ceiling. He gave J.D. a scowl. "Since I did the cooking, y'all ought to make her do the dishwashing."

"Don't tell me how to run things, Boots. She'll be washing the supper dishes."

Boots sidled up to the dry sink and scooted the plates onto the counter; a fork dropped and clattered to the floor, leaving a smear of beans. "Then you best remind me of that," he snapped, rolling the cigar to the corner of his mouth, "since y'all think my mind is going. I'm liable to forget." With his hand gripping the counter's rounded edge to keep him balanced, Boots bent down to pick up the fork.

J.D. held the door open for Josephine, and they went out into the yard.

She looked at him with a silent inquiry, then put her gaze straight ahead.

"What?" he asked when she didn't say anything.

"I was just wondering," she began softly, "why you don't call Boots Father."

J.D. felt like laughing, only he didn't. Because the laugh wouldn't have been humorous. "I haven't called him Father in longer than I can remember. He's always been Boots."

"It's an uncommon nickname."

"The field hands named him that before I could even talk. The story goes it was because he always wore glossy black Hessian boots when he was riding through the cotton." J.D. didn't give her the opportunity to say anything else on the subject, having already said more than he should. "Hey, Ace," he called across the space separating him and the corral. "Where's that red with the crippled calf?"

"We grafted her to the paint."

J.D. nodded.

The boys were earmarking the last of the calves that would be moving out to the spring range. The mother cows that had been separated from their babies were bawling, sending the dogs to lie down a distance away in the bushes. Only Toby came out to investigate, giving a yap now and then when one of the boys whistled. There were those calves that would stay behind because they were born late and newly branded. Some of the yearlings wouldn't make the trip, nor would cattle unfit for travel.

Hunkered down at the wagon, Rio painted grease on the axles. Hazel had jacked up the front and taken off the wheel for repairs.

Pivoting on the ball of his foot, Rio said, "Hey, boss, me and Hazel found Luis's fiddle in the barn. What do you want us to do with it?"

J.D. thought a moment. Luis had been a fine fiddler, entertaining the boys around the campfire many a night. J.D. realized the old cook was going to be missed in more ways than one. "Put it in the wagon. Birdie knows how to play it passable enough."

Drawing up to the wagon, J.D. skimmed a thoughtful gaze across it. The interior woodwork was clean and bright. The harnesses and reins were spread out on the grass, the leather having been rubbed with balm to a supple gleam. The water barrel had been filled with sweet well water to swell its seams closed. Hazel must have seen to the sourdough jar and chipped away the hardened dough and splatters of dried batter. Sunshine reflected off the gray porcelain that could hold five gallons of the best biscuit-making goo a cowboy could ever want.

"I expect you'll be wanting to get the sourdough starter going," J.D. said to Josephine. "Flour's on the back of the buckboard, so's the salt. Hazel can heat up some water."

She didn't look too enlightened when she replied in an offhanded manner, "I'll wait until later to do that."

"I thought you had to let it ferment in the sun today so it would be good for using in the biscuits tomorrow."

"Oh, yes," she quickly said. "Of course . . . I should do that . . . right away." She bit her lip, then abruptly announced, "I've forgotten something in my room. Pardon me a moment."

J.D. bent his head against the sun's glare to watch her walk swiftly toward the house. Clad within the baggy seat of his pants, he could just barely make out the urgent sway of her shapely behind as she minced her steps. She disappeared around the side yard, leaving J.D. to ponder once again why in the blazes he'd hired her.

Grabbing the rusty knob to the back door, Josephine twisted it quickly. She winced as pressure squeezed a cut she had on her forefinger. Bringing her finger to her mouth, she sucked on the wound and let herself into the kitchen. Upon seeing Boots at the sink, she stopped short. She'd forgotten he'd be between her and her room.

Boots turned his head to stare at her.

Lowering her arm, Josephine murmured, "Excuse me." Then she went on to her room. Once inside, she closed the door and headed straight for her valise at the foot of the bed. Lifting the lid, she snatched up the now tomato-stained cookbook and began to flip through the pages for a recipe on sourdough starter. She reached the end. Nothing. Surely she'd just missed the recipe, so she thumbed to each page and read the title. But once at the end again, to her dismay, there was nothing. There were two biscuit recipes. Baking powder and buttermilk. Neither was sourdough.

Josephine lifted her chin. What was she going to do? J.D. McCall expected her to make sourdough starter, and she'd implied she could.

After tucking the book away, she sat on the messy bed. A flyspecked light blazed through the window where the curtains were parted. From behind her door, she heard Boots rattling pans. He seemed to know something about cooking. After all, he'd made the dinner last night and the lunch today. And with the claim the cowboys preferred his meals above others.

Josephine got an idea. She left her room and strolled into the kitchen ever so casually. "Hello," she greeted.

Boots's back was toward her, and he apparently didn't hear her.

"Hello," she said louder.

This time, he turned and barked, "What was that?"

"I said hello."

"What for?"

"Because—"

"What are y'all doing in here?" His watery blue eyes sported resentment. "Come to spy on me, have you? Well, you can tell J.D. that I haven't dropped dead." He jabbed a soapy thumb into his chest. "The ol' ticker is pumping."

"No, Mr. McCall, I haven't been sent."

"Don't call me Mr. McCall. That's a hell of an attitude to address somebody old as Mister."

For Josephine, formally addressing her elders was second nature. She hadn't thought to offend him.

Boots went back to the dishes.

"I'm sorry," she offered. "I didn't mean to upset you."

For the first time since she had made his acquaintance, Boots held his tongue, not giving her a glance or a nod. It would appear she'd been dismissed. She had to think of a different way to get his attention. He seemed to say the most when he was criticizing.

"I guess I'd better get back outside," she remarked while taking a backward step for the door. "I'm going to make sourdough starter. My recipe has been in the family for decades. It's sure to make the best biscuits you'll ever eat." She tried to remember what J.D. had said about the ingredients. He'd only mentioned flour, salt, and hot water. She hadn't learned anything about measurements other than what she'd read last night. "If you insist, I could tell you how mine's made."

Unfortunately, Boots didn't insist.

Josephine retook her step and strategically moved forward so she wouldn't have to yell. Without Boots asking, she began to tell him the recipe as if divulging a guarded secret. "First you take . . ." She envisioned the jar in the yard. It was fairly large. "Um, you take ten teacups of flour. And some salt. Then you get water and . . ." Boots still didn't face off with her. "And you boil it until it's boiling hot—"

"Good gawd." Boots turned his head in her direction. "Y'all haven't got the brains of a grasshopper. To make sourdough starter, you need four quarts of flour, a dash of salt, and warm water—not boiling.

Stir it to a medium-thick batter, cover it, and put the jar out in the sun." He gave her a slanted look that said he truly did think her brain was smaller than a grasshopper's. "Anyone who tells you different is full of horse wind."

Josephine might have taken offense at his reference to her intelligence, but he'd just saved her from a disaster. "Well, perhaps I will give your method a try."

"If you know what's good for them boys, y'all would." Then he turned to the sink once more.

Josephine thoughtfully chewed the inside of her lip. "Would you like to help me with supper . . . Boots?"

He paused but didn't look at her. "Why are you asking me that?"

"Because I thought you might want to."

His body relaxed, and his head seemed to settle onto his shoulders. "If I don't have anything else to do."

Leaving, Josephine quietly closed the door. It was obvious Boots didn't want her there. His displeasure had been perfectly clear by his grumbling at the lunch table. But in spite of how he felt about her, she could use him to her advantage. Having Boots in the kitchen with her could prove to be an asset. His obstinate opinion on her every move could very well save her from botching things a second time. She'd just cook things the way he said, and everything would turn out as it should.

As Josephine started for the yard, she took a small measure of satisfaction for having just outsmarted Boots McCall. After all, he'd said she had a brain the size of a grasshopper's.

CHAPTER

→ 6 ←

After exchanging words with Boots about the recipe, Josephine went outside and prepared the sourdough starter without mishap. Then she helped J.D. stock the wagon with all the freshly cleaned cooking implements and the supply order he'd had filled at Mr. Klauffman's store. There was an entire drawer devoted to remedies. She asked J.D. about them, and he told her what they were: quinine, calomel, black draught, and horse liniment—to be used on either man or animal. Whiskey was for snakebites and doctoring. Josephine hoped they wouldn't have to uncork the bottle.

There were so many hidey holes on the wagon to be packed, she lost track of them. Josephine wasn't able to stay until the end. J.D. told her it was time to prepare supper.

Inside, she loaded the stove with wood and left the dampers to the specifications J.D. had used for the breakfast meal. She had barely struck a match to light it when Boots came sauntering in, a tabby cat padding after him. He slid a stool toward her, picked up the cat, and sat down.

"I would've been helping Peavy with the calves, but

they've got it covered," he said gruffly. "So I figured I'd watch y'all make a hell of a mess again."

She held her tongue.

"For frying steaks, you need to close off that oven damper," he criticized, his big-knuckled fingers spreading through the cat's fur to stroke its back. "Otherwise they aren't going to cook right."

She gave him a half smile and did as he suggested.

Josephine hadn't been looking forward to facing the slab of beef, but she'd had no choice. She'd set it on the counter, picked up a knife, and would have begun arbitrarily cutting if Boots hadn't stopped her.

"Good gawd, y'all cut it with the grain like that, it's going to taste like it was sawed right off the horn of some old bull. You bring the blade *against* the grain."

She wanted to believe him. But suddenly, her oh-so-smart plan had a major flaw. He might tell her how to do the job because he wanted to show he was right; but by the same token, he wanted her to be let go from her position. It could be he'd purposefully steer her wrong.

She glanced at him. There was no mistaking he was crabby by the way his brows shot down at the bridge of his sunburned nose. But he stroked the cat with a light, gentle touch. He'd said he disliked cats. Seeing him contentedly petting the tabby curled up in his lap was a contradiction of that statement. Perhaps he was known for saying one thing but really meaning another.

"What's the matter?" he scoffed. "Is your thinker plumb puny? Cut the beef the way I say."

She gave him a final appraisal and immediately made up her mind upon seeing the hostility in his narrowed eyes. Whatever he said, she'd do the opposite. "Thank you," she replied, turning her focus back on the meat, "but I think I'll do it my way."

"The wrong way," he assured in a cross tone.

Despite her decision, Josephine vacillated with the butcher's knife in her hand. She tried to rationalize beef cutting. There didn't seem to be a right way and a wrong way. Meat was meat. With a shrug, she lowered the blade and cut it the way she'd originally planned.

Once she'd had the meat in jagged slabs, she closed her eyes a moment to recollect what the recipe had said about frying steaks. *Salt and pepper. Roll in flour. Drop into a hot pan.* With a nod of her head, she set out to work, while Boots gave her a lecture on how to cook the meat, all the while adding cheeky commentary about the digestive benefits of creamed corn on toast as opposed to beef.

After the last potato had been peeled—a process that had sliced the skin off one knuckle and given her a cut on another—Boots changed the subject from corn to the present vegetable in hand and said ungraciously, "Y'all can't cut those too big."

"Yes, I know," Josephine said, agreeing with him even though she didn't. She cut each potato into quarters, dumped the mound into the large pot, poured water from a pitcher over the top, and set them on the back of the stove between the skillets of frying meat.

"Those were too big, you numbskull," he warned.

Putting her hands on her hips, Josephine had all she could stand. He could lead her down the wrong path if he liked, but she'd rather not be called a name. "I believe you have an ulterior motive here."

"Y'all're damn right I do," he admitted to her satisfaction, but his next reply was anything but satisfying to her. "I've got to eat what you're cooking, and I don't like tough meat or lumpy potatoes. J.D. made up his mind to keep you on, so if I can't have my creamed corn on toast, I want to sink these old teeth into a decent steak. But what y'all've got going in here is like to break them off to the root."

After his fit of temper, Boots stalked off—at the precise moment the steaks sizzled in dry pans and the potato water sputtered over the side of the pot.

Josephine salvaged what she could, then set the

table. The long pine trestle supported a collection of cowhide-bottomed chairs. Many of them were wired up in one place or another, evidence of efforts to repair past abuse. The table was bare of even an oilcloth. Though there weren't enough cups, plates, and silverware that matched, she arranged the items in a relative order.

With a last look at her handiwork, she went and rang the triangle. Now all she could do was hope for the best as she returned to the kitchen.

She took one of the heavy platters of steaks from the countertop and brought it into the dining room to set in the middle of the table. Gazing at the pile of meat, she hoped nobody would notice the underside had been cooked to a crispy black. She made several trips until the table had been spread out with the food. Pouring the coffee from the heavy pot had proved challenging to say the least. Dribbles of the dark liquid splashed onto plates, the table, and the napkins.

Boots was the first to arrive. He eyed the fare with a finicky gaze, then gave her a smug smile before sitting. J.D. arrived next, followed by what seemed like an endless stream of cowboys, until all eighteen of the chairs were spoken for. Nobody but Boots had sat down.

J.D.'s tan hand rested on the bow back of his chair. He'd removed his hat; aside from shaving, she couldn't recall ever seeing him without it. Around the crown of his head, his hair was dented, the longer ends mussed and unruly. In fact, all of the men were hatless. Some leaned into their chairs, others shuffled in their boots, and Rio chewed on the end of his mustache. They all appeared tired and hungry.

And they all were looking at her.

"I reckon now's the time for proper introductions," J.D. said, shifting his eyes from her to the table. "Boys, this is the new cook, Miss Josephine Whittaker. Miss Whittaker, these are the boys." Then he proceeded to name each one individually, starting at his left. "This here is Gus Peavy."

"Ma'am," Gus replied with a tip of his head.

"That's Jidge Dooly," J.D. continued, and so did the "ma'ams."

"Orley Woodard, Dan Hotchkiss, Seth Winters, Birdie Tippett, Ace Flynn, Print Freeland, Rio Cibolo . . ."

Josephine tried to remember all the names, but there were so many of them.

"And you're already acquainted with Hazel and Boots," J.D. concluded.

One-Eyed Hazel said, "Ma'am."

Boots said nothing.

Feeling uncomfortable with the stiff formalities and gazes on her, Josephine offered, "Please sit down and enjoy your supper."

There was a shuffling of chair legs, and the cowboys all took their places and began to pass the platters around. Josephine could hardly stand to watch as they served up their plates. The only noise was the scraping of spoons in the two bowls of mashed potatoes and the clink of the steak platters as they were passed around the table. She couldn't stay and wait for their reaction, especially when Boots was inspecting every dish with disdain.

Excusing herself, Josephine went into the kitchen.

She should have listened to Boots. He'd probably been right about the steaks because he'd been right about the potatoes. They'd turned out undercooked in the middles. She'd had a hard time mashing them and had been unable to get all the raw lumps out.

Josephine looked at the plate she'd fixed for herself. Drawing the stool up to the counter, she sat down and picked up her fork. A sharp knife was necessary to saw through the stringy meat, never mind that the steak was barely chewable. The potatoes were bland and unpalatable. They needed a sauce or a dollop of butter—neither of which she had. Taking a drink of coffee, she found that the brew was weak and bitter. At the bottom of her cup was a whole Arbuckle's bean. The coffee she'd had before had never looked or tasted like this. She'd assumed the beans would boil down to nothing, but they were still just as whole as when she'd dumped them in.

After eating what she could, Josephine dropped her chin and closed her eyes. What would Pearl Larimer do in a situation like this? Go into the dining room and proclaim she was a fraud, then demand Rawhide pay her anyway? Not likely.

With a heavy sigh, Josephine pressed her fingertips to the bridge of her nose. She had no answers. Unlike Pearl, she would rather run away from her present set of circumstances.

I want to go home.

But she had no home. What she had shared with Hugh was no longer welcome to her—as if for a moment she would think about going back to him. Never. Her childhood home on Madison Square had been sold upon her father's death to pay his debts. There was nothing in New York for her anymore. But New York and its society was all she knew. She was lost out here . . . lost in a house full of men who expected too much from her. She never should have lied. But if she hadn't, where would she be now?

"Coffee," somebody called from the dining room.

Josephine straightened and wearily rose from the stool. Using a folded towel, she lifted the heavy pot from the stove and brought it into the dining room.

Nearly every man around the table indicated his need for a second cup by sliding his mug toward the right of his plate. She obliged. Not a one said the meal or the coffee was horrid. She had a good mind to say it herself and get it over with.

J.D.'s was the last cup to refill. Their gazes met. She thought for sure she was in for a reprimand. But he merely said, "Next time, grind the beans and make the coffee twice as strong."

She nodded, then took her leave, wondering idly why he hadn't mentioned the bad steaks and potatoes. In the kitchen, she returned the pot to the stove. If she'd done this poorly for Hugh, he would have let her know in exact words how displeased he was.

Unbidden, his voice surfaced in her mind.

What good are you? You've got no money anymore. Your name is associated with scandal now that your father killed himself. You aren't a good wife, Josephine. You're a nothing. You can't even give me children. The sight of you repulses me.

The crackle of the stove's dying coals brought her back to the present. What she'd envisioned as a consummation of passion and romance had turned out to be a marriage of limitations and dependence. For her, there had been no magical bridge from her parents' home to Hugh's Fifth Avenue residence where she would become an adored wife and the pride of her husband. Her courtship had been a sham. The moment she'd said "I do," she'd become nothing to her husband.

It was because of her disappointment in Hugh— and in herself for believing him—that she'd begun to read the Beadle's books. She'd dreamed of being one of the heroines, free to love and be loved by a man who would release her from the spell of disillusionment. She'd so wanted to be swept away from the cold and lonely house, into the arms of . . . Rawhide Abilene.

But after six years of marriage, and being the recipient of Hugh's ultimate betrayal and ugly accusations, she'd had to accept that where love was concerned, happy endings were the myths of novels.

J.D. walked through the quiet house carrying an alarm clock. The lights in the bunkhouses had been turned down an hour ago, as were the lanterns in the front room. Navigating his way through the darkened area, J.D. went into the shadow-cast dining room. Josephine hadn't reappeared from the kitchen after supper. They'd all left the table with the dishes spread out, coffee cups empty, and hearty appetites not nearly satisfied. Though the steaks had been tough as bullhide chaps and cooked to black on the bottom, they hadn't been as bad as Boots's corn specialty. At least he and the boys had been able to sink their teeth into something without it going soft in their mouths.

The table had been cleared and wiped down to the plain boards. Not a sound came from the kitchen, and J.D. wondered if he'd come too late. Josephine might have ignored the dishes and gone to bed. But as he neared, a faint yellow fan of light spread from beneath the closed door. He let himself into the kitchen, stopping shy of the counter when he saw Josephine.

She sat slumped over on the stool, her slender arms flat on the ledge of the dry sink, acting as a pillow for her head as she slept. The stove had been cleaned, and all the dishes and utensils had been stored. Fanned open at her elbow was the same book, the pictures and print appearing suspiciously like a dime novel. Her face was toward him, the lashes of her eyes thick and sweeping against the light blush color the sun had painted on her cheeks today.

In order for her to be sleeping so soundly, she had to be physically exhausted. He knew firsthand how it felt to be so tired. More than once he'd fallen asleep in the saddle.

J.D. approached her, thinking maybe he'd worked her too hard. But he told himself he'd asked nothing less of her than he would have asked of Pete Denby. Then again, Pete Denby wasn't a woman.

After setting the clock on the counter, J.D. let his hand fall on her shoulder, and he gave her a light shake.

"Miss Whittaker," he said in a low voice. "Um, Josephine, call it a day and go to bed."

She apparently thought she was already in bed because she rolled over. If he hadn't caught her beneath the arms, she would have tumbled off the stool. Now her spine was to the counter, her back arched with breasts thrust forward. Though she still wore his shirt, there was no denying the enticing curves. Her eyes fluttered open, and she stared at him.

"Time to get up already?" she mumbled in a sleep-silky voice.

"No."

"Then what are you doing in my room again?"

"You're in the kitchen."

She turned her head a little, but from the position they were in, she couldn't view the room. From his perspective, she was nearly eye-level with the buckle of his belt and the fly of his pants.

The semidarkness couldn't hide the flush on her cheeks. She struggled to sit up. He aided her by pulling her upright. Unprepared for the spiral of heat he felt where her gaze had been, he released his hold.

One of his concerns about hiring her had been the boys fawning over her and not keeping their minds on their work. He hadn't included himself in that category, and it surprised him now that he wasn't immune to her.

A slender hand was lifted to her forehead, creased by a frown. "I must have accidentally fallen asleep while reading."

"Go to bed." He reached for the clock he'd set on the counter. "Here."

Her eyes fell on the round clock with its nickel housing and glass dial. Then she took it from him. "Thank you."

"You know how to operate it?"

A grudging "No" whispered from her.

He pointed to the stem and wide bell on the top. "Every night before you go to bed, twist that a few times. It'll ring at three o'clock."

"How do I turn it off?"

"You don't. The ringer runs down until it's played out. It should chime for a short minute."

"Oh."

A thin silence hovered over the room, broken only by the steady *tick-tick-tick* of the alarm clock.

J.D. folded his arms across his chest, trying to think of something worthwhile to say before leaving. He didn't talk to many women. There were two chippies at Walkingbars who knew him intimately, but beyond that no woman had ever caught his attention. He had no one to blame but himself for not pursuing a courtship with one of the finer ladies in town. The separation of his parents was always at the back of his mind. His mother had had every right to leave Boots. Most likely, the same thing was in the cards for J.D. if he got entangled with a set of petticoats. Right now, with his many ambitions for the McCall Cattle Company, any kind of involvement that lasted longer than a night didn't fit into the scheme of things.

With her figure once again hidden by the billow of his shirt, J.D. recalled how soft Josephine had felt when he'd helped her sit up. "You better turn in. It's going to be a long day tomorrow."

"I wanted to wash out my blouse."

"I think it's done for."

She forlornly gazed at the lump of mottled fabric in the dry sink. "I think you're right."

Unfolding his arms, he ran his rough fingertip down the length of her nose to its sunburned tip. He wasn't an affectionate man, so he didn't know where the idea had come from to touch her intimately without any reason other than he wanted to. "And it looks like the brim of that fancy hat of yours isn't any good, either."

Her flush deepened to crimson as her eyes lowered. His gaze was fixed on the fullness of her mouth when she spoke softly. "The Dauvray wasn't made for wagon cleaning."

"I reckon it wasn't." Before he did something he'd regret, J.D. backed away and tucked the flats of his big hands into the slashes of his pockets. "See you in the morning."

Then he left for his room, feeling strangely as if he were headed in the wrong direction.

CHAPTER

→7←

The alarm scared Josephine to death when it went off at a dark hour. It seemed the bell rang for an interminable length of time before the peal finally petered out and at last ceased. By then, her eyes were wide open and her pulse still tripped from the start she'd had by waking to such a racket.

Standing in her underwear, she splashed water on her face and arms and wiped a cloth over her upper body. She dressed quietly in the clothes she'd worn the day before. Her blouse was no longer wearable. She wondered what she was to do clothing-wise for the next couple of weeks, but she'd never approach J.D. and ask him for another shirt and pants.

After plaiting her hair and pinning the heavy coil up, she'd gone into the kitchen and turned up a lantern while fighting off her lingering drowsiness.

She lit the stove and began her day with the first item on her list. Coffee. The only recipe she could use was the one in the cookbook. She doubled the amount of beans, this time looking in the section that described the grinder; she found one in the larder. Once the coffee was on, she made the oatmeal.

An hour later, she set the thick and sticky mush on the table with canned milk and sugar.

The cowboys had barely sat down before they were up and off again. She speculated everybody's mind was on the cows that had been bawling since the fringes of dawn had approached. J.D. came and went as quickly as the others.

She was elbow-deep in dishwater when he entered the kitchen with a set of clothes folded over his arm, as well as a hat and a pair of boots.

"You'll never last in those shoes and that hat. You'll need these." He set them down on the counter and left before she could thank him.

She dried off her hands and looked at the hat. It was broad-brimmed, just like the type J.D. wore. Picking it up, she examined the tooled leather and the inside rim where a stain of sweat made it appear well used. For some reason, she was compelled to sniff the brim. It smelled like J.D. She brought the bundle to her room, where she tried the hat on.

Gazing at her reflection in the small mirror, she almost had to laugh. The hat put her eyes in shadow, making her look like a true cow woman. The kind she'd read about in the Beadle's.

"Howdy, Pearl. Nice hat you've got there," she said to her reflection.

"Why, thank you, Rawhide," Josephine replied to herself.

She examined the boots. They hadn't belonged to J.D. They were far too small in size. The burnt-brown leather was scarred, and the heels had seen a good number of days. She sat on the edge of her bed and unlaced her old shoes to try on the boots. She thought surely they were the wrong size because her foot wouldn't fit. But after pulling and wiggling, she was able to stand up and push her heel in. They fit perfectly.

She took a test walk after both boots were on. She felt different in them. As if she could walk through anything and it didn't matter if it was mud or horse droppings. Boots were made to get messy, unlike her smart leather shoes that she'd had to worry about the luster of the grain and always mind her step.

Josephine had wanted to thank J.D. before they left, but by the time she finished in the kitchen, packed away the cookbook and alarm clock in her valise, and carried her wicker case outside, she knew that getting close to him would be impossible.

The yard fairly swam with movement. The wagon had been hitched up to a team of four mules. Boots sat on the bench seat, and One-Eyed Hazel made a check of the straps that held the water barrels in place, while the dogs darted past with high-pitched barks and wagging tails.

Hazel approached and took her valise as she wandered toward the front of the wagon to search for J.D.

Knowing that her thanks would have to wait, Josephine lowered her hand as Rio Cibolo rode up to her on a glossy roan. A string of tin cups and rawhide hobbles swung from the horse's long neck. "Morning, ma'am. Mighty fine breakfast you served up this morning." Then he winked at her.

She knew he had to be jesting.

"You'd best get in the wagon, Miss Josephine," Rio said. "We're moving them out." He leaned forward and held a hand out to her so she could step up into the high bed.

She took his offered grasp, automatically going to clutch her skirts but coming up short. Leveling her boot onto one of the wheel spokes, she pushed off the ground and situated herself on the spring seat that dipped when she sat down. She crossed her ankles and brought her feet back, only to have them hit a box that had been stored beneath her.

"That's where the boys keep their hobbles and other stuff," Boots blustered, his elbows resting on his spread knees. "I don't know what else they've got in there, 'cept that J.D. told me I can't throw anything overboard."

When she made no comment, he added, "If something bothers me, I've been known to toss it over the side."

Meshing her hands together, she pondered Boots's implication that if she annoyed him he'd get rid of her.

Boots shifted in his seat, adjusting his belt. It was then that she noticed that he wore two belts. The second belonged to a holster, in which a very big and lethal gun was strapped to his left hip.

"Are you sure we'll need that?" she asked, not comfortable with a revolver beside her. "We're traveling in a group. No one would dare rob us."

"Danger is never where you think," Boots said simply. Then he fired back with, "What's the matter? Y'all don't think I can hit anything?"

Before she could reply, he withdrew the cumbersome gun by holding its butt in his shaking hand. "I could shoot the hat off of J.D. if I had a mind to." He aimed the gun at J.D.'s head as he rode toward them.

"Boots, put the goddamn Remington back in your holster," J.D. hollered, spurring his horse into a prance, its hooves kicking up flecks of dirt. He reined in next to the wagon. "You're liable to shoot me, you old son-of-a-bitch."

"I don't know how I could," Boots snorted. "Hazel wouldn't give me the bullets for it. Said y'all told him not to."

"Damn right."

"Then what good's the gun to me if it don't work?" To prove his point, Boots centered the tip of the barrel on the tabby cat rubbing up against a porch post. He curled his knobby finger over the trigger and squeezed. *Click*. The mechanism gave off a dry, hollow note. "Nothing. Deader than a beaver hat."

Click. Click. Click.

"And like to stay that way," J.D. replied, his reins tight in his fist to keep the horse from dancing. For the first time, he looked at Josephine. She suddenly felt self-conscious wearing his hat and clothes, as if she needed his approval to be in them. He gave her a slight nod, and she opened her mouth to thank him, but he spoke first—in such a low tone that she had to tilt her head extremely close to his in order to hear him.

"In the back of this wagon in a box marked horseshoes is a loaded gun. If for some reason you two run into trouble, you give it to Boots. He'll know how to use it."

She was barely able to meet J.D.'s eyes when he pulled away and spoke in a loud voice. "Miss Whittaker, you watch this old man and make sure he doesn't throw anything off the wagon. If something rattles in back, don't let him give you the reins so he can go investigate. He once tossed a crate of shoeing jewelry because he didn't like the sound the nails and irons were making."

"Annoyed the hell out of me," Boots muttered under his breath. "And y'all think I'm deaf."

"You're deaf when you want to be." Having said the final word, J.D. turned his horse around before Josephine could speak with him.

Boots swore a string of spicy words as he shoved the gun back into its holster. Josephine kept her gaze forward. She was anxious to be on their way and see how the cowboys would maneuver everything.

J.D. ran his impatient horse out a ways down the center of the road leading to the end of the corral. Josephine watched him in fascination as he withdrew his hat and pointed it at arm's length before him as if to signal the direction. The cowboy behind him and two others at their flanks let out a whoop.

The whole cavalcade moved out in a jumpy rush, as if it had been held down too long. Boots kicked the brake free and just about threw the leather lines away as the mules jerked forward in their traces.

"Get on, you mules!" he called with a bit of undisguised cheer in his tone.

Josephine slanted a discreet glance at him from

beneath the brim of her hat. Boots's eyes were merry, the lines at the corners etched deeper into his hairline as he genuinely grinned.

Looking behind her as they turned, Josephine watched One-Eyed Hazel lift his hand in a gesture of good-bye from the porch, while Rio followed the wagon with at least four dozen spirited horses and a bevy of scruffy dogs. The riders behind him controlled the herd through the corral where one side of the wire fence had been dropped down.

Josephine faced forward and leaned into the hard-backed seat, her thoughts in a jumble. At this time last year, she'd been waiting for the arrival of her summer wardrobe from the dressmaker and had been planning a spring cotillion. Her tiny world had been shaped by a conventional and unobtrusive pattern whose moral clichés and attitudes she'd never had the foresight to question or doubt. Her first mistake had been to trust her husband; her second had been staying with him as long as she had. She'd had inklings that not all was right, but she would remember the Hugh she'd fallen in love with during their courtship. He'd been charming and witty, and she'd never been so happy.

Once they married, he changed. Their entire relationship crumbled to a stern reserve that Hugh imposed on her. Feelings would sometimes skim over her, but she had never reacted to them, as it was forbidden for a lady to ask her husband about his financial affairs. Of course, going to her mother would have been no help; and even if she'd wanted to, she'd lost her mother the Christmas of 1868 to a heart ailment. Nor could she have turned to her father for advice, for he had been absorbed in the Tilden offices, a two-room establishment staffed by himself and three clerks.

The door to his office had always been open, but he usually ignored anyone who came through it. He almost never looked up from his maps and ledgers, and when he did, he rarely said anything. As a child, she'd been allowed to visit on two separate occasions. Most visitors found it prudent not to start a conversation with him when his head was down, and many simply walked away after having decided to say what was on their mind in a letter. Andrew Tilden answered all his letters personally. Though he had been self-absorbed, he wasn't selfish. He supported many charities and attended dinners regularly. It was because of his involvement on Wall Street, with financiers and brokers, that he'd lost his life. But Josephine didn't want to think about that right now.

Sighing, she held on to the bend of metal that was anchored on the side of the wagon seat. What would her parents think of her if they'd been alive? Surely they would be shocked. But no more shocked than she herself. For if the truth were being told, she would have to admit that she liked the wild enthusiasm of the pending excursion into the unknown. Because this time she had control of the situation. She knew what was expected of her, and gender played no part in it. She had been treated as an equal since coming to the McCall ranch. Though she didn't delight in some of the chores she'd been given, she found an uninhibited freedom that she'd never experienced before.

She held a cook's position, and those duties had been plainly stated to her. Unlike the duties of a wife, where subservience ruled the roost and there was no questioning allowed.

Boots gave a little holler of joy as the cowboys held the herd in an unbroken file of bawling and mooing, with dogs barking and dashing back and forth and the whistles of men as they cut through the grass on horseback.

Josephine contented herself for the first time since coming to Sienna. This was the beginning of a new adventure, and maybe she'd come out of it more like Pearl Larimer from the Beadle's Issue No. 639, *Rawhide's Wild Tales of Revenge in Sienna*.

Her gaze fell on J.D., who rode in the lead some

ways ahead. The way the sun glinted off his brown hair that fell below his collar, and the striking pose he made sitting tall on that big white horse, she couldn't help thinking he looked a lot like how she'd pictured Rawhide Abilene.

J.D. could have sworn he'd seen a little smile out of Josephine as they'd left the yard. He'd turned his head for a moment to make sure everyone was filing in the way they should and had let his gaze drift to her. She'd had a slight curve on her lips as she adjusted the brim of her hat to fit more snugly over her hair. One hand held on to the side of the wagon seat, while the other rested in her lap. Her eyes darted from this to that as she took in all of the motions with an animated expression. She hadn't caught him gazing at her, and he'd turned away before she could.

Riding through the pasture with its tender rye grass and clover, J.D. couldn't help thinking the expressive sight of Josephine Whittaker was a far cry from the woman who'd busted into Sheriff Tuttle's office ranting she'd been robbed. Maybe his treating her like one of the cowboys had done her some good.

As the sky blossomed into a ribbon of oranges and blues, he and the boys kept the herd strung out well yet close enough to let them feel one another. They crawled past the top pasture, an area also referred to as the Tepee Range. J.D. liked the solitude up here and came as often as he could.

During his reflections, as the hawks rode the updrafts from the ridges, he would sit on the grassy precipice and think that he was untouchable. A calm freedom would overtake him, and he'd tell himself that he'd done all right in spite of everything. Though he was twenty-eight, he had broad aspirations that reached beyond what he already had. The more land a cattleman owned, the bigger he could expand his operation. There was a handsome parcel—one hundred and sixty acres—that Buffalo Creek flowed through at the southernmost point, and he'd been meaning to buy it on his next trip to town. But each time he went into Sienna, he inevitably got sidetracked by something and never made it to the land office.

The available property was sort of inside his, like the middle arc of the letter C. The land had been vacant for years, and nobody had filed a claim on it, as eighty percent of the boundaries were tucked into McCall land. That left expansion nonexistent for any interested parties. Homesteaders would likely never file on the dormant parcel, because after proving up for a year they wouldn't be able to use the desert rights which entitled them to another one hundred and sixty acres. J.D. already owned the surrounding land.

He relaxed in the saddle and let his body sway with Tequila's easy motion. He slowed his pace and fell back to let his left and right point riders, Gus Peavy and Jidge Dooly, take over the lead. The cows were strung out for almost a mile with the sun flashing on their horns. Orley Woodard and Dan Hotchkiss, the swing men, steered the group, while Seth Winters and Birdie Tippett rounded out the ensemble as the flank men. In drag, Print Freeland and Ace Flynn ate the dust. All but the two point riders shifted positions daily to relieve those on the dusty side and those riding drag.

Glancing over his shoulder, J.D. frowned when he saw that the wagon had veered south under Boots's guidance. Reining left and turning around, he nudged Tequila into lope. The horse was full of vigor, eager to run and work away winter idleness and shed his heavy coat. All the horses seemed filled with a rough playfulness that taxed their riders and kept the dogs scurrying.

The chuck wagon ambled along closer to the middle, but at the side of the winding group to keep the dirt and debris at a minimum from coating the interior. The mules had gained speed as if Boots wanted to beat the herd to the noon stop as Luis always had. This was Boots's first jaunt behind the wagon's reins on such a grand venture. He'd always accompanied Luis, but Luis had done the driving. Luis had been known to take the shortest route—trail or not—and J.D. guessed that Boots was aiming to do the same. Only Boots wasn't as capable a driver as Luis had been, and J.D. didn't need the wagon busted up.

Boots saw him bearing down on the wagon, and J.D. could swear the old cuss clicked his tongue and set those mules off faster.

"Slow 'em down," J.D. called as he fell in line next to Boots's side of the wagon.

"Can't do that," Boots rebuffed without looking at J.D. "Got to get to Willow Creek before the boys so she can set up the victuals."

"She can set up once we're there." J.D. kept Tequila in a fast trot. "Pull back on those reins, and slow the mules down."

Boots remained silent, and J.D. glanced at the anxious expression on Josephine's face. "Reach over," he told her in a loud voice, "and put pressure on that brake lever. Push it back."

"Don't you come near this brake," Boots warned.

Josephine stayed put, confusion and indecision in her eyes as she held on to the bench seat for support.

J.D. fought to control his anger. "You're headed for the sagebrush. You don't know straight up about driving this wagon through it."

"Watch and see for yourself." The gauntlet had been thrown down, and J.D. was supposed to leave Boots alone while he proved himself to nobody but himself. He made no bones about the fact that he owed nothing to any man, and in return he expected nothing from anyone. After he'd retired himself from sitting astride a saddle some years back, he'd acquired the habit of considering himself invincible. J.D. imagined that Boots thought his whole destiny was in his hands now. But J.D. couldn't let him go on with his foolishness and find out for sure, because there was somebody else's safety to think about.

Galloping, J.D. shifted his reins from his right hand to his left, intending to jump on one of the mules.

The unrelenting fast and rickety sounds of squeaking harness leathers and the jingle of brass rings made him spur Tequila on. Boots immediately gave a loud holler of "Whoa!" to the mules. Then he spit the cold nub of a cigar from his mouth, the butt barely missing J.D.'s thigh before it hit the dirt.

"Hazel wouldn't cotton to having you ride on one of his mules without them being properly saddled up," Boots sourly proclaimed, the four leather reins still woven between his fingers. He sat hunched over the box, his blue eyes sharp and fiery. Sweat beaded beneath the lower lashes and above his gray brows.

"It wouldn't have been an option if you'd stopped when I asked."

"What are y'all going to do?" Boots inquired with a stinging verbal venom that prickled the hair at the back of J.D.'s neck. "Send me back home?" He went so far as to drop the reins and stand up. "Give me a canteen, missy, so I don't dry up on the walk."

Josephine shifted her gaze between J.D. and Boots before venturing in a soft voice, "Is he really walking back?"

"Sit down, goddammit," J.D. barked.

Boots's knee joints cracked as he sat down with a snort of disgust. "William wouldn't have stopped me. He was a son a man could be proud of."

J.D. didn't think; he reacted. He began yelling. "What do you want me to do? Kill myself? Would you be happy if I was dead like William and Lewis? Then you'd have three fallen sons instead of two. Wait, mine wouldn't be a death on the battlefield, so it won't count as glorified." He clenched his fist on the stitched horn of his saddle. "Do you think it's easy living? At least my brothers don't have to remember. I do. I have to live with memories I don't care to think about, much less talk about. But because I'm here to remind you that I didn't fall under Yankee fire like my brothers, you make me pay for their deaths every damn day.

"Hell, if it'll make you feel any better, I'll give you the bullets for that Remington and you can shoot me yourself. It won't be as good as a yellow belly doing it, but one bullet should be as good as another." Fumbling at the row of bullets he kept on his gun belt, J.D. fingered a few out of their slots and threw them at Boots. They clattered at his feet, one bouncing off the tip of Josephine's boot. "Go ahead. Load up. What are you waiting for?"

"Y'all've got no call to be going on with her sitting here," Boots said, not moving for the bullets. "This is between me and you."

"You worry about her now?" J.D. countered. "A minute ago, you didn't give a damn about her or yourself when you were running these mules hell-bent for leather toward that sage."

"There's a road there!"

"None that I can see."

"Then y'all aren't looking, because Luis drove through this sage dozens of times and you never told him to slow up."

"I could trust Luis's judgment."

"But y'all can't trust the judgment of your own father."

J.D. shook his head, gazing downward with a cynical smile, then facing off with Boots. "You're my father when it suits you, and that hasn't been a hell of a lot in the past twenty-eight years."

Boots cursed his hide, then stood again and attempted to put his leg over the side so he could disembark. "I'm going home."

"The hell you are." J.D. put his hand around

Boots's arm, reacting angrily to the deflated intonation in Boots's voice. "Sit down!"

Their eyes locked in a silent but volatile battle. Unspoken retorts hardened Boots's wrinkled features. J.D. was breathless with rage, afraid that his temper would get out of hand and he'd hurl Boots onto the seat. He had to get out of there before he did further damage. He let Boots go and repeated in a calmer voice, "Sit down. You're going to drive the wagon."

Boots didn't readily move, and J.D. backed away, his thoughts swirling ahead of him on what to do next if Boots really did intend to walk home. Luckily, J.D. didn't have to contend with that problem. Boots slid back onto his seat, tucked his hands into his armpits, and stared dead ahead.

J.D. gave Josephine a glance. Her uneasiness was readable in the expression on her pale face. Rather than make any atonements for his outburst, he kept quiet about what had just transpired between him and Boots. It was nothing he cared to elaborate on for her, anyway. "Are you still set on taking the sagebrush route?" J.D. asked after an eternal few seconds of silence.

"It's the shortest way."

"I reckon throughout this drive you'll be taking the shortest way."

"Y'all reckoned right."

"Then I've got to ask Miss Whittaker if she feels safe traveling with you." At the mention of her name, Josephine's chin rose. "If she doesn't, she'll ride with me."

Josephine's eyes widened, and her mouth opened, then snapped shut. Then she changed her mind and spoke her piece after all. "I don't think riding on the back of your horse would be comforting to either of us. I'll stay where I am."

Nodding once, J.D. said tightly, "If you're not at Willow Creek by noon, I'll send Rio after you."

J.D. spurred Tequila and took off in a smooth lope that turned into a gallop. His outward anger had abated somewhat, but there was still that fury beneath the stoic facade he'd planted on his face. Boots sent him to the limits, more often than not pushing him over the edge. They rubbed each other the wrong way, and he wasn't sure how much longer they could go on fighting before one of them went for the jugular. Boots was undoubtedly mulling over the same thoughts, and J.D. was glad Colt bullets didn't fit in a Remington revolver.

CHAPTER

→ 8 ←

The ride to Willow Creek had been rough going. Boots made the mules trudge through the gnarled sage. Fragrant gray branches snapped and broke beneath the animals' hooves. Contrary to what Boots had told J.D., there was no trail. At least none that Josephine had seen.

After long, tedious hours of travel, they finally reached the meeting spot at Willow Creek, which was nothing short of a dried-up gully.

Building a cook fire took know-how. Know-how Josephine didn't have. She was forced to rely on Boots. He kept a steady stream of wood coming from a storage bunk beneath the wagon, and she took the initiative to light it. She didn't question him as orange flames climbed skyward in what could only be considered a huge bonfire.

Minutes later, the fire blazed so hot, the sparks erupting from it shot to the canvas on the chuck wagon and began to burn a hole.

"Good gawd!" Boots yelled. "Look at what you did!"

"*I* did?" she replied over the roaring din.

A horse and rider bore down on them, just as Josephine looked for something to put the canvas fire out with. There was a water barrel anchored to the wagon's side, but there was no way she could lift it.

"Get out of the way!" J.D. blared within inches of Josephine, as he threw his leg over the saddle and ran to the water barrel. He grabbed the coffeepot, dunked it, and splashed water over the flames.

Josephine dashed to the front of the wagon and looked for something to help with. A stack of blankets was within her reach. Snatching one, she began to whip the end across the hole that was burning into a large gap.

Between both methods, the fire sizzled to a smoking end. The damage had been kept to a minimum, but a sizable black-edged circle had come precariously close to burning up the back of the chuck's cupboard.

The fire in the cooking pit had calmed down a bit but was still burning so hot that Josephine kept her distance.

J.D. tossed the coffeepot on the ground and stared at Josephine and Boots—who had stood there the entire time without doing a thing. "What happened?"

"She made the fire too big," Boots quickly offered. "The damn thing burned out of control."

Josephine bit her tongue. She couldn't fathom why she didn't immediately put the blame where the blame belonged. Perhaps because she saw Boots's hands trembling so badly he had to put them in his trouser pockets to control them.

"Is that true, Josephine?" J.D. asked, his eyes hard like flints.

She hated that she was afraid of the tone he used on her. Even after she'd become a married woman, her father had still been able to make her fearful of his reprimands when he spoke to her in such a way.

The Josephine with backbone who had told J.D. McCall not to call her Cookie had disappeared. Her hard-gained self-command failed, and she reverted back to what she did best.

She apologized.

J.D. swore beneath his breath.

"I've never built an outdoor fire before. I didn't know how much wood to use."

To her surprise, his anger was no longer directed at her. He vented on Boots. "You were here. You should have stopped her. You've seen Luis light a cook fire a hundred times. You know how it's done."

Boots licked his lips, sunlight catching on the stubbled gray whiskers on his chin. "I'm not a baby-sitter."

"You're not much of anything," J.D. shot back.

Josephine's shock was probably nothing compared to Boots's. His expression tightened, his face paled, then he stormed off.

She knew what it was like to receive such a belittling remark. If only J.D. knew how much he'd just hurt his father. "You shouldn't have said that," she caught herself saying. "It was unnecessarily cruel."

With an oath, J.D. kicked some dirt over the containment rocks holding back the fire. "You don't know the way of things. Stay out of it."

Josephine concluded that something horrible lay buried between J.D. and Boots. It had to do with two sons who had died during the war. And probably a whole lot more.

At that moment, Rio reached them, his herd of fine-looking horses in tow. He dismounted and stood back to gaze at the damage. Shaking his head, he said, "I reckon dinner won't be hot. That fire won't settle down in time to cook it."

He was right.

At noon, half the crew came in from the trail expecting a satisfying meal, while the other half stayed to control the herd. Dinner was canned tomatoes, with a side order of curses and even a few mutterings about her being a jinx.

Packing up hadn't taken any time since she hadn't unpacked anything. Rio had repaired the hole in the canvas with a tarp.

The rest of the afternoon, her thoughts wandered from Boots to J.D.

She had never known a man who had as many changing faces as J.D. McCall. He could be hostile one moment and caring the next. She'd witnessed the way he went after Boots, yet she'd watched him softly stroke the ear of his dog. He'd told her to get dressed in her ruined clothes, then given her a set of his. She didn't understand him. She had only truly known the characters of two other men: her father and Hugh. Both had been self-absorbed. Her father had never known the truth about her deceitful marriage. And her mother had died thinking her only child had been blissfully happy.

She wondered if men like Rawhide Abilene existed outside the pages of a book. Men who would risk their all for their love. Men who were daring yet honorable and kind. For Josephine, based on past experience, there just wasn't such a man.

"We're at the bed ground," Boots said, pulling Josephine out of her musings.

She and Boots hadn't exchanged a single word since leaving the disastrous dinner spot.

"This is where we set up camp for the night." There was a slight breeze in the air, and Boots grappled to swing the team around so that the wagon would be headed into the wind.

The terrain was rocky and sparse. The sagebrush had thinned, giving way to native bushes she couldn't put a name to. Sparrows flitted about in a stand of hawthorns. The sun began to hang low, though there was at least a good three hours of daylight left. In the near distance, a short range of mountains was cast in a golden hue.

After pulling back on the brake and wrapping the reins around the handle, Boots eased himself to standing. He faltered some, and Josephine automatically put her arm out to steady him. Their eyes locked. To her amazement, he didn't snarl at her to let go. His fingers felt like parchment in her own as he stamped his feet and shook his legs a little, no doubt ridding himself of the numbness that had set in. She felt it, too, though probably not nearly as much as he did. Letting her go, Boots shifted to the side of the wagon box and let himself down. Once on the ground, he stood back and waited for her. Wordlessly, he extended his own weathered hand to aid her in disembarking.

She took it with the same silence he'd given her, then walked around to get the circulation moving in her own limbs.

Josephine inhaled the sweet air and let her gaze travel in a slow circle as she turned in place. No signs of cattle dust came from any direction, nor was there a single hint of the cowboys who herded them. All she could see was gently rolling land. All she could hear were the sounds of birds and the buzz of insects. It was as if she and Boots were the only two people for a hundred miles.

An unexpected calm claimed Josephine. She never would have guessed, but she *liked* it here. She liked the solitude. The dull greenery. The sky that seemed made especially for her.

She told herself that lunch was over and that there was no sense in worrying about that failure. For dinner, she was going to fix those hungry and tired cowboys a meal they could really appreciate. And even personally hand J.D. McCall his plate. One that she could be proud of. She could do it. She had to prove to all of them that she wasn't a jinx.

But more importantly, she had to prove her worth to herself.

After getting several small fires going, Josephine accidentally stumbled onto leaflets of handwritten recipes that had been stashed in one of the wagon's assorted compartments. She'd been looking for the spices when she came upon the pieces of yellowed paper marked by oil splotches from grease splatters and various other food stains she didn't recognize. J.D. must have returned the recipes after he'd done his thorough cleaning. They probably belonged to the last cook, Luis.

Josephine skimmed through them. There were some for pies, meats, desserts, and vegetables. Even one for "Best Six Shooter"—which she quickly realized was a code name for coffee. The ingredients for all were listed in large quantities. Elated, Josephine selected several for the evening meal.

Boots had set up the drop table in the back of the wagon, anchoring the leg in a small area of ground he'd leveled. Now she had a counter to use. The first order of business: the stew. Then the sourdough biscuits. Since tackling a pie seemed too overwhelming, she'd opted to attempt a dessert she thought she could make on her own with the dried apples she found in the wagon.

While Boots smoked a cigar and sat on an overturned crate at the fire roasting a plain, fat stick he'd picked up, Josephine set the slab of meat on the clean table and began cutting it into cubes. Her untutored fingers were blundering and clumsy, and she forced herself not to get discouraged. She'd had no practice in this art. Her hands knew how to write a letter in perfect penmanship, to embroider a beautiful border on a handkerchief, and to arrange a lovely bouquet, but they hadn't been trained to work this way. They knew only the labors of decoration and display.

Boots didn't come over to investigate when she dusted each piece of meat—fifteen pounds' worth; she'd weighed the cubes on the scale to make sure she had the designated amount—with flour and pepper. He stayed where he was, stirring the ashes of the fires that were now banked into red-hot coals.

It dawned on her then that everybody had a job outlined for them but Boots. All she had heard was that he was to drive the wagon. When the wagon wasn't in use, he wasn't in use.

Though Boots's temperament was far from pleasant most times, she was beginning to see that perhaps some of his gruffness was a way to hide his lonely heart. And his failing memory. Apparently, he'd known how to make a fire but had forgotten. That once realized, he'd been afraid. She'd seen it in the tremor of his hands and the stoop of his body.

"Mr. Mc—" Josephine stopped herself with a shake of her flour-coated hands. "Um, Boots, could you be so kind as to show me where the Dutch ovens are kept?" She knew where they were but wanted to give him something to do.

"Beneath the box."

"Could you be clearer?"

"Good gawd." He stood and walked toward her. "The box. The only box."

When she didn't move for the box, he swore again.

"That box," he said, pointing to the four-foot-high cupboard, then shifted the aim of his finger below it.

"Oh, yes, thank you."

She retrieved the ovens and dumped the meat into them. Then she lugged each one to the fire. Next came the sourdough biscuits.

"If you've nothing pressing, I was wondering if perhaps you could talk to me while I make the biscuits."

"Talk about what?" he asked suspiciously.

"Whatever you like."

With a shrug, Boots dragged his wooden crate over and settled in to watch.

Josephine retrieved the sourdough jug, lifted the lid to peer inside, and was instantly taken aback by the bubbling goo rising up the sides of the porcelain keg. Her first reaction had been that it had gone bad, but Boots leaned over and nodded.

"Good batch."

She glanced at the recipe and began following the

instructions with Boots's "helpful hints," although she gave them more merit now after concluding he'd been right about the way to cut meat.

Immersed in stirring the salt and lard into the flour, she didn't readily hear Rio ride up to them. The nicker of horses caused both her and Boots to look up at the wrangler traveling with his remuda.

"The boys are about an hour behind me," he said, dismounting and slapping the dust of his pants. "Something smells good."

A pulse-quickening panic rushed through Josephine, who swiftly thought he was joking with her. She delicately sniffed so as not to be detected.

He was right!

Something did smell good. It was her browned meat, now covered with the right amount of water, potatoes, some skunk eggs—that's what Boots had called the onions—and a pinch of cayenne pepper. Pleasure rose inside her until it came to the surface in a smile. "My stew," she declared with a fair amount of modesty.

"What are you going to name it?" Rio asked, heading for the water barrel and grabbing the dipper.

"Name it?"

"The cook always names the first stew on the trail after a member of the drive. Usually somebody he's got a pet peeve with."

"Oh." Josephine worked some sugar into the dough as she pushed the mass into the counter to incorporate it. Boots had explained that she had to knead the dough with the heel of her hand, not pound it. She didn't know what *"knead"* meant, but she figured it out by the way Boots was demonstrating with impatience in the air. "Why, I don't have a personal vexation with anybody," she said, putting her weight into the task of flattening the sourdough, then folding, then flattening again.

"Luis always did," Rio replied after taking a drink. "Inevitably, somebody came riding in and unsaddled his horse by the chuck and let hair and dust fly, or a newly hired hand tried to sneak a peek in the pot without permission. Could be not putting dirty dishes and eatin' irons in the pan when he's through. You take your pick, and that's who you ought to name the stew after."

Josephine thought a moment as she pinched off a piece of the kneaded dough and rolled it into a ball. "Can't I name the stew after somebody for another reason?"

Rio shrugged. "Never been done before, Miss Josephine, but you're the cook." Then, to Boots, he frowned. "Why didn't you unhitch the team?"

"Not my job."

Stomping over to the mules, Rio shot back, "At least get the grain out that's under the seat while I unharness them."

"I got nothing else better to do." Boots stood from the crate and went toward the front of the wagon.

The oft-repeated phrase that Boots spoke got Josephine to thinking.

Sliding the box out from beneath the seat, Boots declared, "Good gawd. What'd y'all pack in here? Iron weights? It must weigh a ton . . ."

The rest of his words were lost, as the beginning of an idea was forming in Josephine's head.

Something was wrong.

J.D. rode toward the camp thinking he could smell Luis's stew. That same aroma that had welcomed him after a long day in the saddle and made his mouth water. Like it was now. Surely he was imagining things. The afternoon on the trail had taken its toll on him. He was dead tired, covered with dust, and thirsty. He was thinking up things that weren't real.

There was no sign of Josephine as J.D. reined in. Behind him, the muffled lowing of cows drifted nearer. The boys were moving the herd to the bed ground, getting them quiet and settled in for the night.

After approaching the wagon and dismounting a goodly distance away so as not to send any stirred-up dirt into the cook's pots, J.D. led Tequila by the reins. Rio showed up around the wagon's billowing canvas cover.

"Hey, boss," Rio said around a lump of something in his mouth. J.D. noticed the kid was holding on to a piece of white biscuit dough. "We heard you coming in. Miss Josephine said supper's almost ready." Rio took the reins into his free hand.

"That a fact?" J.D. replied. Inhaling the strong aroma of coffee, he couldn't help asking, "Who's at the fire? It doesn't smell like Josephine's work."

"No, boss, it doesn't. But it is. She's got stew. And she's making biscuits." He gave a wistful sigh. "She's an amazing woman."

Rather than mull over Rio's infatuation with Josephine, J.D. let his gaze fall on the lump of dough. "Is that any good?"

"Raw, it don't taste too bad. I wouldn't know what to compare it to. Luis never let me near the endgate when he was at it. But Miss Josephine doesn't mind."

Loosening the leather in the cinch ring, J.D. undid the saddle strap. "She doesn't know she's not supposed to let anybody close while she's cooking."

"I reckon not."

J.D. hoisted the saddle off Tequila. "Throw that blanket on top, would you?"

Rio obliged and removed the sweaty blanket from the horse's back. Draping the thick fabric upside down on the saddle J.D. was holding, Rio said, "I'll brush him down for you."

"Obliged." J.D. walked toward the fire, where a myriad of cast-iron pots sat over the coals. He flung his saddle on the ground to use as part of his bedroll later. Removing his gloves and tucking them into the pocket of his chaps, he turned to see what Josephine was up to. He didn't find her at the drop-down table at the back of the wagon. So he went over to investigate. He heard rattling inside the bed of the wagon. Walking to the front, he climbed up and sat backward on the seat. He poked his finger through the part in the canvas.

All he could see was Josephine's hind end. She was on all fours. The billow of his shirt fell softly to the wagon bed floor, and if he tilted his head a certain degree, he could see a slice of snowy white around her waist that had to be her corset. His gaze caught the lace-cupped swells of her breasts when she suddenly shifted and scooted toward him without looking where she was going.

She shuffled and moved the heavy supplies, the bags of flour, coffee, and pinto beans. She slid some cans to the left and lined up the molasses jugs next to her thigh. Her knee bumped into the long black branding irons, and she muttered something he couldn't clearly make out. An ax was to her right, and she picked it up.

He couldn't help saying, "I don't suppose we'll need that to cut the biscuits you've got on."

"What?" Still in her bent-down position, she turned her head toward him, ax in hand. A piece of her fiery hair had come loose from its crown of entwined braids. She didn't wear any ribbons, nor did she have on his hat. He was able to make out the oval of her face and the glimmer of surprise in her brown eyes.

He nudged his chin up a little, gesturing to the implement in her tight grasp. "What do you need the ax for?"

Her gaze landed on the sharp end. "Boots."

"Yeah, I've felt like chopping him up myself."

"No," she returned sharply. "I would never think such a thought about that dear old man."

J.D. widened the opening in the canvas by taking both sides in his hands. "Then we must not be talking about the same person."

"Of course we are. I'm getting the ax for Boots."

"What for?"

"You'll see."

Josephine raised herself up to her knees and stood. She had to stoop over so her head wouldn't hit the top of the bowed canvas. Stepping over her valise, she came toward him without another word. J.D. held the canvas open for her, then jumped down and lifted his hand. She planted the ax handle in it rather than her fingers. Then she turned around so she could back down by putting one boot on the hub while the other dangled.

Tossing the ax, J.D. reached up with both hands and circled her waist with his palms to pluck her free. At first she wouldn't budge, then she let go, and he swung her to the ground. She twisted free of his grasp, a blush rising across her cheeks.

"That wasn't necessary," she said, fussing with the stray lock of hair, trying to get it to stick back with the others and not having much success.

"Maybe not," he returned, inexplicably enjoying the color of discomfiture on her face. Picking up the ax, he handed it to her. Then he went to the water barrel and dipped the ladle inside. After a long, satisfying drink, he laid the dipper down and wiped his mouth with the back of his hand. He looked up, surprised to find her gaze still pinned on him. Most notably his lips. "I thought you were going to give Boots that ax."

"I—I was," she stammered. "I mean, I am."

She took off in the direction of the gully, the unwieldy ax pulling her shoulder down. Once at the edge, she called for Boots, who must have been walking along the dry banks.

The scene that had passed between him and his father earlier replayed in J.D.'s head. *You're not worth much of anything.* J.D. shuddered. As soon as he'd spoken the biting words, he'd been sorry for them. But there was no taking them back, and that made J.D. want to try harder to get along with Boots.

J.D. folded his arms across his chest and leaned

into the wagon's sideboard. Boots appeared, cradling an armload of long and short branches and squaw wood. Aged by years of damage and recovery, his body tilted forward, his hips stiff as he walked up the shallow incline of loose pebbles. His bowed legs seemed pained as he approached Josephine and, without ceremony, dumped his load at her feet. Hands that had once amazed J.D. by their dexterity in whittling fancy figurines now appeared swelled up like hams, making J.D. wonder how Boots could even work the buttons of his plaid shirt. J.D. observed his father, really looking at him for the first time in a long, long time.

Boots was getting on in life. Sure, he grumbled about it, but J.D. never paid him any mind because Boots grumbled about most everything.

Josephine passed him the ax, and Boots grasped the handle in his hand. He reached over and separated a length of wood from the others. Gripping the handle in both his hands, he steadied himself as he pulled the sharp ax head back.

J.D. pushed his hip away from the wagon and began walking. "You're going to whack off your foot," he offered to Boots, truly not wanting him to injure himself. J.D. intended on chopping the wood for him. But Boots ignored his warning, and the blade came slicing down barely missing *Josephine's* left boot. She jumped back with a gasp.

"Good gawd, look what y'all made me do!" Boots yelled at J.D., tossing down the ax with disgust. The fallen tool kicked up a small cloud of dust.

"You shouldn't be splitting wood, Boots. It's too much for you."

"Well, that's a hell of an attitude. Why don't you just take me out to pasture, then, and put me down?"

Josephine stepped between them. "Please," she said, "don't do this."

But Boots was already stalking off.

"I wish you hadn't said what you did." Josephine's

gaze was on Boots, who'd squatted on the crate he'd returned by the edge of the fire, but her words were for J.D. "You implied that he was feeble."

"He is. And I don't mean that in an unkind way. It's just a fact. He's too old to be cutting wood. He could hurt himself."

Her gaze moved to his, but she didn't speak. Instead, she bit her lower lip.

"What were you really going to say?"

"I'd better check the biscuits." She turned to leave, but he caught her softly by the upper arm and made her face him.

"It's not my place to interfere," she said at length.

"But I'm asking."

She licked her lips. "You have to let him try, and if he fails, the only person he's failed is himself. It's a lot better than not doing anything at all." Then she ducked from beneath his hold and went to the wagon, leaving him to ponder the weight of her words.

CHAPTER

➜ 9 ➜

Josephine had burned the biscuits. She could smell their scorched bottoms without even looking.

She struggled to remove the deep pots from the fire, keeping the hot wire handles wrapped in a cloth as she brought them to the endgate. As she lifted the lids and pried a biscuit loose from the bottom with a fork, her dreary suspicions were confirmed by the dark brown underside.

The fork in her hand felt as heavy as the disappointment in her heart. Her cooking thus far had been going so well. She'd thought tonight would be the night she served a perfect meal. If she hadn't been arguing with J.D., she might not have burned the biscuits.

Reaching for a plate, Josephine began to stab the biscuits and take them out of the pot. They made a *clunk* noise as they hit the tin. Her irritation should have been directed at herself; she was to blame for their overcooked state. But she wasn't feeling rational and laid the blame solely on J.D. McCall for upsetting her. If he could only understand how lucky he was to have Boots with him. Josephine would have given anything to have a second chance with her own father. Were she to be so graced, she'd make more of an effort to involve herself in his life and try to form a closer relationship with him. Most especially after her mother had died.

But that wasn't to be so, and a tiny part of her resented that J.D. still had the opportunity to mend his fences with his father but would rather chop down the posts entirely before making a move to fix them.

Josephine set the plate of biscuits next to the Dutch ovens, which now were supported on a board Rio had constructed on the wagon's side. The two boards ran the length of the chuck, and that was where Josephine had stacked the plates and laid out the napkins and the silverware, as well as coffee cups. This, Rio had told her, was how Luis operated. Every man served himself in single file, with the line moving smoothly.

For the past half hour, the cowboys had been coming in and making the small camp flourish with activity. They set their saddles around or near the fire, then collected their bedrolls, which had been stored in the chuck but had since been laid out on the grass by Rio after he unhitched the team. Everything seemed so precise and methodical to Josephine. Who would have thought men could possess perfect order and organization?

The last thing she needed to do was get the big coffeepot. Turning toward the fire, she was bent on taking the five-gallon pot from its hook over the coals, but when she reached for it, J.D. stopped her with a light touch on her wrist.

"Pot stays on the fire. The boys like it hotter than the underside of a saddle blanket after a long ride."

"Do they?" She didn't want to acknowledge where his fingers connected with her pulse. Her skin felt hotter than the pot's bottom would be, the intimate contact sending currents through her. She'd felt this way when he'd helped her from the wagon. She didn't like it. Well, yes, she did. And she didn't want to. That was the problem.

"They do." She sensed his gaze on her, examining and trying to determine her thoughts. She grew even more unnerved.

"I'll remember that," Josephine replied, then pulled her arm away, unable to meet J.D.'s eyes.

Retreating to the wagon, she made a final check of the area, smoothed her hands down the white towel apron she'd tied around her waist earlier, then stood aside and waited.

She waited in vain. Nobody came. But they were looking at her. Boots included. They sat on their bedrolls, some smoking cigarettes, some with hats on, some with hats off. All with boots on and hands washed—she could tell by the dirt that remained from their wrists up. Glancing at the expressionless faces, she thought the worst. Maybe none of them was willing to risk indigestion again. She couldn't blame them. But the stew. It did smell good. Rio had said so. Why wasn't he first in line?

"Well . . ." she ventured, wondering if there was a hidden triangle somewhere that she was supposed to sound. "You can eat now."

Boots was the first to leave his post at the crate. He made his approach and whispered in a low tone that wasn't at all reminiscent of the gravelly mine-shaft voice she'd first heard him use on her. "Y'all've got to call it like it is. Say something like 'It's all right with me' or 'Grab a plate and growl.'"

"Pardon?"

Boots gave her a deep frown, as if she were testing his patience—something she knew full well he lacked. "Good gawd, are y'all going deaf? I said to call the grub like you're supposed to. Say 'Come an' get it!' and say it like y'all're calling in them mountains over there."

"Oh." Josephine cleared her throat. "Um . . . come and get it."

"Not loud enough," Boots critiqued with a snort.

Josephine gave him a scowl, put her hands on her

waist, and yelled as loudly as a lady of her station could yell. "Come and get it!"

The cowboys got up as one whole, proceeded toward the wagon, then fell into line as if they'd just been invited to dine at Delmonico's.

Josephine stayed put, eyeing all those who were partaking of her latest offering. Helpings weren't generous. A bad sign. Some even passed up the plate of biscuits. How could they tell they were burned on the bottom? Her question was soon answered.

One of them, she believed he was Print Freeland, picked up a rock-sized biscuit in his wide fingers and examined its bottom. He put the biscuit back to rights, opting not to put it on his plate.

Josephine wanted to die.

She couldn't just stand around and watch them pick apart her meal. It was too much to bear. She escaped and went around the other side of the wagon. She took a short walk to the dry creek bed and made her way down the incline. At the bottom, she found a suitable boulder and occupied it. With her elbows slumped onto her knees, she didn't strike a very ladylike pose. She barely had time to ponder her next move before her privacy was invaded.

She heard tiny pebbles rolling down the embankment and recognized a pair of scruffy boots and the long legs encased in denims without bothering to look at the person wearing them.

Josephine didn't move to remedy her poor posture. What was the need? J.D. had already seen her state of defeat, her gloomy slouch. Here she sat in his baggy men's pants, with a shirtfront dusted in peppery flour and an apron smeared by the now brownish blood of raw meat. Indeed, she was a chuck-wagon cook. A bad cook, but a cook just the same. Her clothes were stained, and she probably smelled like stew and burned biscuits.

She tilted her chin up, and a strand of hair fell in her eyes. She viewed J.D. through the russet fringe.

"Can't I have a moment to myself?" she mumbled, her breath fanning the hair away from her mouth. She was not feeling herself. Decorum, above all else, was a value she most adhered to.

"I don't mind that you do, but the boys were wanting a word with you."

"I already know what they have to say."

"Do you?"

"I do." Josephine straightened, her spine stiffening. Brushing the hair from her forehead, she said, "They wish to tell me my stew is tough as cowhide chaps, my biscuits aren't fit to throw, and the coffee is hideous."

"Not quite."

She gazed at him askance, taking in his features beneath the dying sun. He appeared tanner, taller than she recalled. It had to be the sunset and her position below him. Regardless, he cut quite a handsome picture with his windblown hair tousled against his shoulders and minus his hat. She got caught in the lure of his eyes. Blue yet gray.

"What is it they want to say?"

"Come with me and find out."

Wistfully holding on to a sigh, Josephine rose and followed J.D. to the wagon, where some of the cowboys were lined up for—she blinked—second helpings.

"The stew is just like Luis used to make," Rio commented with a smile as he scooped another plateful.

"The coffee don't taste like sheep dip anymore," the one she thought was Ace Flynn announced from his spot at the fire.

"The biscuits ain't half bad when you cut the bottoms off 'em," another next to him responded. She thought his name was Orley Woodard.

"Yup," Gus Peavy added from the line at the wagon. "If we had some of that White Goose's syrup, these biscuits would sop it up okay."

"That's White Swan, you numbskull," Boots threw

in from his perch on the crate, a biscuit in his hand. "Y'all never seen a swan, so you think that bird on the tin is a goose. Well, it's not. It's a trumpet swan."

Gus shrugged his bony shoulders. "It don't make no never-mind to me. I like it whether it's a goose or a swan."

"Miss Josephine, pour me another cup of that stuff you call coffee," came the request from Dan Hotchkiss. "It's just the way I drink it: plumb barefooted and boiling hot."

Josephine gazed at J.D. "Am I too obtuse to realize I'm being made the brunt of a joke here? Or are they serious?"

"They're serious."

Josephine swallowed the lump in her throat and walked to the coffeepot, where a folded towel lay over the iron rod. She gathered the pot, faltering in her steps a moment to adjust to the dense weight that seemed only half of what it had been when she'd filled it. Had it been full, she never would have been able to lift it. She went to the first man but was unable to heft the pot up high enough to pour. He helped her out.

"Obliged, ma'am."

"You're welcome," she replied woodenly, still not believing what she was hearing.

Josephine made several more trips around the encampment with the smoke-blackened pot, the men refilling their own coffee cups. When she was finished, she went to the wagon to collect herself. With her back to the group of cowboys, she willed away the happy tears that had gathered in her eyes. It had been so long since she'd had such a concentration of approval, she didn't know how to handle her emotions. Sniffing quietly, she bit her lip and smoothed her hair, tucking the wayward strand behind her ear. She rounded the wagon's edge just as J.D. was fixing himself a plate.

"Aren't you going to eat?"

"Yes," she replied softly. "I believe I will."

Josephine helped herself to a small quantity of the food, too overcome to do more than sample the stew just to form her own opinion. She took her plate to the endgate and stood, her gaze following J.D. as he made his way to his spot with the others. Both of his hands were full—one holding a plate and one a steaming cup of coffee. He half crossed his feet while still standing, then scissored down to a squat, never spilling a drop from either cup or plate. Balancing his meal with his hands, he let his knees move outward so that the calves of his legs could bear the burden of his weight as he sank to the ground where he'd unrolled a heavy blanket. Though the motion appeared difficult, he'd pulled it off with unerring grace.

The coffee was placed by his side, the plate leveled on his knee. He dug in, and she quickly looked away as his eyes rose to hers.

"It *is* like Luis's," J.D. said, adding his own view of the stew with a somewhat amazed tone.

Josephine picked up her own fork and sampled the meal. The stew wasn't half bad for a dish heavy with meat and potatoes and no demi glaze to thicken the sauce.

Conversations came to a lull while the group ate Josephine's supper. The occasional snap of the fire broke through the silence as she remained standing to eat. She'd sat too long in the wagon. Besides, there wasn't much time to eat, anyway. She'd be doing all these dishes soon.

When everyone had had his fill and the second pot of coffee had been put on the fire, Josephine brought out the dessert. She'd found another lidded pot that she'd put the dried apples into and poured several cans of milk.

"What's that in there, Miss Josephine?" Rio asked as she removed it from the edge of the fire, where it had been sitting in a half-dead bank of coals.

"Dessert."

Rio declared, "Whoo-ee. Dees-sert!"

There had been a rousing line for the apples, but when Josephine put a spoon in them they weren't soft. In fact, the apples had barely puffed at all. They didn't look too good. Perhaps it was the artificial light. J.D. had gotten several kerosene lamps burning on the sideboard and the endgate.

Though everyone helped himself to a large portion, the dessert was inedible. Josephine knew that with her first taste. She'd been trying to mimic nutmeg baked apples with warm cream. The dried apples hadn't softened; they were hard and chewy in milk that was neither thick nor creamy. And the nutmeg had been grated too large for it to delicately flavor the dessert.

"Please," she felt compelled to state, "don't eat the dessert. It didn't turn out right."

Cowboys, she soon realized, had strong sweet tooths. Despite her warning, they managed to choke some down. But before long, calls to the dogs were made, and the tins were laid aside for the animals to eat the leftovers.

Josephine didn't want to end the best meal she'd cooked so far on such a sour note. She climbed into the wagon interior, collected her handbag, and brought it to the endgate where she could dump out its contents.

A small gold case with her pearl-white visiting cards plopped out, followed by a writing tablet with pencil attachment in her French pocketbook, a case containing a comb and mirror, a folding fan, a silver thimble, miniature button hook for shoes, some coin change, and her well-worn copy of *Rawhide's Wild Tales of Revenge*. The last to come was the tatted-edged handkerchief in which was tied a pound's worth of butterscotch candies. She undid the knot and proceeded to the campfire.

"Candy, anyone?"

"Good gawd," Boots said in a flourish of spirit. "What kind?"

"Butterscotch."

She had no trouble divesting herself of the treats, some of the boys helping themselves to two and three pieces. When she came to J.D., he took two, and her gaze followed his hand as he popped the caramel-colored candy into his mouth. He sucked sticky butterscotch from his thumb and raised his smoky gaze to her. Swallowing tightly, she turned and hurried to the back of the wagon with only a dozen of the sweets left.

As she replaced the contents of her purse, she glanced at the group sitting around the fire. The cowboys worked the candies in their mouths, rolling the hard lumps from left to right cheeks, dragging the butterscotch across teeth, and smacking lips. The blatant appreciation brought her joy, and she gloried briefly in this shared moment where she was more than the cook but seemed to be a comrade as well.

"Say, Miss Josephine, you never said who the stew was named after," Rio remarked, crunching his candy and opting to take another from the blanket he was sitting on.

"Oh." Josephine had almost forgotten. Closing the clasp on her purse, she left it on the endgate as she made her way toward the fire. "I'm not naming the stew after somebody with whom I have a disagreement. Were that to be the case, there is no one here that I could name. In spite of my failures, you have all been generous with your patience. And I can only say on my behalf that I'm certain my endeavors will get progressively better." She absently wrapped the string of her apron around her forefinger, then unwound it, mindless of what she was doing. "I've opted to name the stew after someone I feel is very important to this grand undertaking. He is a person without whom I wouldn't be here."

She glanced at J.D., who was staring pointedly at her. She couldn't retain the contact when she announced, "Tonight's stew has the distinct honor of being called Boots's stew."

"What was that?" Boots piped in, his eyes crinkled. "You're talking to my bad ear. What was that y'all just said about me?" he repeated.

"I've named the stew in your honor."

"Good gawd, what for?"

She smiled, undaunted by his bristling. "Because you drive the chuck wagon, and if it weren't for you, I wouldn't be able to get to the cooking sites. Your kind presence is essential to my job."

She thought she heard somebody to her left mumble, "Boots McCall isn't kind." Turning, she believed the mumbler was Orley Woodard.

"There, sir, you are wrong," she returned softly, so as not to have Boots hear what was being spoken about him.

Her gaze returned to the stoop-shouldered man, his cheek puffed by the candy in his jowl. She couldn't be certain because of the fire's red cast on his lined features, but she thought she recognized a blush on his wind-dried cheeks. "Well, good gawd, this puts the pressure on me. I don't want you ever to ruin that stew. If you do, I'm changing its name to Adelaide after Eugenia's mother—and don't mistake my generosity for praise. That woman is as long-headed as a mule, and with a bray to boot."

A murmur of laughter circled the campfire. Josephine smiled despite herself. She didn't condone slander, having known too well its biting sting. But in this case, she let the matter drop, as she didn't want to spoil the jovial mood of the group.

She dared a glance in J.D.'s direction. He sat with his back butted against the swell of his saddle, knees bent toward his chest, his eyes flat and unreadable. She wondered if he was angry with her for naming the stew after his father—a person he clearly didn't feel was deserving.

Well, she couldn't worry about him. To each his own opinion, and she felt in this instance Boots needed to be reminded of his worth. And that was the truth. He truly did play a significant role in this venture. In spite of his taking the wrong road, he'd gotten her there just the same. She didn't know how to handle a team and would have been of no use at all.

Josephine turned away, trudging back to the lighted wagon and rolling up her sleeves in the process.

The boys began to break up, Ace Flynn and Print Freeland going for the fresh horses Rio had watered and fed earlier. Others removed boots with sighs, wiggled sock-covered toes, and settled in on their blankets to light cigarettes and play cards as the fire's glow caught them in its light.

Josephine listened as one of them started telling a story. She caught bits and pieces as she rounded up the dishes and placed them in the huge dishpan. Rio came to her aid with hot water he'd set to boil earlier.

They worked together silently, and she suspected he was lending an ear to the tale as well. Some of the words were salty, with a quick mutter of apology and a hasty glance in Josephine's direction, which she calmly ignored. She could have told the storyteller she was no stranger to swearing and save him from embarrassment. But she'd rather not encourage him.

Within the hour, she and Rio had done up the dishes. The stories had turned to joking and joshing on every condition of life from the cradle to the grave. There were two subjects, she noted, they stayed clear of: home and their mothers. Periodically, Rio became the brunt of their jokes. They'd ask him if his hands looked like prunes yet or if he was planning to set up housekeeping any time soon. When they ribbed him in such a way, they called him Little Mary. He retorted by reminding them that all the horses were in his care and it went unspoken that not a one of them—the boss included—could ride without his permission. He also reminded them that *he* could have the luxury of uninterrupted sleep while every man in the outfit except the boss and the cook would have to stand two hours of night guard. This sobered the bunch. They began to quiet down after that and snuggled into their bedrolls.

Earlier, Boots had told Josephine she was the lucky one because she got to sleep in the wagon where the varmints couldn't sneak into her bed. She'd counted herself lucky, too, as soon as he'd told her. The water damage from the fire had dried out, and she'd put her bedding away just prior to serving supper.

Rio hung his wet dish towel over a bar on the box. "Luis always turned the wagon tongue to the North Star before he called it a night. I don't reckon you're strong enough to do it on your own, Miss Josephine. I'll do it for you," he offered in a tone that was too sugary for her comfort.

"Thank you." Josephine tagged behind him, gazing skyward with Rio, trying to figure out what it was he was looking for. "Which one is it?"

"That big one there." Rio pointed. "Right in the Little Dipper."

Josephine couldn't tell where he was aiming. She felt his gaze on her profile, then his warm hand as he took her fingers in his and raised her arm to the bright pinprick winking from its dark blanket of smaller speckles in the galaxy.

She couldn't concentrate on the designated star; her energies were focused on the liberties Rio Cibolo had taken with her. Granted, he was an appealing young man with his sunny blond hair and devil-may-care stride, but that was just that. *Young man.* She had to be his senior by at least several years.

"Oh, yes," Josephine replied, trying to ease away. "I see it now."

She had some success. She was able to lower her arm without trouble, but Rio remained close by her side. Josephine grew flustered. She wasn't flirtatious by nature, not that she wanted to flirt with him, but she felt awkward with the need to say something. Anything.

"Why don't you show me how to move the wagon? Perhaps I can do it myself tomorrow."

"I don't mind moving it for you, a'tall. It'd be my pleasure each night."

"I wouldn't want you to go to any trouble."

"No trouble," he drawled in a voice so smooth it melted on the night air like sweet taffy.

Rio moved up to what she assumed was the tongue. It was propped up by the neck yokes, the harnesses hung upon it in an orderly array. Rio kicked out the yokes, realigned them, then took up the tongue and nudged it over with a great show of brawn. Josephine wondered if it was that heavy.

"All there is to it," Rio announced, then took up a tarpaulin and covered the tack. "Keeps the dew off so the leather doesn't spoil."

"I think I can manage that."

"Well, it's like I said. No trouble a'tall." She noted that Rio hadn't shaved, but his pale beard could probably stand to grow a week before it became noticeable. Unlike J.D., whose firm jaw was already shadowed like midnight by this evening's supper. Not that she'd overly noticed when he'd been in line filling his plate. Well, she had noticed. Just a little . . . actually a lot more than she should have.

Rio didn't readily move on. He stood next to her, his eyes on the North Star once more, as if he were looking for something. Josephine folded her arms beneath her breasts. She was beginning to feel the evening's chill and was about to excuse herself politely when Rio said, "You know why we point the tongue to the North Star?"

"No."

"So that we can take our direction from it tomorrow morning. This is our trail compass."

"Hmm." Josephine couldn't think of anything useful to add. "Well, speaking of tomorrow morning, it's coming too soon for me. Thank you for your help," she said, then scooted toward the wagon wheel as Rio took one of the lanterns from the sideboard and hung it on the tongue, apparently as a kind of beacon to the men who were tending the cattle in the dark beyond the limits of the camp light.

Rather than climb into the wagon immediately, Josephine went back to the endgate, where a little hot water was left in a bucket. She made a quick perusal of the cowboys and saw that most of them were slumbering with their hats over their faces. Some slept on their sides, making that impossible; but for the most part, heads were cushioned by the swells of their saddles. Boots was asleep closest to the fire, and she imagined the warmth felt good seeping into his joints.

Josephine spotted J.D., who had crushed out his cigarette and was eating his second butterscotch while gazing at the sky. His arms were behind his head, and one knee was bent over the other. He seemed relaxed and contented. But more importantly, occupied. She didn't want anyone following her.

Picking up a cake of soap, lifting the water pot, and flinging a dry towel over her shoulder, Josephine left the wagon. She traipsed off toward the hawthorn bushes that had earlier sported a host of sparrows. Her steps were cautious, her eyes wide, as she made her way through the near-dark. She should have brought a lantern with her, but she didn't want to attract any attention to herself. Especially since Rio seemed bent on getting her attention this evening.

Something scurried to the right, and Josephine gasped. Stopping, she strained to get a better look. She picked up a rock and threw it. Having a good aim, she hit the long, dark image on her first try. Nothing. It didn't move. Cautiously, she inched forward, another rock in hand. She threw it. The snakelike image remained still.

"It's just a stick," she said to herself, feeling foolish for being afraid. But this was the wide open.

Continuing, Josephine still minded her steps, careful to search for any night creatures that had come out from under rocks. She reached the hawthorn, ducked behind it, and set the water and soap on the ground. After flipping the towel over a dense, thorny branch, she deftly unbuttoned her shirt. Slipping her arms from the long sleeves, she removed the garment and tossed it beside the suspended towel. She longed for a decent bath, to submerge herself and scrub away the trail dust and grit that seemed to cover her from head to toe. She didn't like being dirty. At least she could wash before crawling beneath the covers.

The chilly air caused gooseflesh to rise on her arms as she bent down to get the soap. The moment she did, a big bird swooped into the brush and rustled the leaves, apparently not seeing her. Rising, Josephine screamed as she stared at a pair of large yellow eyes and a pointed beak. She darted from the bushes with her hand over her racing heart. She blindly ran away from the hawthorn and smacked into something solid with strong arms.

"What are you doing?" came J.D.'s nonplussed voice.

She exclaimed, "I believe I just encountered an owl!"

Wings flapped overhead as the bird took off from the brush.

"Yeah, that was an owl. A big one, too."

"I stared right into its eyes."

"Is that right?" She saw a white flash of J.D.'s teeth.

"Yes!" Then Josephine frowned. She was being made fun of. "I've never seen an owl up close like that."

She grew aware of the fact that J.D.'s hands gripped her bare arms and that his chest was pressed next to hers. To say the least, their pose was compromising.

"Is that why you're running around in your underwear?"

"I beg your pardon?" Then Josephine remembered

she was in her sheer shift and satin corset. With pants on. "Oh . . ." And again with more horror. *"Oh."* She wiggled free and took a step backward. She clasped her arms around her waist in an attempt to conceal herself. Her halfhearted actions proved futile. Her nipped-in waist wasn't nearly as scandalous as her cleavage. But to change the course of modest coverage by moving her hands to her breasts would only cause unwanted attention to rove upward. So she remained frozen to the spot.

Before, she'd been wary of the poor light; now it was a godsend.

"W-what are you doing out here?" Josephine stammered.

"Checking on you."

"I don't need any checking on."

"No?" His reply was riddled with doubt. "You were running blind before I caught you. No telling where you would have ended up. Maybe halfway back to the ranch."

She didn't appreciate his humor and said with ill temper, "I was startled." She shivered. Both from the memory and the cold.

"You better put some clothes on."

A good suggestion. One she intended to adhere to posthaste. She turned to leave, and to her chagrin the scrape of his boots over the ground indicated he was following her. "You needn't accompany me."

"But what if the owl comes back?"

"I'm certain it's not. I scared it off."

"I reckon you did with that scream."

Once back at the hawthorns, Josephine paused and abruptly turned around to save herself from J.D. approaching any further. But he'd been too close to her behind for her to put any distance between them now. It seemed as if he stood on top of her, his height intimidating. Her mouth went dry. She could smell the sting of campfire smoke on him. A pleasant kind of odor that clung to the cotton fabric of his shirt. The darkness worked to enhance her sense of smell, while her vision was suffering terribly no matter how wide she opened her eyes.

"Do you mind?" she finally said when he didn't have the decency to go back the way he'd come.

She detected the faint buttery sweetness of butterscotch candy on his breath as he leaned closer to her and said, "No, I don't mind."

With his warm presence skimming over her exposed skin, her mettle faltered a degree, but she rallied with, "Well, I do."

"I'm not leaving until you're finished." He straightened and folded his arms across his chest.

What was she supposed to say to that? No man had ever imposed himself on her while she took care of private matters. Her state of half-undress should have been cause enough for his immediate departure.

She had to try her best to get him to do just that, but she ran out of ground before she even gained any. "I'm quite capable of . . . of . . ." Her words trailed. No lady would dare mention such a thing as washing herself to a man who wasn't her husband. And even then, the opportunity would not present itself to be openly discussed. She and Hugh had never once spoken of personal grooming. "What I have to do is of a private nature."

"You'll be private behind the bush."

Josephine clenched her fingers into fists at her side. "I will ask you once more to please return so that I can do what I need to do quickly."

"If you were a man, I'd do just that. But you're not. And I saw the way Rio was with you."

Flabbergasted, she blurted, "What?"

"I don't need any of the boys lurking off in the dark after you to take a peek at what you're doing."

"Then how do you explain your presence?"

"I'm not watching. I'm guarding."

"Guarding?" Josephine had never heard anything so ridiculous. She didn't need guarding. She, of all people, who walked the streets of Manhattan unescorted on many occasions, didn't need protection from her fellow man. She'd learned how to walk quietly through the streets, seeing and hearing nothing that she ought not to see and hear, recognizing acquaintances with a courteous bow, and friends with words of greeting. She never talked loudly or laughed boisterously, so as not to attract the attention of unknown passersby. But if all that failed, and an undesirable made untoward comments or laid a hand on her person, she knew how to execute a blow with her parasol.

"You needn't guard me," she said at length, wishing he wouldn't stand so close to her. She would have taken a few steps backward, but if she did, she'd feel the stab of thorns from the hawthorn. "I'm capable of fending off a stolen impropriety before it happens."

"Stolen impropriety?" J.D. returned, and she could have sworn he gave a lopsided smile at her expense.

"You know perfectly well what I mean."

"Yes. I think I do." His face inched closer. Josephine's breath hitched in her throat. "But you're not fast enough to get out of my way should I decide to steal an impropriety from you."

"I wish—"

But he cut off her thought with his velvet-warm mouth covering hers in a slow, exploring kiss. Shock ran through her, tingling and needlelike across her skin. He tasted like the flavor of her favorite candy, butter and brown sugar, melted together . . . just like their lips. Like a silly girl, she felt her knees tremble. She was too mature for this . . . this folly. Too wise to succumb to him. But his lips were more persuasive than she cared to admit. A heady sensation claimed her, the air surrounding them suddenly growing thick and sultry.

Drugged by the expert touch of his mouth on hers, she felt a far-off thought bob to the surface of her mind: *It would take more than a bash with a parasol to thwart J.D. McCall.*

Worse yet, had she been holding one, she wouldn't have used it.

In J.D.'s arms, with his lips against hers, she was transported into a tangle of passion she knew nothing about. Her emotions spun a lustrous web around them, and she blocked out all reason. Her feelings were unlike any she'd ever known.

Her fingers dug into his shoulders as she clung to him. She could feel the tension of firm muscle beneath her light touch. His body next to hers was hard and enduring, as if he could lift her with a single sweep of his arms.

The night seemed darker, more seductive. The sounds around them seemed richer. She herself felt more complete. For the first time, everything in her, from head to foot, was feeling the same current of sensation: glorious.

She abandoned herself to the kiss for an endless moment, just until reality set in from some unknown place in her mind, and she remembered who she was. Who *he* was. Then she grew quite sober. Breaking away, she fled behind the hawthorn bush to calm her racing heart.

CHAPTER

⇥ 10 ⇤

J.D. had made a mistake hiring a woman cook. He'd made an even bigger one by ignoring reason and kissing her. Less than eight hours after the fact, he still didn't regret that he'd put his arms around her and enjoyed the feel of her soft lips against his.

Had it been anybody else, J.D. would have called him stupid—just before he fired him for trifling with the underwear-clad cook. J.D. couldn't give himself walking papers. Any more than he'd knock himself over the head by putting more into what had happened than truly had. So he'd kissed Josephine Whittaker. So he'd liked the feel of her in his arms. He kept telling himself it wasn't *her* exactly, but rather a woman wearing satin and lace . . . and his pants. But there was no mistaking the lady in question was Josephine. She'd smelled of wood smoke and sourdough batter, of apples and cinnamon. He knew leading into the kiss whom he was tangling with, and that had made the stolen moment all the more tantalizing.

J.D. was treading on dangerous ground. He was admitting his attraction to the cook. Last night, he'd told himself the only reason he was following her was to make sure nobody else did. Especially not Rio, who liked to dally with the ladies—and most every lady liked Rio to dally with her.

Rio Cibolo was experienced and as smooth as any glass of fine brandy when it came to encouraging women. Whenever he was in money after payday, the chippies at Walkingbars cut cards to see who would have a turn with the wrangler first.

J.D. hadn't liked the heat of rivalry that had hit him out of nowhere when he'd seen Rio cozying up to Josephine at the wagon. He didn't think Rio was fool enough to step out of bounds on the drive. But just in case, J.D. had taken it upon himself to be her protector.

Trouble was, who was going to protect her from him?

This morning, J.D. hadn't awakened to the accented voice of his former cook. Josephine, in her crisp northeastern tone, had said, "Come and get it." Even if she hadn't spoken, J.D. would have been awake.

The cool morning sluiced over him, making him lie beneath his blanket a moment longer than usual. Josephine had been rattling and banging pots and pans for an hour and a half. He'd opened his eyes and given up on shutting them again. Not to mention, she must have propped that alarm clock he'd entrusted to her care on a turned-over metal bucket. The resounding ring had been quickly muffled; she must have put the offending clock beneath her pillow until the chime played out.

The noise, the clatter of utensils, and the delicious aroma of coffee awakened the boys, who rolled over in their sougans. J.D. stretched and put his boots on. One by one, the boys followed suit, rolling their beds and dumping them near the wagon, then making their way to the washpan to get the sleep from their eyes.

J.D. was last in the breakfast line. Holding an empty bowl, he moved forward, his eyes on Josephine. She gave him a quick glance, then finished serving Dan's oatmeal. The cowboy nodded his thanks and went to the fire, leaving J.D. alone with Josephine.

"Mornin'," he said, picking up an empty coffee cup.

"Good morning," she replied, her eyes downcast.

"Did you sleep all right?"

"Just fine." She lifted her eyes to his. "And you?"

"Fine."

They were both skirting around the issue, and he sensed she knew it, too. He felt he needed to say something about the kiss they'd shared, but he wasn't sure how to broach the subject.

She plopped a spoonful of mush in his bowl and said, "Sweetener is on the endgate."

He didn't move. "Josephine . . . about last night—"

"Excuse me, but I need to check the coffeepot." She whirled away and went to the fire.

J.D. held back, watching her. Seeing her with her hair in a neat coil and his old shirt covering her in a way that made her appear lacking in form, he couldn't stop reliving the way she'd felt in his arms. Soft and inviting.

After she'd run off behind the bush out of breath, she'd told him to go away, but he hadn't. He'd stood guard, listening to the splash of water as she quickly washed herself. When she'd reappeared, her shirt was buttoned up to the collar, the towel thrown over her shoulders as if she intended it to be armor. Silently, she'd walked past him back to camp. He'd left her at the wagon, and that had been the end of things.

Only this morning, in the sunrise-tinged sky that cast Josephine in its golden light, J.D. wasn't so sure. Last night might have just been the beginning.

Josephine hadn't slept well.

How could she have allowed J.D. to kiss her? She'd promised herself that after what Hugh had put her through, she'd never let a man be in charge of her emotions again. But what had she done? The moment J.D.'s lips had touched hers, she fell into a chasm of wonderful sensations. Ignoring her conscience, she'd stood there and enjoyed the kiss. A flame of feeling for total intimacy had captured her, and she'd done nothing to stop him.

J.D. had reminded her that she was a woman. A woman who'd had her hopes and dreams dashed. Who thought that the ultimate happiness came through love and marriage. But she'd been in for bitter disappointment because she'd been born with money. And yet she was still a woman who craved companionship . . . and who longed for children in spite of nothing to show from a six-year relationship.

This morning, she'd truly thought she could put what happened behind her and face J.D. with casual indifference. It wasn't that easy. He was such a large presence. He was tall, and he was built tough. Wherever he stood, he stood out. Wherever he spoke, his voice was the deepest. And after she'd left him at the chuck wagon, wherever he went, her gaze had quietly followed.

As soon as breakfast was over, the camp presented a scene of vigorous activity. There was the dull thunder of hooves on the soft earth as Rio brought the horse herd in on the run. Ropes cut the air from all directions as each cowboy roped his own mount for the morning drive. Saddling was quickly accomplished, and the shouts to move out before the sun got a head start were constant.

During all the hubbub, Josephine washed the dishes, pots, and kettles and noisily stowed them in the wagon. When she was finished, Boots poured water on the fires, filling the air with the stench of wet wood ashes and greasy dishwater.

Bedding and duffles had been rolled up and left for Rio to load back in the chuck wagon after breakfast. The wrangler wasn't nearly as attentive toward her this morning, having all he could do to keep up with the steady pace at which things were happening. J.D. and the cowboys rode off, then Rio hooked up the teams while Josephine finished the last of her duties with slow motion.

She was sore and stiff all over. She'd been tired and aching the night before, but she'd attributed it to all of the cleaning she'd been doing. But this morning, her backside hurt so much from the spanking it had taken on that hard bench seat of the wagon, she longed to take the pillow from her bedroll and sit on it. She would have if she thought Boots wouldn't make a comment. But he most surely would have; her sitting on a pillow nursing her tender behind would be too tempting a picture for him to pass up.

Even if she had named the stew after him.

"Y'all about done?" Boots asked, having managed to hoist himself onto the bench seat with little more than a creak of his joints.

"I'm ready." Josephine took one last survey of the cupboard, making sure the panels were closed tightly and the endgate secure. Then she walked down the side of the wagon and braced her hand on the edge of the seat. With a hop, she climbed on board. Without skirts to hinder her, she clunked her booted feet straight out in front without any care, then folded her hands on her trouser-clad lap.

"With y'all wearing those britches and that hat, you're fitting in with me and the boys," Boots said around the stub of his cigar. "I used to think of you as trouble when y'all first came out to the ranch. But after what you did last night, with naming the stew and all like Luis would have done, I'm not thinking of you as a woman no more."

Josephine didn't know whether to be flattered or depressed.

* * *

J.D. had gone ahead to search for the best noon camping location, as well as water. Its scarcity weighed heavily upon him, but he held out hope that there had been enough snowfall in the mountains for the high country grass to be plenty and the streams full. The natural grasses on the plains suited the herd, and as they plodded along beneath a sun that had grown pleasantly warm, they foraged on rye and bunch grass and the occasional white sage. Cane grass and alfileria weren't sprouting up the way they should. The dry winter worried J.D. If they didn't get some significant rain, the range land surrounding the ranch wasn't going to be able to support the cattle they'd left behind.

Heading east, J.D. caught up with the boys as they came west. He nodded to Gus and Jidge, Orley and Dan, then rode toward the end where Seth and Birdie managed the flanks, and finally to Print and Ace.

Print spurred his piebald in a spurt of energy, Ace lagging from the leeside, not far behind him.

"Hey there!" Print shouted through the muffle of his bandana. J.D. swung his kerchief over his nose so as not to choke on the dust.

Ace whistled through the noise. "Get on up there!"

Their calls were directed toward the slower cattle to get them to catch up with the rest of the herd.

J.D. moved in alongside them, helping to stave off a yearling that was heading into the brush. "Ho! Move it! Move it! Move it! Yee-haw!"

The cowboys slapped their legs with their gloved hands and zigzagged back and forth behind the herd to keep the animals together and moving in the right direction. They hardly ever touched the cattle, a true sign of knowing what they were doing. It didn't take a heavy hand to deal with animals.

J.D. nudged his spurs into Tequila's sides, bent on scouting the chuck wagon, whose cloud of dust couldn't be seen from this distance. Though Luis had made his own way, he never strayed far from the obvious trail. Boots wasn't likely to lag behind for long. His absence made J.D. wonder if he'd encountered some kind of trouble.

The saddle horses made a close pack as J.D. went past them, Rio putting his fingers on the brim of his hat. J.D. nodded, then took off in a lope in the direction of the camp they'd broken this morning.

Covering the ground at a swift gait, he was mindful of the go-downs—the burrow holes of gophers and prairie dogs. A false move, and a horse or a cow could snap its leg. Mice and rabbits crept out from sage and grass to sniff suspiciously at the tainted air of man-made scars as he sped by.

Fifteen minutes later, still no sign of the chuck or Boots and Josephine.

Another five minutes of covering the terrain, and J.D. knew something had gone wrong.

There were occasions when the wagon had to cross a dry, barren section of a stream where the feathery dust, buoyant as mist, enveloped her and Boots, settling softly on the canvas and provisions like yellow snow. She choked on the arid grit in the air, wiping her face with a handkerchief she'd fished from her handbag. In spite of the unpleasantries, Josephine was glad the river was dry.

She didn't know how to swim.

Some two hours after they'd left camp, they'd come to their first indication of any kind of water at all. It was a pitiful-looking tributary, with skimpy greenery on the fringes. The banks were bald gray mud.

Boots set the brake and gazed at the thin trickle of water. He looked at the clearest spot, which flowed down the center over small rocks. The sun reflected off the rippling paths made by skimmers that barely touched the surface as they jetted across it.

"We should fill up the water barrel since half of it got used up putting out that fire." But as Boots's gaze further assessed the area, he shook his head. "But we won't get any from here."

"Why not?"

Boots motioned upstream with his head.

Josephine then saw the decaying body of a bloated cow.

"Luis said that boiling killed the germs, and what germs weren't killed it made no matter as a cow-puncher's stomach was made of iron. But I'm not drinking water that killed a cow."

A shiver worked through Josephine. She didn't like this place.

"Might as well make the stop worthwhile. There's a dead scrub over there. Its branches will do fine for the cook fire." Boots wrapped the reins around the brake handle and stepped off the wagon seat.

Josephine wanted to check her pans of bread and her pot of soaking beans, so she climbed down after him, feeling the stretch in her legs. Boots had chastised her for not covering the spotted beans with water last night to soften them up in time for tonight's supper. And he'd declared her bread dough looked too spongy.

On a quick inspection, she saw that both looked fine, but the water from the beans had sloshed from beneath the lid a little and wet the inside of the cupboard.

Raising her hand to the sun, Josephine gauged that it was getting close to noon, and they hadn't been told where to make camp. Come to think of it, they hadn't caught up with the herd, nor had they seen the steady stream of dust being kicked up by the animals.

"I haven't seen any dust for a while," Josephine ventured.

Ambling toward her with his arms laden with wood, Boots quickly answered, "Don't worry, I know where we are."

"I wasn't, but—"

"Get in the wagon."

Josephine folded her arms beneath her breasts. She would have really taken offense if she hadn't heard the slight tone of anxiety in his voice. Rather than argue with him, she did as he said and took her spot on the seat. He joined her after throwing the dry sticks and bits of wood into what he'd called the possum belly under the wagon bed.

Boots kicked the brake free, popped his blacksnake, then gave a yell and urged the frisky teams into a run.

He kept up a breakneck pace due south, crushing grass and bouncing over rocks in their way. She wasn't keen on compass points, but she remembered what Rio had told her last night about the North Star. To her way of thinking, they were going in the wrong direction.

She held her tongue for a good ten minutes. But after she glanced at Boots and noticed the sweat beaded on his brow and dripping down the side of his neck, she had to ask, "Are you certain of our course?"

"I am," came the heated reply. Then he did something that put her instantly out of sorts. He shoved the four lines of leather reins at her. "Take over. Take over."

Josephine was helpless to do anything else. The reins felt uncomfortable in her unaccustomed fingers. She didn't know how to thread them through as Boots had done, and there wasn't an opportunity to ask him. He'd reached into his back pocket and taken out a large red handkerchief and was swabbing his face. His complexion seemed ruddy, his perspiration increasing. He moved his gaze from left to right, then stared dead ahead with a befuddled expression.

Dear Lord . . . they were lost.

J.D. picked up the wagon tracks near a dingy riverbed with a low flow of water. Steering Tequila around a cluster of greasewood, he headed south—the apparent course they'd taken. Why in the hell would Boots go toward Dixon?

The terrain was rough and rocky with stones the size of a man's fist, this area once belonging to a wider and wetter portion of the Haymaker River; but the water source had since been dammed up by the beavers in the higher elevations, and what came through now was just a hint of what the flow once had been.

He left the area behind him, winding upward toward a flat section mottled with buffalo grass. From there, the grove imprinted by the wagon wheels was easier to read, and J.D. was able to regain his earlier pace. The countryside flashed by, an undulating expanse of desolate prairie occasionally broken by a lone scrub or sagebrush. In the far distance, he caught sight of a moving blur. Sunlight radiated off the white canvas, making it an easy mark to spot.

The chuck wagon.

"Pick 'em up," J.D. ordered Tequila. The white gelding kicked his hooves into a smooth run and sped toward the wayward wagon.

Riding up next to the chuck, J.D. closed in on the driver's side, ready to lay into Boots with a streak of cussing. But once he got within the level of the box, he saw that it wasn't Boots behind the reins. Josephine held them.

"Stop those mules," J.D. hollered above the ring of tack.

Boots looked up in confused surprise, but the expression on Josephine's face was one of instant relief. She hesitated, clearly uncertain how to go about stopping a moving team of four mules.

J.D. motioned with one arm. "Pull back."

Josephine didn't exactly follow his directions, but she managed to get the job done by practically lying flat on her back. "Whoa! Whoa! Whoa!" she chanted, her knuckles white on the leather ribbons.

Easing his own mount to a standstill, J.D. crossed his hands over the pommel of his saddle. "What in the hell are you doing out here?"

J.D. could have sworn he saw Boots pale a shade beneath the brim of his old hat. His brows creased into deep furrows, and his hands looked unsteady.

"I don't remember," Boots mumbled in a tone quiet and forlorn—so unlike his normal baritone. J.D. could barely hear him or comprehend that the words belonged to Boots.

"Never you mind about him," Josephine responded. "It's my fault."

Boots's gaze lifted to her. She was undaunted by him, continuing with her explanation while she fidgeted with the slackened reins. "I wanted to see what it was like to drive the wagon. Boots told me I was going in the wrong direction, but I didn't believe him." She wet her lips, looking down, then up and past Boots, who continued to stare at her. "He's steered me wrong before, that's why I didn't think he was telling me the truth this time. He said to go the other way, but I thought you'd gone this way. That's why we're here."

J.D. looked from Josephine to Boots, waiting for Boots to lash back at her or, at the very least, make some sarcastic remark.

Boots sat there, looking china-fragile and totally unlike his hard-edged self. His shoulders slumped forward, making him appear short when he really wasn't.

"What happened?" J.D. finally asked Boots, not fully convinced Boots would hand over the reins to a woman, much less Josephine Whittaker.

The short whiskers on Boots's leathery cheeks glistened in the sun. "She said all that needs to be said."

"I'm glad you came along when you did," Josephine said in a rush. "I suppose this means dinner is going to be a little late. Just where do we go to make camp?"

J.D.'s eyes narrowed on her, taking stock of the way she refused to meet his gaze. She'd handed the length of reins over to Boots, who wove them through his gloved fingers. "First, you turn around. Then follow that ridge over there about five miles until you get to a spot known as the Belanger Cliffs. Boots has been there before."

"I know where it is," he snapped, the old piss and vinegar coming back.

"I reckon you do," J.D. returned calmly, determined not to start a full-blown argument with Boots. Swinging Tequila around, J.D. said, "Take care over these rocks."

J.D. nudged his horse into a gallop, but not fast enough to leave the chuck in the lurch. The mules could hold their own pretty well and cover a lot of ground in a short amount of time, even with the wagon in tow.

Josephine watched J.D. move out, her hands curled in her lap while she sat in silence. If he hadn't found them, she wasn't sure what they would have done. She'd carried on in the direction Boots had pointed them, uncertain how to turn the mules around, and uncertain that they truly were going the wrong way. At least now J.D. was here. He gave her a sense of relief, but she remained troubled by Boots's disorientation.

Boots finally asked, "What'd y'all do that for?"

"What?" But she knew full well.

"Tell J.D. what you did. I was the one who got us lost. How come y'all said it was you?"

"I was thinking of what you told J.D. at the table the other day."

"I say a lot of things to him."

"You said you wanted to be shot in the head if you got forgetful." Her eyes were settled on the man they discussed as he trotted ahead of them.

"I didn't mean it."

"I would hope not."

"Is that why you said you got us lost? Y'all are afraid I might just have Hazel do me in because my memory is going?"

"That's nothing to joke about." Her voice faltered,

then she stared pointedly at Boots McCall. "You may think you're entertaining when you make such morose commentary, but taking your own life is serious." She inhaled a gulp of air. "My father shot himself in the head. I can assure you, I was not laughing when I found out."

Then she faced forward, dismissing Boots—for once, before he dismissed her.

CHAPTER

→ 11 ←

The fire's snapping warmth began to loosen up J.D.'s stiff joints and the aches of bones that had been broken. Sunset had come and gone, and in the early night campfire flames shot skyward to consume the darkness. Flickering shadows promenaded across faces absorbed in telling stories between puffs of smoke and sips of coffee.

Rio, who'd disappeared once he finished his supper and put his dirty dishes in the wreck pan, returned with J.D.'s saddle and saddlebags slung over his shoulder. He set them in front of J.D., who mulled over what to do about the wrangler's steady flirtations with Josephine.

A glance in her direction, and J.D. saw that she sat on the wagon seat with a lantern at her hip and her nose in a book. Wearing her oversized shirt, the sleeves rolled partway up and the hem billowing into her lap, she didn't look like Rio's type. Her hair drooped at her nape, its twisted confines ruffled. It was no wonder none of the other boys paid her anything more than passing attention or engaged her in conversations that went beyond the polite. Gus Peavy and Rio were the only two hands who had seen her up close in her fancy suit the day she'd arrived at the ranch. And Gus had a girl he was sweet on in Sienna, so he posed no threat, but Rio was always looking for a good time.

"You planning on doing anything tonight?" J.D. asked over the rim of his cup.

Slouching with his hands in his back pockets, the younger man replied, "I got some hobbles that need stitching."

"That all?"

Rio's eyes shimmered with unspoken humor in the light, as if he knew what J.D. was getting at. "You need me to do something special?"

"Nope." J.D. washed down the last of his beans with his coffee, then stood as a way of dismissing the kid. Rio sauntered off to heat water for the dishes, and J.D. cursed himself for not being blunter and coming right out with what was eating at him. But if he did, it might look like he had designs on Josephine himself, and that would be purely false. No sense in giving the boy the wrong idea.

J.D. dumped his dishes in the pan, then went toward the wagon's front. She held the book up close, a strand of hair curling past her cheek. She turned to the sound of his steps, managed to sit straighter than she already was, and slipped the book beneath her behind. "Yes, boss?"

For some reason, the question grated on him, and he had a good mind to tell her not to call him that. But it was his own insistence that had her choosing either boss or J.D. He wished she would use the latter, though even that form of address had its flaws. The foremost being a level of intimacy. It didn't matter that the boys called him that. They were all men. But with the row of buttons on his shirt in a line down the curve of her breasts, Josephine was definitely not one of the boys.

J.D. put his weight on his left hip and took on a stance of casual indifference. "Supper was fine."

"There were rocks in the beans."

"Yeah, I found a few." J.D.'s molar had hit one and thought for sure he'd be requiring a trip to the dentist.

"I thought the little pieces were broken beans." She tucked the curl behind her ear. "Who would have thought the company wouldn't sort through them?"

"They always slip a few pebbles in to make the sack weigh more. Then I get charged the extra."

"That's not right."

"No, but that's the way it is." Pushing his hands into his pockets, J.D. looked at the sky, then at Josephine, who waited for him to say something. "What are you reading?"

"A book."

"I figured that. What's it called?"

She shifted, as if he could see what the title was beneath the flare of her hip. "It's just a book. You wouldn't be interested." She paused, then asked, "Is there something you wanted?"

He wanted to find out what he could about her. Why was it that Josephine Whittaker had come out West all by herself? She'd never offered the information, and he'd never asked. That just wasn't done. A man's business was his own. Just like a woman's should be. Most of the women out here had hard-luck tales. Those told by the ranch widows were looked upon with compassion. A lot of the girls at the saloons recounted colorful stories when they talked about why they'd taken up the life of sin, mostly while crying into their handkerchiefs.

Josephine was no Walkingbars' floozy. Nor was she a woman made for the West. So what was she doing here?

He knew that getting to know her would prove fruitless. She'd be leaving soon, so it was best to keep things indifferent. But he'd have to try hard to keep it that way. "Can you reach in the back for my bedroll?"

Josephine made sure the book was facedown, then ducked to go inside the interior of the wagon. He was sorely tempted to take a peek at the cover, but she came back in a few seconds. Her hair looked worse for the wear, its bun coming completely loose when she hit her head on the fore bow shaping the arc in the canvas. She gave him the rolled-up sougan, then quickly struggled to make some order out of her hair. Unbidden, the image of the long cinnamon-colored curls tumbling down to her hips surfaced in his mind.

Her fingers were nimble as they first unbraided, then rebraided the long coil that had fallen free of its crimped pins. A long glimmer of silver reflected from the dusty wooden floor of the wagon, and J.D. reached for it. He lifted his arm and handed Josephine the pin.

"Thank you," she said quietly, averting her eyes from his once she had the hairpin in her grasp.

J.D. should have turned away and gone about his business, but he stayed put, mesmerized by her styling her hair. J.D. tucked the sougan beneath his arm and said, "You see the fiddle while you were in there?"

"Yes."

"Mind getting that, too?"

"No."

She rammed the last pin home, the final effect decidedly neater but no less wispy than before. In a moment, she came back with the black leather fiddle case and handed it over. "Obliged," J.D. said, then could think of no other reason to prolong his stay. He took off to set up his bed.

J.D. laid out his blanket, then adjusted his saddle and bags. "Dan and Orley, you boys'll be on bobtail guard, then Gus and Jidge take over at midnight."

"You boys going to give us some music to sing by?" Dan Hotchkiss asked while refitting his boots back on his feet.

Singing was supposed to soothe cattle; J.D. didn't know for sure why. Unless it was that any sound, be it soft and crooning, could drown out the spooking noises of the night. He'd been on enough bobtail guards to know that if he wasn't singing in a quiet tone—bad as he was at carrying a tune—any little sound could make them leave the country. Even if that sound was something familiar like a horse shaking itself or the jingle of spurs.

Two men would circle around the cattle, keeping their horses at a walk. If it was a clear night, so quiet you could hear the bedded-down cows breathing, one man would sing a verse of a song, and his partner on the other side of the herd would sing the next verse. If he didn't know the words, he'd make something up. And they'd go through a whole string of songs that way, sometimes until their voices grew hoarse.

J.D. reached over and handed Birdie Tippett the fiddle case and asked him to play. Birdie wasn't as talented as Luis, but in desperation a man overlooked a lot.

Boots sidled his crate closer to the fire where he could warm his feet. "Birdie can't carry a tune in a corked jug," he commented, crossing his stockinged feet at the ankles and folding his arms across his chest.

"Better than you can," J.D. remarked while getting out a tin of oil so that he could work it into the leather of his saddle.

Boots snorted, then took out his latest whittling project and began to shave off the rough spots.

Opening the case and lifting out the instrument, Birdie examined the wood grain and the strings. He brought the fiddle to his chin, tested a few notes, then made some adjustments to the strings.

Seth Winters dragged out a mouth organ from his shirt pocket and knocked the tobacco crumbs loose from the holes. Birdie made a big show of limbering up his neck and shoulders by shrugging them a few times and tilting his head. Then he placed the fiddle snugly against his bristled chin.

" 'Little Black Bull,' " Birdie said, and Seth nodded.

The tune was pleasant. Nothing fast and hard to follow. Mostly the same musical verse was repeated when telling the story about a bull coming down from the mountain, with the refrain of "A long time ago." J.D. sang the words in his head, an old habit he'd picked up to keep the monotony from closing in on him. He must have sung a thousand songs while doing line work one winter.

While the notes of the fiddle embraced the group by the fire, J.D. oiled his saddle. He periodically glanced in Josephine's direction. She'd put her book away and sat on a blanket, using the rear wagon wheel as a back support. She crossed her legs in front of her, her feet—encased in the old boots—keeping time with the music.

As the two men moved right into another song, he wondered if she missed the highfalutin dances that she'd no doubt gone to. Big to-do ones where she'd most likely worn velvet or silk . . . and perhaps danced with a man named Hugh.

He started to think about who she would have danced with, if she'd had a favorite partner . . . why she wasn't married at her age. He guessed her to be halfway into her twenties. He was getting close to thirty, and he felt he had a good reason why he hadn't tied the knot. But for a woman, especially a woman from the type of society his mother was from, not being married by her late age was cause to be labeled an old maid.

Birdie and Seth had played more than a dozen songs when Birdie took a break to straighten the kink from his neck. Seth wiped his mouth with the back of his hand.

Gus made a comment about Luis listening in from up above.

Print added, "Luis was a good friend."

Somebody ventured, "It don't matter where a man goes after he passes on. If he was a friend, you'll know him when you meet up again."

Then Boots put his plug nickel in, the knife in his

knobby fingers going as still as the piece of wood in the other. "I'd know an old cowboy in hell with his hide burnt off."

His observation was one of the few things J.D. was in agreement with Boots about. He went so far as to voice his accord. "I bet I'll meet up with a few who've crossed my path."

Boots raised his eyes to stare at J.D. over the fire's flames, but he offered no sarcastic undertones— which took J.D. greatly by surprise.

"I imagine you and I will be there together," Boots remarked, moving the tip of his knife into the wood once more. "Eugenia will see to it I won't get anywhere near her. Just as well. I don't like harp music." Then, to Birdie, he called, "Aren't y'all going to play anymore?"

"I ran out of songs. Don't know anymore."

"Good gawd, what kind of fiddle player are you?"

"A bad one," Birdie replied in all honesty.

"Don't any of you other numbskulls know how to play that thing?" Boots threw out to the boys.

J.D. noted they all had sorry shakes of their heads . . . all but Josephine, who suddenly looked at her hands. He suspected she was withholding something.

"Miss Whittaker, do you know how to play a fiddle?" J.D. asked.

She lifted her gaze to his. "I was given tutelage on the violin."

"Same thing as a fiddle if I'm remembering my music studies correctly," J.D. said offhandedly.

Boots grumbled beneath his breath, "Eugenia would be glad to know all the money I paid that book scholar, Archer, was good for something."

"Give us a song, Miss Josephine," Rio urged, pitching his smoke butt into the fire and sitting straighter. "I'd surely like to hear anything you could offer us. I'm sure it'll be as sweet as an angel's song."

J.D.'s mouth fell into a thin line. He was curious himself about Josephine's playing abilities, but he wouldn't go so far as to state she could play like an angel. If her violin playing was anything like her cooking, even Toby would run for cover with his paws up over his ears.

"Go ahead, Miss Josephine," Birdie added. "I'm played out. It would sure be a treat to listen to somebody else."

Josephine was anything but modest about the talents she possessed, which J.D. couldn't exactly name at the moment. In fact, she was appearing downright shy when she rose to her feet to take the instrument from Birdie.

She apologized before she even strummed a note. "I'm not very good. I can't read music. I play by ear."

"How can y'all play with your ear?" Boots inquired.

"That's a figure of speech," she replied. "I can't read sheet music, or, rather, I can, it's just that all those notes . . . well, I got them all mixed up. So instead of reading the pieces, I memorized them inside my head after my tutor played them."

She gently examined the fiddle, her slender fingers gliding over its dull and beat-up surface. Bringing the instrument to the point of her chin, she tentatively ran the bow across the strings. She made numerous adjustments, so many that finally Boots complained.

"Are y'all going to play it or what?"

"I'm tuning it. I'm not sure, but I think I have them the way they should be." She worried her lower lip. "It's been a long time . . ."

J.D. put aside what he was doing so he could better concentrate on what she would play. Like the rest of them, he was interested to hear what she had to offer. She wouldn't know "Bury Me Not on the Prairie."

Taking a deep breath, and remaining standing, Josephine positioned the fiddle, then closed her eyes. J.D. kept his gaze on her. She seemed so set on what she was doing. So in tune to the instrument alone.

Then she began to play, and J.D. was just as awestruck as the rest of them.

Professor Lindstrom had been Josephine's tutor when she was nine years old. He'd given her lessons for eight years before she'd decided the violin wasn't for her. She'd rather play the piano like the rest of her friends. But even then, she'd had to practice harder because reading music was so difficult for her. A year later, she gave up on the piano, but she continued to play her violin when the mood struck her. Once, at the Beauchamps' party, Josephine had been coaxed into playing for a roomful of people. Tonight was only the second time she'd performed for an audience.

As Josephine played one of the first pieces she'd put to memory—Bach's violin concerto in E major—she thought back on all those lessons she'd suffered through. All the times she'd been made to read Francesco Germiniani's *The Art of Playing the Violin,* she never thought that any of it would come to practical use. But it had. The reason she'd relented tonight was that J.D. had asked her to play. She wanted to show him she was capable of doing something well.

The concerto came to an end, and Josephine only caught herself missing a note several times. It was amazing what one could retain in the mind, even when unused. On the last note, she opened her eyes and lowered the violin.

Gazes on her were fixed; nobody moved. Dear Lord, they'd hated the classical composition. But she didn't know any popular tunes.

Her eyes fell on J.D. He sat motionless. She swallowed.

"I, um, am a little rusty," she said without preamble. Then, before anyone could tell her to stop, she vowed to win them over with a Vivaldi *allegro non molto,* appropriately the spring piece from the "Four Seasons." She went directly into the introduction, her fingers working hard to press the strings down in order to create the right sounds. The melody was slow and lilting, with a series of connecting chords.

Aside from the varying pitch of music echoing from the horsehair bow across the violin strings and the occasional snap of the fire, the air was still and quiet. There seemed to be divine timing as a log gave a rendering *pop-pop* and flares of orange shot skyward as the tempo of the piece changed to a faster, more intricate pattern. Her fingertips whisked over the fingerboard, stopping some strings and vibrating others.

She concluded the lengthy Vivaldi with a flourish, feeling her hairpins loosen. As she claimed the last dynamic notes of the melody, her braid had uncoiled, its end falling to her waist. She braced herself for another cool reception, but when she looked out into her leather- and denim-clad audience, her heart stopped. There seemed to be tears glittering in the boys' eyes.

With the exclusion of J.D., everyone was wiping his eyes with a handkerchief. Boots blew his nose loudly into a square of red, then wadded the linen into his pants pocket.

Not accomplished at organizing witty remarks on a whim, one suddenly came to Josephine, too timely to let slip by, and she spoke it in the hopes of salvaging her pride. "I guess tomorrow's breakfast will be boiled violin."

Boots spoke in a harsh whisper, his gruff voice clogged with uncharacteristic emotion. "There'll be no such thing. Good gawd, y'all made me think of my burial."

Mortified, Josephine blurted, "I'm sorry!"

"Don't be. Made me think of it in a good light." Boots blotted his eyelids with the pads of his thumbs. "I'd like to hope I could be hearing your violin music when I'm on my way down."

"It made me think of my sweetheart," Gus said.

Then Rio added with misty eyes, "Made me think of home . . ."

". . . and mothers," Birdie finished.

"Sisters, too," Seth said.

Josephine was flabbergasted. "You liked my playing?"

There was a round of nods, even a slight one from J.D. Well . . . *well!* She gave an inward smile to herself, then an outward one to the cowboys. "I'm glad you did."

Boots stood from the crate and ambled to his bedroll. "I'm turning in. I don't want a bunch of rawhides watching me get older . . . and gawddamn sentimental."

"Been a long one," somebody said.

"Yup," another seconded. "Sunup'll be here just when I get the blankets warmed up."

"I won't be sleeping long when I'll be dragged out to nighthawk," came a reply from Jidge.

Josephine watched as those who hadn't removed their boots did so now. The blankets were turned down and crawled into. All but J.D., who leaned against his saddle, his hat dangling over the horn. He had a cigarette clamped in his mouth, and he took a puff.

Josephine settled the violin back inside its case, then she took the instrument to the wagon and placed it beneath the front seat. She paused a minute to muse. It had been a long day. One that had begun with disaster—Boots getting them lost, then the beans not turning out the way they should have. But it had ended on a better note thanks to Professor Lindstrom.

Josephine smiled, then went to the other side of the wagon, where she could wash her face with water from the barrel and not be seen by those who hadn't yet drifted off to sleep.

A bath was long overdue. Washing up in water

wasn't her idea of getting the grit off. She didn't dare ask J.D. if there would be some kind of accommodation for her. He thought she was trouble enough.

As she ran a wet cloth across her face, she relived his expression in her mind. Tonight, when she'd played, he'd gazed at her with . . . what? Admiration? She couldn't be sure. Respect, perhaps? Hugh had never respected a single thing she'd done.

Rolling up her sleeves, she wiped the dust from her elbows. She would have gone out a ways and really done the job proper, but last night was too fresh in her thoughts. J.D. following her . . . kissing her. She almost wished . . .

No. She shook her head.

The snap of a twig behind her caused her to turn. J.D. approached, having come from a line of brush in the distance. He dropped his cigarette and ground it beneath his boot.

"Evenin'," he said in a drawl that was as smooth as honey.

"Good evening," she replied, the cloth still in her hand. She froze for a moment, then propelled herself into action and let the wash rag go so she could dry her face off. Her hair was still a mess. She hadn't thought about its disarray until now—when J.D. was gazing at her face, her disorganized coiffure.

"You didn't tell me you were a violin player when you were selling yourself for the cook's job." He'd reached her, standing only a few feet away. She noticed he was a lot less dirty. Was there a creek nearby she didn't know about? His hair was wet and combed back, the ends waving softly behind his broad shoulders.

"I didn't think playing the violin could land me the job," she replied.

"It would've impressed me a lot more than your proclaimed archery skills."

"Indeed?"

"Sure."

Josephine fussed with her hair, feeling utterly self-conscious with the way he kept looking at her. Her palm smoothed down what she could, but the fine wisps wouldn't lie flat. "I'll have to remember that the next time I'm giving my résumé to a potential employer."

Frowning, J.D. leaned toward her and stretched his lean right arm above her head. He braced his weight on his hand and looked down to talk to her. "Why is it a woman like you is looking for work out West? Aside from the fact that you were stranded in Sienna. What made you come out this way alone in the first place?"

She was taken aback by his query. The truth wasn't something she could tell him. She'd never admit to running away. She had no choice but to embellish and hope he believed her. "I'm a woman of independent means. I had no ties keeping me in New York, so why not venture westward and see the rest of the world?"

"I wouldn't call Sienna the rest of the world." Tobacco and camp smoke clung to his shirt, putting a pleasant tang in the air surrounding them. "Where was it you were heading when you got your money stolen?"

Her honest answer wouldn't be saying too much. "San Francisco."

"I can picture you there."

She could, too. But, oddly, she was beginning to picture herself here also. Out in the open with a chuck wagon, a violin, and cowboys who got misty-eyed. The horses, the cows, the dust. Even Boots. She didn't feel so wholly out of place. She wondered why not. Still, the idea of moving on was still an appealing one. A hotel with room service and a big brass tub brimming with warm soapy water was quite alluring.

"So can I," she admitted.

J.D.'s mouth was dangerously close to hers. "Yep. You belong in a city like that." His deep voice caressed her, raising the fine hairs on the nape of her neck. Her breath caught in her throat. She stilled, not moving a muscle. Not daring even to breathe. She waited . . .

Ever so lightly, his lips brushed across hers. A stirring hint of warmth, and a soft graze of his mouth. She had no opportunity to appreciate the kiss or to return it with any ideas of her own. If he'd meant the brief meeting of their mouths to tempt and tantalize, he'd succeeded. More than succeeded. She felt an instant chill across her skin the moment he stood back.

"You better go to bed." His eyes were dark as he wet his lips; she wondered if the gesture was a conscious one. As if to taste her . . .

"Yes . . ." she managed to reply.

" 'Night, then."

"Good night."

Josephine watched him go. It wasn't until she was tucked beneath the soft blankets inside the wagon that she truly allowed herself to relax. She closed her eyes tight and willed J.D.'s face from her thoughts. But he kept resurfacing in her mind's eye, just when she was ready to doze off. Her last conscious thought was of how J.D. had looked when he'd ridden in for supper with the sun behind his back. He'd been covered with trail dust, his gloves tucked into the band of his chaps and his hat brim hiding the expression in his eyes. If she hadn't known any better, she could have sworn he'd been Rawhide Abilene in the flesh.

CHAPTER

→12←

J.D. scanned the ribbon of plodding cows with a practiced eye, looking for any signs of flight or trouble. The drag men yelled and whistled to the stragglers, ever pushing. The pack of dogs panted alongside the herd, tongues hanging and dripping saliva, patiently waiting to do their jobs when the need arose.

A mother cow and her fresh-licked calf sneaked off at a right angle from the others to seek relief from the pressure of the relentless pace.

Whistling between his teeth, J.D. called, "Toby! Bring 'em!"

The scruffy white and black dog charged off in a spurt of canine energy with vocal barks. Nipping at the ankles of the unruly charges, Toby brought the bellowing, kicking mother and her calf back to the ranks.

In a gesture of respect, J.D. nodded to Toby. "Good boy."

Dust rose in choking white clouds that put a film of gray on the herd and the men riding horseback. The chalklike powder cracked J.D.'s lips under his red bandana. His hat brim kept the grit from sifting through his hair, but the long ends were exposed and had become pale.

What grasses had managed to sprout up were dying beneath the sun. Scrub littered the landscape like precious nuggets in a miner's tin—few and far between. Out of the horizon jutted the mountain they'd be cutting into three days at the most. He hoped the winter had been kinder to the hillsides, leaving them lush with budding aspens, cottonwoods, and willows, the ground covered by bluegrass, cowslips, and currants. But until then, they all suffered the parched terrain with quiet tolerance.

Blinking at the dryness in his eyes, J.D. settled into the saddle wishing he had Josephine's violin music in his head rather than the lowing of cows.

Never had he heard such notes played on that fiddle. Luis did the instrument proud with his renditions of western tunes and cowboy lore, but what Josephine had played had been celestial. It made him think of the stars in the sky and see them in his mind without looking heavenward. He wouldn't have thought anyone could have such a talent, but she'd surprised him. She'd surprised them all.

Reluctantly, J.D. admitted to himself that she was fitting in on the trail. But that didn't mean she fit in with his life.

He had nothing in common with Josephine. He couldn't talk to her about what was important to him. She didn't know the way of things. Ranch life was what he was good at. It was what he knew. Every bit of it. Inside and out. It was a part of him. No matter what he and the boys would start talking about, whether it be a long-awaited letter from home, or the weather, or what was happening in town, the conversation always took a turn toward cattle.

Eugenia McCall hadn't had the West in her. He kept in touch with his mother through infrequent letters. At the end of her correspondences, she obligingly asked after Boots as a postscript, but nothing more than that. He'd write back when he got the chance. Those times when he sat at the big dining table with paper and pen, he fumbled for how to phrase his thoughts. He wasn't much of a letter writer, having nothing to say to the woman who had borne him. Not that he didn't love her; he just didn't know her anymore. She'd been gone five years and hadn't come for a visit. He didn't expect her to. Nor would J.D. travel to Boston to see her. But it wasn't that he didn't care.

Just as Eugenia knew where she needed to be, J.D. knew where to hang his hat, too. He wasn't a plantation owner's son anymore who could afford to be idle or go where he wished on a whim. He was a cattleman employing more than a dozen men who depended on him. He had thousands of cows that didn't give a man a day of rest, no matter what the season. Leaving, even for a short time, was impossible for him.

J.D. eased back in the line, preparing to tell the drovers on his side about the water situation they'd be heading into the next couple of miles. They'd gone over it at the dinner stop, but whenever cattle got wind of water it could spell trouble, especially if the water wasn't enough to quench their thirst. The best plan to keep them under control was a plan that had been gone over a half-dozen times.

Turning in the saddle, J.D. caught sight of the chuck wagon, satisfied to see that Boots wasn't going off half-cocked today. J.D. wasn't wholly convinced by Josephine's story about her being the navigator. What puzzled him more was, why would she cover up Boots's mistake?

It would seem that the two had struck up an odd alliance of sorts. They seemed to be sharing a secret, an ill-formed bond of some kind that J.D. couldn't figure.

There hadn't been a single day gone by that J.D. had felt as if Boots was his ally. And deep down, buried in a place where J.D. would not feel the hurt, he was a little envious of Josephine.

* * *

Josephine sat next to Boots, her hand on the brim of her hat to keep the dust from sifting into her eyes worse than it already was. The heavy air was thick with the powder and the odor of cattle.

Resting her raised arm for a moment to get the circulation back, Josephine shook out her hand and leaned a little into the hard, uncomfortable seat. The small of her back hurt; her spine felt bruised. Her behind still hurt. She was achy. She was dirty.

The country was as flat as her palm, with little or no shade. When would they get to some trees? Some water? She'd jump in the first puddle she saw, as long as it was shallow enough for her to sit in without the water coming past her waist. Was anyone else bothered by the endless dust? The smell?

Apparently not Boots.

He sat to her left, his gloved fingers loosely holding on to the reins. His head periodically bobbed; his chin would come down toward his chest, then snap upward as he dozed.

The team of four mules, without directions from the driver, took it upon themselves to veer off from the grooved road that ran parallel with the herd. As they started to swerve left, Josephine opened her mouth to tell Boots what was happening. But before she could say anything, the wagon wheels hit a series of washboard flutes. The chuck bounced like a baby on its father's lap.

Josephine nearly flew out of her seat. Blindly grabbing for anything to keep from taking flight, she gripped the iron rail and Boots's shirtsleeve at the same time.

"Good gawd!" Boots hollered as he managed to get the team back on the beaten path. "Let go of me!"

She did, but only after they were safely traversing the old rutted cattle road.

Boots gave her a severe frown, the dust thick as fur on his brows. "What'd y'all go and knock me off the road for?"

"You drove us off the road." Then she added gently, "You were sleeping."

"I was?"

"It's the heat. I'm sleepy, too." She wasn't really, but she didn't want Boots to know that.

From the line of cowboys ahead, J.D. swung around and headed their way. As he approached in a canter, dust puffed beneath his horse's hooves, and the fine powder fell off his cotton duster and the edges of his hat. He reined short of the wagon and fell into pace with them. A red kerchief was tied at the back of his neck, the triangle-shaped front over his nose.

When he tugged the kerchief down, the lower portion of his face was a shade darker than the slash of his exposed forehead where the fine grit paled his complexion.

"We'll be coming up to Long Creek in the next mile," he advised. "I want you to stay off to the left, just the way you have been doing. We're going to have to turn to keep the cows from running."

"So y'all said," Boots replied, hunched over with his elbows resting on his knees. The jangle of tack minced his words.

"And I'll say it again." J.D. pushed the kerchief back into place and sternly warned, "Keep to the left."

"I heard you."

"Just making sure."

J.D. looked pointedly at her while touching the brim of his hat. "Josephine."

Then he spurred his horse forward and rode off. Her gaze followed him, as did her thoughts.

"Why'd your father shoot himself in the head?"

Boots's blunt inquiry caught her so off guard, he could have knocked her over with his words. She spied him gazing intently at her, waiting for her reply.

Josephine had nobody to blame but herself. She *never* would have mentioned the details of his death if Boots hadn't said such a thing to J.D. about Hazel doing him in. She'd felt sorry for Boots when he'd gotten them lost. She'd seen the confusion on his face, the desperation. For Josephine, the way her father had died was a scandal. The gossips on Fifth Avenue had had a field day. The New York papers gave the incident front-page coverage, and yet his obituary was short and to the point. Nobody seemed to remember all Andrew Tilden had done for the city.

Instead, society's tittering had feasted on him taking his own life. The viperous talk was a constant source of humiliation for her whenever she went out in public—which became increasingly rare. She wasn't so wounded as to let the painful words affect her grief or make her hide forever in shame. It was just that *suicide* was a word associated with . . . cowards. She'd been told this by Hugh, who never let her live it down.

Andrew Tilden had been one of many to be ruined by what they were calling Black Friday. But only two others had taken the same way out of their despair.

Josephine licked her dry lips, suddenly longing for a cold drink of water to soothe her throat, which had gone tight. "My father's money was invested in Wall Street, and when the market crashed this past September, he was financially ruined."

"He did himself in because he lost all his money?"

She didn't like the tone of Boots's voice. It grated with caustic and judgmental censure. "I suppose you could say that, though I don't—"

"Let me tell y'all a thing about money," Boots cut in as he faced forward, his profile grim. "I used to have a forty-room home that any Southerner would be proud to sip a julep on the veranda with me. I built up a cotton plantation from nothing more than resolve and ingenuity. Then the gawddamn war came and took our livelihood away from us. That gawddamn war . . ." he repeated softly, the words fading on his lips. His slack mouth hardened. "And when it was over, those Yankee bastards took me for all I had.

I ended up with nothing but a pile of debt and taxes that I couldn't pay. They got the house and all the land. All I had left was Eugenia and the boy there."

Boots's gaze strayed to J.D. riding toward the drag men, and Josephine couldn't tell what Boots was thinking.

"Y'all didn't see me blasting a big hole in my head," Boots spat, pitching his burned-out cigar over the side of the wagon. "But I'll admit, I did my share of liquor tossing."

Josephine's heartbeat tripped against her ribs. "That was a very unkind thing to say."

"Maybe. But it's the truth. Money can be made again if a man has a willingness to work for it."

"You didn't know my father. You didn't know the situation he was in. He . . ." But she couldn't finish her defensive line of thought, because part of what Boots was saying was the truth. A stronger man wouldn't have given up. Her father had her to live for, and yet she hadn't been important enough for him to fight back and start over.

Lowering her chin, Josephine held on to her tears. "I don't want to talk about it anymore."

"Suit yourself."

And that was that. In the seven months since she'd buried her father beside her mother, she'd made excuses for him. Not only to herself but to Hugh. To her friends. But there was no excuse, and Boots knew it.

How she disliked him for having the nerve to speak what she'd been thinking in her heart. Just when she was feeling compassion toward him, he went and said something hurtful. She could see why J.D. didn't get along with Boots. He could be mean-spirited without even trying.

The herd smelled the trickle of water in Long Creek, scant that it was, a mile away. They bawled and moaned for a drink. Gus and Jidge had to hold the strong leaders back, while down the line Print and Ace whooped and cursed, popping down their ropes to keep the weaker ones going.

The herd thundered into the flat wind that carried the smell. J.D. swore thickly.

"Hi-ah! Hi-ah!" J.D. called as Toby cut off a half-dozen heifers set to stampede.

Jidge, Dan, Birdie, and Ace were on J.D.'s side, and they went into overseeing the cows, many with their tongues hanging out, dry and dusty, and eyes sunken. Their tails went up, and they broke into a hurried and heavy-footed trot. J.D. wanted them to turn right, so Gus dropped back, and Jidge started pushing the herd over. Orley and Dan followed up the same way, and so did the flank and drag men, until the cattle were cutting a curve. This way, they'd protect the drags from harm by saving them a couple hundred yards since they were the weakest of the bunch.

Even with their precise maneuvers and the reliable horses and dogs, they couldn't stop the inevitable. The whole herd moved like one big animal and lit out for the water.

Birdie's horse cut up some, nervously dancing as the cattle surrounded it and pressed in. Birdie tried to turn the dun, but he wore Mexican spurs with long rowels and bells on them. His horse kept shifting to the left, then the right, trying to get away from the cows pressing in. All the jerky movements caused Birdie accidentally to catch his big spur in the cinch ring. J.D. watched as he struggled to free his boot, but he couldn't get it out.

The dun began to buck, trying to fling Birdie out of the saddle. His Colt six-shooter went sailing, then the Winchester. Without a moment's thought, J.D. rode directly into the herd and headed straight for Birdie's thrashing dun. If the cowboy fell off, he'd be trampled to death.

J.D. got alongside Birdie's horse, made a grab for

the cheek strap, but he missed. He tried again, this time successfully getting hold of it. Swinging his leg over his saddle, he prepared to dismount, but his own spur caught on the cantle. For several paralyzing seconds, J.D. was stretched out between Birdie's horse and his own. The dun was moving like a maniac, while Tequila shifted to stay still so that J.D. could get free. He did so, landing on unsteady feet. He held on to the pommel of Tequila's saddle, keeping the horse close for protection.

Reaching for the quick release knot on Birdie's cinch, J.D. got it on the second try and gave the latigo a firm jerk. A stirrup smacked J.D. on the side of the head, and the saddle came off just as Birdie—minus the boot that he'd slipped his foot out of—went through the air. He crashed in the dust with a grunt, falling in the midst of running cattle, the dun taking off with nostrils flared and ears back.

J.D. snagged the back of Birdie's collar and yanked him onto his feet toward Tequila; the horse had enough sense to stay still with cattle mooing past. Pressing Birdie between Tequila's belly and his chest, J.D. waited for help.

Seconds ticked by with agonizing slowness as the cows went around Tequila, their flanks bumping into J.D.'s legs. Finally, Ace and Jidge came, Ace hauling Birdie up into his saddle and getting him out. J.D. snatched Tequila's reins in his gloved hand, slid his boot into the stirrup, and mounted. He rode a quick zigzag path through the herd to the edge where Ace had let Birdie slip out of the saddle to his feet.

J.D. couldn't stop and ask him how he was. Instead, he and Ace joined Jidge and the other boys in trying to control the herd.

Once the cows hit the creek and churned it to mud, they'd lose any chance of drinking what little there was. Loping around the crying group of animals as they stood in the sludge, J.D. noted several were down. Two newly born calves, a few of the old heifers, and a three-year-old that had given birth two weeks prior to them setting out. He couldn't find the calf.

There was nothing he could do. The cows would eventually calm, but until then he and the boys were fighting a losing battle trying to subdue them in such a big cluster. Eventually, they'd spread out and could be put into ranks again.

J.D. turned Tequila so that he could check on Birdie. When he got there, Birdie was still pretty well shaken up. Wincing, he held his left arm, the bone between wrist and elbow obviously broken.

Breathing heavily, Birdie said, "I would have surely been dead if you hadn't come in and got me. I owe you."

"You don't owe me anything."

The rumble of the chuck wagon as it careened toward them had J.D. glancing up. Boots brought the four mules in at a breakneck pace. Abruptly, he leaned back and gave the reins a stretch to get the mules to stop. Blindly grabbing for the brake handle, he yelled in a well-deep voice, "Whoa! Whoa!"

Dust and pebbles sputtered in the wagon's wake, easing down to a drifting of powder as Boots brought the chuck to a sliding stop. The mules brayed with their lips curled and yellowed teeth bared. Ears pricked with their disgust at being the brunt of such backward treatment. Boots neglected their grunts as he wrapped the reins around the handle and stood.

"What in the hell happened?" he asked Birdie, whose face had gone a paler shade.

"They ran for the water," Birdie managed to get out between his cracked lips.

"Y'all broke your arm, you nitwit."

"First break of the spring," Birdie said, his face a mixture of pain and elation. "I win the pot."

The boys had been putting money into the broken bone fund all winter, and whoever broke the first bone of the season won the money. There was something like thirty dollars in the quart glass jar the boys kept beneath one of the floorboards of the bunkhouse.

Josephine made a soft gasping sound that caused J.D. to gaze at her. She stared at Birdie's contorted arm. "Where are we going to find a doctor? Is there a town close by?"

Birdie shrugged. "J.D.'ll set it."

She looked at J.D. "You have medical training?"

The way she said it, with such incredulous doubt and wonder, he couldn't help laughing as he ran his hand through his hair to push it out of his eyes. He'd lost his hat in the scuffle; no doubt it was pretty well thrashed by now. "I've got no more training than anybody else around here."

"But he needs a doctor." Her eyes widened as he brought his hand down. "Your forehead."

"What about it?"

"You're bleeding."

J.D. didn't feel anything.

"Good gawd, he's just got a gash on the side of his head," Boots broke in. "I've had worse."

J.D. lifted his hand back to his temple, brought his fingers down, and looked at the smears of blood. "You know how to sew, Miss Whittaker?"

"I embroider," she replied without pause, but her brows had come down in a questioning frown.

"Same thing." J.D. wiped his hand on the seat of his pants. "If I need stitches, you can sew me up."

She made a slight breathy noise from deep in her throat, and he wondered if she might be sick. He'd meant to get a reaction out of her.

To his amazement, she didn't faint or puke. She merely straightened and put her hands together in her lap. "My best stitch is the lazy daisy, but don't expect too much if you want anything fancier."

CHAPTER

⭑ 13 ⭑

Rather than continue on to the bed ground, J.D. gave orders to make an early camp at Long Creek. Josephine built cooking pits and got her fires going. Water covering the beans she'd put in a Dutch oven to soak had spilled over in the chuck cupboard and seeped through the cracks to the spices on a shelf below. After a cursory inspection, nothing else seemed to be ruined. Her keg of sourdough starter was all right, too. But no matter how much she wiped down the sides before and after each use, the sticky batter managed to seep through the lid and cake the outside.

There had been a lot of commotion going on for the past hour. The cowboys tried to settle in the herd. The animals had been deprived of water and were making their displeasure known. The endless crying was wearing on Josephine.

Just as she covered the lid to a roast with hot coals, J.D. rode in with Birdie. The cowboy sat astride his horse, holding the reins in one hand. That he'd gotten back in a saddle with a broken arm amazed her.

Rio had been taking care of the horses a close distance away and came over to relieve both men of their mounts. J.D. walked toward Josephine, tugging off his gloves as he approached with a rolling stride that she'd come to recognize as his alone. She noted that the blood on his temple had dried, his hair sort of stuck together in that spot. Birdie's gait was taxed, his body movements stiff and awkward. He kept his broken arm tucked close to his side. From the grimace twisting his face, it seemed his threshold for pain had all but worn out. She couldn't imagine having to work in the physical state he was in.

Without a word, J.D. went past her and flipped open the cupboard doors. After snatching the full bottle of whiskey, he stole a coffee cup she'd set out. She used it for measuring, having already filled and dumped flour from it for the biscuits.

Tugging the front tail of his shirt free, J.D. wiped out the inside of the cup with the hemmed edge of muslin. He dragged Boots's crate from the front of the wagon and moved around to the eastern side so that Birdie could sit without the setting sun blinding him. The cowboy eased himself down, the flagrant curses spoken beneath his breath not going unnoticed by Josephine.

J.D. popped the liquor bottle's cork and poured a healthy amount into the coffee cup.

"Have a drink, pardner," he told Birdie, pushing the mug into his good hand.

"Don't mind if I do," Birdie replied, then took a generous swallow.

J.D. searched through the drawers, fingering the brown-glass medicine bottles so he could read the stained labels. He chose the one marked laudanum. Then he found some linen strips that Josephine kept with the flour sack towels. Lastly, he collected a butcher knife.

That spread panic through Josephine, and she blurted, "What do you need the knife for?"

"What do you think?" His blue-gray eyes held her still.

"I don't know."

"Then you better stick around and find out. I'll need your help."

If there was going to be any limb severing, she didn't want to see. She wondered if there was a way for her to sneak a drink of that whiskey for herself. She'd never tasted hard liquor before aside from whatever had been in that bottle Boots had given her after her tomatoes had exploded.

J.D. turned his back to her, the sunset casting his hair in hues of amber and gold. For the first time, she noticed he was without his hat. No wonder she'd been able to stare into his eyes.

The leg bottoms of his denim pants were splattered with mud. A hole in the seat caught her attention, the gash in the fabric just below one of the pockets that hugged the slight curve of his behind. When he moved, a sliver of red showed past the blue denim. His drawers. Josephine averted her gaze, but her mind burned with the image that could only be labeled as alluring. But for the life of her, she couldn't explain why.

Hugh hadn't worn his trousers as tight as J.D. did. Perhaps that was it. Nor had her husband ever gotten a rip in the twill covering his seat. He was too concerned about his appearance ever to be found in such a state of disrepair. Funny how J.D. wasn't at all concerned about his appearance in front of her. That was one of the things that attracted her to him. His ruggedness. The way he'd roll his sleeve cuffs up or, as he'd done just now, untuck the front of his shirt and leave the back in.

"Get a bowl of water." J.D.'s instructions intruded on her thoughts, and Josephine did as she was told. Collecting the big bowl she'd intended to use for mixing the pie crusts, she went to the sweating barrel, positioned the bowl beneath the spigot, and opened the flow of water.

When she returned to the endgate with the bowl,

she set it down and waited. Silently, she watched as J.D. gently unbuttoned Birdie's shirt. The light touch that he had, the concern for the other man's discomfort, rested as soft as a down feather next to Josephine's heart.

Once Birdie's shirt was off, he sat with the upper portion of his long johns exposed. Josephine was about to turn away to give the cowboy his privacy, but J.D. called her.

"Fill up his cup with more whiskey."

Josephine picked up the bottle from where J.D. had left it and gave Birdie a liberal refill.

His eyes, watery from the violent pain, met hers. "Obliged, Miss Josephine."

Josephine wanted to weep. This was the same cowboy who'd played violin music last night. And here he sat in misery with his left arm fractured.

Returning the whiskey to the endgate, Josephine noted that none of the other cowboys had come in. Boots wasn't in view at the fire, and she idly wondered where he was.

After making a quick check of the beans and poking the slab of meat with a fork, she returned to J.D. He'd gotten Birdie out of his underwear sleeves.

Birdie's hairless chest and his lean torso were as white as chicken skin, but from his neck up and his wrists down he was tan—except for that pale band high around his forehead that all the boys had from their hats.

"Get me the gutta-percha that's in the wagon bed," J.D. said without looking at Josephine, who remained a respectable distance away. "It's in an Arbuckle's bag beneath the front seat next to the jewelry box."

Josephine had seen the coffee bag before but hadn't looked inside. She easily found what she needed and came back to find J.D. examining Birdie's crippled arm. Birdie stared straight ahead, his eyes fixed on the wrought tripod that supported her bean pot over the fire.

J.D. rested Birdie's arm back in his lap, then turned to her and took the coffee bag. The gutta-percha was a waterproof cloth. She'd seen it used for various things but hadn't known about its use in setting fractures. Reaching for the knife, J.D. stuck the sharp tip into the edge of the cloth, then brought it down and sliced out a piece about a foot square.

She'd forgotten about the bowl of water that he'd asked for until he poured some of the laudanum into it. Then he grabbed one of her towels and dunked the whole of it into the bowl. She was afraid to tell him she'd already used the flour sack to wipe down the endgate after mixing her biscuits.

J.D. wrung the cloth out and went back to Birdie.

"You know this is going to hurt like hell."

Birdie nodded.

"I'll do it quick."

Another nod, this one less evident.

J.D. turned to Josephine and looked at her. The expression in his eyes was stony with purpose. "Go into my duffle and get some neckerchiefs. Then dump the cigars out of Boots's cigar box and bring me the box."

"All right."

Josephine had to climb into the wagon and weed through the bedrolls until she found J.D.'s. She was uncomfortable searching through his personal belongings. She didn't unearth any manly articles she hadn't already seen on or in her own bedroom bureau. A change of underwear, a couple of shirts, hairbrush and toiletry articles. There was a bar of soap that gave off J.D.'s scent.

Replacing the soap, she found the bandanas and was crawling out of the wagon when a strangled moan ripped through the glow of sunset.

Josephine bit her bottom lip. Poor Birdie . . .

She snatched Boots's cigar box, opened the lid to the aroma of tobacco, and put the cigars on the wagon bed in front of the seat. When she returned to J.D., he was wrapping Birdie's straightened arm in the laudanum-soaked towel.

The cowboy's shoulders slumped as he drank his third mug of whiskey. J.D. wrapped the strips around the towel and secured them in place with two knots. He cut the remainder off with the knife.

J.D. took the cigar box from her and sliced the lid from the box, then proceeded to dismantle the rest of the hard-board sides and bottom until he had strips about four inches wide. Using the remaining bandages, he loosely wrapped the soft cotton around Birdie's arm for padding before he aligned the cigar box splints over them. That done, he used an extra length of strip and held everything in place.

When J.D. was finished, he wrapped one bandana around the bandage, then tied the other two together and made a sling out of them for Birdie to slip over his head and tuck his arm into.

Birdie was on his way to being drunk. His eyelids slipped over his eyes, his body went slack, and a smirk crossed his lips. Well, not exactly a smirk. He smiled. Lopsidedly.

J.D. reached for Josephine. Her breath hitched, and she stood motionless. She had no opportunity to move out of the way once she realized that he wasn't going after her but rather the bottle of whiskey resting on the endgate she was backed up against.

He gave Birdie a healthy pour, then stuffed the cork into the bottle's mouth. "I'll make up your bedroll."

"Obliged, boss."

J.D. left the remains of the cigar box for Josephine to tidy up. He was about to go around her when she remembered his wound and said, "What about your head?"

He raised his hand, felt around for a second or two, then shrugged. "If I was going to bleed to death, I would have by now."

"Don't you want to wash the blood out of your hair?"

"As much as I want to wash this dust and mud off me, but I don't see any signs saying there's a bath house in the vicinity."

She didn't like it when he talked to her as if she were dim-witted. Squaring her shoulders, she said, "I'm not amused. As soon as you've got Birdie settled, come back and I'll take a look at you."

He didn't reply, or gaze at her, as he continued on. She had the urge to stamp her foot and squeeze her fingers together into tight balls. But she didn't. Instead, she lifted the cloth on her biscuit oven, deemed the dough balls risen enough, then put them on the fire. She examined her pot roast—a good-size chuck of beef that she'd salted and covered with flour hours ago. The juices bubbled, and nothing smelled burned. She lifted the lid to the beans. Steam gurgled up from the lumpy mix—minus the little rocks this time. After breakfast, she'd gone through the amount she needed and picked them all out.

When J.D. called him, Birdie staggered toward his bed, refusing the help Josephine offered. She supposed just because his arm was broken didn't mean his pride was.

She lit a kerosene lamp, waved out the match, and went to put the whiskey away. Looking to see if anyone was watching her, she sniffed the cork and wrinkled her nose. It smelled horrible.

"Good gawd, what'd y'all do that for?"

Josephine started. Boots came up to her from the side, his gaze burning on the dismantled cigar box.

Guiltily putting the bottle in the cupboard and closing the door, she explained, "Birdie needed splints."

Boots frowned. "You should have splinted him with something else, dammit. Now my stogies are going to lose their flavor. Where'd you put them?"

"On the wagon floor."

"The wagon floor?" His tone soured even more. "The night air is going to ruin them. Give me a jar."

Josephine hunted one up from a drawer and handed it to him. Stalking off, he muttered about her being greener than a pile of manure. She didn't know what he was talking about, but she didn't care for his tone.

The cowboys began riding in before J.D. came back to the chuck wagon for her to examine him. She spied him smoking a cigarette while talking to Gus Peavy and Jidge Dooly near the remuda where Rio was brushing down their horses.

Josephine called the boys to supper, then took her meal later. She ate what she felt was a marginal portion. Her appetite wasn't as hearty as that of those around her. She found that the rigors of the trail and the trials of cooking preoccupied her too much to sit and relish a supper plate.

When the last of the coffee was gone and Josephine put on another pot for the nighthawks, she passed out the remainder of her precious butterscotch candies, saving one for Birdie and one for herself in case of an emergency.

Having already put water on to boil for the dishwashing, she filled one of the wreck pans half with it and half with cold water to cover the mound of dirty dishes. She rolled up her sleeves and dug in, relishing the small amount of warmth and suds, wishing there was a whole tub of it to soak her entire body.

Rio stood and came over to help while the others conversed in soft tones.

"Nice night," he said, readying the rinsing tub. A shock of his white-blond hair fell across his brow.

"I suppose it is," Josephine replied to be polite.

Taking up a towel, Rio asked, "You aim to be a ranch cook, Miss Josephine? Or are you out West looking for a husband?"

The bluntness of his question caught her by surprise. And to make matters worse, J.D. had come near. A quick glance at him, and she wasn't all that sure his presence was unintentional. He grabbed a thick towel, folded it twice, and lifted the lid on the coffeepot to check the brew. Anybody would know that the coffee couldn't possibly be done yet. He lingered at the fire. Hunkering down, he held that position, well within earshot of anything Josephine would say.

"Well, Miss Josephine?"

Rio's voice pulled Josephine's gaze off J.D.'s wide shoulders. She stared at the wet dishcloth in her hand, then swished it across a plate. "No, I most surely did not travel west looking for a husband."

"Why not?"

"Because I don't need one."

"But a man out here would treat you right. A man like me could show you—"

"Fall into bed, kid," came J.D.'s deep voice from behind. "Miss Josephine has to see to me."

She turned, nearly bumping into J.D., who stood so close to her she could feel his body heat.

Rio didn't readily set down the plate he was drying. "But we're not done yet."

"You are now," J.D. replied in a tone that said the matter was settled.

Adding the tin to the stack, the wrangler mumbled his good nights.

Josephine watched him retreat, then turned her attention on J.D. She had thought he didn't want her to tend to him. Secretly, she'd been relieved. But now that he'd come, she couldn't back down.

He remained near, and she took a step toward the light to set her wash rag down. "Well . . . come here, then." She'd tried to make her voice sound composed, but, to her ears, it had wavered. She had never done any kind of doctoring.

J.D. drew next to her. There was no place to sit, and she didn't know where the sewing things were kept. So she stood there blankly.

Opening the cupboard, J.D. slid a drawer open and collected a rawhide pouch. He brought it out, opened the gathers, and dumped the contents on the endgate.

A small pair of scissors, a single spool of black thread, and various needles stuck in a tiny cloth remnant came out.

"Use the smallest needle." He pointed to the one he wanted.

She could barely nod but didn't go near the needles. "I'd better wash the cut first." Moving around him, she dunked her dishcloth into the warm water, wrung it, and came back to J.D. The dried blood in his hair looked terrible, the locks falling over his forehead and making her unable to see the extent of the damage. With a gentle touch, she began to wipe his hair clean with light, even strokes.

J.D. kept his gaze on her as she worked, while she made every effort to avert his direct stare. Her knuckles brushed the smooth skin of his forehead as she used two hands. One to steady his head, the other to stroke the cloth over his hair to push it out of his face. A stubborn lock wouldn't stay back, so she ran her fingers through the length, amazed at how cool and silky the strands felt.

Once his hair was out of the way, she could clearly see the cut. A jagged gash ran from the end of his eyebrow upward to his hairline. In spite of no fresh blood coming from the wound, it looked terrible. Even to her untrained eye, the gap was a definite candidate for stitches.

"What do you think?" he asked, the vibration of his voice moving through her and sending pinpointed tingles across her skin.

"I think you better have a drink of that whiskey."

J.D. cracked a smile. "And what about the doctor?"

Her eyes flew to his. "I only drink sherry."

"Or corn liquor."

"That was an emergency," she blurted.

"And what's this?"

Cause for a pound's worth of butterscotch candies. Biting her lower lip, she murmured, "A critical situation. I can handle it."

"I hope so. I don't want to look like I'm wearing a tapestry on my head. Just do some simple stitches, and that's good enough."

Nodding, she picked up the needle and threaded it while J.D. poured a small amount of whiskey into a cup. Rather than drink it, he grabbed a flour sack cloth and dipped the corner into the drink. He brought the liquor-laced towel to his cut and pressed.

Gritting his teeth, he closed off a distinct curse. Then he repeated the process. When he was finished, what liquor remained in the cup he drank with a toss of his head.

"Okay, go ahead," he said, cocking one hip against the ledge of the endgate.

Josephine brought the needle up but found she had trouble focusing on the area that needed her attention.

"Hold still," she commanded.

"I'm not moving. That's you who's swaying."

"Oh . . ." She lowered her arm. "Maybe we should sit down."

"Maybe I should forget about this."

She shook her head. "No. I can do it, it's just that you're too tall." She spied Boots's crate by the wagon hub. "Sit on that."

J.D. dragged it over and sank onto the wood. His bent legs were in the way, and she couldn't get close enough to him until he spread them. The compromising position made her throat go dry, and she wet her lips before proceeding.

She had to put her palm on his forehead once more and tilt his head toward the kerosene light. She felt his inner thighs on either side of her as she moved even slightly. Trying not to think about the tender skin she was going to puncture, she pretended that his cut was just two pieces of fabric that needed fusing together. A quick prick, and then one stitch. Another, and then another.

She began talking to distract her from thinking

about the reality of what she was sewing. "I noticed you have a faint scar on your chin. How did that happen?"

He was silent a moment, then said, "I got in a fight with my brother."

"William or Lewis?"

He cocked his head, and she nearly pricked her finger. "Don't move."

"How do you know about William and Lewis?"

"You spoke about them to Boots our first day out."

"I don't remember."

Slowly pulling the thread, she asked, "So which one was it?"

"William." J.D. grew thoughtful, and she allowed him his silence, hoping he would expound on the incident. A moment later, he did. "I was twelve. Me and him had already developed into a pair of hot-heads. We had Boots to blame for that. He taught us that if we didn't stand up for ourselves, nobody else would.

"For a while, I thought about going into the horse-breeding business. It's a cardinal rule that nobody rides the horses without permission. William took off on one of my best stud horses.

"When I found out, I went after him and tackled him to the ground. We hit each other and did a pretty good job of getting our respective messages across."

Josephine leaned toward J.D. for better lighting. "I can't imagine beating up a sibling over something silly like that."

Tipping his chin up, J.D. said seriously, "It wasn't silly to us."

"What did your father do?"

"Hell, when Boots found out, he slapped us both on the sides of our heads. Even though I'd made out better in the fight, it was William who got Boots's praise for taking it like a man." J.D. became pensive once more. "To Boots, the eldest son is everything."

"And is that what William was?"

"Yes. Lewis came next. Then me."

"They both died during the war," she observed, steeling herself for another stitch. "Did you fight, too?"

"Yes."

"I didn't have any brothers, so I never experienced what it was like to have a loved one go off to battle. It must have been hard."

"You have any sisters?" He quickly changed the subject.

"No. I'm an only child."

J.D.'s eyes closed for a moment, and she wondered how much pain he was in. He hadn't flinched or winced once.

"You ever lived anyplace besides New York?"

"We had a summer house in Connecticut. Other than that, this is the first time I've ever been this far west."

"And going farther west still."

Josephine vaguely nodded, feeling as if San Francisco was thousands of miles away. Getting there seemed utterly inconsequential at the moment. She was needed here. And she liked that feeling.

"Have you ever been to New York?" she asked, wondering if J.D. McCall had ever seen her world.

"I came from Mississippi to here. Never been anyplace in between but small towns. I wouldn't go to New York for anything."

"Neither would I." The declaration slipped out before she could catch herself.

"You don't have any family there?"

She thought of Hugh, then replied, "No."

A lull passed between them. As the campfire had slowly died, the cowboys' conversation had died with it. She and J.D. were the only ones still awake.

When she reached the point where she needed to snip the thread, she battled a sudden attack of light-headedness. If it hadn't been for J.D. reaching out and putting his hands on her waist, she might have faltered backward.

"I'm all right . . ." she managed, but she could hardly hear herself speak. The firmness of his grip fortified her, and she was glad when he didn't let her go. With scissors in hand, she made a quick snip, and that was that.

Opening her eyes wide, she stood back to view her handiwork. The stitches weren't exactly even, but they'd done the job. *She'd* done the job! And without the butterscotch candy that had been tucked in her pocket.

"There." She set the scissors down and gazed at J.D. "I'm not going to faint. You can let me go."

But he didn't. He stared up at her face. "I didn't think you had it in you to go through with it. You proved me wrong."

A little nervous, Josephine gave a shaky laugh. "Well, I hope you don't get hurt again so I have to prove it to you a second time. I'd much rather sew the hole in your pants instead." Then she blushed, realizing what she'd just said.

Awkwardly backing out of his embrace, she put her hand on the endgate and nearly toppled the whiskey bottle. "Well . . . I hope your head doesn't hurt too much."

"I've had worse. I'll survive."

She threw herself into cleaning up the sewing things. J.D.'s hand came down over hers and stilled her fingers. Her eyes moved to his.

"Thanks."

She had to clear her throat in order to speak. "Maybe you better not thank me until you take a look at it."

"I'm sure it's fine."

"You said plain stitching. I believe I went too fancy."

"It'll do."

The nicker of a horse with the remuda, the low

night songs of the two boys on the nighthawk, and the lowing of the cattle surrounded them. Josephine felt oddly at peace. She could have easily snuggled into J.D.'s arms and rested her cheek against his chest. The thought felt so comforting . . . so right.

J.D. hesitated, and she wondered if he was thinking the same thing as she was. But then he said, "You should get some sleep."

In spite of the trying day, she wasn't tired. "Yes . . . I suppose."

"Good night, then."

"Good night."

He left, and Josephine finished what little dishes had been left to wash. Then there was nothing left to do but climb into the wagon bed.

Once inside, she took off her boots, easing her sore feet out of the insteps. The scratchy woolen covers clawed at her as she tried to get comfortable beneath them. She groped in the dark for the alarm clock and made sure it was set. Then her hand fell by her side and she stared at the bowed ceiling and waited for sleep to claim her.

Her thoughts drifted to fragments, and she reluctantly admitted that she had wanted to impress J.D. since the moment she first met him. With her cooking, with her cleaning, and tonight with her doctoring. She was finding out that she wasn't as useless as Hugh had proclaimed. There was a lot she could do.

And probably more here than in San Francisco.

Josephine was awakened by J.D.'s voice, very close to her ear. At first, she thought she'd dreamed him up. How could he be in the wagon? She hadn't felt anyone climb in. But the breath tickling her temple brought her around, though not to full coherency. She blindly reached for the alarm clock to shut it off, thinking that the noisy bells were what had woken her. But her hand didn't make contact with the cold brass. She touched solid warmth. A man's chest encased in a heavy fabric shirt.

Sitting upright, she opened her eyes wide but couldn't see clearly.

"What's going on?" she mumbled through the disheveled tendrils hanging past her brows.

"You have to get up."

Disbelief feathered her words. "It's three-thirty already?"

"No. Midnight."

Josephine groaned.

"I need your help."

The odor of campfire and tobacco pressed in on her. "Did you hurt yourself again?"

"No. Are you dressed?"

That got her full attention, and Josephine opened her eyes wide. "Yes."

"Come with me." His deep voice wrapped around her, the close confines of the wagon making the situation worse. She could hardly move without bumping into him.

"Where?" she asked, holding her breath with wonder. Where did he want to take her?

"Get up, and I'll show you."

In spite of herself, Josephine was curious. She struggled to sit up, her head brushing his. She froze. She couldn't exactly see him, but she felt him. And he wasn't even touching her. The hairs on the nape of her neck prickled, deliciously.

He moved away before she could put order to the spiraling sensations that were burning her nerve endings.

"I need to put my boots on."

"I'll wait outside."

She joined him in a matter of minutes, her eyes adjusting to the lantern light in the clearing just ahead. Tied to one of the branches of a sorry bush was a calf.

J.D. walked toward the mottled brown-white cow, and Josephine followed behind.

"We tried grafting her," J.D. said as he adjusted the rope around its neck and knelt down, "but none of the heifers would take her. Her mother was killed in the stampede. She's a doggie—an orphan."

The orphan calf made a low sobbing noise, its black nose wet and reflecting the kerosene light. Despite it being a smelly cow, Josephine felt sorry for the poor thing.

"I'm going to need you to bottle-feed her."

Josephine took in a sharp breath. "What?"

"Bottle-feed her." J.D.'s brown hair fell over his collar as he gazed at her with all seriousness in his eyes. "Luis used to if we ever lost a heifer. You've got canned milk in the wagon, and there's a box with bottles and nipples."

"But . . ." Josephine couldn't think of a good excuse. She'd longed to be a mother to Hugh's children, but they hadn't been blessed with any. She hadn't been able to . . . well, that's what Hugh had told her. It was her fault they had been childless. How she'd longed to hold a baby in her arms and nurture it. She felt she had all the right motherly instincts—but they were for a child. A real baby who smelled like heaven. Not a calf with big brown eyes and a slobbery tongue.

The calf lifted its nose and sniffed Josephine's scent. Then it cried. Such a pitiful sob. Josephine cringed.

She stood motionless. Then, after a few seconds, she fit her hand into her trouser pocket and fished out the butterscotch she'd tucked away. Popping the candy into her mouth, she looked at J.D. "Do I have to sing to her while I give her the bottle?"

CHAPTER

→ 14 ←

J.D. was on his way back from the slow rise of Haymaker Mountain where Reliance River spilled through the gaps in the granite. What he'd found had put him at ease. The river was full and crystal-clear. It was good water, and there was plenty of it.

By late morning, they'd left the brush country behind, where everything that grew had thorns on it except for the willows. Bull pines had begun to take over, and red-winged blackbirds chattered and chirped in the cottonwoods. Goldenrod scattered the ground, pushing up between the dead pine needles, while lichens covered the trunks of trees.

As J.D. rode an overgrown path down to where the herd and chuck were winding their way up the more widely traveled road, the squeak of his saddle was his only company. An alder branch brushed the side of his head as he leaned away from it in the saddle. He was reminded of his cut and grew agitated. He'd washed his face this morning, looked in the mirror, and stilled when he saw Josephine's handiwork. He had three embroidery-type flowers across the side of his forehead. Swearing silently, he'd done the best he could to cover them with his beat-up hat.

The crown rode so low, he could barely see. He

hadn't confronted her about what she'd done, having the feeling she thought she'd done exactly what she should have. As long as nobody had to see him stitched up like a lady's pillow, he could live with the stitches—and hope like hell the black threads wouldn't leave a five-petaled scar.

As J.D. left the thickets of alders, the white and yellow pines spread out far enough for him to get a clear view of the herd as they progressed up the hillside. He caught sight of the chuck wagon with the calf trotting behind, tied by a rope.

J.D. disliked asking for favors. Within twenty-four hours, he'd gone to Josephine twice. And now he was about to embark on the third time. Only this one required a physical effort he wasn't sure she could manage.

"I don't understand why I have to give the calf a bottle. Why can't you milk one of the other cows?" Josephine asked, her hands resting on her knees.

Boots shifted in the seat, taking a puff on his cigar. "Beef cows don't cotton to being milked."

"Then why don't you keep a dairy cow?"

"Dairy cows lead to a milking job twice a day. Who's going to do that? Besides, what would a cowboy want with milk? He don't put it in his coffee because he doesn't need his breath to smell like a calf's. Better he smells like whiskey and tobacco."

Josephine wasn't placated. "I just wish there was another way."

"Use the canned cow like I told you."

Yes, he'd told her. A half-dozen times to make sure she'd gotten it right. To the milk she was to add some molasses to make it sweet, some soda, and some salt to prevent dehydration.

This morning, before she'd even had the coffee on, the calf had been crying something awful, and she'd given it the first bottle. The midnight feeding had been fixed by J.D. for her to give the calf. So not having known any better, she'd fed it plain canned milk this morning. The animal hadn't really liked it. It had cried for a while and nosed the bottle out of the way but eventually slurped its tongue over the nipple and dribbled milk down its chin while fussily drinking the whole thing.

Josephine's only knowledge of a cow was that she dished it up in a stew. How did J.D. McCall expect her to tend an animal she knew nothing about?

As if her thoughts of the man had conjured him, J.D. broke through the brush and headed directly for the wagon. He sat tall in the saddle and at ease with the stride of his horse. The sun-streaked ends of brown hair spilled beyond the collar of his duster coat, and his hat tipped low over his eyes. She couldn't see his forehead and wasn't sure how his injury was faring.

He reined in and spoke to her above the jangling rattle of the harnesses. "Can you ride a horse?"

She raised her brows and pulled her spine straighter. "With a sidesaddle."

"Think you could ride astride?"

"I could try."

"That'll do."

"Do for what?" she asked, dread inching its way up her spine. She didn't like the sideways manner of his approach. Asking her a question before giving her a hint of his intentions.

"I'll be back." Then he rode off, leaving her to ponder what she was getting into.

Josephine turned to Boots. "What was all that about?"

Boots cracked a half-smile. "My guess is he's putting y'all on the line before we get to the water so them cows don't run for it again."

Her palms moistened at the thought as she gazed

toward the string of cattle. Their horns seemed sharper, their bodies more barrel-like. She was no match for persuading them to do anything.

J.D. returned a quarter of an hour later with a tall, sandy-colored horse. The animal was heavy in the flanks and had a long black tail that swished like a whip. It tossed its dark mane, and leg muscles surged to get going.

Dread worked through Josephine, and she fought the rapid rise in her pulse.

The horse had been saddled with a western saddle and fit with a bridle rather than the rope halter the cowboys and J.D. favored. Wooden stirrups fell on both sides of its belly. Yes . . . this was definitely no sidesaddle.

"Her name is Peaches," J.D. said. "She's gentle."

Josephine didn't think she looked gentle.

Boots called for the mules to stop, and he set the brake. "Get on out if y'all're going."

Josephine hesitated, unsure she wanted to go.

"Come on," J.D. called. "We've got to get you up front where I can tell you what to do."

Reluctantly, Josephine disembarked from the chuck. With her feet planted on the ground, Peaches was even taller than she'd first thought. Boots cracked his whip over the mules and took off, leaving Josephine in a cloud of dust.

J.D. sidled closer to her, pinning her between the horses so he could hand her Peaches's reins. The mare shifted its weight, and Josephine worried about how she'd mount up. Her legs weren't long enough.

Leaning forward, J.D. dropped the reins into her hand. Peaches started walking, taking Josephine along.

"Quit that," J.D. reprimanded the horse, taking the side of its bridle and putting an end to its motion. Then he gazed at Josephine, who stood mutely there holding the reins. "Mount up."

"I've never gotten on this kind of saddle before."

J.D. held Peaches at bay while instructing Josephine. "You're on the right side. You always mount up on her left. Put your left boot in the stirrup and swing yourself into the saddle."

Josephine struggled with the reins and lifted her leg. She couldn't reach the stirrup. At the academy, they'd had mounting blocks.

J.D. jumped down so he could assist her. "Wrap those reins around the horn, and get them out of your way."

She did so as he squatted down slightly so that he could grip her calf.

"Push up."

She tried but lost her balance when J.D. picked her foot up to lead it toward the stirrup.

"Put your hand on my shoulder," he ordered.

Her fingers fell on his collar, brushing the hair that curled softly.

"Push up," he said again. Then she felt his hands on her derriere, and he was propelling her upward before she could react to the intimate contact and become flustered over it.

She would have sailed right over the saddle had he not caught her by her upper arm and held her in place. Fumbling for the saddle horn, she fervently clutched the hard tab of leather. Her legs were spread apart, and the hard leather of the saddle rubbed next to her inner thighs. This wasn't a position she was used to or felt comfortable in.

J.D. had his hand cupped over her knee. She hadn't been aware of it until he gave her upper leg a playful slap, then turned away while saying, "Get ahold of those reins."

The heavy leather felt peculiar in her grasp without gloves. She correctly positioned them in her hand so they made a nice, even droop on either side of Peaches's neck. She couldn't get used to the dangle of her legs against the mare's wide girth, but her feet seemed to fit all right in the stirrups.

"Keep to my right," J.D. said, then kneed his white horse into motion.

She didn't have to knee Peaches. The mare followed along quite nicely in a trot that Josephine settled into, and she became more at ease.

Soon, they caught up to the men at the head of the cattle, and J.D. called for her to ride up to him and stop.

"We're going on to the banks," J.D. informed Gus. "Start spreading them out. Lead cattle downstream, so the drags get clear water when they come in."

"It's covered, boss."

J.D. nodded and surged ahead, Josephine close behind. She was finding out that riding astride was easier than sidesaddle. She had a better grip, but in this position her behind didn't sit firmly on the leather, and she bounced a bit.

They came to a marginally wide river with sand sloping up the banks. Assorted pines fringed the area, a verdant canopy entirely different from the drab they'd left behind after breaking camp. There were several tiny pools made by impressions in the sparkling gray granite. They didn't appear to be deep, and, with the shallow depths, surely the water had to be warm. Sunlight glistened off the surface, so inviting that Josephine longed to get her feet wet.

J.D. turned left and followed the water downstream to a spacious meadow rich with grass.

Stopping, J.D. faced her. "We'll make bed ground here and camp where we came from."

That was fine with Josephine.

"We'll go back, and I want you positioned upstream. When Gus starts bringing in the leads, don't let any of them get past you and try for the water at your back. You got that?"

"How do you propose I fend them off?"

"Ride in front of any strays, and get them going back in the right direction. Peaches is a good cutting horse. She knows how to head 'em off. You just have to tell her where to go."

Josephine had no more opportunity for last-minute guidance. The chuck wagon approached, and directly behind it came the herd. The cows cried and hollered, most taking the grade at a run. The boys had their work cut out for them, dodging and chasing those animals that took it upon themselves to leave the mass and get out on their own to be the first ones to take a drink.

J.D. whistled between his teeth, and Toby shot from the pack in a black-and-white blur, ready to follow J.D. and pick up the slack. Josephine held her stance, Peaches pawing the soft earth. The mare was determined to do its job, and Josephine didn't have a moment to think about the situation before she was forced to react to it.

A brown-and-white painted cow came hurtling toward her, and she had to rein Peaches sharply to the left and hold on as the mare jumped into action. Her hat flew off her head, but she didn't give it a second's thought. As soon as Peaches had the cow back with the others, another slipped free, and the mare was after that one, too.

This went on for an undeterminable length of time. Josephine developed cramps in both her sides, and in tenderer spots of her anatomy she ached cruelly. When at last the herd was stretched out along the Reliance River farther than her eyes could see, J.D. came toward her on his horse.

Tipping his hat at her, he said, "You did all right, Jo."

His compliment surprised her, but his calling her a nickname did so even more. She had never been addressed as Jo her entire life. Perhaps now J.D. considered her one of the boys since she hadn't fallen off Peaches or ridden in the wrong direction. Regardless, she wasn't sure how she felt about being one of the boys in J.D.'s eyes. She rather liked it when he looked at her as a woman.

But in a sweeping gaze at her shirtfront and pants, she saw she was splattered with freckles of mud. And she wouldn't doubt some cow droppings were mixed in there somewhere.

She did look like a man, and she smelled like a cow. It was no wonder J.D. called her Jo.

Obligated to reply, Josephine murmured, "I just held on, and Peaches did the work."

J.D. gave her a smile that would have caused several ladies to swoon in the finest salons. "Don't discredit yourself. You know how to stay in a saddle."

Josephine glanced to the chuck wagon in the distance. Boots and Rio were in a conversation next to it while the wrangler held on to a shovel and dug out some pits for the fire. Wanting nothing better than to strip down to her underwear and sink into one of the pools, Josephine had to put that thought on hold and resign herself to standing and cooking for the next couple of hours.

As if J.D. could read her mind, he said, "We can have cold roast and biscuits for dinner. We're all going swimming as soon as the herd settles in. You can join us if you want."

Without hesitation, Josephine replied, "I'll tell Rio not to chop the wood yet."

J.D.'s soft laughter followed her as she steered Peaches in the direction of the wagon. His voice stayed with her and she replayed his earlier words. *You did all right, Jo.* Even if he had referred to her as one of the boys, at least he'd given her his approval. Josephine was immensely pleased with herself.

"Forget about the wood for a while," Josephine said to Rio with a grin. "It's a cold dinner today. We're all going swimming."

"What in the hell would we want to do that for?" Boots wanted to know.

"To clean up," she replied, undaunted by his sour tone.

Josephine swung her leg over Peaches's rump and slid out of the saddle, her stomach pressed against the mare's belly. Both feet hit the ground, and a nerve-splitting current raced through her body. She was so stiff and numb that once she dismounted, she could barely move. She hobbled toward Rio with the reins in her hand, but each step was agony.

"You look a little sore there, cookie," Boots said around the cigar in his mouth. "We got liniment in the cupboard for your fanny."

She shot him an angled gaze. "I don't need any."

Boots chuckled.

Josephine frowned. She hated it when he was right.

J.D. leaned his back against a rock with a smoke clamped between his lips, enjoying the pulse of spring water being parted by his long john-covered chest. No doubt about it, the water was damn cold; but near the surface, the temperature was warm enough to be tolerated, and these pools weren't all that deep. Besides, J.D. would have lain back in one even if ice was floating by. At least long enough to scrub up with a bar of soap—which he'd already done.

He'd washed his clothes, scrubbed his underwear with him in it, then lathered his body and face. He meant to shave once he got out.

Around him, the boys frolicked in the shallows, while some were submerged in the little pools like himself. The mood was considerably lighter than it had been in days. Even Birdie had gotten his feet wet up to his knees before taking a spot in the sun with the whiskey bottle. J.D. had seen no reason not to let the man have his due. Birdie had ridden hard today, and if he wanted to get drunk for his time, that was fine by

J.D. Under normal circumstances, liquor wouldn't have been tolerated, but with Birdie's broken arm there were allowances to make.

A jay swooped past, and J.D. followed it with his gaze toward the section of stream that was around a bend and secluded. That was where Josephine had gone off to. After everyone had eaten a plate of dinner, she'd walked on shaky legs, with a blanket over her arm, her valise, and a bar of soap in her hand.

J.D. had watched her walk with such a favor to her stride that he'd felt bad for her. Because she'd be feeling a lot worse come tomorrow morning when all the soreness really set in.

But if he'd had to do it again, he would have had her on Peaches once more. He'd needed the extra hand, and this time there weren't any casualties when the herd had gone for water. She'd been a real asset.

"Y'all don't get me started on them Yankee bastards."

Boots's exclamation drew J.D.'s attention. Once Boots got on the subject of Yankees, there was no stopping him.

"I saw one coming down the road at our place, and I met that damn blue-bellied abolitionist with a shot straight in his fat paunch. He laid in the brush and bawled like a steer for three days before he died in a fit. The yellow-striped scum."

J.D. knew of no such incident. It was a span of time neither he nor Boots ever talked about. J.D. hadn't filled him in on what he'd done with the Confederacy, nor had Boots told him what had happened to the plantation while he was gone. J.D. knew some from Eugenia. His mother had told him Boots was never without a pistol strapped to his waist when he went out to watch his cotton fields go fallow from neglect.

"Them gawddamn Texans is full of it when it comes to knowing what happened in the war. Cowards, every last one of them good-for-nothing Rawhides."

Boots had dragged his rickety crate near the shore and was whittling. The shavings scattered across his lap.

Rawhide was a derogatory term for the Texas cowhands who had a habit of mending whatever broke down or fell apart on the trail—from a bridle to a wagon tongue—by tying it up with strips of rawhide. J.D. saw no call to be labeling the hands from other regions; he'd done enough fighting in the war, and it had gotten him nowhere.

"Did you really shoot a man in the gut, Boots?" Ace asked, scooping up handfuls of water and rinsing off the soap from his shoulders.

"Yes. And I could shoot a sidewinder going backwards." Boots laid the whittling in his lap, drew the gun from his holster, and took aim. *Click.* The empty chamber sounded like a stick snapping in two. "Gawddammit all to hell." J.D. was the recipient of a disgusted snort. "How am I supposed to show these boys some fine shooting when I don't have any bullets?"

"Don't need any bullets, Boots. There are no bluebellies out here."

Without a retort, Boots rammed the revolver back into his holster and took up with his whittling. A frown as deep as a canyon stretched across his weathered forehead.

J.D. slathered the bar of soap across his fabric-clad chest, took another puff of his cigarette nub, then tossed it downriver. Working up a good lather in his hands, he washed his hair, then slid below the water's surface to rinse. He came up feeling better than he had in days.

Standing, he got out of the river. He sludged through the murky shallows and went past Boots, who looked up and began to laugh.

"What in the hell do you call that?"

J.D. knew without asking what Boots was referring to. He'd left his hat on the shore, along with the clean clothes he'd washed.

"Y'all've sprouted a flower garden."

J.D. glared at the cowboys and dared them to make a comment. Grabbing a blanket, he wrapped it around his middle to ward off the chill seeping through his skin to his bones. Then he decided to check on Josephine.

Not that he had any intentions of spying on her.

He believed a man, or a woman, was due some privacy when the need called. And in this case, Josephine was due some to herself. In three days' time, she'd proved she could hold up. J.D. merely wanted to make sure she was where she was headed and not halfway downstream into the Utah Territory.

With Josephine, he could never tell what was on her mind. Or Rio's, for that matter. He'd slowly inched his way toward Josephine's little spot in the trees around the bend, until J.D. had lost sight of him some minutes back.

So it wasn't spying on J.D.'s mind; it was putting together where Rio had gone and making sure he wasn't where he shouldn't be.

Skirting a patch of larkspur, J.D. came upon a thicket of birches dense enough to give a man cover but thin enough to view through. Rio Cibolo had positioned himself so as not to be seen on the other side and was peeking between the young branches.

J.D. managed to temper his anger, but the emotions inside him were thunderous.

"See anything interesting?" J.D.'s tongue was thick with sarcasm.

Rio jumped back and swung around, his fine wet hair clinging to the side of his face. "N-no, boss."

"Looks to me like there's something, or someone, you were watching." J.D. moved forward.

Backing away, Rio dove his hands into his pockets and took on a casual stance. "Nothing worth your time. I was thinking to go back to the wagon for some . . ."

The rustle of thick grass sounded behind J.D. as

Rio's voice faded, and when J.D. turned around the wrangler was gone.

J.D. should have moved on, too, knowing full well who Rio had been looking at. But his gaze fell back on the spindly birches. A slice of frilly white, a hint of creamy skin, and a cloud of cinnamon-colored hair took shape through the leaves, and J.D. couldn't help but stay a minute and see for himself what Rio had been so entranced over.

Josephine hugged her knees while she sat on a boulder in her shift and bloomers, with her long curly hair unbound and half dried by the sun. She might as well have been wearing nothing as much as the damp underclothing concealed her shape. Sheer as the fabric had gotten from being wet, it molded itself against her generous breasts, the side of her nipped waist, and the flare of her hip. His view was of the profile her body made with the early-afternoon sunlight glistening across her droplet-kissed skin.

He'd never looked at her in the broad daylight with so much of her to see. She was well defined in all the right areas. His mind relived the kiss they'd shared. The way she'd felt in his arms, the press of her breasts against his chest.

At the thought, he couldn't disguise his body's reaction to her, and he was glad she couldn't see him.

Rather than allowing his gaze to linger over her, he moved it elsewhere. He needed a minute to get his control back, and visions of her bare arms, the cascade of her hair, and the cling of her chemise across her breasts weren't going to help him.

A corset lay out in the sun to dry, along with both sets of clothes he'd given her. She had her valise open on the shore, an unfamiliar calico skirt spilling over the edge.

The grass behind him crackled again, and J.D. cursed himself for staying so long. His mind whirled with explanations to hand over to whoever had caught him nosing around.

Just as he turned, Toby barked while wagging his tail.

"Toby," J.D. rushed in a low voice. "Quiet."

Another bark was J.D.'s reply.

"Who's there?" came Josephine's distressed cry.

J.D. swore and debated walking off and not answering her. But Toby trotted through the birch—leaving enough of a wake to expose J.D.—reached the valise, and began to sniff at the contents.

Clasping her arms tightly around herself, Josephine widened her eyes when she saw him. "What do you think you're doing?" She made an attempt to tuck her feet closer to her body but ended up sliding down the slippery rock.

J.D. never had the chance to answer. The current pulled her under.

Chapter

➤ 15 ◆

Water gushed into Josephine's mouth as she frantically clawed her way to the surface, gasping and sputtering for air to fill her lungs. She was able to steal a gulp before being sucked toward the bottom again. Smooth rocks beat against her bare feet; her legs had gone numb from the icy cold. Heavy rushing sounds filled her ears, and her nose stung.

She felt as if a hand had closed around her throat and squeezed her in its death grip. She couldn't breathe. And though her eyes were open, she couldn't see. A knot had formed within her stomach, begging for release, but she couldn't free herself from its tight confines.

She lost the ability to judge time and motion rationally. The minutes became endless and indiscernible, her journey down the river immeasurable. She didn't know how far she'd gone or where she'd end up. One cataclysmic thought pushed its way to the forefront of her mind: She was drowning, and she was helpless to save herself.

A burst of the current flailed Josephine upward. She opened her mouth to scream but only managed to get out, "H-h-h—" instead of "Help."

Nobody would hear her over the din of the river's

roar which had shut out all sounds in her head but the cadence of its power. J.D. had to have seen her fall in. But how could he get to her? He'd be swept away, too, and then they'd both end up . . .

Josephine couldn't finish the thought.

Blindly reaching to grab hold of anything she could as she bounced over larger rocks, she wasn't able to grip a life line. The boulders beneath her slapped her thighs, but they were submerged too much for her to use as a safety net. If only a fallen tree came in her path. But how would she know until it was too late? She had no control over where she went. And she was growing tired of fighting.

Fatigue engulfed her, and she slipped under the water once more. It was a hard fight to the surface, and once she made it, she went right back under again with only a broken breath to see her through to her next upward battle.

A blackness began to surround her, and the crashing in her ears began to ebb. She let herself go into the dark place, too cold to struggle.

A solid touch ramming against her side gave her the energy to reach out in a last-ditch effort to stop herself from buckling under.

The muscles of J.D.'s forearm hardened beneath her groping hand as she desperately clung to him. She struggled to hold on to his arm, her fingers digging into fabric, then finally through to the taut skin beneath. Hope welled inside her.

But her relief was short-lived. They bobbed down the river together like the cork on a silk fishing line. She felt herself being pulled to the right, her shoulder socket aching from the strain and water crashing over her head. She tried to help J.D., but she didn't know how. Her legs wouldn't work the way she wanted them to.

An eternity seemed to pass, and then the current lightened enough so that her feet made contact with soft sand and pebbles. She tried to stand up but faltered. The faded red of J.D.'s long johns where a line of buttons were snagged and half undone across his chest came into focus as she leaned toward him.

His arms came around her waist and pulled her flush against him as he kept walking backward, drawing them both to the shore.

Once they left the river behind and were on dry ground, Josephine staggered to her knees, taking J.D. with her. Together they fell onto the mossy bank, he on his back, she flat on his chest. Her cheek pressed against the knit of his clothing, her eyes closed. The sun's rays didn't send down enough warmth to stop Josephine's trembling.

J.D. ran his palms down the curve of her back and up again, holding her close but not saying a word. She could hear his ragged breathing and the fast, steady thrum of his heart as it beat against her ear.

She coughed, breathing in shallow, quick gasps to regain her bearings. Somewhere overhead, a bird sang. A fly buzzed close by. The drone of Reliance River seemed far away.

Swallowing with difficulty, Josephine found her voice. "You saved me."

"Yeah," he replied, the vibration of his slow drawl rumbling through her breasts where they pressed against his chest.

J.D. fell silent after that, and Josephine didn't know what else to say. She was appreciative of his daring rescue, but the simple fact was, if he hadn't been spying on her, she wouldn't have fallen into the river. It was his fault he'd had to jump in to get her. But after he'd saved her from a sure drowning, she couldn't exactly point that out.

Josephine couldn't seem to stop her shivering no matter how hard she tried. She felt frozen through. The shallow pool of warm water that she'd dipped into and washed herself in had been so welcome. She had no idea just how frosty the river was until she'd been caught in it. Now she was cold. Colder than she could ever remember being. Her back teeth actually chattered together, and she couldn't feel her lips even when she bit them in an effort to stop the incessant clicking of her molars.

Before she knew what was happening, J.D. rolled over, taking her with him until she was pinned beneath his body. He put most of his weight on his elbows and gazed down at her. Water from the ends of his wet hair dripped onto the tip of her nose and into her eyelashes. She blinked the moisture away.

Unbidden, the crazy thought came to her that she didn't really mind the stubble that darkened his chin. And the stitches at his temple reminded her of his rough edges. Both added to his strong constitution in such a way that she found herself more attracted to him than if he'd been clean-shaven and void of any facial imperfections.

She didn't want to think about the shocking position they were in, only that with him on top of her, she felt somewhat warmer. Now, if her teeth would quit dancing a four-quarter beat . . . but she just couldn't stop.

Without warning, J.D. dipped his head toward hers and covered her mouth with his. He kissed her. Nothing deep and passionate. He just kept brushing his lips against hers. Soft. Fluttering. Over and over. Pressing his perfectly sculpted mouth to the corners of her lips that were reserved for smiles and frowns, and making her forget about being so bone-chilled.

She shivered, only this time the waves were delightful and pleasant. At the base of her throat, her pulse tripped into an erratic beat, equally matching J.D.'s. Their breathing came in unison, and she couldn't remember how miserable she'd been seconds ago. Her teeth quieted; perhaps it was because his tongue traced the seam of her mouth, then slipped inside to give her a kiss more intimate than she had ever known.

She breathed in, dizzy yet completely coherent. The effect of his kiss was slow and drugging . . . as if she'd had more than her limit of sherry. She felt the stirrings of reckless abandon in her heart. This could be dangerous. But it was the danger that entrapped her . . . made her *want* to keep kissing him. And more.

The heat from his legs tangled with hers caused her senses to reel. Her breasts ached, the nipples sensitive against the lawn of her chemise. Blood pounded in her brain, and her thoughts spun.

This was madness. An exquisite madness. His hard body atop hers. Him making her feel utterly feminine, desirable, and even wanton, for the first time ever.

Her hands lifted to touch his broad shoulders and glide over the hard strength of muscles that led from his neck to his rigid biceps as he kept his full weight from crushing her. The firm contours of his body tucked neatly into her curves. She became acutely aware of the explosive sensations he gave her there, of the impassioned need that took hold of her.

The tips of his fingers skimmed across her side and upward to the edge of her breast, then upward to cup her . . . to tease her nipple. In spite of the touch being so pleasant and heady, she panicked. No matter how good what he was doing to her felt, she knew what would come next. With Hugh, after they'd made love, she'd always felt hollow and disappointed. She didn't want to feel that way about J.D.

Josephine moved her head. "No . . ."

J.D. stopped and leaned his head back. His eyes were dark in spite of their grayish-blue color. The irises were wide and fathomless. His mouth seemed more chiseled, his jaw set harder. He frowned, then shook a lock of hair from his lashes.

"I . . ." she mumbled. "I feel better now . . . thanks."

"Yeah, your teeth stopped chattering," he said, his voice low and deep, sending a ripple across her skin.

She stared at him, wide-eyed and vaguely aware that her lips were tingling. That the skin around her mouth felt tender from the abrasion of his scratchy beard.

"Just so you'll know," he said, her gaze leveled on his lips as he spoke, "I wasn't gawking at you in your underwear."

Josephine felt uncharacteristically snappish. "Then why did I catch you staring at me when your dog trampled through those trees?"

"I wasn't staring at you—"

She cut him off. "Your eyes were right here." She let her fingers slip away from his arm, and without pondering the repercussions of her action, she laid a palm to the center of her cleavage.

He didn't give her the satisfaction of saying she was right. Instead, he put the blame elsewhere. "I was there checking up on Rio."

"What does Rio have to do with your staring at me in my underwear?"

"Plenty. He was staring first."

All she heard was his late admission. "So, you *were* looking at me in my unmentionables."

His eyes smoldered. "Dammit, yes, I was." He rolled off her then, and sat up. "What do you expect? I'm a man, and you're a woman."

Well, she'd finally gotten that matter cleared up. He did think of her as a woman. A woman named Jo.

Josephine pushed herself to sitting as well, absently flipping a tangled mess of hair over her shoulder. As she did so, the brunt of what J.D. had said hit her with a gale force, and she gasped, "Why was Rio watching me?"

"I reckon he liked the view."

Josephine wondered if J.D. had liked the view, too, but she'd rather die before she asked him. It was bad enough that she'd have to contend with facing the wrangler again knowing what she did. And him knowing what he did about her while she wore next to nothing.

"We need to get started back," J.D. said, and rose to his feet. For the first time, she noticed he was in his stockings.

"Where are your boots?" she asked, attempting to stand herself and not getting very far. Her legs felt like the mush she'd cooked for this morning's breakfast.

"Some mile or so back where I left them when I jumped in after you," he replied, extending a hand to her.

Reluctantly, she took his offering, and he pulled her upward. Her balance wasn't what it normally was, and she nearly smacked into his chest. But she put her hand out to keep a respectable distance between them, then immediately brought her arm to her side. "How are we supposed to get back?"

The flicker of amused light in his eyes said he thought she was joking. "Walk."

She gazed at her bare feet and groaned.

They hadn't gotten more than a few yards when J.D. cursed, reached down, and peeled his socks off. Tossing the sodden pair of woolens at her, he barked, "Put these on, and quit saying 'ouch.' "

She didn't like his menacing tone. She couldn't help it if it came natural for her to voice her discomfort every time a pine needle jabbed the tender arch of her foot or a sharp pebble caught between her toes.

Without a word, she squished the too-large stockings over her feet, and they set out again. This time, she bit her tongue before she'd utter a single whimper. But her feet still hurt even with the socks on, and her legs were chafed from the ride on Peaches. And her derriere felt as if she'd been swatted with one of her frying pans.

J.D. walked fast, and Josephine did her best to keep up with him. Her gaze kept falling on wet and dirty fabric that molded next to his behind. He had a build that demanded her attention. Her infatuation with his muscular physique made her even more upset—at herself, but she took it out on him.

As she hobbled along, she mouthed words to his back. Mostly, she called him childish names. He could bring out the worst in her, and she shocked herself by the way he made her emotions run high. Usually, she was quite tepid in that department, having restraint. Or, at least, tamping down what she was feeling so nobody would know.

Out here in the wide open, it was as if she'd been given permission to express herself. Even though she didn't say the words out loud, she felt better by the time they reached the spot where his boots were strewn in the grass. He paused for a minute to slip them on—minus his socks—and by the time they came to the bend where she'd left her valise, she'd run out of rambling sentences to mouth at him.

It was a good thing they got to the pool when they did. Josephine couldn't walk another inch. She dropped to her knees on the cushioned ground and held on to a moan as pain shot through her every joint. She was done for. This was it. J.D. would have to find another cook to do his bidding this evening, because she wasn't going to make it to the chuck wagon tonight.

J.D. collected her—*his*—clean clothes and stuffed one pair of pants and a shirt into her valise along with the skirt that had spilled out. She'd intended to try it on now that she'd taken in the lacings of her corset. But she hadn't had the opportunity to see if the garment would fit.

His tanned hand fell on the whale-boned item with its fancy embroidery, ribbons, cording, and hooks. She had spread it open to dry, and the corset was flimsy yet stiff in his grasp. He seemed to linger over it longer than necessary before shoving it into the case and flipping the lid closed with the toe of his boot.

Reaching down, he snagged the leftover shirt, trousers, stockings, and her pair of run-down boots.

"Put these on, and let's go." He tossed them at her lap.

She wanted to yell at him, "You've got to be kidding!" But she held her tongue. *Guts*. He wanted a woman with some backbone. If she didn't go along, he might strand her there. Then she'd have to camp out alone. She'd heard the baying of the wolves from her bed. They'd come out when the moon was full . . . and scavenge for food.

Josephine blew wayward curls from her vision and began to dress. Each move she made reverberated through her body until she truly was on the verge of crying.

At last she was dressed except for her boots, which she just couldn't put on. She held them in her grasp and went after J.D., who'd gone on seconds before her.

The hour had to have been approaching three. The cowboys must have finished up in the river a while ago. Those not on the cattle guard were sprawled on blankets playing cards by a low-burning campfire. She didn't look for Rio. She didn't want to see him.

When she approached the wagon, she had the misfortune of having Boots meet her. He gave her a keen once-over with those hawkish eyes of his, then he had the audacity to say loud enough for the boys to hear, "Y'all've got an imprint of J.D.'s long john button on your cheek."

Then he laughed, the sound echoing around them and making her painfully uncomfortable—as if he knew precisely what had been going on between her and J.D.

"In Texas, them bastards ride two or three horses," Boots orated with zeal, "eat what's in the wagon when they're on the trail, and work for twenty-five dollars a month. Then they come up Wyoming's way looking for a job, and they expect to have ten horses at their disposal and eat pie three times a day. All for thirty-five dollars a month."

"That's right," Orley seconded. "We work twenty-six hours a day."

"You damn bonehead, don't y'all know there's only twenty-four hours in a day?"

"Yup," Orley said with a dimpled grin, "but we stand guard two hours every night."

Boots spat onto the ground. "Good gawd. There's no talking to y'all."

They had all settled onto their bedrolls around the campfire after their cold swim. Supper had been cleared away, and evening was being spent cleaning guns, oiling saddles, playing cards, and telling stories.

Leaning into the bow of his saddle, his hat—somewhat reshaped, but still tired looking—slung over the horn, J.D. gazed into the starlit sky. Around him, the conversation droned and familiar noises abounded. There was talk about tomorrow's ride, a call was made for a full house in the card game, and the rub of an oiled cloth next to leather made a rhythmic squeak.

Earlier, Josephine had staved off playing the violin, claiming she wasn't up to it. Like the others, J.D. had been disappointed.

Sitting up, he stretched his legs. Josephine sat on the wagon seat mending holes in the socks he'd given her to wear from the river back to camp.

J.D. rifled through his gear, came up with a pair of pants, then stood and made his way toward her.

He put his hand on the seat. "You think you could sew these for me?"

Her chin lifted. "When I'm done with these."

"Mind if I wait?"

"No," she replied softly.

He took it as an okay for him to climb up next to her. He had to slide the lamp a little out of the way, then he sat down. He noticed that she was repairing the sock so that he could hardly tell where there'd been a hole. "How are you feeling?"

Surprise lit her face, as if she hadn't thought he'd ask. "I'm all right."

"I suppose Boots told you we've got liniment for what ails you."

"He told me."

J.D. cracked a half-smile. "I take it you aren't going to use any."

"I'd rather not smell like that greasy tin."

"So you went as far as lifting the lid, huh?"

He caught a profile of her frown. "Yes."

A moth bumped into the lantern glass. J.D. swatted it as he leaned his elbows on his knees. "Who taught you how to sew like this?"

She didn't miss a stitch. "My mother."

"I imagine you miss her."

"She's been gone for nearly six years." Her voice grew distant. "And, yes, I still miss her."

"Your father?"

Her hand stilled. "He died less than a year ago."

"And you've been alone since?"

Josephine gazed at him, and he saw reservation in her eyes. "I've been lonely." Then she picked up the scissors and cut the thread.

He knew loneliness, too. Though he was surrounded by the boys most of the time, the nights were his. The winters were the hardest when he was cooped up inside with Boots. He'd walk through the quiet house and long to hear a woman's voice. He'd wonder what it would be like to sit by the stove while it was snowing and share a cup of hot coffee together. Or to lie side-by-side in the bed and read. Then snuggle beneath the covers and touch . . .

For a long while, J.D. had held these thoughts at bay. But Josephine was a constant reminder of femininity. Her voice, her softness, her curling hair. When she was near, he felt something was lacking in his life.

Her hand reached out to him, and, like a fool, he'd hoped she wanted to take his hand in hers. Instead, she said, "I can sew your pants now."

Grudgingly, he handed them over to her as Rio came in from checking on the remuda. The wrangler walked right on past without so much as a tip of his hat.

Earlier, J.D. had watched Rio and Josephine doing the dishes. As far as J.D. could tell, she and the wrangler hadn't said much between them during the cleanup. He'd noted she stood away from him as much as she could given they had to work side-by-side. And she hadn't met his eyes when he looked at her.

Knowing of no cowboy code that said a hand couldn't share a bath with the cook if he wanted to, J.D. was undecided about how to handle what had happened at the river. The best way would be to let it go. But then again, if Josephine was interested in Rio, maybe he ought to know.

"What do you think of Rio?" he came right out and asked.

She knotted the end of her thread and shrugged. "What do you mean, what do I think of him?"

"Are you sweet on him?"

She nudged him in the side with her elbow when she adjusted the pants in her lap; he wasn't altogether sure it was an accident. "I don't have any kind of infatuation with him. I'm certain I'm years older than he is."

"How old are you?"

"Were we sitting in a parlor, I wouldn't tell you."

"Good thing we're not."

She sighed and locked her gaze onto his. "I'm twenty-five."

"How come you're not married?"

"How come *you* aren't?" she returned so quickly he almost felt the blow.

His statement was simple. "I've never been in love."

"Then you have good reason."

J.D. stared at his boot tips. "Going by how Boots and Eugenia ended up, I probably will be a bastard of a husband."

She pricked the back of his hand with the needle. "Jesus!" he complained. "What'd you do that for?"

"Because sometimes you make me very angry and I forget myself." Her cheeks were hot with color. "You're nothing like your father. Can't you see that? Quit trying to blame Boots for everything. He has his flaws but also his good points. You can take after him or not. It's your choice. You're responsible for the way you live your life."

Dumbfounded, he returned, "Where the hell is this coming from?"

"Something that I have and you apparently don't: experience. I had a chance to be my father's daughter, but I did nothing because I was afraid he'd reject me. Well, now it's too late. You still have time. Do something. If you don't like who you are, make changes." With that, she threw the wad of denim at him and said, "Finish your own pants." Then she climbed over the seat back and disappeared through the flaps of canvas.

CHAPTER

✦ 16 ✦

The next day started out clear with one big cloud serving as a canopy for them to pass under. But by the time Boots tucked the wagon into a small area of grass, relatively far from any trees, the whole sky had closed in with heavy, purple, inky black, and saffron clouds.

It was nearly as dark as nightfall when the rumbling came from the distance. Its cacophony was bold as brass and crashed like metal cymbals. And yet no rain fell. Just this ominous sound that had the mules braying and pawing the ground while the dogs barked at the eastward wind.

When dinner was finished, the lightning began. The massive, many-fingered bolts that splintered the stormy black were still a long way off but nonetheless dramatic to view above the lower treetops that angled down the hill they'd stopped on. Josephine had been in her share of electrical storms in New York, but she'd always been ensconced in the safety of her own home. Being so exposed left her uneasy.

She stayed close to the chuck wagon, while Boots held out his palm to give the mules treats to quiet them. Josephine tried to put her mind on other things besides the brewing storm.

She gave the calf its bottle, hesitantly petting the wiry hairs on its head to calm it from the storm. As the milk dribbled down the fuzzy chin, she thought of how her cooking had gone thus far today.

Breakfast had been fried hasty pudding, a cold and clotted leftover from yesterday that she hadn't thought tasted that bad with molasses poured on top like the cowboys had asked for. Her cooking was improving by little degrees. And after she put the empty milk bottle away, she intended to try her hand at pie making, storm or not.

With each move she made to gather ingredients, she had to keep hitching her waistband to keep it from sagging. Since she'd taken in her corset the day before, J.D.'s pants no longer fit her in the waist, and even the hips seemed too loose. She would have put on the skirt if it fit, but she found that she rather liked the ease in which she could move without the layers of fabric.

She found the cans of peaches in the wagon and decided to make five peach pies, following Luis's recipe to the tee. She read it over a half-dozen times, just to make sure she fully understood the instructions.

Josephine had mixed the dough, then used an old bottle as a rolling pin. She rolled out the pastries a few times after attempts at perfect circles failed. She kept getting tears on the dough when it stuck to the glass as she rolled it back and forth. It was sheer trial and error that made her figure out that if she started in the middle and rolled outward, the chances of getting cracks and holes were less.

Two hours later, and with one big flour mess to clean up, she set the lopsided pies in the Dutch ovens to bake.

In the valley that swelled like a bowl beneath them, a huge lightning bolt seemed to strike backward, from the grass to the pitch sky. Josephine had never seen anything like it. She shivered. The mules fought against their hobbles.

For a time, Josephine sat on a blanket with her back next to a wagon wheel, just watching as the black pall of clouds shut out all remains of the sun. Recurring flashes of sheet lightning filled her entire view and lit up the sky almost as bright as daylight.

The cowboys took turns in large groups riding among the cattle to pacify them. Those mules were going crazy, and she wondered if she should find Rio to have him check their restraints. But the wrangler was busy with the remuda; she could barely see him in the distance as he and two of the dogs circled the horses.

Boots had disappeared, and the handful of cowboys by the coffeepot left when J.D. rode toward her and dismounted as she was setting the pies from the ovens to cool. She'd lined them up with pride, and although they looked a little lumpy, they smelled wonderful.

"What's that you've got there?" J.D. asked while removing his rawhide gloves and stuffing them into the pocket of his chaps.

"Pies," she said with a fair amount of pride. "Peach pies."

J.D. drew up, lowered his head, and inhaled. "They smell real good."

He'd been nice as could be to her today, and she felt a niggling remorse for having jabbed him. But he'd forced her to it by saying he'd probably be a bad husband and practically blaming his parents for it. He didn't realize that he had the power to be who he wanted.

For the long years of her marriage, she'd told herself that Hugh was only being the kind of husband society expected him to be. Controlling and domineering toward his wife. Only now she knew better. He'd chosen to treat her poorly, and for that she resented him. But she was angry at herself more for having allowed herself to be overshadowed by him. She should have made changes years ago, but she'd been afraid.

When J.D. went to the water barrel, Josephine took a spoon and stuck it into the hot pie. Steam rose from the tiny hole she'd made, but she had to know for certain that her creation tasted as good as it smelled. She blew on the golden dough and the wedge of peach, then popped it into her mouth as J.D. came back with his face and hands washed and his hair wet above his ears.

She chewed discreetly, then swallowed. Heavenly. Simply heavenly. She couldn't begin to believe it, but she'd baked something that tasted like peach heaven.

J.D. stopped in front of her, reached out his arm, and brought his finger to her lips. She was so stunned, she simply stood there. Frozen. He ran his forefinger across the corner of her mouth and then to the seam. "You missed some."

Horrified that she'd been found out sneaking a taste of the pies, Josephine was helpless to do anything but lick the remains from her lips, J.D.'s callused fingertip still pressed against the evidence. She tasted pie, but she also tasted the lingering traces of the soap he'd just used.

The electrified moment put her completely out of sorts. His nearness was overwhelming; the intimacy of his finger pressed to her lips upset her balance and rational thoughts. There was no other way to describe what had just transpired between them: this was her first purely sensual experience, and she hadn't even been kissed.

How was it that J.D. could make her feel so coveted while barely touching her? Did he know he did this to her? Was it intentional?

She breathed a sigh of relief when at last he lowered his hand. But she had the feeling he'd enjoyed every second of their encounter. As if it was his way of getting back at her for last night. She'd no doubt upset him; now he wanted to upset her—only his tactic wasn't as vocal as hers. He chose his charm. His eyes were observing, his mouth impossible with a disarming smile.

Had the sky not crackled with an ominous current she couldn't ignore, she might have said something she would have regretted. A lightning tree of blinding white exploded skyward, thin branches thrusting up to the heavens. Then came a *bang*. Not a rumble or crack of thunder. But a distinct *bang*.

It sounded like gunfire.

J.D. must have heard it, too. His eyes instantly left hers, and he cocked his head to the copse of low-lying trees.

Bang! Bang! Bang!

Before she knew what was happening, he grabbed her by the shoulders and shoved her behind him. He pulled sideways until they were hidden by the cover of the chuck wagon. Then he unceremoniously pushed her to the ground. She fell on the hard earth with a groan.

"Stay down," he warned while unholstering his gun and peering around the wheel of the wagon.

"What is it?" Josephine asked in a small, terrified voice. Though she feared his answer. She knew what gunfire sounded like.

"Keep quiet, and don't move."

She wanted to heed his warning, but she began to tremble inside at the thought of a band of outlaws in the brush shooting at them. She had nothing of value to steal. She would gladly surrender whatever it was they wanted. But in *The Lariat Thrower and the Lawman Strike a Deal,* Beadle's Issue No. 57, the banditos had wanted more than gold trinkets from the women passengers in the stage. They'd wanted . . . it was too horrendous a thought for her to complete.

Another crescendo of thunder split the air, seemingly sizzling the very ground they were sitting on. She could see the calf's feet in the space between the wagon bed and the ground. The small animal danced a bit, then began to bawl. Josephine felt the sting of a hundred needles coursing through her body. They reminded her of the shock she'd get from touching a brass doorplate after walking across the salon carpet on a breezy day. She quivered, trying to shake off the static, but she couldn't. Her skin tingled; her lips felt numb. Her fingernails hurt.

Bang! Bang!

During a lull in the storm's symphony, the gun report echoed through the clearing. Then everything seemed to happen at once. One of the mules broke free of its hobbles and took off in a run, a thick and heavy branch from a nearby spruce severed from the rough trunk with a splintering crash, and J.D. sprang to his feet, with revolver poised, to chase after whoever was doing the shooting.

J.D. ducked behind a stand of firs, his finger curled snugly over his Colt's trigger. There was a break in the shooting to reload. J.D. had counted off six shots. But that didn't mean he was in the clear. The gunman might have more than one revolver.

As far as J.D. could tell, none of the bullets had made a direct hit into the wagon or the surrounding camp. The shooter had to be a pretty piss-poor shot, or he hadn't been aiming in their direction. The latter more than likely, since nothing had been hit. Still, that didn't alleviate the blood pounding at J.D.'s temples. He didn't cotton to gunfire of unknown origin within the vicinity of his camp.

Sprinting down the embankment, J.D. kept hidden in the tall brush until he came to the edge of an area that opened to a small clearing made from fallen trees. Many stumps littered the grass, the once towering trees now fallen and decaying. Scanning the terrain for signs of movement, J.D. tightened his finger over the curl of metal when he caught a glimpse of a hat. But he didn't move in and start shooting without asking questions. It was a good thing, too.

The man in the clearing was Boots.

His holster sagged at his hips, slung real low and with deadly-looking intent. He trudged over to one of the horizontal pines and set up some battered, rusty cans, then backed off to take aim.

"Where in the hell did you get those bullets, you old son-of-a-bitch?" J.D. bellowed into the ruffling wind as the storm kicked up another flash of lightning.

Boots spread his bowed legs apart, cocked his hips somewhat, and raised his Remington with a shaky arm. Before he could take a shot, J.D. leveled the sight on his Colt barrel, aimed, and picked off every one of those cans with a precision that sent several skyward before they tumbled into the grass.

Turning with a start, revolver drooping to his side, Boots scanned the brush with hooded eyes. J.D. stepped over a log and showed himself, the realistic thought running through his mind that Boots had a loaded gun and might use it against him.

But Boots didn't go off half-cocked usually, and for that J.D. was somewhat reassured.

"Where'd you get those bullets?" J.D. demanded once he was within Boots's hearing distance.

Boots clammed up—a rarity for him. He looked at the dull silver revolver in his grasp, then at J.D., as if he were hoping the gun would vanish into thin air and he wouldn't have to answer for his actions.

Reholstering the Remington, he took on a defensive attitude, papery hands braced on his narrow hips. "I found them in the wagon."

"Found them, my ass." J.D. tugged his hat lower. "You stole them from one of the boys' duffles. Peavy and Freeland carry Remingtons. Which one of them did you rob?"

Boots's mouth thinned. "I found them, gawddammit. I'm no thief."

J.D. wouldn't get a straight answer from him. He'd figure out which one of the two men was short bullets, anyway. Not knowing right now didn't make any difference.

"You could've been struck by lightning, you old fool."

Boots shot back with the rumble of the thunder, "And wouldn't y'all just be dancing on my grave if I was."

"Contrary to what your opinion may be of me, I don't wish you six feet under. But I do want you out of here right now."

"Don't give me orders."

"Somebody has to. You're not thinking. What in the hell possessed you to come down here in the middle of an electrical storm?"

Boots kept quiet, a thinly disguised mask over the pride that marked his age-lined facial features. A realization dawned on J.D. Boots had wanted to prove, if only to himself, that he was still man enough to be a crack shot with a gun. J.D. knew Boots could defend himself in an emergency; but other than that, he didn't want Boots to have a gun at the ready in case it accidentally went off. That conversation at the river about him shooting Yankees must have put the sharp-shooting idea into his head.

Folding his arms over his chest, the hem of his duster flapping at his calves, J.D. asked, "Just how many of those blue-bellies did you kill, Boots?"

His cornflower-blue eyes shot to J.D.'s. "Good gawd, y'all never asked me that before."

"I reckon I was too long in getting around to it, then."

Boots took hold of his weighted holster belt and pulled it up a notch to keep the revolver from slipping down to his ankles. He opened his mouth to speak, then must have thought better of it, because his lips closed together. Instead, he began to climb the hillside.

His balance was unsteady. He reached out to

branches to give him a lift as he sought sure footing. J.D. followed him upward, the notion to extend a helping hand at the back of his mind, but he didn't act on it. He'd already taken the shine off Boots's make-shift shooting gallery; he couldn't very well add insult to injury by suggesting Boots was too feeble to take an incline on his own.

The lightning had become less frequent and the thunder less potent as it drifted toward the horizon. A few grumbles, a far-off flash of light, and the rustle of leaves played through the embankment as J.D. moved slowly behind Boots.

Perhaps it was the recklessness of the storm that made J.D. throw caution to the abating wind. "Hell, I don't care how many of them you shot. I killed my share, too. But for what? We all went off fighting for a way of life that was dead as soon as that first shot was fired. It was all a damn waste."

Boots stopped abruptly in his tracks and pivoted with surprising steadiness. Fire spat from his gaze. "Damn your hide to hell. Your brothers died in that war."

"And it was a waste," J.D. said evenly. "They died for nothing."

J.D. waited for Boots to hit him on the side of the head, but the blow never came.

"I'll tell you why my boys died." Boots pointed a trembling, bony finger in J.D.'s face. "They died for honor. They died killing the Yankee bastards that were running through our fields and spoiling our womenfolk." A drop of spittle dotted the corner of his mouth. His shoulders trembled, and J.D. thought he'd never seen Boots look so weary. "I wish I'd shot more of those blue-bellies than I had. But at least I got one, gawddammit." His next words came out in a rush, and in hindsight J.D. knew that if Boots had realized what he was about to reveal, he would have kept it to himself. "There was one who had your mother down in the fields. She was always walking off to the cabins like nothing had changed. I told her not to go out alone, but she didn't listen to me. She never did.

"I came on them . . . it was the blue coat that caught my eyes against the gray of the plants. He'd pinned her to the ground and was going to force himself on her. I called out, and when he looked up, I shot the bastard between the eyes. He laid dead on your mother, with her screaming at the blood. Good gawd, I could shoot to kill back then . . . and I could now, too . . ." His gaze lashed out at J.D. "But y'all never give me any damn bullets. Y'all've turned me into a pile of worthless manure."

Stumbling, Boots blindly groped to steady himself but couldn't grasp the nearest branch. J.D. put his hands on Boots's shoulders, their eyes locking in the process. The fragile emotion in Boots's eyes was gone before J.D. could define it.

"Let go of me," Boots demanded.

J.D. hesitantly obliged.

Boots managed to get turned around and keep climbing without falling. J.D. remained where he was, disquieting thoughts racing through his mind. Eugenia had never told him about being attacked. In all the ensuing years after he'd come home, and with all the trouble between him and Boots, never once had Eugenia spoken up and said the words that would have profoundly affected J.D.

J.D. mused on private memories, only this time they left a burning imprint on him. One that he couldn't ignore or ride away from.

Josephine had been right. For a long time, he'd been underestimating Boots.

Josephine remained huddled behind the chuck wagon, peering through the spoked wheel to look out for J.D. It seemed she had waited forever, the gunmetal clouds overhead slowly traveling eastward, when Boots appeared. His stride was stiff yet purposeful as he walked toward her. She rose to her feet and dashed out to meet him.

"Where's J.D.? What happened?"

Boots didn't look at her, nor did he stop. "I expect he's on his way." He went right on past. She didn't have the chance to chase after him. J.D. came into view as he climbed over the hill. His expression was tight with strain.

"What happened?" she asked, hoping to get a reply out of him.

"Boots was target practicing. No big deal."

"But Boots didn't have any bullets."

Beneath drawn brows, J.D.'s eyes leveled on Boots. He sat on his crate, an unlit cigar clamped hard between his lips as he gazed into the flames of the fire pit. Seeing J.D. staring so intently, Josephine didn't say anything further.

Three hours later, under a hazy sky that had no trace of the storm in it, those boys not on the herd watch came in for supper. Rio had taken Dan Hotchkiss and Jidge Dooly with him to look for the runaway mule but had come back empty-bridled an hour ago. The wrangler hadn't been too distressed as he'd unsaddled his horse downwind from the chuck. He'd said Old Wednesday had a taste for sweat-soaked saddle blankets and sweet oats and would come back as soon as she was hungry.

Supper wasn't any big to-do. Josephine had fixed what she knew she could with fairly certain success: beef stew and biscuits. She wanted to win them over with her peach pies. She'd hidden them on the sideboard on the opposite side of the wagon so they'd be a surprise.

As she made the coffee rounds, she was anxious for everyone to finish so she could serve up dessert. Orley wanted another biscuit. Birdie asked if it would be an inconvenience for her to get him the bottle of laudanum from the cupboard. She couldn't refuse him;

he'd ridden in the saddle all day without a complaint. Now that he was reclined, the stress wore across his face like an old blanket: thin and not tolerating much.

After taking care of the two men, she paused at the coffeepot once more. "Anyone else?" she asked.

"What's your hurry, Miss Josephine?" Gus asked as he chewed the bite of stew in his mouth that he'd sopped up with his biscuit. "You've been doing the two-step around the fire all night."

"No hurry," she insisted, just as the clatter of tins came from behind her. She whirled around. She couldn't readily see anything amiss.

Then Jidge went and said, "Mule's back."

Old Wednesday appeared around the endgate of the wagon. The mule strolled toward them with peach pie smeared all over its face. It moseyed over one of the five empty pie tins visible underneath the wagon, with the nerve to put a hoof in one and stomp down. It made a loud smacking sound, tongue coming out and swiping the flaps of hair-freckled lips.

Horror couldn't begin to describe how Josephine felt. Those pies had been the pride of her heart, and she had baked them for the boys' after-supper surprise. All her hard work had fallen victim to a smelly mule with big, ugly, yellow teeth.

It came as a mindless reflex. Josephine bent down, grabbed a long piece of firewood from the stack by the pit, and hurled it Old Wednesday's way. Rather than hitting her mark, she merely threw dirt and dust over the food and cooking utensils on the endgate. The pan of biscuits fell as the scared mule made a quick-turning getaway.

Josephine, who had heard firsthand the score of expletives her father used to rattle off when he voiced his darkest ire, let out a string of cuss words hot enough to singe the animal's tail off.

She was barely aware of Boots's "Good gawd, the cookie can swear like a buffalo hunter" as she took off after Old Wednesday. She didn't give any conscious thought to the inappropriate vulgarity of what she'd said or what she'd do to the mule if she caught it.

Josephine ran toward the spruces, the mule's backside disappearing into the tufts of greenery.

J.D.'s voice caught up to her. "Slow down!"

She couldn't. From where the spurt of energy came, she didn't know. But she had a fiery stamina and determination that fueled her steps. She could actually run fairly fast as she hopped over the twigs and small rocks in her way. With no clinging skirts and layers of petticoats to tangle in her scissoring legs, she was more agile than she imagined. There was only one drawback: her pants were slipping.

Knocking a branch out of her way, Josephine grabbed her waistband as she entered the thicket in search of Old Wednesday. She couldn't see mane or tail of that dingy mule in the dense shrubbery.

Strong fingers clamped over her right shoulder, and Josephine was jerked backward, just as her trousers fell down her hips to ride precariously low on her thighs.

She felt a hard chest behind her as J.D. crushed her to him in an effort to get her to stop. Something lanky and metal bit into her shoulder blade, and she winced beneath the discomfort of the bridle. She would have struggled if she thought it would do her any good. Going against J.D. was futile. He had the upper hand over her in strength ten times over.

"Where do you think you're going?"

Unable to face him, she huffed, "After that damn pie-snatching mule."

"Then what?"

She didn't know. Maybe yelling at it would make her feel better. She turned beneath his arm so she could look into his eyes. The pants inched a little farther down. "I'll worry about that when I catch it."

"You aren't catching any *damn* mule." His laughter

was teasing. "I didn't think you had it in you to cuss like Luis."

Josephine ducked out from his grasp. "I usually keep peppery words inside."

"No need to on my account."

She clutched the waistband and tried to wiggle the unyielding fabric up her drawer-clad hips. Funny how the pants wouldn't return to their former position the way they had come down. She'd have to unbutton the fly. But surely not in front of J.D.

"Pardon me." She stalked off. She heard him follow her by the jangle of the bit and bridle that rode over his shoulder with the reins obviously riding down his back. Her retreat was difficult at best, the hems of her pants stacking at her booted ankles. When he didn't let up in his pursuit, she turned around, both hands on the waistband. "Do you mind?" she blurted out.

He answered in a low tone, "Mind what?"

Disregarding the eyes blazing down into hers, she explained, "In case you hadn't noticed, I'm having some trouble here."

"I noticed." He took a casual step toward her, the breadth of his powerful shoulders seeming wider than ever. "I noticed at supper, and I noticed when you ran off. And I'm sure as hell noticing now."

The rich timbre of his voice melted through her. Warm and sugary, like he could be a butterscotch candy in her mouth. A familiar shiver of awareness jolted her. He took another step closer. She couldn't move . . . she couldn't think clearly.

When he dipped his head toward hers and kissed her, she forgot about holding on to her pants. Her arms came around his neck, and she gave herself over to the insanity of the moment.

CHAPTER

⇒ 17 ⇐

J.D. savored Josephine's mouth against his as she returned his kiss with reckless abandon. They were chancing a perilous journey, but it would seem neither of them cared about the repercussions of such an uncharted course.

The soft, feminine weight of her arms around his neck was a seductive invitation. Her fingers slipped into his hair, knocking his hat askew. The feel of her fingertips as they moved through the strands to touch his scalp with a light caress heated his insides.

His lips seared a path down the arched column of her neck. She swayed into him as his teeth caught her lobe, and he pressed a kiss to her ear. Soft curves molded next to him. Wherever they touched, his body ignited from the contact. He was conscious of her every contour. The lushness of her breasts, the span of her waist, and the flare of her hips veiled only by the thin cotton of drawers.

Recapturing her mouth, his kiss was more demanding this time. His hands spread down her back, to the nip of her waist and the softness of her underwear. He'd never kissed a woman half-dressed in man's clothing. Oddly, he found Josephine more erotic dressed thus than he had any of the women at Walkingbars in their fancy silk wrappers.

Enjoying the kiss, the sensations of her mouth against his, and the feel of her next to him, he wrapped his arms around her midriff. Disjointed thoughts ran rampant through his head like a stampede. The way she kissed led him to believe she wasn't a total innocent. He wouldn't think anything less of her if she'd fallen to temptation before. But he didn't want to start something with a woman who thought she knew what she was doing, only to regret an encounter the next morning. J.D. figured he had to ask her what she wanted to do. He'd give her the out if she opted to take it.

He murmured against the sweetness of her mouth, "Where's this going?"

"Going?"

He caught her full lower lip between his teeth as he spoke. "I think you know what I mean, Jo. We've been going along for the ride since the first night out on the trail. Do you want to get out of the saddle with me?" Her lips touched his like a tiny whisper. "We could get thrown on our butts. I'm not making any promises."

"Neither am I," she mouthed against him. "I don't want to run away from you anymore. I have to find out . . ."

"Find out what?"

"Why you're different."

Her answer took him off-center. He would have thought she'd go into some song and dance about why they couldn't be together, and he was willing to accept that. But her coming back with a consenting reply floored him. Maybe he was hoping she'd tell him to go to hell. That he'd gotten things all wrong.

J.D. lifted his head and gazed into the upturned face and pair of eyes staring into his. Good God, she was an attractive woman with her amber eyes, ivory skin, and ripe mouth. He couldn't just take her down to the ground and make love to her. She deserved better. But, dammit all, she was offering. Any man would do it. Most especially a cuss like himself.

Then why wasn't he acting on the moment rather than analyzing it? Maybe he wasn't as much of a son-of-a-bitch as he thought he was. Maybe—

Old Wednesday suddenly stomped into view and trotted over as if they were lost friends. The long-eared mule drew up to Josephine without her knowledge and began scratching the side of its jaw on Josephine's shoulder. Her eyes widened, and she clung to J.D. in an effort to shrug away.

"Quit that," J.D. scoffed to the mule. He moved Josephine to his side, slid the bridle from his shoulder, and gave Old Wednesday a light slap on the neck with the reins. "You pain in the ass."

Old Wednesday stood there, batting fringy lashes at him.

Josephine struggled to look over her shoulder at her shirt back. "Why, that no good . . . she smeared peach syrup on me."

J.D. fit the grazer bit in Old Wednesday's mouth, then the headstall over the mule's perky ears. Tying the throat strap, he gathered the reins in his hand.

Old Wednesday had saved him from an explanation to Josephine. He didn't want her to think that he was the type who trifled with women, then brushed them aside. She wasn't like the girls at the saloon. Romping in the hay wasn't her style. She'd no doubt want more than the physical. Women like Josephine needed to be shown affection by being able to unwrap presents of store-bought trinkets, given bouquets of hothouse flowers, and taken on surprise buggy rides for sunset picnics. None of those things was in J.D. His mother had expected all and more from Boots; and when she hadn't gotten them, she'd left.

J.D. knew too well what eastern women expected. Their views pretty much stayed the same, even on the less populated frontier. Josephine was trying hard to fit in, he'd give her that. But she was only temporary. She had plans to move on. She'd be better off in a big city where she could have all the comforts of the life she'd been accustomed to. So there was no reason to start anything up, just to watch it ride away.

"We better get back to camp," J.D. suggested. "Rio'll probably come looking after us."

Josephine nodded, her expression unreadable in the shadows that crossed the thicket of brush. She turned around, fiddled with the buttons on her trousers, then slipped them up and back into position. That done, she faced him once more. A curl the color of a slow flame fell over her brow, and he couldn't help brushing her cheek with his knuckles.

He was reluctant to leave, yet at the same time wanted to get out of there as fast as he could. A haze of feelings and desires were hitting him all at once, and he couldn't sort them out. "Let's go," he said, his voice thick and foreign-sounding to his ears.

To his misplaced disappointment, he was sorry when she followed after him.

They reached the spring range in early afternoon the next day, and J.D. put everyone to work as soon as the stock was taken care of. There was a lot to do at the line shacks that would serve as bunkhouse and kitchen for Orley, Dan, Seth, and Print over the next several months.

Rodents and other small creatures had moved in during the winter, and the mattresses had to be aired out and repaired. The blackened chimney pipe to the potbelly stove had been clogged up by a bird's nest. The floors were coated with grime, while the windows barely let in enough sunlight through the webs of spiders. Lying dead in the sills were numerous bees, black flies, and yellow jackets.

J.D. unbuttoned his duster with gloved fingers and let the lapels hang open as he crossed the span of green grass toward the chuck. One moment he'd been freezing, wishing he'd had two sets of long johns on with the wind slicing through him, the next he was sweating beneath the partial sun. The weather up here was damned fickle.

It had rained an hour ago, just enough to settle the dust. A few silver-trimmed clouds lingered, the last traces of the electrical storm that had passed through. After a good night's sleep, the rest of them would start back for the ranch at sun-up tomorrow. They'd cut their way south for a spell so they could follow the railroad line back home. It was a tradition to see who could reach the Wampum Saloon first. Everyone always made it there by noon and spent the rest of the day soaking in the spoils of the payroll. J.D. had consorted with the boys, doing his share of liquor tipping and dallying with women. Only this time, he was thinking about what to do with Josephine. He didn't want her in the saloon, but he could see no other place to put her.

"Hey, Jo," he called to her as he approached. Since she hadn't made any prior protests about the nickname he'd fastened on her, he opted to use it again.

Josephine's back was to him. She'd been washing the pots and pans from the shack, and they were laid out all around her to dry.

Turning, she shaded her eyes with a damp hand.

"You want to go for a ride and see where we put the cattle?" He hadn't really expected her to care, but he'd wanted to spend a little time with her, just talk to her. Show her more of what his world was all about. He was hoping she'd be open to the suggestion because he had something to give her, and he felt awkward about doing it in front of the boys.

"I suppose. As long as we don't have to go faster than a walk, scale any steep mountains, or ford any rivers."

"I can manage that." J.D.'s heartbeat kicked up. "I'll have Rio saddle Peaches."

"All right." She wiped off her hands on her apron before removing it. Her pants didn't sag, and he guessed she must have put to use that length of rawhide he'd left on the endgate after coming in last night.

A quarter hour later, they were riding through patches of fir with the occasional view of Deerflat Lake in between the boughs.

J.D. felt more comfortable on horseback when he was with Josephine. This was what he was familiar with, and it served as a reminder of who he was.

A cattleman, first and foremost.

"What's over there?" Josephine asked.

J.D. followed her questioning eyes to the slight dip in the terrain, then an expanse of valley, and beyond a thick ridge of trees. "Rough country," he replied. "A lot of timbered breaks in there that look like the foothills of a mountain range. Beyond that, a bunch of coulees head out on a big level divide, covered with grass and scattered with bull pines. A man could get himself killed in there, even on an experienced horse."

"Are there rattlesnakes?"

J.D. cracked a smile. "Where we just came from. The plains are alive with them as soon as the sun heats up the ground. Some coil beneath the shade of a greasewood, some stretch lazily in the sun, some crawl around. All are quick to coil, rattle, and strike if you approach them."

Josephine's face paled a shade. "Do you think it will be warm enough on the way back?"

"Nope."

Catalpa, box elder, and white ash flourished, creating a private retreat for them to pass through. Overhead, a bird chattered from a branch. Tequila nickered, and Peaches replied.

"Stop a minute," J.D. said, pulling back on the reins as she did likewise.

"What's wrong?"

"Nothing." He reached into his duster pocket and came out with seven folded dollars. Then he fished for the coin at the bottom of the lining. He'd thought about paying her eight dollars for the week rather than the seven twenty-five he owed her, but he wasn't sure how she'd react to the overage. Maybe she'd think he was trying to pay for some extras.

"What's that?" she asked when he held out his hand to her.

"Your week's pay."

Her eyes widened as she took the money. "Oh . . . my." She clutched the currency, as if mesmerized. "You don't know how much this means to me. It's the first bit of money I ever earned."

"You deserved it. Put it someplace safe."

She stuffed it into her pants pocket.

By paying her, J.D. was pushing her one step away from him. He was giving her what she needed to get to San Francisco. He was reluctant to accept that, but he had to.

Nudging his horse, and Jo doing likewise, they continued on. J.D. felt as if he needed to know all there was about her before she left.

"Why is it you came West, Jo?" He caught her averting his gaze. "The truth."

Josephine stared ahead when she replied, "I thought the West would be an adventurous place to see."

"What gave you that idea?"

She sighed. "If you must know, the Beadle's."

"Those dime novels?" J.D. held a chuckle at bay. "Is that what you've been reading at night? They aren't worth the paper they're printed on. It's all a bunch of exaggeration. I read one once."

"I realize now that they are grossly overstated, but the elements of ro—" She stopped herself. "That is to say, the fiction is still enjoyable."

"Why did you head for Sienna?"

"It was described in *Rawhide's Wild Tales of Revenge in Sienna*. The author said there were red brick hotels, fine restaurants, and an opera house."

This time, J.D. couldn't keep the humor from his voice. "I doubt Sienna will ever have anything like that. It's just a mudhole town. Always will be."

"I have come to that conclusion myself."

"So what are you going to do in San Francisco?"

She turned her head toward him, her eyes meeting his for a few seconds. Then she looked away, her grip on the reins tightening. "I haven't quite figured that out. I doubt there is a high demand for archery instruction."

"You could be a cook in some fancy restaurant."

Shadows fell across Josephine as they rode beneath the boughs of alders. "You've got to be kidding."

"Not really. You've been coming along. I'll bet you could bake a cake and ice it up pretty good with candied stuff on it."

"Don't lie—I thought we were friends."

Friends? The word hit J.D. sideways. He had never thought of himself as a friend to anyone. He was boss to the boys, an acquaintance to Zev Klauffman at the mercantile, paying customer to Billy, and a good time to the girls in town. As for Boots, J.D. was a pain in the ass. Surely no son, and definitely no friend. Come to think of it, inasmuch as J.D. felt a part of the community, he could honestly say he had no one in particular whom he called friend. Neighbor, yes. Friend, no.

Why Josephine's assumption struck him as humbling, he couldn't figure.

They'd ridden in silence for a while when Josephine quietly asked, "Tell me more about your brothers."

J.D. damned himself as he revealed what he kept closely guarded in his heart. "The first time Eugenia sat me down in the parlor and read me the official military letter, I suffered with her, but I didn't cry. When William died, I wanted to enlist more than ever. But I stayed behind because Eugenia begged me to; she'd even taken to bed and swore she'd wither if she lost another son to the cavalry. So I remained home."

"And Boots . . . how did he take the news?"

"He didn't talk to any of us about it. He shut himself up in the stables." J.D. tried to relax the tension from his shoulders, but he found he couldn't. "The second letter came six months later. Eugenia didn't have to say a word to me. Her expression said it all.

"I was raised within a strong faith and church, and I asked her if God could have kept my brothers from dying. And she replied, 'God is all-powerful, and he could have prevented it if he wished. But it was his will they be taken.'"

A knot of anger had welled inside him as he recounted. "So I told her I'd never go into one of her damn churches again."

Josephine caught his eyes and softly asked as they rode out of the cover of trees, "Have you ever told Boots any of this?"

"No."

"Maybe you should one day . . . perhaps sooner rather than later."

J.D. made no comment.

"How is it you came here?" Josephine queried through the clop of the horses' hooves. "Boots speaks with an accent from the South sometimes. Even you do to a small degree."

J.D. reined Tequila left, up a slight grassy knoll. "I grew up in Mississippi on a cotton plantation."

"Really? I can't picture you there at all."

"I was. All my life until I was nineteen. After the war was over, I worked my way across the plains, building bridges in Illinois and laying railroad ties in Nebraska. I eventually made it out here and worked for a man named Dillard. When he died, I started the

McCall Cattle Company, in 'sixty-eight. I sent for Boots and Eugenia once I was settled. Eugenia only came to make sure Boots wouldn't go off his own way, then she went back to her folks."

If J.D. ever married, his bride would keep whatever she had coming into the marriage. His reasons were simple: Eugenia's property had become Boots's when she married him. For a time they'd prospered, but after the war there'd been nothing left. Once out West, Boots had mismanaged the funds her father had sent with risky ventures such as a stud farm that had failed.

J.D. had seen the dismal breakdown of Eugenia's independence. It wasn't something J.D. wanted to repeat. He didn't care at all about what a woman had of value. Though he was no baron, he was doing all right financially and didn't need a thing from anyone, much less his wife.

"And your folks?" J.D. inquired. "What did your father do?"

Josephine licked her lips. "My mother was the chairwoman of numerous charities. My father was a Wall Street speculator."

"I read about the market crash some months ago." The merc got copies of the *Laramie Press* when the train came through, but J.D. couldn't recall the details of the fallen market, as it hadn't directly affected him. "Paper said it put Wall Street under obligations only Fifth Avenue could repay."

"Yes," came Josephine's far-off reply, and her profile took on a thoughtful set. She said nothing further, and he had no opportunity to continue the conversation.

They reached the crest of the knoll. In a verdant valley below, spots of brown and white cattle grazed on rich grass. A broad streambed cut through the greenery. Ace, Seth, Dan, and Orley rode through the herd, Toby and the other dogs chasing after strays.

Josephine shaded her gaze against the blaring sun as it popped out from behind a solitary cloud. "It's lovely. I almost wouldn't mind being a cow."

J.D. laughed. "You want to go down there for a better look?"

"All right."

Kneeing Tequila, J.D. started down the incline, Josephine keeping to his right. He made no attempt to hide the fact that he was watching her. He had no business staring at her the way he was, but he liked the Josephine he was getting to know. He liked having her around more than he ought to.

"You know—" he began, but the rest of his words vanished in a jolt to his body. In the next second, his reins went slack in his hands, and his feet were out of the stirrups. The air was full of the acrid smell of burning hides.

When he looked up, Josephine was sprawled on the ground with a vacant look on her face. Peaches was still bucking, hooves kicking up tufts of grass.

Knowledge flared through J.D., and he swept his gaze in a quick circle. He caught sight of a pile of dead cattle, a horse minus its rider, and Toby running frantically to and fro in front of a prone object.

J.D. couldn't remember hearing any sound, but he knew what had happened.

"Are you all right?" he quickly asked Josephine.

"Y-yes . . ." Her eyes were half-lidded, her lips quivering. "What happened?"

"Lightning strike." J.D. sat up in the saddle and swerved left to capture Peaches's reins. Without dismounting, he drew Tequila close. "Whoa . . . whoa . . ." He was able to calm Peaches enough to quit bucking, then he wrapped the reins around his saddle horn. Calling over his shoulder, he hollered, "Crawl over to that short scrub and stay over there. You hear?"

She nodded mutely and started inching her way on her behind.

J.D. hunched over Tequila's neck and took off in a fast lope to get to the man on the ground. Lots of cowpunchers had been killed by lightning. J.D. had been knocked off his horse several times because of it. The first time he'd ever seen a ball of fire coming toward him, it had hit him like a blow on the head. When he'd come to, he was lying under Tequila while the rain poured down on his face.

A soreness instantly spread from the top of J.D.'s head to the bottoms of his feet. He figured the only reason he and Josephine had been spared was that they'd been spread out. The cows were close together, and they'd generated the heat that had attracted the lightning. Dammit all, but the rider had been in the thick of those cattle. It had looked to be Orley.

Lots of times J.D. had ridden around the herd, with lightning playing and thunder muttering in the distance, when the air was so full of electricity that he could see it flashing on the horns of the cattle, and there would be balls of it on the horses' ears, and even on his beard—little orbs about the size of peas.

But J.D. hadn't seen any of that today. The strike had come from a harmless-looking cloud.

The frightened cows bawled and scattered as J.D. reined in and dismounted just as Dan and Seth came barreling over on their horses. J.D. knelt in front of Orley, who was on his side, his hair mopping his temple, his face lopped over and pressing into the moist earth.

Dragging off his rawhide gloves, J.D. placed a hand gently on the cowboy's shoulder and rolled him onto his back. Across his face and neck, the skin was burned like toast. His eyes were closed, his mouth slack and opened.

J.D. felt for a pulse but got none. His own heartbeat was roaring through him; his fingers trembled.

Dan crouched down and laid a palm on the cowboy's shoulder. "Orley?"

Seth took Orley's gloved hand into his and gave it

several sharp pats. "Orley, partner, no time for beauty sleep."

J.D. left his fingers on the column of Orley's neck, hoping to feel the beat of life through the man's veins. But nothing.

"Orley, come on now," Dan yelled to his swing partner. "You get the hell up."

Ace Flynn was the last to ride up, fling himself from the saddle, and hunker down to assess the cowboy. "Orley, boy, it's Ace. Pick 'em on up. Time's a-wastin'. Cattle to move."

But all their talk was to no avail. Orley Woodard lay as still as the Stetson by his side.

The mood at the line camp was somber. Orley had been laid to rest in the back of the chuck wagon. J.D. had said tomorrow they would take his body to the nearest train stop and arrange to send him home to Sienna where his family would be notified.

Josephine had been too stunned to weep, but inside she was falling apart. Just last night, she'd tossed the good-natured cowboy an extra biscuit. And now . . .

Sniffing quietly, Josephine opened the fiddler's case and took the instrument out.

Everyone had gathered outside by a large bonfire. Dusk had come, and the night sky was lit up by the flames that rose toward its blanket of stars. The cowboys stood in a circle around the fire, their hats held in their hands. Even Boots had been solemn when J.D. had told him the news.

After J.D. had left her to ride toward the cattle, Josephine waited for him, her body aching so badly she thought she would never walk again. Every nerve ending seared with pain as she'd struggled to get to the place where J.D. had told her to go. She'd scooted and half crawled, in shock over what had happened yet still not understanding what had hit her. One minute she'd been on Peaches, the next instant she'd been on the ground.

With shaky hands, Josephine held the fiddle. Firelight played off the gloss of the wood as she ran her fingertips across the strings. Everyone was waiting for her to play a farewell song to their fallen partner. Josephine didn't think she could do it. Her emotions were unsteady, her legs just as weak. She stood in front of the wagon, it now serving as a makeshift tomb for one of their departed.

Surprisingly, it was Boots who began the Lord's Prayer. The others followed—all except J.D., who stood with his feet spread apart and his hat dangling in his fingers from arms that were behind his back. When the prayer was finished, a round of "Amens" came from the group, then eyes fell to her.

Josephine swallowed the thickness from her throat. Slowly, she raised the violin to her chin. Closing her eyes, she envisioned Orley's weather-beaten face. His smile. His humor. His expressions. She put them to memory, then began a tune that she had learned long ago. She knew no name for the piece. It was something she had picked up somewhere along her life, but the melody had haunted her then. And it haunted her now. The notes were not overly sad, but they were touching and gentle. They carried a lullaby sound, of high and low octaves. A special beauty that she had found in no other song.

When she was finished with the piece, she lowered the fiddle to gaze at the boys. Several wiped their eyes of unabashed tears with bandanas that got wadded back into pockets. A few loud sniffs filled the night. Boots even blew his nose. Everyone seemed to have a place to put Orley's memory.

Everyone except J.D. He was lost, and she knew why. Having no faith was like living without hope. He stood alone, his height tall and proud. Not a single sound came from him; not a single emotion showed in the glow of the fire.

Josephine put the fiddle away, then closed the lid. She looked up once more, caught J.D. watching her, then she fled. She had to get away. She knew she was going to cry, and she didn't want anyone to see her.

Running blindly behind one of the shacks, Josephine pressed her back to the rough wood and buried her face in her hands. Oh, why did everything out here have to be so harsh and violent? Why did Orley have to die?

Firm hands touched her shoulders, and Josephine's eyes flew up from her palms to see J.D. gazing at her.

She could have easily fallen into his embrace, but she held back. "You don't even care that he's dead. I know you don't believe in God anymore, but—"

"At night, when I ride alone on Tequila with just the cattle for company, I look at the high and bright stars. And I get to thinking about heaven . . . about my brothers being up there—if there is a *there*. I don't doubt such a place exists, but I'll never see it. William and Lewis are going to have to do without me and Boots in the hereafter." J.D.'s voice was laden with a broken whisper. "I do care, Jo. I care more than you know. But death is a way of life out here, and people part ways. You have to accept it, or you can't move on."

"I don't want to accept Orley is dead," Josephine lashed out. "It's not fair."

Tears streamed down her cheeks. She could taste them on her lips. She took in a gulp of air, and J.D. pulled her closer to his chest. She leaned into him, unable to help herself. Being held by J.D. and kissed by him was something she couldn't deny. He was different, and she knew that by his touch and the way he looked at her. She didn't need anything more to prove it to her at the moment.

It felt good to be in his arms, and she wanted to stay there until the ache in her heart went away.

CHAPTER

❖ 18 ❖

Henry Tascosa owned the Wampum Saloon in Bircher. There wasn't much to the town—if a person could call it that. Just the saloon, a livery, an abandoned U.P.R.R. boxcar that served as a post office and trading post, and a set of railroad tracks that ran down the middle of the only street. There was no depot house, only a solitary bench that looked over the double row of rail irons. If rain fell, a person got wet waiting; if the sun beat down, a person was cooked well done by the time the train showed up.

The Wampum had started out as the trading post but grew into a hangout for the ne'er-do-wells—mainly the buffalo runners who still roamed these parts. Having reached its maturity, the town now had a colorful past to boast. Bircher's youth had been gaudy, with liquor, gunfights, and the fast-growing cemetery that had begun with the deaths of the railroad track layers, the troops that had pushed through, and the first hide men.

None of the original so-called founders came back this way. Mostly, Bircher was born out of the hide men's need and had matured into the sordid place it was today because of their fondness for liquor and squandering money. The inhabitants were a wild, reckless bunch.

If J.D. could have sent Josephine someplace else, he would have. But there was nothing settled up for miles, and the Wampum was familiar to him. He knew how it operated and what to expect from Henry.

J.D. and the boys headed for the Wampum after putting up their horses and the mules in the stable. Rio had turned the remuda out in a ramshackle corral adjacent to the trading post. The chuck had been rolled into the livery's faded, whitewashed building until the morning train rolled through to take Orley to Sienna. Boots had volunteered to ride back with the young man's body.

Grief had kept the group solemn this morning as they'd broken camp. After breakfast, Jo had asked if she could use the old hip bath in the shack, and J.D. had had Rio fill it up. J.D. had gone down to the river and washed the trail dust off him; a few of the boys hoping to impress any women that might be in Bircher had done likewise.

On the ride over, things had been quiet—even Boots had been silent—and it still hung around them as the McCall outfit stepped through the narrow doors of the saloon knowing one of their company had departed. Josephine kept by J.D.'s side, her gaze drinking in the dark interior. J.D. tried to view the place through her eyes, and it looked a lot worse.

The Wampum served as a saloon and eatery, with a hotel upstairs that could accommodate a half-dozen patrons if they took single rooms. A rickety flight of stairs connected the two levels, and decorating the stairwell wall was a bevy of Indian paraphernalia.

Henry Tascosa had an aversion to Indians, even though he'd made a profit off them. When he'd operated the trading post, he'd turned a good business, and this was his way of showing what a redskin would give up for a bottle of firewater or a cup of coffee. He claimed the objects were his trophies: the buffalo-horned headdress, knife and sheath, beaded moccasins, cedar pouch, vests, deerhide leggings, bow and quiver with arrows, quilled breastplate, and assorted tomahawks.

The saloon was occupied by a group of hide hunters wearing wide-brimmed beaver hats, fancy shirts that at one time had been bright in colors, high-heeled boots, and leather vests. The weather didn't dictate that they wear the heavy buffalo skins they made their living from.

Five men sat in the corner playing a game of cards, while Henry stood behind the bar sipping from a chipped coffee cup that contained anybody's guess.

Silver-haired, Henry had an angular face just boxy enough to make a man uneasy when he stared too long. A large glass jar with the lid affixed rested on the counter before him. Inside there appeared to be a coiled snake. A rattler.

So this was the hunters' new vice: snake betting.

Boots ambled toward the bar, hooked his boot on the rail, and ordered a bourbon. Birdie, Print, Judge, Gus, and Rio followed, while J.D. held back with Josephine.

She wore his baggy shirt and loose-fitting trousers, which was fine by J.D. He didn't want her attracting attention. Although it was no secret she was a woman, what with the style of her hair and the blue hat tied by ribbons under her chin.

One other woman occupied the Wampum. She stood on the upstairs balcony that overlooked the main floor, with her arms resting on the railing. She worked one of the hotel rooms. He'd seen her here last winter and figured she'd be long gone by now. Apparently she made enough to keep her going, though why she'd want to stay in Bircher, J.D. could only speculate. Her hair was the color of brass, and she wore tights that looked like she'd been melted into them.

"Who's that?" Josephine asked in a low tone, her gaze turned upward on the chippy.

"Just who you think she is," J.D. replied, taking Josephine by the elbow and guiding her to one of the vacant tables. With his cuff, he brushed the ashes and crumbs from the top where he had pulled out a chair for Josephine. "Sit down, and we'll order some dinner. Then I'll get you a room."

She nodded and sat, her gaze lingering on the woman, then lowering to the group of men in the corner. She didn't hold her eyes there long. "You're going to get a room, too, aren't you?"

"We all are."

Relief slackened the tension squaring her shoulders. She gazed at the tabletop. "Is there a menu?"

"Nope."

"Oh."

"You get whatever Henry's cooked for the day. Mostly it's stew."

Josephine brushed off a few leftover crumbs from the table. "I don't care what it is."

Today, words between them had been going pretty much in this direction. Very shallow, with just enough to keep a thin conversation afloat.

J.D. missed Orley something fierce, but he hadn't said any church words, and he wasn't going to. It just wasn't in him anymore.

Last night, he'd finally let Josephine go, reluctant to lose the feel of her in his arms. He'd let her have one of the line houses to herself, while he and the boys and Boots had settled into the remaining two. Nobody had said anything about the tight arrangements, but it had been on J.D.'s mind.

Josephine was complicating things. He couldn't take for granted how he and the boys did things while she was along. She made him worry about her. He'd never worried about anyone, much less his own welfare. He took what came his way and dealt with it then. But with Josephine around, he had to think ahead and deal with the circumstances beforehand so as not to put any of them in a situation that would be sticky to handle.

Rio came over to the table holding a dripping mug of beer. He scraped back a chair and sat. Foam wet his mustache, and he chewed on an untrimmed end at the corner.

"You see that rattler on the bar?" he asked.

As soon as Rio said the words, Josephine's eyes darted to the jar on the counter.

"There's a snake in there?" she said in a rush.

"Yep," Rio replied. "Henry's takin' dollar bets on who can leave their hand on the jar while the rattler strikes. First man who can wins the spoils." Rio wiped the suds from his mouth with the back of his hand. "I aim to win."

"You do that, kid," J.D. replied, leaning into the back of his chair and stretching his legs out. "If Henry cleans you down to your spurs, don't come asking me for money."

"I've got plenty of money," Rio boasted, giving Josephine a sidelong glance. "I'm wallowing in the velvet. In fact, I'll buy Miss Josephine her dinner."

"No need. I've got it covered." J.D. crossed his ankles and gave the wrangler a tight frown. The kid may have been long on money at the moment, but he wasn't long on brains. He'd be busted before the sun rose. Between the snake game and the woman who'd just descended the stairs with a sway of her skirts, young Rio was doomed.

"I, um, I'll let you do that, boss, if you insist." The wrangler gave the chippy a few furtive glances that she enthusiastically returned with a painted smile and a batting of kohl-lined lashes. Rio tipped his hat to her as she paraded by. Without a good-bye, Rio rose and went to the bar to enter into the good-natured laughing the boys were doing with the prostitute.

Boots stood on his bowed legs, bourbon in hand, and did his share of the jesting. J.D. felt a fleeting sense of injustice. Nobody should be having a good time without Orley. But Orley wouldn't have wanted them to mull around long-faced. He would have wanted them to drink to his memory.

J.D. didn't put down a lot of liquor. Large quantities did nothing for his concentration, other than to fog it to a shade of gray. He didn't like being without his wits, especially in the Wampum Saloon, where anything could happen at any time without any warning.

Henry came over to the table, an army revolver strapped to his thigh. "Hey, J.D. Figured you'd be in around now."

J.D. put his fingers to the brim of his hat. "Henry."

The saloon owner's gaze strayed to Josephine, raking across the column of her neck where her collar was buttoned at the base of her throat, then downward to the swell of her breasts. "What have we here?"

A blush crept across Josephine's cheeks.

"She's my new cook."

Henry laughed. "Shaw outfit had itself a *cook,* too."

J.D. kept his tone level, but with clear intent. "Don't let your mouth overload your hardware, Henry. She's what I'm saying she is."

"Sure, J.D." Henry nodded, though J.D. didn't believe the other man's opinion had swayed. "What can I get for you?"

"Whatever's on the stove, a beer for me, and a coffee for the lady."

Henry moved on to the corner table, where the runners were boisterous and asking for more whiskey.

J.D. tucked his feet beneath his chair and leaned forward. "I'll have Henry bring your plate to a room."

"I can eat down here with you," she replied, unaffected by the loud guffaws filling the small area. "I'm not offended by those men. I've already met them."

Quirking a brow, J.D. said, "What?"

Josephine fidgeted with a button on her cuff. "My father brought men such as those to our home for business discussions in his study. Of course, they were wearing cutaway suits and top hats, but they were of the same nature. Loud and offensive to get their respective points across. Although I doubt those in the corner have much of a point to make at all. Who are they?"

"Buffalo runners."

"I've read about them."

"In the Beadle's?"

"Yes. But those few that trod across the pages were of a more admirable character than I suspect those five are."

"I told you the Beadle's weren't long on fact. I've never met a runner who was admirable."

A short time later, Henry returned with plates of stew, the lumps of meat in them tender in spite of their chunky appearance. The boys ate at the adjoining table, the chippy hovering nearby in case one of them called for another drink. Boots had consumed three bourbons to J.D.'s casual eye and was on his way to a good drunk.

Boots had never been a hard drinker, but on the trail he let his suspenders down, so to speak, and tied one on with the boys. He usually never lasted beyond the first half hour of card playing. He would manage to haul himself up the stairs and fall into the first unoccupied room he came to, and he'd sleep through the night until morning.

The only trouble with Boots when he was drunk was that he was more ornery than ever.

As J.D. slid his empty plate to the center of the table and washed down the last bite of his meal with the remains of his beer, Boots slurred, "Y'all're so dumb, you couldn't pour piss out of a boot if the directions were writ on the heel."

"Boots, shut your yap," Ace threw back with a

slight slur; then he looked glassy-eyed at his companions while raising his glass. "Let's drink one for Orley."

That sobered them up to a degree, and even Boots joined in without further slander.

Josephine set down her fork and, to J.D.'s surprise, quietly lifted her coffee mug in salute before drinking the last of the brew.

Rising, J.D. went to Henry at the bar, paid for a block of rooms, then collected the key to number two. He went back for Josephine. "Come on. I'll get you settled."

She rose and followed him up the stairs. When he reached the top, he turned to see her lagging behind, staring intently at a quiver of arrows and a bow suspended on the wall.

When she came to him, he proceeded down the hall a few short yards, inserted the key in the lock, and swung the door inside.

"It's not much," he offered by way of an apology.

The air in the room was stale, but at least the bed was made, so the sheets must have been laundered. Sometimes guests weren't so lucky. The wrought-iron frame for the bed was banged up, the coverlet and extra blanket sporting a few moth holes. Other than that, it wasn't bad. There was a pine washstand and basin of water that had a few dead gnats on the surface. The window shade was drawn, but pinpoints of light from the late-afternoon sun speckled through. Besides the bed and the washstand, no other furniture filled the room.

J.D. went to the door and checked the lock for soundness. If somebody wanted to break in bad enough, they could. He made sure the key worked on the inside, then clasped Josephine's hand and laid the key in her palm.

"I'm going to the livery to get your valise," he said while turning away. "You lock the door after me and don't open it for anyone."

He crossed the threshold, closed the door, then waited to hear the lock's tumbler engage as she turned the key. When the bolt clicked into place, he took the stairs.

Josephine had fallen asleep shortly after J.D. returned with her valise. She'd looked to see if a flock of bedbugs inhabited the mattress. Deeming the sheets free of vermin, she'd stripped down to her underwear and crawled in. In spite of the ruckus going on below, she'd drifted into a heavy, dead sleep. When she awoke, the room was dark.

She'd left a lamp by the side of the bed, so she sat up and struck a flame to light it. A soft orb of yellow flickered to life, and she turned up the wick. Padding on stockinged feet to the window, she lifted the shade's jagged edge and looked outside.

There were no lamps to illuminate the street. Just a moon that wasn't full and gave off barely enough to see that nothing stirred.

Letting the shade fall into place, Josephine went to her boots and checked to make sure her seven dollars and twenty-five cents was still tucked inside. Of course it was. But she'd had to make sure. She brought the money out and stared at it. Of all the money she'd had at her disposal, this was the first time she could recall ever actually touching the currency. All of her shopping trips had been put on the boutique's ledgered accounts—which Hugh had taken care of at the end of the month.

This was a monumental step for Josephine. At last she knew the value of hard-earned money, and she truly appreciated it.

After tucking the money away once more, she sat back down on the bed and pondered what to do. She fumbled for her alarm clock. She had to unwrap it from her extra pair of drawers; not having to wake up to its insidious bells in the morning, she hadn't even wanted to hear the dreaded thing ticking.

She was depressed to read the hands: three-fifteen. Good Lord, was she becoming accustomed to waking at this hour without the clock to give her a boost out of bed?

Sighing, Josephine stared at the locked door. She hadn't heard anyone come up to bed. They might have, but she'd been so tired she hadn't noticed.

A chorus of loud male voices rose from below, and Josephine strained to hear what they were saying. She couldn't be sure who they belonged to. Was that Rio's laugh?

Josephine walked softly to the door, wincing each time the bare floorboards creaked, and pressed her ear against the wood. The voices came again, only this time more heated. What was going on down there?

She hesitated a moment, her fingers on the key. She should go back to bed . . .

"Kiss my ass if you can catch it!" The distinct challenge roared through the hallway, and Josephine backed away from the door. Her heartbeat skipped a measure. It sounded like somebody was right outside her door, but there were no footfalls.

Slowly, she crept closer again. That same voice was now a little muffled when it said, "You goddamn cowpoke."

It had to be coming from the stairs. Then, to confirm her suspicions, boots fell hard on the treads and descended below.

Josephine ran to the bed and sat down, worrying her fingers together. There was going to be a fight . . . she knew it. Would guns go off?

In *Rawhide's Wild Tales of Revenge in Sienna*, Rawhide had had to shoot his way out of a barroom brawl, with Pearl tucked next to his hip as they walked backward through the saloon. The daring hero had shot up all the bar glasses on the shelves before gunning the chandelier chain in two, creating havoc as he fled from the scene.

Josephine's eyes strayed to the door. What if J.D.

was down there? And Boots . . . and the others? She was certain they could fend for themselves. But, still, that didn't alleviate her fears. Trouble was brewing, trouble of a Beadle's kind. This she knew . . . this was the one thing the books couldn't have embellished. Because she'd read Rawhide Abilene say that very line about catching his behind to one of the no-accounts at the bar . . .

J.D. had been playing cards most of the night after the novelty of the snake had worn off. Rio had lost himself some seventeen dollars before he quit and went upstairs with Lottie.

All of the boys had taken at least a half-dozen tries, but no one had been successful. Even Boots put his dollar in, but he hadn't been able to keep his hand on the glass when that rattler struck out. The mug on the bar had built up with a good deal of ante, but no one was winning it. J.D. suspected the spoils weren't going to be all Henry's good fortune but some of those runners, for one of them had probably caught that rattlesnake and had a stake in it.

Amusements like these weren't uncommon. Even the toughest hombre had a hard time not flinching when that forked tongue slithered back and forth and the fangs were bared as the diamond-shaped head jutted forward. Reflex kicked in, and the mind reacted to the danger by automatically moving away. J.D. had learned his lesson some seven years ago when he'd fallen victim to the game. Since then, he'd never bucked the odds, and it had saved him a lot of money.

Once most everyone was having a high time on liquor, the runners and the cowboys had mingled together for a game of twenty-one. J.D. had watched for a spell to see if the game was clean; when he deemed it fair, he joined in.

Boots had taught J.D. how to count by playing blackjack. It was one of the things he hadn't learned from his tutors. Boots wasn't much of a talker when he played. Mostly, he'd chew on a toothpick and study his cards, sometimes so long he made J.D. antsy. By the time he was eight, he knew better than to cut a deck, touch his cards before the deal was done, or expose his own good fortune with a smile. Boots had told him, "Never show your opponent your true feelings, you'll give him the advantage." J.D. had taken that to heart, for he never much showed his feelings about anything.

Another hand was dealt with the greasy cards. J.D., four of the hide hunters, Gus, Print, and Jidge were the only ones in. Boots had gone to bed an hour ago, Rio hadn't returned from his date with Lottie, and Birdie had gone to his room after he'd fallen into a pit of drunkenness he'd be sorry for when he woke up.

J.D. was tired. The backs of his eyes felt like sandpaper, but he sipped the hot coffee in his cup and stared at the upturned jack he'd been flipped. From where he sat, he had a good vantage of room number two. He could see the left edge of the jamb and tell if someone was snooping around in the hallway.

The music, if he could call it that, had quit a half hour ago when the runner at the grubby piano had fallen facefirst onto the keys and Henry had lost his voice.

Snores broke through the calls for cards at the twenty-one table.

"I'm out," Jidge said, shoving his cards to the middle.

"Me, too," Print seconded.

"Hit me," Gus declared, and he was dealt a ten of hearts on top of his seven of clubs. He swore and threw in his cards.

J.D. nodded for a card and was given a three of diamonds. Visible was his jack, but underneath was an eight of spades.

Two of the runners who'd asked for cards folded,

while the other two stayed in the game. When it came time to show their hands, J.D. went first.

"Blackjack," he called after a swallow of coffee.

The first runner, a man by the name of Witchal, snorted. "One of us is a dirty, lyin' cheater. And it ain't me. I've got me the eight of spades." He flipped his cards, and the eight of spades rose to the top like cream.

J.D.'s eyes narrowed. They'd been playing for four goddamn hours, and he hadn't seen a single sign of double dealing or card swapping. What in the hell had happened?

Witchal ran his stubby fingers through his wiry beard, then began to slide the pot toward his side of the table.

"No one is going to call me a cheater," J.D. said. "So it seems we've got ourselves a problem."

Witchal had stood, stuffing the coins and greenbacks into the slit of his pocket. Without a word, he began his ascent up the stairs.

"Problem?" he spoke over his shoulder. "We don't have any problem. Kiss my ass if you can catch it."

J.D. gritted his teeth. Jidge leaned toward him. "You aren't going to let that stinkin' hide hunter walk away with your money?"

"I'll catch your ass," J.D. threatened, "then I'll kick it up your throat."

"You goddamn cowpoke," he shot back.

To call a cattleman a cowpoke was the gravest of insults. J.D. couldn't be certain who threw the first punch, his heavy gaze still on the runner who'd tromped back down the stairs; but after that, all hell broke loose.

Somebody overturned the table. Cards went flying, and so did fists. A shot glass broke, and the whiskey bottle beaned Jidge over the head.

Witchal ran to the table with the ungainly lumber of the buffalo he hunted. J.D. ducked right, and

Witchal's hammy fist swung through air. With a round punch, J.D. got the man in the hairy jaw, snapping his head to the side. His bulky weight put him off-center, and he fell over.

J.D. turned to see Gus and one of the runners in a heated battle, Gus on the losing end. Picking up a chair, J.D. swung the legs into the other man. Stunned, he gazed briefly at J.D. before crumbling with a moan.

Gus swore, then latched himself onto the back of another man who'd just given Jidge a coldcock. He rode around on him like he was a bronc, his legs hugging the girth of the runner; star spurs jangled like can openers, and that runner tried like all get-out to pry Jidge off him. J.D. backed away to stand below the staircase, trying to see who needed help.

Swerving to avoid being hit by a flying coffee mug, J.D. observed Witchal staggering to the bar. His hands encircled the rattlesnake jar. Then he picked it up, caught sight of J.D., and threw the jar at him.

Oh, shit! J.D. sprang to the left, just as glass fragments splintered behind him on the paneled wall. The ominous quaver of a ribbed tail buzzed near. Frozen so as not to garner the snake's attention, J.D. lowered his eyes, looking right, then left.

The snake was within striking distance of his boot. It appeared to be two feet of coiled energy, fiercely agitated judging by the rumble of that loose, horny rattle that shook. Its forked tongue darted in and out maliciously. The diamond-shaped head lifted, jutted back, and poison fangs gleamed like two miniature needles just as it thrust forward.

J.D. grabbed for his Colt, but he could see he was too late. He stiffened, waiting for the pricks on his leg, but they never came. The snake suddenly flailed and writhed, its head pinned to the floorboards by a single arrow shot to the side of its neck. After seconds of struggle, it fell still.

"Jesus . . ." J.D. said hoarsely, his revolver dead in his grasp.

He glanced up at Witchal, who was glancing up the stairs. J.D. turned his head to see Josephine standing on the landing. She had her underwear on; his shirt covered most of her, but it was unbuttoned. Her stockinged feet were spread apart, and in her hand was the bow that had been tacked on the wall.

"Jo?" he called up to her.

"I . . . I held the position of Lady P-Paramount at the Manhattan Archery Club." She trembled visibly, the bow in her hand slipping from her fingers. "But to . . . to be fair . . . I must say . . . that I could have . . . missed just now."

Then her eyelids slipped closed, and she dropped like a dishrag to the floor.

Chapter

→ 19 ←

Josephine felt a wet cloth pressed against her forehead. Whatever was beneath her was soft. Warm fingers stroked her hair from her brow. She wanted to linger in the darkness, lazing in the gentle feel of the hand on her skin. It was with great effort that she opened her eyes.

J.D.'s face came into focus. She blinked a few times, looking past him to the wall behind. Her bearings came to her. She was in her room. Obviously on the bed. The mattress dipped where J.D. sat next to her.

"You're a hell of a shot," he said, his words echoing through her muddled head. She still felt fuzzy. She was loath to think she'd actually fainted. With everything she'd been through this past year, she had never succumbed to the clutches of feminine weakness.

Everything came flooding back to her. She'd thrown on a shirt as soon as she heard that man on the landing. Then she'd unlocked the door, just to peek through the crack. That's when she'd seen the fight start down below. It had been a furniture-tossing and barehanded brawl, just like in *Rawhide's Wild Tales of Revenge*. She'd crept out a little farther when J.D. disappeared from her view. It was then that the man at the bar picked up the snake jar. Josephine had run to the landing before the glass crashed.

She couldn't believe it now, but some logical reasoning had taken over, and she'd known precisely what to do in the moment of crisis. It had been as if she'd become Pearl Larimer. Cool and composed. In control and out to save her man.

She'd pulled the bow from the wall, stolen an arrow from the quiver, and taken aim as soon as the glass crashed. Without any hesitation, she'd fired at the snake before it lashed out at J.D.

The bow had been accurate . . . the arrow straight. If it hadn't been . . . she didn't want to think about that.

"I got it . . . didn't I?" she asked, her voice sounding weak to her ears.

"In the neck."

"Not exactly my intended mark."

"Close enough."

"I've never killed anything before."

"I didn't figure you had." J.D.'s palm slid down her face and cradled her cheek. His fingertips were rough and callused, but she found his touch light and considerate.

"Did anybody get hurt downstairs?" she asked, licking her dry lips.

"Nah. Henry broke it up. Everybody's gone to bed." He withdrew his hand, and she missed his warmth. His hair shone in the lamplight, subtle shades of brown and burnished coffee. She liked the way he wore it—pushed straight back from his forehead without a definite part. His cut looked a little better; her stitches had done the job. He wasn't wearing his hat, and she spied it suspended on one of the footboard knobs.

Just seeing his hat there, so casual, so intimate, made her feel safe. She enjoyed being with J.D. McCall. Much more than was prudent. She was drawn to him in ways she shouldn't be.

She couldn't understand or define this physical attraction that seemed to have a path of its own. It had come upon her quickly, without warning, and she didn't know how to sort through her feelings.

She had been courted by Hugh for nearly a year before her emotions of love had evolved fully and reasonably, before she'd committed herself mind and soul to him. Their engagement had lasted a respectable ten months before they were wed. She had had time to plan and arrange her life with him. But as she looked back, she saw that she had never taken a stand for what she believed. She had had no relation to her own life, her own way of thinking.

Josephine had never considered herself a free thinker, a woman of whim and careless action. But she was thinking along those lines now.

When she gazed into J.D.'s face, she was physically moved. Passions stirred. He was in her room . . . alone with her.

"Are you feeling all right?" he asked, his gray-blue eyes contemplative.

"Hmm," she replied, not really focusing on his words but on his lips as they moved. She wanted him to kiss her, but she could never ask him to—not even if she *was* a woman of whim.

J.D. ran his fingers through his hair, the ends ruffling on his shoulder. "How would you feel about my sleeping in here?"

Her heartbeat tripped.

"When those runners got a look at you in your underwear on the stairs, they took a lot more notice than when you'd been buttoned up in my clothes." His eyes narrowed speculatively. "A pair of them have a room at the end of the hall. They were pretty drunk when they went in there, but I wouldn't put it past them to mosey on over and pay you a call."

Josephine's confidence spiraled. She may have shot an arrow at a snake, but a man? She knew she couldn't do it.

Recovering from his offer, she asked lightly, "Don't you have a room?"

"I did. Boots is snoring on my bed." Standing, J.D. went to the door. "I can sleep on the floor. The room's right next door." He put his hand on the doorknob. "If anybody walks down the hall, I'll hear them."

Josephine sat upright, the damp cloth falling into her lap. "No," she blurted. "Stay."

When he turned around, she added, "I'll feel much better knowing you're here. Those men . . . they looked dishonorable."

J.D. leaned against the side jamb, his head nearly brushing the top, and folded his arms across his chest. "Dishonor isn't the half of it."

He strode to the bed. Josephine scooted back against the pillow. "Are you tired?" she asked, unable to think of anything else to say. She couldn't deny the spark of excitement over the prospect of his staying in her room with her.

She was treading dangerous waters, waters that she didn't know how to swim in. What should she do?

She hadn't planned any kind of romantic liaison with him when she'd invited him to stay. She had just wanted his company. But she couldn't deny that she wanted to kiss him. To feel his arms around her. To be comforted and safe in his embrace.

"I'm tired," he replied. "But I drank too much coffee to go to sleep." Taking the extra blanket off the end of the bed, he spread it out on the floor. "I'll blow the lamp out so you can."

"I'm not sleepy anymore," Josephine said, flipping her braid over her shoulder. "I hate to say it, but I've gotten somewhat used to this abominable hour of the night. It seems like I ought to be doing something. Mixing biscuit dough. Or putting on a pot of coffee."

J.D. removed his boots and lay down. Peeking over the bed's edge, Josephine frowned. He had put his hands beneath his neck to support his head. She reached behind her and tossed him the pillow. The downy square hit him on the shoulder, and he looked at her while dragging it under his head.

"Thanks."

"You're welcome."

Josephine leaned back once more, studying the hat dangling on the bedpost. She grew entranced by it, the soft glow of the lantern playing across the room. She felt . . . protected. The wrought rails of the bedstead pressed into her shoulders. Sliding downward, she bent her knees and pulled the covers over her.

"What time are we leaving?" she ventured quietly.

"I reckon when everybody drags themselves out of bed." His voice drifted up to her. "Why? Are you in a hurry to get back to Sienna?"

"No . . . but I was thinking you might be." She bit her lip. "Somebody might be waiting for the cook's job."

"I wouldn't bet on it." A pause stretched between them. "I suppose you're sick of the outdoors and are ready for a nice hotel room in San Francisco."

She leaned over once more, staring at the top of his head. He had crossed one leg on top of the other and closed his eyes. The blanket was barely draped over his middle and the length of his legs.

"I don't mind the outdoors. I like parks."

He lifted his head and looked at her. "Parks and prairies are two different things."

"Yes, I know. Each has its own beauty." It was too easy to get lost in the way his gaze traveled across her, so she lay back down.

"I'm surprised to hear you say that, Jo. I'd figured you to prefer fountains over creeks." He didn't give her the opportunity to comment. "You sure you don't want the light out?"

"I'm sure."

A span of silence separated them. Then J.D. said, "I hear something ticking."

Josephine sat up. "It's my clock."

"Where is it?"

She put her feet over the side of the bed. "In my valise."

Earlier, she'd moved her valise on the floor. It lay open close to J.D.'s head. She moved around him, collected the clock, and rolled it in her petticoat once more, then snapped the lid on her case and put it next to the wall. Turning, she said, "It has that same effect on me."

She paused. J.D. was staring intently at her. She should have been self-conscious in just the shirt and her underpinnings with him gazing at her so. But she wasn't. She had longed for Hugh to give her that same heart-stopping skim of his eyes, but he never had. She'd talked herself into staying in love with him. Telling herself that he would love her in time.

She'd fooled herself. And just when she'd thought it could get no worse, he'd told her the real reason he'd married her: for her bank account.

Josephine swallowed, sadness drifting across her memories. She still wanted her dreams to come true, only she was afraid to reach out to them. She still wanted to love somebody . . . to have somebody love her.

"What's the matter, Jo?" J.D. asked quietly.

"I was just thinking . . ." Unbidden, her eyes filled with tears.

"Come here," J.D. said, his voice a rich timbre that caused her to shiver.

She took a step toward him, feeling shy yet daring at the same time. She'd fantasized about a moment like this, one that was driven by sensuality. Though the descriptions hadn't sizzled off the pages, she'd felt the loving emotions between Rawhide and Pearl when they had kissed.

When J.D. stood up, she moved closer. Keeping words to himself, he held his arms open to her, and she went to him.

They kissed, soft and exploring. Her heart thumped erratically. He was so compelling, his magnetism so potent, she didn't want to think about consequences. This had been coming for a long time. She'd thought about it; she'd accepted it. What was to happen was inevitable. Somewhere along the trail, an intangible bond had formed between them.

She had tried, and been unsuccessful, to ignore the strange aching in her body when he held her. When he kissed her, she was his Pearl, he her Rawhide. Only it wasn't pretend. This was real. What she was feeling was stronger than any ink-written lines . . .

This was real life. Her life.

The strong hardness of J.D.'s lips against hers aroused a hunger within her. She fit herself tightly into the circle of his arms, pressing against him.

A brief quiver rippled through her when his hands slipped inside the open shirt to caress her back, her spine, and upward to the nape of her neck. Blood coursed through her veins like an awakening river. She wasn't inexperienced, but this was so new. Like nothing she'd ever felt before.

He swept her into his arms and carried her to the bed. The mattress dipped by the weight of his knee as he laid her down, gazing at her with passion-darkened eyes. "We can't go back."

She searched his face, then met his eyes. "I know."

Bringing his head lower, he kissed her once more. It was as if their words released her. As if they allowed her to abandon herself to the torrent of desire and heat that had been building in her.

She could feel his uneven breathing against her crushed breasts, the jolt of his thigh brushing her hip.

This was shameless . . . she was shameless. But she felt no guilt. Just need . . . and warmth. A space that had to be filled with caresses.

Her skin tingled when he pulled back to slip her arms free of the shirt and toss it over the side of the bed. Softly, his breath fanned her ear, as he dipped low to kiss her, then undo the ribbon at the scooped neck of her chemise. His mouth came to hers, nibbling, arousing, as he slowly inched the fabric at her shoulders down.

His lips were persuasive, making her impatient. Each new kiss sent spirals of ecstasy through her. Her hands explored the broadness of his back, the stretch of cotton across his shoulders. With a thread of self-consciousness, she reached in the front when he broke the kiss, to undo the column of buttons.

At each one, her fingers trembled. She had never undressed a man before . . . a man had never undressed her before. J.D. gazed down at her, his hair dusting her hands when they rose to the last button at his throat, where his pulse visibly jumped. He pressed a kiss to her knuckles.

Once the checkered fabric was parted, she glided her hands inside, noting that he wasn't wearing the long johns she had seen him in before. Her fingers touched marble-smooth skin.

She ran her palms down his side, feeling the strength of his ribs, the contours of his body. Then she raised them once more to his chest and the sprinkling of dark hair between his flat nipples.

He was perfection, sculpted to an artist's rendering, yet big and broad. He put to shame the men who sat in offices for hours a day. J.D. McCall worked beneath the sun, building muscle, his skin taking on a hue of honey where it was exposed to the rays.

Her hands explored the hollows of his back. The waistband of his denims where the fabric stretched.

His firm lips explored the sensitive skin between her neck and shoulder, leaving dancing kisses in their wake. He moved lower, and lower yet, until he came to the swell of her breast. He eased the chemise down and bared her to his gaze.

A fleeting dart of embarrassment assailed her. No man had seen her naked. And J.D. had all but said her figure was imperfect in Mr. Klauffman's store . . .

Josephine stiffened, uncertain, feeling very exposed. But J.D. murmured against her, "It's too late,

Jo," then he nuzzled her breast. He kissed the fullness of the sides, then inward to the crest. She moaned as a wave of shock gripped her. It was as if her senses had intensified, that everything she felt was magnified a hundred times over.

She arched her back, her emotions whirling and skidding, as his tongue traced her, sucked her. The combination of the two drove her to a torturous arousal.

His hands slid across the silk covering her midriff, then lower as he eased to his side so he could have full access to her. She still had reservations about how he viewed her, yet she waited . . . wondering . . .

"You're pretty, Jo. Soft and curvy in all the right places." He ran his thumb downward, to her most intimate place; he stroked her ever so gently. His circular movements made her crazy. Reassured and no longer fearful that he wouldn't find her body to his liking, she caressed the strong tendons in his neck, trying to pull him close; but he stayed away, giving her a torture so pleasurable she could hardly breathe.

His hand moved magically, in a way she could have never dreamed. She gasped in sweet agony, welcoming the release that had been so tight within. His hand caressed her thigh as she burned where he touched her.

Breathless, she felt like her body was half ice, half flame. She wanted more, needed there to be more. He'd fulfilled her in a way she had never known, yet she wanted to be closer to him.

J.D. leaned back, stripped off his shirt and denims, then tugged on the cord of her drawers. He slipped them over her hips, along with the chemise.

They were both naked.

She didn't dare look at him, but her gaze had a will of its own. She drank in his strength, his maleness. Seeing what she had only imagined . . .

Coming to her, J.D. enfolded her in his arms,

kissing her, rousing her tongue in a playful dance. Her legs opened with a will of their own, a driving need of their own. She welcomed him into her body.

They shared a joining of exquisite harmony. This was bliss. She knew it. Everything she had been told about repression and distance was wrong. How could she detach herself from the melting tempo that bound them? She could not. So she went with it, allowing herself to fall. To be passionate.

The pleasure was pure and explosive, rocking her to her toes. She had felt wondrous before when he touched her with his hand, but this was different. This was a togetherness that weakened all her defenses.

This was heaven on earth.

The feel of his rough skin over hers brought her to new heights. Her arms locked around his neck, her lips crushed his. And the fire spread throughout her, to a degree that stunned and shook her.

A raw sensuousness made her eager to respond to him, to move with him. She couldn't control her outcry of delight when the rocking experience of moments before returned to a higher degree of surrender. She couldn't disguise her emotions any more than she could cover them with a mask. She felt; she wanted; she enjoyed.

She moaned aloud with the erotic pleasure that coursed through her, J.D. kissing the sigh on her mouth as he shuddered. Every inch of her tingled, and she savored the feeling of satisfaction he left in her.

With his head cradled on her shoulder, Josephine held him to her, eyes closed, heart filled with wonder.

She had finally done what Hugh had accused her of.

She'd slept with another man.

J.D. nudged the door closed with the toe of his boot, then walked quietly to the washstand and deposited one of the cups of coffee he'd been holding.

The small room was cast in a hazy yellow glow that

came from behind the drawn window shade. The morning time was closing in on ten o'clock. Josephine was still in bed, lying on her side, the curve of her hip barely covered by the sheet. Her eyes were closed; she hadn't been awake for some hours now. Not since they last made love.

The words were hard for him. "Making love" meant you deeply cared about the person; it meant you had passionate feelings for her. He'd never thought of his time at saloons with girls as making love. That had been pure sport. He'd bought and paid for what he'd gotten. But with Josephine things were different.

So now what? He wasn't sure. For the first time, J.D. wasn't sure what he wanted.

Taking a sip of piping coffee and walking toward the bed, he studied Josephine while she slept. Her hair had come undone from her braid, and the waves of fiery auburn covered her shoulders like a shawl. Her skin, the color of ivory, looked pale and soft in the veiled daylight. The sheets were twisted through her legs, the end draped across her middle. He couldn't see her breasts; her hair fell over them.

A contented feeling radiated inside J.D. The kind that worked around his heart after he'd had a satisfying day in the saddle or after he'd helped a heifer birth a calf. He wasn't a man of much luxury. He took pleasure in the simpler things in life. Like watching a sunset or sitting up on the Tepee Range looking out at his spread. He didn't like complications. He liked routine.

So why, then, was he feeling so damn good watching Josephine sleep? To his recollection, he'd never stood back and enjoyed the beauty of a woman while she was dreaming. And just what was Jo dreaming about?

J.D. cocked his hip, took another swallow, then sighed. Maybe he shouldn't have let things go so far.

He'd known he was playing with fire. She wasn't made for his kind of country. She wouldn't be happy here. So why was he thinking otherwise? Why was he imagining her lying in his bed at the ranch?

And why had he told Rio first thing this morning to back away from Jo?

Recalling the incident, J.D. saw himself as a gallant hero—the kind she would have read about in one of her books. He'd cornered Rio and asked him his intentions. Rio had replied, "A man's got to try and steal a kiss from a pretty girl." It had been all J.D. could do not to punch the kid in the jaw. He'd told Rio that the first kiss he stole from Josephine Whittaker would see him kissing his job good-bye.

Though why J.D. had made such a point to put the other man at bay, he couldn't be sure. All these thoughts about Jo at the ranch would never be. J.D. shook off the memory of how good Josephine had felt in his arms. Of how fine she'd been to kiss . . . to explore. One thing he'd found out, she wasn't inexperienced.

A cord of jealousy tightened around his ribs, making his breathing tight. He had no right to feel the way he did. What she'd done in the past was no business of his. Because he was plenty experienced himself. But that didn't stop him from wondering something fierce. Who had she been with? Had she loved him?

Josephine stirred, slipping onto her back, taking the sheets with her yet not high enough. Her hair fell to her sides, and her breasts were exposed to his gaze.

He lingered a moment, the flames of the fire inside him stirring. Then he wrenched himself away, set his cup aside, and bent down to grab the clock from her valise. The underclothing that she'd wrapped it in was soft and satiny against his fingertips. He was surprised that he had any feelings left at all where the skin was hardened over by calluses one on top of the other.

He turned the clock around so that he could examine the settings for the alarm time. Twisting the dial several times, he stopped when he had it pointed directly on the ten.

Collecting his cup, he put the clock on the washstand next to the coffee he'd brought Josephine. The boys had been up for a half hour; some were downstairs nursing their bottle fatigue over breakfast and a pot of Arbuckle's, while some had gone to the livery with Rio. Boots was up and about, and the last J.D. had seen of him, he'd been walking across the street toward the bench to wait for the train.

J.D. didn't want anyone knowing where he'd spent the night. It was better to leave Josephine alone, have her wake up on her own, then join them in the saloon as if nothing had happened last night.

With a final lingering gaze, J.D. turned and left the room.

The blare of the alarm's bell bolted Josephine upright. She was momentarily disoriented, and it took a few seconds for her eyes to focus. Then she kicked the covers off and tripped out of bed with the intention of stuffing the clock beneath the pillow. But the peal ran down by the time she reached it; she nearly knocked over a cup of coffee on the washstand in the process.

The room quiet now, she grew more alert. Gazing around, she looked for J.D. Not a trace. The aroma of coffee filled the corner where she stood, and she laid her fingertips on the handle of the mug.

J.D. had been there.

Walking slowly back to the bed, she sat down on the rumpled coverlet. How was she going to face him? She was almost glad he wasn't there. She'd have time to collect herself.

She'd never, *ever* done anything as impetuous as she had last night. What must he think of her? That she fell into bed with whatever man was available when the mood struck her?

Josephine mulled over her options as she reached down for her valise. Lifting the case onto the bed, she rummaged through it, her trousers and shirt on top. Folded on the bottom were the skirts and blouses of the original owner.

Pausing, Josephine thought about trying them on, then opted against it. She didn't want J.D. to think she was chasing after him.

Josephine dressed in J.D.'s old clothes while going over in her mind just what exactly one said to one's boss after having spent the most incredible hours of her life with him.

"Thank you" seemed hardly appropriate.

The Union Pacific No. 76 chugged into Bircher at high noon. J.D. went up to the conductor and explained the circumstances to him. A boxcar was opened, and the cowboys lifted Orley's sheet-wrapped body inside.

After paying for Boots's fare, J.D. put him on the train. Boots stood on the platform, his eyes bloodshot and his legs a little wobbly.

"Get Klauffman to make the arrangements," J.D. called up to Boots. "Tell him I'll be paying for the casket. Then you have him send a telegram to Morris Crossing."

Boots barely paid him any mind, his gaze latched onto the boxcar as the sliding door was shoved closed.

"And get somebody to ride out to the place so Hazel can come into town and get you in the wagon. You hear?"

Boots snorted. "Good gawd, what do y'all take me for? A nitwit? I ought to get me a hot-blooded stallion and ride my way back to the house. But if I get throwed and break my neck, don't go burying me under that gawddamned peach tree. I don't want any bird shit splattering on my tombstone."

With that, he disappeared into one of the two passenger cars connected to the engine.

J.D. shook his head as he walked off toward the chuck. Jo was already on the seat waiting for him. The calf was tied to the rear making mewing sounds and sniffing the air. Seeing as how Josephine wasn't up in time this morning, J.D. had fed the calf its breakfast.

Jo sat with her back straight, her clothing neatly buttoned, and her frilly hat over her perfectly plaited braid. She looked nothing like the seductive woman he'd been lying next to for the latter part of the night. He'd been imagining her in a dress. A blue calico with white petticoats underneath. A forget-me-not–colored dress for a woman he was likely never to forget.

Pushing himself up, he settled in beside her and grabbed the lines. Their thighs brushed, as did their elbows. She scooted over.

He smiled. "No need."

She smiled back, soft and tentative. "I suppose not."

The train's whistle blew, and the engine's wheels began to turn. By little tufts of steam, the No. 76 gained speed and pulled out of Bircher.

The boys removed their hats and waved them at the boxcar that carried one of their departed, then Rio whistled between his teeth for the dogs that weren't staying at the spring range and moved what was left of the remuda out into a run.

J.D. flicked the reins on the mules' rumps, and they joined the procession. The cowboys mounted up and trotted alongside the train for a spell.

"Look behind you," J.D. said in what he hoped was a casual tone, his elbows leaning on his knees. "In the wagon. Right there in front."

Josephine turned around, then faced forward. "What am I looking for?"

"Something new."

She reached in back once more, then came up with what he'd wanted her to find. A gray Stetson that hadn't seen too much wear with a fine leather band. He'd picked it up at the trading post, glad that somebody had cashed it in last week. "Oh," she said with awe in her voice. "You bought yourself a new hat."

He gazed at her with a half-smile. "No, Jo. That's for you."

"Me?"

"Yeah. Since the other hat I gave you washed downstream." His eyes returned to the road. "That one you've got on isn't worth the price you paid for it. That Stetson'll keep the sun off your face."

"I . . . I don't know what to say."

"Don't say anything. Just put it on."

She slipped the ribbon bow free of her eastern hat, took it off, then placed the Stetson on her coil of braids.

"Well?" she asked.

"I like it."

Her eyes brightened. "Thank you . . . um, boss. It was thoughtful of you."

His brows furrowed. "You call me boss again, I'm liable to take the hat back."

She was quiet a moment, then faced forward. She put her feet on the ledge of the box. "I want you to know that last night . . . well . . . it's just that there was only one other, and he . . . he isn't a part of my life anymore."

The clop of hooves over the earth rang out between them.

"I've never done anything like last night before," she said with quiet emphasis. "I . . . I just wanted you to know."

J.D. didn't reply as promptly as he should. He appreciated her candor more than he could ever say. "I'm glad you told me, Jo."

CHAPTER

→ 20 ←

Each day ran into the next as they traveled toward Sienna's outskirts. For Josephine, the sunsets came too swiftly. She liked the time spent after supper the best, when the dishes were done and she could sit by the fire and listen to the tales Gus Peavy spun, with commentary from Birdie Tippett, who appeared to be on the mend. J.D. had given him a fresh bandage, and Birdie had scoffed that he wasn't an invalid.

These moments of reverie usually progressed into a familiar order. One of the boys would ask to grind some of the Arbuckle's coffee in the hopes that he'd be the one to find the stick of striped peppermint candy that was packed in every sack. Print Freeland had been the lucky one the other night. Then she'd play the violin for a while, trying to pick up some of the camp songs they would sing to her. She was able to carry the melody of "Bury Me Not on the Lone Prairie" fairly well.

She made peach pies again their second day out. Unfortunately, she burned the edges this time, and they hadn't looked as good as the ones Old Wednesday had stolen. But they tasted fine enough for everyone to have two helpings.

There wasn't an opportunity for her and J.D. to be

alone together for any length without causing attention. While they rode on the wagon together, they talked. She listened, mostly, to his plans for the ranch. It meant a lot to him. She had never put so much hope into a property; for her, a house had been merely a house. She hadn't thought about land and what it could do for a person. To J.D., his land and his cattle meant the world.

Although she discussed her parents with love and admiration, she didn't tell him that her father had committed suicide. Even though Boots knew, she doubted he'd tell J.D. He never asked, but she sensed he was waiting for her to tell him about the other man she'd been with. There was no point in bringing up Hugh's name. She had left him behind.

They were able to keep up a faster pace without the cattle to slow them down, and J.D. had told her they'd be at the ranch by late this afternoon.

She swayed to the lumber of the wagon as it rattled across the rutted road. J.D. held the reins and leaned back to prop a foot up.

She formed a question that had been on her mind. "What does 'J.D.' stand for?"

He gave a half-laugh. "I wondered when you'd get around to asking. Most people do sooner or later." A smile curved his mouth. "Jefferson Davis. Boots was an admirer of the soon-to-be-elected congressman. My mother wanted to name me Gilbert."

It was Josephine's turn to laugh. "I'm glad Boots got his way."

"He always does. I wonder what the old cuss is up to."

"What is there to do at the ranch once we get back?" Josephine asked, thinking of Boots herself. "You don't have the cows anymore."

"I've got a lot of cows," he replied. "We didn't move them all out. There were some too old or weak to be moved, and I've got some calves that were born days before we left. I'll need to brand them."

"What about Freckles?"

J.D. gave a sideways glance. "Who's Freckles?"

"My calf." It was amazing how easily the words slipped free. Josephine would have never thought she'd be inquiring about a slobbering animal's welfare.

"You named it, huh?" J.D. said with a soft chuckle.

"Of course I did." Josephine folded her arms beneath her breasts. "I couldn't keep calling it 'it,' or Adelaide like Boots started doing."

"Adelaide? That's my grandmother's name."

"I'm aware of that. Boots doesn't like her."

"Boots doesn't like anyone."

"I think he likes you." Josephine gazed at the panorama of sage as it rolled by. "You two never give each other a chance to become friends."

J.D. frowned. "We've got too many differences to become friends."

"Being family is a start that you can't ignore." She plucked a piece of lint off the fabric at her knee. "I've seen how Boots is. I truly believe he thinks he's not needed. That you don't trust him."

"I don't."

"Why not?"

"Because he's old and foolish. He doesn't think." J.D.'s eyes narrowed on the double row of ruts. "Why are we talking about this?"

"Why not? We've talked about a lot of things these past days. Mostly how important the cattle company is to you. But you never talk about Boots. I talk about my parents. You never talk about yours."

"There's nothing to say. Eugenia lives in Boston with her mother, and Boots lives out here with me."

"Don't you miss your mother?"

J.D. grew pensive. "I do."

She wondered how he felt about his parents' separation . . . how he would feel about divorce. Divorce was not widely common. Its social pressures and prejudices inflicted injury on all those it concerned. It was a source of revelation, about manners and attitudes, and not everyone accepted that divorce was the best way for both parties. Had J.D. ever considered his parents' divorce, or was he one of those who preferred to keep marital bonds tied, even though that meant stretching them out for miles as the individuals went on with their lives without each other? She wouldn't ask him. She was afraid of his answer.

"Would you ever go to Boston to visit her?" Josephine ventured.

This time, his answer was immediate. "No. I don't like big cities."

For some reason, Josephine's hopes fell. What had she been thinking? J.D. McCall didn't care for "citified ways." His mother had been a city woman, and she'd gone back to the place she knew best. It could be this way for Josephine as well, though where she was running was certainly not back to the scene of the hideous offense. She was going to another place, another city that in many ways would be like the one she'd left.

In San Francisco, she'd have conveniences and luxuries that the open West did not provide. Her employment opportunities would be broader, and the hiring of a woman with her character would be more acceptable. She'd been thinking about what she'd do once she got there . . . perhaps see if a publishing company could use her reading services, or perhaps finally get hired as a hostess in a restaurant. She would be in a more familiar setting. In a city with an affluent population. And with people of her own breeding and background. But did she really want to surround herself with such shallowness again?

No city position truly excited her. Not after she'd seen the excitement of the West through her own eyes instead of Pearl's.

All this time, she'd wanted to run from a place where the citizens were oppressive and tunneled inside their rules and decorums—perhaps to a place that ran on the very same principle. Did she truly want to be guarded by rigid society once more? It was all she knew . . . until she'd come to Sienna.

Sienna had not been what she'd dreamed of as a safe haven, but when she reflected on it now, she could do so with a slight smile of fondness. Mr. Klauffman had been more than kind, and even Effie Grass had been accommodating. Also, Sheriff Tuttle had offered her money to see her through. In New York, people like these would be swallowed by those who took advantage.

Josephine didn't want to think she was growing accustomed to the bones that lay bleaching in the sun or the bawling of cows and the nickers of horses. She didn't want to think that she was becoming attached to the notion of cooking for a large group of men, but she sort of was, now that her errors were less frequent.

And what of J.D. McCall himself? She was . . . fond of him. More than fond. But she feared losing her heart so soon. Hers had been battered. Severely. She couldn't risk being hurt again. Not yet. Not when the wounds she'd had inflicted on her were still just as raw as they'd been the day Hugh had accused her of being an adulteress. And when he'd publicly humiliated her. For that, she couldn't head blindly into another relationship. No matter that she saw J.D. as vastly different from Hugh, she just could not allow herself to fall in love with J.D.

They rode the rest of the way in meditative silence. The sun was settling in the western sky when they ambled down the drive to the ranch. Toby and some of the other dogs raced to greet them. She and J.D. were the last to return home. Rio, along with the cowboys, had moved ahead of them just after dinner. In the end, it had been just J.D. and Josephine with nothing but a faint line of dust ahead of them to guide them back.

J.D. steered the chuck around to the front of the house and engaged the brake. Boots sat in one of the rawhide chairs on the porch, a tabby cat in his lap. His knobby fingers were buried in the fur as he stroked the cat behind its ears and on its back.

"Y'all raised a hell of a lot of dust coming in here," he commented, making no move to shoo the cat from the cradle of his legs.

J.D. didn't respond, but Josephine gave Boots a soft smile.

The corners of his mouth twitched but never went up enough to be considered a full-fledged smile back at her.

One-Eyed Hazel came out from the barn. "Boss. Good to have you back," he said, then his voice went down an octave. "Sorry to hear about Orley, boss. He was a fine hand. Me and Boots, we went into Sienna yesterday and saw to Orley's momma and poppa before they took Orley home."

"You rode into Sienna?" J.D. asked, a slight lift of incredulity in his tone. "That's thirty miles round-trip. You went in just to see if Orley's folks were all right?"

"It was Boots's idea. Actually, he insisted."

J.D. shot his gaze to Boots. He shoved the cat off his lap and stood on bent knees. "Get the hell off me, you gawddamned cat." He made a big to-do about brushing the cat hair off his trousers, then he glared at J.D. "I wanted to buy some cigars. I was all out, so I made Hazel take me. I forgot Orley's kin was coming in."

Josephine could clearly see that Boots was embellishing. He'd gone into Sienna to make sure Orley was properly taken care of and that his parents were not unduly distraught. How could Boots be such a mean old thing one minute and so sweet her heart ached the next?

J.D. removed his hat, forked his fingers through his hair, then said, "I'm obliged you were there, Boots. Hazel."

"Sure, boss."

"I'm sure Mr. and Mrs. Woodard very much appreciated your being there," Josephine added. "It was very thoughtful. Of the both of you."

Boots was having a rough time with the consideration being put his way. He shuffled toward the porch rail, grabbed hold, and snorted. "Well, I figured y'all would be coming in about now. No need to put up a sweat in the kitchen. I've got the stove covered. It's good eatin's tonight." With a crooked-toothed grin, he proclaimed, "Creamed corn on toast. Y'all's favorite."

Boots came into the kitchen as Josephine finished the dishes. He took up his spot on the stool and stared at her. She was getting better at ignoring him when he tried to eyeball her to death. She went about her duties, paying him no mind.

After a while, he stated, "You skewered a snake to save J.D."

She glanced at him, surprised that he'd bring that up. To her, it seemed like it had happened a long time ago. "I had a lucky shot."

"That's not how the boys tell it." Boots scratched his jaw. "They say that only somebody who knew what they were doing could have hit that snake."

"I've had archery training."

"I reckon you have." He grew thoughtful a moment, then said, "Y'all joked with the boys at the supper table."

"Did I?"

"Jidge made a comment about the biscuits being plumb good when you refilled his coffee. Y'all said it was because you didn't flavor them washers with leather no more."

"Hmm." Josephine had learned that *washers* was

the term used for biscuits when they were tough as an old boot. The comment had come naturally to her; she hadn't thought it over until Boots brought it up. But she *had* been joshing with Jidge Dooly.

Pausing with the soapy washrag in her hand, Josephine straightened. She never had been very adept at light banter. At parties, she allowed those around her to carry the conversation, not wanting to say something inappropriate to one of Hugh's guests.

"I never would have pegged you," Boots was saying, drawing Josephine from her thoughts.

"Pegged me for what?"

Boots gazed at her, the stubble on his chin glistening white in the early lamplight of the room. His gray hair fell over his ears, and his watery blue eyes appeared tired. He stood and went toward the dining room door. "Pegged you to be one of us." Then he pushed the door open and let himself out, leaving Josephine to ponder his words.

She remained motionless for a time, trying to come to terms with what he'd said. She tried her best to fend off the feelings of sentimentality and a sense of belonging. She couldn't stay here . . . she didn't want to stay here. Or at least that's what she tried to convince herself.

A while later, J.D. came in through the back door with Hazel. They carried a plain metal bathtub and set it in the middle of the kitchen floor.

J.D. raked his hair from off his brow. "I figured you may be wanting to use this."

Josephine felt as if she'd been sent to heaven. A bath. A real one. "Yes, I would," she replied.

Hazel, who had removed his hat in her company and was twisting the brim in his grasp, scooted backward toward the open door. "I'll pump some water."

"Thank you, Hazel."

"Ma'am."

Then he disappeared, and Josephine hunted down

the big soup pot so that she could heat the water. The coals in the stove were still hot from Boots's use for the creamed corn—which had sent a grumble around the table. Just to be on the safe side that the fire would be hot enough, she added another piece of wood.

"You do that like you know what you're doing," J.D. commented as she swung the door on the stove closed with a folded towel.

"I believe I am finding my way around."

Leaning up against the counter, he smiled. "You didn't know squat about a kitchen until I hired you, did you?"

"As a matter of fact, I knew quite a bit. Only not the actual mechanics of cooking that went on in the kitchen. But I was skilled in how to check the organization of the larder and the menus."

"At your parents' house?"

Josephine stilled. He had her there. She could fess up with the truth, or she could hedge. Her eyes met his. He was giving her every opportunity to be truthful. But she couldn't. Not yet . . . not to him, not to anyone.

"Yes, in my parents' house."

Hazel returned with two buckets of water. After pouring one into the tub, he poured the second into the pot on the stove. After repeating this ritual a half-dozen times, the tub was full enough for her to use.

J.D. and Hazel departed, and Josephine pulled the shade down on the door and slid the curtains closed on the windows. She went into her room, got the toiletry articles she needed, and went back into the kitchen.

With the fire burning softly in the stove, there wasn't a chill in the room as she disrobed. She tested the water with her fingertips. Wonderful. Josephine pulled the pins from her hair and stepped inside the inviting water.

Once in the tub, she scooted down as far as she could so that her entire body was enveloped by the bone-melting warmth. She closed her eyes and stayed that way for a long time before soaping her body and washing her hair. She had saved some clean water for rinsing, then stood and dried off with a towel. She dressed in the cotton nightgown that had been in the valise, then collected her brush to sit next to the stove.

She'd just finished running the brush through her hair enough times to leave the ends fuzzy, when a knock came on the door that led to the dining room.

"You out yet, Jo?"

Josephine felt as if the air was charged with the timbre of J.D.'s voice. "Um, yes."

"I was going to take a bath myself when you're through."

If Josephine had known that, she wouldn't have stayed in so long. She went to the door and opened it. "I didn't meant to be so long. If you had told me . . ."

"No need. I wanted you to take your time." J.D. stood over her, seeming taller and broader than any man she'd ever met. His hair curled over his collar, his shirt wasn't buttoned to the top, and she could see the play of dark hair on his chest at the opening. When she gazed downward, she noted that his shirt wasn't tucked into his denims, nor did he wear any socks or boots.

He looked relaxed. And comfortable. As if they should be getting ready for bed together. As if they could be holding each other beneath the covers and talking about the day's events. It was a strange feeling, wanting to share things like that.

"I'll help you empty the water," she offered, putting a hand to the ribbon at her throat. The nightgown was nothing lavish by any means; she'd had the finest satin and silks. But the simple cotton didn't make her feel any less feminine. She wished she had a robe for it; the material was thin, and in places she wasn't sure the light couldn't filter right through.

"It's getting too late for that. I'll use yours if you don't mind."

"Oh . . . no, I suppose I don't."

"That is, unless you've gotten the bottom as thick as silt with all that dirt you've been carrying around."

She froze, then quickly peered into the tub.

J.D.'s laugh had her turning around. "I was kidding, Jo." His eyes creased very slightly at the corners.

"Yes, of course."

He brought his fingers to her chin and tipped her face up to him. "You're awfully pretty with your hair unpinned." His lips touched hers. Light; soft; dreamy. Her eyelids slipped closed. She kissed him back. Just enough to torture herself and make her want him in the worst way.

J.D. pulled back. "I'd love to, Jo, but I'm wearing five days' worth of the trail." His mouth pressed quickly over hers. "Wait for me?"

"Where?"

"On the porch. Boots may pretend he's deaf, but he can hear when the mood suits him."

Josephine nodded with a knowing smile. "I'll wait for you."

J.D. pushed open the screened door and let himself onto the porch. Josephine sat in one of the rawhide-bottomed chairs he and Boots had made some five years back. Eugenia had wanted a porch swing, but Boots had never gotten around to it, and now there was no need.

Josephine wore her nightgown but had gathered a shirt from her room before leaving. The evening air was pleasant for May, a slight chill, but with the leftover warmth of the day still collected in the wooden planks to make the porch comfortable.

Taking a seat next to her, J.D. put his legs out in front of him. He'd thrown on a pair of clean trousers and a shirt. Nothing else. He hadn't wanted to take the time to dress fully. He wanted to be with Josephine.

The atmosphere over supper had felt so comfortable, J.D. wasn't in any hurry to look for another cook. And none had come his way while they'd been gone.

In the distance, coyotes called. It was too early for crickets, but silver-winged moths were attracted to the soft slice of light that poured out from the living room. The insects batted and bounced off the screen.

Jo had tucked her feet beneath her on the seat of the chair so that the fullness of her nightgown covered her knees and the length of her legs. Her hair cascaded over one shoulder. She hadn't braided it, and he hoped it was because he'd told her he liked it down.

"You tired?" he asked, feeling as if he was at his first dance, trying to win over the prettiest girl in the room.

Her reply came softly. "A little."

"It's been a long day. If you want to turn in . . ." he began, but couldn't get the rest of the sentence out. He didn't want to be accommodating, but he felt he owed it to her. She'd been riding on a hard bench seat for the better portion of ten hours.

"Do you want to turn in?" she asked, her chin lifting from the fold in her nightgown as she gazed at him.

"Naw, I need some time to settle down."

"Then I'll stay and sit with you for a while, if that's all right," she added in a rush.

"I'd like that, Jo."

Across the yard, the tabby pranced out of the barn and took off in a run toward the pasture. A few seconds later, a kitten appeared, then one of the other barn cats came out, collected the tiny ball of fur in its mouth, and traipsed back inside through a wide crack in one of the boards.

"Looks like we'll have some more mousers around here." J.D. put his arms on the rails of the chair. "Boots's cat is a get-around tom."

"Boots claims he doesn't like that tabby, but I think he loves it to death," Josephine said. "I never had a

pet when I was a child. I think I would have liked to
have a cat."

"You want to see the kittens?" J.D. asked, then felt
like a fool. Of course, she could care less about some
free-ranging cats. She didn't even like animals, so
she'd probably hate the smell of the barn.

"I don't have any shoes on."

"Neither do I, but I'll carry you over."

"I'm too heavy," she blurted.

"No you're not."

"But you said—"

"Never mind what I said in Klauffman's. I was full
of it."

J.D. rose and held out his hand for Josephine. She
took it and stood. They walked to the middle of the
porch and down the steps, then he swung her up into
his arms. Her feet dangled over as he crossed the yard.
He didn't mind the prick and dig of the occasional
rock or sticker. Holding Josephine made the trip
worth it.

She didn't feel too much for him. In fact, she felt
just right. Though she'd trimmed down some since
he'd hired her on, he liked the voluptuous curves she
still had.

Once he reached the barn, he had to put her down
to lift the latch. The inside was dark, but he knew his
way around to the rafter where they kept a lantern and
a box of matches on the ledge.

"Stay there," he said, then struck the match and
brought the large space to light.

The floor had been raked out, the hard-packed dirt
easy on his feet as he went back for her.

"My guess is they're up there." He pointed to the
hayloft, then took her hand. The distance to the tall,
wooden ladder was short, and J.D. stepped aside so
Josephine could climb up first.

She put her hands on the edges but didn't move.
"It's not that far up. I'll be right behind you. Lift the

hem of your nightgown and tie it in a knot so you won't trip over it."

She reached for the white bottom, and he helped her take the fullness and twist it into a single knot that raised the hem up to her knees. "You're all right," he reassured her.

Josephine put her foot on the rung and climbed. J.D. stayed directly behind her, his feet on the rung just below hers. Once at the top, she leaned over onto the sprinkling of hay. J.D. reached her and went around. He put his hands on her shoulders and helped her up.

She climbed to her knees, then stood.

He brushed a piece of hay from her hair, then squeezed her hand. Walking toward the large opening that was closed off, J.D. pushed one of the doors open. A pulley was on the outside. They used it to haul the bales of hay to the loft.

The scents of night mingled in to stir with the grassy scent of straw and musty wood. From the corner came a mewing sound. The open hay door let in enough starlight for J.D. to make his way over, his hand still holding Josephine's.

"There they are," he said, bending to one knee. "Looks like five of them."

"They're not all yellow like Boots's cat."

"Nope. Black and white like their mother. Except that one. It's got the stripes."

The mother cat lay on her side, the kittens curled around her, several nursing.

J.D. straightened and took Josephine to the opening. From this position, they could see above the house's rooftop to the bluffs. A bat flew over the chimney and flapped off into the darkness.

Sitting down, J.D. took Josephine with him. She sat by his side, and they looked out together.

"It's so quiet here," Josephine reflected. "I never thought I'd like the quiet, but it's nice. I got so used to hearing the sound of horses and the voices of people on the street below my window, I didn't think I could sleep to anything else but noise."

"Some people can adapt, I reckon . . ." His voice trailed as he thought of Eugenia. "And others can't."

A light wind fell through the opening and ruffled the hay. A few stalks blew across Josephine's bare calf. One tumbled into her lap. J.D. plucked it away, then put his hand on her shoulder and gathered her close to his side.

He wasn't good at expressing his thoughts and opinions. What was on his mind wasn't something he could just say. He needed to consider every corner of the corral before he declared any promises.

"Were you in love with that man?" he asked in a quiet tone.

He felt Josephine stiffen a little, but he didn't let her go. His fingers grazed the soft fabric of her sleeve as he caressed her arm.

"I believed myself to be," she replied. "I . . . yes, I was. It's not fair to say that I wasn't. I did love him. But I don't anymore." She turned to him. "I don't want to talk about that tonight. I'd rather not talk at all . . ."

Leaning into his chest, she kissed his cheek, then his mouth. J.D. slipped his arms around her waist and brought her to him as he lay back in the hay, taking her with him. The softness of her nightgown inched higher up her thigh. His one hand cupped her buttocks as the other slipped across warm skin. She wore no underdrawers. The realization left him eager to touch all of her without the constraints of clothing.

His lips brushed hers, then he pulled back and brought her gown over her head. Within seconds, he'd divested himself of his own clothing and spread the garments out as a makeshift bed to keep the slivers of hay away.

Lying atop the scattered clothing, he brought Josephine to his side once more, stroking the valley of her waist. He explored her breast and brushed her tight nipple. Then he took her into his arms.

There was a certain urgency this time, unlike the slow hours they'd shared in the Wampum Saloon. He needed her, like he'd needed no other woman.

Pinning her beneath him, he buried his hands in the curls of her sweet-smelling hair as his mouth swooped down to capture hers. She returned the kiss, lingering, testing. She parted his lips with her tongue and took control of the kiss.

He sensed her eagerness, and without any preludes other than blinding need, he took her. The pleasure was pure and harmonious as they moved together. Their legs intertwined. Blood pounded through his heart.

A moan slipped through her lips, and he caught it with his own, pressing a kiss to her as he joined her in the outcry of release.

He savored the feeling of her, keeping her close, feeling her breath on his heated skin. Feeling himself inside as the turbulence of their lovemaking pulsed around him.

J.D. didn't want to let her go. Not now, or ever. But he feared that if he pushed for her to stay right at this moment, she'd run. And that was the last thing he wanted her to do.

Instead, he'd have to show her all she'd be missing if she left here. Because he didn't want to let her go.

CHAPTER

→ 21 ←

J.D. spent the next several days showing Josephine the land surrounding the ranch, hoping to convince her he wasn't a fly-by-night rancher. He took her on a line ride so that she could get an idea of the boundaries. The barbed-wire fences weren't his idea, but the encroaching homesteaders had made them a necessity since last year. Those line fences seemed to have no beginning or end, stretching for miles down through gullies or up over hills and ridges. Camps, all just a day's ride away from the main house, had been established for the cowboys on repair duty. Each was nothing more than a framed shack with a stove and a bed.

Boots maintained the camps for J.D. Hazel would hitch up the buckboard for him, and Boots came out to make sure the places were usable. He'd also ride down the endless miles of fencing to mark off the places it needed to be repaired.

Yesterday, J.D. had taken her to the top of Tepee Range so that she could have a good look. He'd pointed out the direction of the one-hundred-sixty-acre parcel he intended buying. She'd asked him about the bluffs and the pond, the size of the spread and the number of cattle he had, then she'd asked about the road that led to Sienna.

That had put a damper on J.D.'s easy mood. Her wanting to know about Sienna was something he'd hoped she would have gotten out of her mind. Obviously, she was still set on leaving, in spite of the nights they shared together.

After their first night back when they'd gone to the loft to see the kittens, they'd met there each subsequent night. J.D. looked forward to those hours he could spend with Josephine in his arms, but he didn't like sneaking around. He didn't want to have to worry about Boots discovering them, or any of the boys. He wanted her in the house with him. In his room. And in his bed.

As his wife.

He'd made up his mind this morning as the dawn had streaked across the sky. While there were still several hours of darkness left, he'd saddled up Tequila and ridden to the Tepee Range to sit and think. He'd left Josephine somewhere around eleven. He'd walked her back to the house and seen her to her room. They'd said their good nights and gone their separate ways.

J.D. was tired of pretending. He'd fallen in love with her. He couldn't be sure when exactly, but he had.

He hadn't been close to many women in his life. The war had come and turned things upside down for him and his family. Balls and barbecues had ceased, just when J.D. was growing old enough to appreciate them. Then he'd gone off to fight, only to return to bitterness and a house that no longer reminded him of home. His trek out West had been one of hard labors. No time for romance or dalliance with a woman beyond what could be paid for in a night's time.

Once he'd reached the Wyoming Territory, he began work for Dillard, and once again, any extra hours were spent on much-needed sleep or short rendezvous in town. He'd been going on this way for too long ever to find one woman and spend enough time with her to get to know her.

Although J.D. sensed there were a lot of underlying layers to Josephine, he knew she was a warm and giving woman. Able to learn what she didn't know and unafraid of the rigors of ranch life. She'd more than proven herself on the drive.

He enjoyed her company. Her smile. Her laugh. He loved to listen to her play the fiddle, and she'd saved his life at the Wampum.

A combination of many things made him love her: beauty, strength, and resolve. But what he loved most about her was her willingness to try. She could do what Eugenia hadn't been willing to do: try and make it out here.

J.D. wasn't sure how he could convince her to stay. But he'd shown her all there was to him, all that he'd accomplished on the ranch. He could do no more than to come right out and ask her to stay as his partner.

And he intended to do just that after the branding party tonight.

Josephine found out quickly that branding wasn't a pleasant thing to watch.

"Fire's hot!" Rio called from the corral.

J.D. nodded and waved his arm to Gus astride his horse in the branding pen.

Birdie began to herd the calves, one at a time, toward the area where the branding was done.

Rio stayed at the fire, while Print and Jidge used their lariats. They roped a calf, one on the forelegs and the other on the hind. The calf was held securely as J.D. took up the handle of the iron and moved in a rocking motion.

Rio handled the earmarking and dehorning, while

J.D. set the iron down to doctor any of the cows' ailments, then castrate the bull calves.

Josephine couldn't stop the tiny scream as he made the cut, then tossed a bloody lump in a bucket of water.

"Big deal," Boots scoffed. "A little cut, and that's that."

She had her hand to her throat, her pulse thrumming beneath her fingertips. "I wasn't expecting him to do that." She swallowed. "I mean . . . doesn't that hurt?"

"What do y'all want me to do? Go out there and tell J.D. I want to be next so that I can tell you for sure?"

"Of course not!" she shot back. Boots was the most infuriating man sometimes. "I was just wondering if there isn't a better way to do that. You know, like giving the poor thing some medicine first . . . or something."

"Nope. Just cut 'em and throw 'em. Then fry 'em."

"W-what?"

Boots gave her a toothy grin. "J.D.'s going to cook them up for supper. We're having . . ." He paused, his face screwed up with concentration, then worry. "I can't remember. It's one of them foreign words. What are they called?" He scratched behind his ear. "It'll come to me if I think hard enough."

Josephine waited. And waited. She didn't want to prod and get him excited. He'd been doing better at home, much less forgetful. She'd still caught him boiling a pot of water dry on the stove, and there were the little mistakes like leaving the back door open and walking off, or going outside without his boots on and gazing bewildered at his stockinged feet. But in his own surroundings, he generally moved with more confidence. She didn't think he was ailing from any disease. He was just feeling the effects of old age and a natural absentmindedness.

"Cajonies!" he declared at last.

"*Cajonies?*"

"Y'all can be a real bonehead at times." Boots fit one foot on the bottom rung of the fence. "*Cajonies* are testicles."

Josephine didn't feel any better having had the word spelled out to her. "I'm not eating any . . . *cajonies,*" she said, tripping over the pronunciation. "I'd rather have creamed corn on toast." Quickly, she realized her error and tried to make a fast recovery. "That is to say, I prefer your style of cooking to J.D.'s if that's all that's on his menu for this evening."

"I'm not cooking tonight, so you're out of luck."

"Then I'll have a plain can of corn."

"Suit yourself."

Josephine folded her arms beneath her breasts and watched J.D. and the others work with the calves. His chaps were dusty from the dirt in the pen as he bent down numerous times to tend the cows suspended between the taut ropes of Jidge and Print.

The back of J.D.'s shirt strained as he knelt over a calf, which despite being roped kicked up a cloud of dust. He didn't make a cut on this one, merely slathered a paste of some sort on its tongue and then nodded for Rio to let it go.

The thought dawned on Josephine that Freckles would have to be put through such an ordeal. Hazel had taken over the feeding of the bottle to Freckles, but Josephine went and visited the calf in its corral by the shed. Freckles was gaining weight and growing into a nice-looking cow. If a cow could be called nice-looking.

As if summoned by her thoughts, the next calf to be branded was her own freckle-faced calf. Josephine stood taller, her arms over the railing. She hated the thought of Freckles being hurt with that iron that burned the hide right off with an M and a small c.

"Why do they have to do this?" Josephine questioned as Freckles struggled in the ropes.

"To declare ownership and to prevent theft," Boots said between puffs of his cigar. "A problem that has always plagued cattlemen."

"But I own that calf. J.D. gave her to me. I don't want a brand on her."

Josephine paused, her words coming back to haunt her. The way she was talking, it was like she was planning on staying. Like she meant to be around to watch Freckles grow up. It was becoming increasingly hard not to lose her heart over a calf . . . or a man . . .

With a frown, Josephine watched as Freckles was doctored and branded.

"Y'all should know about brands," Boots offered. "A brand needs three things. Got to look good and sound good, be easy to run, and planned so it won't fit under any other brand around. An X is always good, so's a bar or a diamond, with any good-sounding letter."

Nodding, Josephine didn't really hear. She was struck by a wave of melancholy. She would miss this place. More than she ever thought possible.

Dust was stirred by an unfamiliar rider coming down the lane. Once at the yard, he dismounted and tethered his horse on the hitching post. Josephine watched as Hazel went over to meet him, and then he came back and got J.D. The two men disappeared into the house.

"Who was that, Hazel?" Boots hollered.

"Matt Sellars. Said Mr. Klauffman sent him."

Josephine had had enough of the branding, so she decided to read in her room instead. She assumed J.D. had business, and rather than enter the house from the front, she went around to the back. At the steps, she plucked up the hem of her calico skirt. She'd tried the garment on that morning and had been delighted it fit along with the plain cotton shirtwaist.

After breakfast, J.D. had cornered her in the larder,

stolen a kiss, and told her she looked sweet in the new clothes. She'd kissed him right back with a smile, missing him the minute he left to go to the corral.

As she entered the kitchen, voices from the living room drifted to her. She paused, not wanting to listen in, but several words had made her still: "I've done a fair amount of ranch cooking."

She inched toward the door to the dining room and eased it open a fraction.

"Klauffman said you pay a decent wage and that this is a good outfit to work for," came a man's voice.

"I appreciate Zev sending you out my way."

"Well, sir, I could surely use the job. I fix a mighty fine stew."

Heartsick, Josephine could listen no longer. She let the door fall into place and went into her room. Sitting on the bed, she felt empty inside. But what was transpiring between J.D. and another cook should have come as no surprise to her.

J.D. had been honest from the start. He'd told her the job was temporary. Only lately she'd . . . Oh, never mind. It was just as well that this had happened. It was the eye-opening she needed. She'd been beginning to think . . .

Pulling in a short breath, she stood and collected the boots she'd discarded this morning in favor of her old lace-ups. Inside the left boot was the money she'd earned to date.

Fifteen dollars. Taking it out, she put it in her handbag, then left the house.

She found Hazel repairing a hinge on the barn door.

"Hazel, I need you to drive me into Sienna. Right away."

He looked up, his expression questioning. "Ma'am?"

"I'm all out of flour, and I need to bake biscuits."

"But last time J.D. was at the merc, he bought enough to see us through to the end of the month."

She clutched her pocketbook to her waist. "It went bad. Weevils got into it."

Setting his hammer down, Hazel straightened one of his suspender straps. "Does the boss know about this?"

"Yes," she lied coolly. "He gave me permission to go, and he said to hurry back because of the branding party tonight. So we better not dally."

"All right." But his tone didn't really indicate he was assured that what they were doing had truly been cleared by the boss.

Once the team was hitched and Hazel led them out of the barn, Josephine climbed up and took a seat. As Hazel clicked his tongue to the mules and they moved into motion, Boots yelled across the expanse, "Where are y'all going?"

Josephine didn't reply. She merely waved and left him to wonder.

On the ride to Sienna, Josephine mulled over the past weeks with a clarity she hadn't been equipped with until now. All along she'd been cautious of falling in love too quickly, but she had practically done just that. Whether she had known a man ten months or a matter of weeks, Josephine had been a fool to lose her heart twice.

Sienna came into view long miles later, and Josephine told Hazel to go to the train depot instead of the mercantile.

"Ma'am?"

"It's best you don't know anything, Hazel. Just take me to the station."

The ramshackle little building was as she remembered it. She opened the door and spoke to Mr. Vernier.

"I'd like to buy a ticket to San Francisco. I believe the fare is eight dollars."

He squinted at her through his spectacles. "Yes, ma'am, it still is."

Opening her purse, she counted the correct amount and handed it to him.

"The train doesn't leave until Thursday," he said while making out her ticket. "That's five days away."

"Yes, I'm aware of that. I just wanted to make sure I had a ticket for it."

He handed her the receipt, then removed his glasses. "Your baggage never showed up."

"I assumed not. But it doesn't really matter now. I can't fit into those clothes anymore." Then she safely stored the ticket inside her handbag. "Good day, Mr. Vernier. I'll see you on Thursday."

"Why did Hazel drive you to Sienna?" J.D. asked upon their return. He stood waiting in the yard as Hazel pulled up the wagon and applied the brakes. Wearing his work clothes, he was splattered with blood, paste, and grit.

Josephine disembarked without any assistance. She'd made Hazel promise not to tell J.D. where she'd gone, and she'd asked him please to confirm her story that she had gone into Sienna to buy some candies— which she had done at the last minute.

"I was out of butterscotches."

She glanced at Hazel, who wasn't a good liar, and she hoped J.D. wouldn't notice that the man couldn't meet anyone's gaze.

"So you drove fifteen miles just to get some?"

"I know how much the boys like them, so of course." Hazel wasn't the only one who couldn't look people in the eye. She herself could barely pass her gaze over J.D. "Did your company leave?"

A frown marred J.D.'s forehead. "He wasn't company."

"Then it must have been business."

"Yes, it was."

Josephine didn't want to find out any more. She noticed a cooking area had been set up by the corral. A pot of water had been started over a fire. "Well, let's not delay the party any more." Her voice sounded cool and impartial to her ears. She held on to her purse as if it were her lifeline, and in the other hand she clutched the paper-wrapped candy. "I've never seen how *cajonies* are fixed."

"All right . . ." J.D. said slowly, staring at her as if he were going to put a hole through her. "Let me get cleaned up first."

Half an hour later, J.D. came out of the house with his clothes changed.

Boots sat on the porch dozing in one of the chairs.

As the screen slammed shut, Boots's head snapped up, and his eyes flew open wide.

"Good gawd!" he hollered, the snuffed-out cigar that had been clamped between his lips rolling across the porch.

J.D. put a hand on Boots's shoulder—the first intimate contact she'd ever seen pass between the two.

"Sorry about that, Boots," J.D. said, then moved to the fire.

Her gaze lingered momentarily on Boots, who hadn't shrunk beneath the touch of his son's hand. The older man watched as J.D. strode toward the cooking area that had been set up.

Josephine's own eyes followed him, too. J.D. had rolled up the sleeves of a fresh blue calico shirt and had tied a white flour sack apron around his middle.

He looked impossibly handsome, with a new richness to his tan and with his hair wet at the ears and combed beneath the brim of his hat. She couldn't recall ever seeing him in the trousers he was wearing. They weren't denim, but a canvas type of duckcloth in a buttery shade like the color of biscuits when they turned out the way they were supposed to.

She tried to remain dispassionate. She would have to go through the motions of the next five days without breaking down.

He took up a big spoon, the kind she used for beef stew, and scooped up a heaping amount of lard. He flicked it into one of the frying pans, and the grease sizzled as it melted. A smile lit his mouth when he saw her, then he returned to the chore of cooking.

Josephine fought against the pangs of love that struck a chord within. She couldn't let herself be in love with him. She just couldn't!

J.D. kept at the frying for most of the supper, removing a pan full of the *cajonies* just as he put more in. The boys, Hazel included, ate them up as fast as J.D. could make them. Rio sat on a bale of hay, periodically asking her if she was sure she didn't want to try one. Each time she declined.

Rio had been excessively polite with her ever since the Wampum Saloon; his flirtations had ceased from that day on. She couldn't be sure why, but she was glad she didn't have to be uncomfortable around him any longer. Perhaps he realized that she wasn't interested in him that way.

Josephine passed on the supper, unable to eat no matter what the fare was. When the cowboys had all eaten their fill, they stayed in the yard to tell stories and drink the bottle of whiskey J.D. had uncorked for them. Even Hazel had lifted his glass when the bottle passed by. She felt guilty for having made him a part of her lie, but she couldn't help it.

Since he'd done the cooking, J.D. said he'd clean up.

"I could use some help, Jo," he said as he stood on the porch.

She wanted to say no, but she caught herself nodding and going to him.

A single kerosene lamp lit the kitchen, and J.D. filled the dry sink. Neither was very talkative as they got the dishes going. After a while, the silence got the best of Josephine, and she said, "Clouds are gathering in the western sky," trying to keep the sadness at bay in her tone. "Maybe it will rain tonight."

"They weren't rain clouds." J.D. dunked another plate into the rinse water. "Rain clouds are dark. Like the gray of a hot iron."

"What are you going to do if it doesn't rain?" She laid the clean plate on the counter.

"We'll lose some cattle. It happens."

"What about Freckles?"

"I don't know, Jo. Only the strong survive. You have to know that about this place. Life can be hard."

She knew. Too well.

J.D. paused and let the forks in his grasp fall into the washtub. He grew still, then he faced her and dried off his hands.

"What's the matter, Jo? You've been acting strangely ever since you came back from town."

"I'm just tired is all," she begged off.

He gazed at her for so long, she lowered her lashes after feeling her eyes fill with tears.

"I planned on doing this another way," he said softly. "A better place than the kitchen." A chorus of the cowboys' laughter from the yard drifted through the open door to the house. "A lot quieter, too."

He put his hands on her waist and brought her close. He smelled pleasantly of soap and campfire smoke. She wanted to lean into him. But she couldn't move. She could barely breathe. Somewhere in the recesses of her mind, this scene made sense. She could see where it was leading, hear what he was going to say. No matter how much she wanted to stop him before he began, she couldn't tell him not to speak.

"Jo . . ." He caught her chin with his damp fingers. "This isn't how it ought to be when a man says what I've got to say, but I'm not much good at the kinds of things you deserve, like flowers and such. I expect you know that already about me.

"I'm just an ordinary man. Nothing fancy. Not like you're used to. All I have is what you see. Nothing much in the bank by way of money. It's all here. In the place, the cattle.

"It's a good way of life, but it's a hard one. It takes a special kind of woman to fit in."

She could barely meet his eyes. Those wonderful eyes of his, so soft and sincere. Her own were filling with tears, and her vision clouded.

"I didn't think that you could when I first saw you, but now I know that you can." He squeezed her waist a little, his fingers slightly trembling against her. "I don't know how to say this, other than to come right out with it. I love you, Jo. Will you marry me?"

Josephine couldn't keep her tears from spilling any longer. They fell down her cheeks, and she took in gulps of air to calm herself.

"I . . . can't," she said on a shaky breath. "I'm sorry. I can't marry you."

She broke free of him and went into her room, blindly reaching for her purse. She fumbled inside for her handkerchief. Her calling card case caught on the lace edge and came out with the square cloth. The ticket spilled out with the gold case and tumbled over her knees. Both fell to the floor, the cards scattering across the bare wood.

When she turned, J.D. stood in the doorway.

"What's that?" His gaze was fixed on the train ticket.

"I'm leaving this Thursday for San Francisco."

"You went into Sienna today to buy a ticket."

"Yes."

"Why?"

"Because you don't need me anymore. You've hired another cook."

"What the hell are you talking about?"

She stared at her ticket on the floor. "That man who was here earlier was answering your advertisement."

"He was, but I didn't hire him."

Her heartbeat tripped. "You didn't?"

"Why should I hire him when I already have a cook?" He smoothed his hair back with his fingers. "I was hoping you'd stay . . . and after we were married, I'd hire another cook then."

Josephine tried to hide her confusion. "But I thought . . ." Her words trailed as she watched J.D.

He slowly bent to pick up one of the cards that had landed faceup. His eyes narrowed as he read the engraving set in the pearl-white paper.

"Is this you?" His head lifted. "You're Mrs. Hugh Whittaker?" he asked, incredulous. Then, with more accusation than statement, he said, "You're married."

Her voice wavered as a tear spilled into her lap. "I was."

"Was?" His brow shot up.

The cold truth touched her lips; then, for the first time, she openly admitted, "I'm divorced."

J.D. felt as if he'd been kicked in the gut twice by a colt. The air went out of his lungs, and it took him a minute to recover. Not only had she bought a ticket to leave him when he'd been making plans for her to stay, but she had been hiding who she really was. He could only deal with one thing at a time.

Divorce.

It wasn't common. In fact, his only knowledge of one being granted was a case of adultery.

If he'd been thinking clearly, he would have immediately acquitted Josephine of any wrongdoing. She had admitted to having only one lover. That had to have been her husband.

But several seconds passed before this sank in. It was too late for him to erase his tightly strained expression. She saw what he was feeling. A combination of twisted anger and an undertone of chilling contempt.

He didn't really mean either of them, but they'd been his first reactions.

"What happened?" he asked, setting the name cards on her washstand. He stood back a few feet from the bed. Far enough so that he could lean against the door frame. He had to put some distance between them so he could think while she talked.

His senses were still tangled up in the sweet scent of her when he'd held her and the softness of her beneath his hands.

Josephine wiped her eyes with her handkerchief, then set it in her lap. "I was married for almost six years."

That didn't matter to him. "Who asked for the divorce?"

"My husband."

The answer wrapped around him and squeezed. "The grounds?"

"Infidelity." She spoke the word coolly and with detachment. She rigidly held her tears in check now, though her eyes were rimmed with moisture. "It was a cruel lie."

J.D. was assailed by desolate bitterness. He believed her. But that didn't help him accept the situation. He didn't know how he felt about divorce.

By outward appearances, Boots and Eugenia were divorced, or should have been. They neither resided together nor spoke to each other. Why hadn't they put a legal end to their sham of a marriage? He couldn't be sure. In all likelihood, it was Eugenia's faith in the church.

J.D. shoved his hands in his pockets to keep from reaching out to Jo and taking her in his arms. He was mixed up. His pride was wounded; his heart was broken. "Why didn't you tell me before?"

She leveled her eyes on his, lifted her quivering chin. "Would you have hired a divorcée?"

He wasn't sure. Probably not. Just because his way of thinking could be narrow at times. He was of the belief that a person only married once; and when two people said "I do," that meant weathering out whatever storm clouded the horizon. If the marriage couldn't withstand the turbulence, then it hadn't been strong to begin with.

He'd seen this with Eugenia and Boots. They had married for social gain. Never mind that they were entirely unsuited for each other. J.D. resented Boots's unwillingness to bend and give; and deep down, he resented Eugenia for not giving Boots a chance in Wyoming.

His parents' bad marriage had been enough to make him look with open eyes when he fell in love. It had made him cautious and careful about his feelings for Jo. But for all his prudence, he'd been caught blindfolded.

"Why did you marry him?" J.D. couldn't bring himself to say the name of her husband, but it echoed in his mind. *Hugh.* Now he knew whom she'd been talking about that first morning he'd awakened her. The name sounded pompous. J.D. hated him for that alone.

"I was eighteen when we met." She toyed with the frills on the edge of her handkerchief. "He was sixteen years older than myself, but he was nonetheless dashing. It was his maturity that attracted me to him. But it was my money that attracted him to me," she said with a chilling indifference that numbed the room.

J.D. remained quiet, letting her take her time. He didn't know what to say in any regard. He'd figured her to have come from a well-to-do household, but he hadn't estimated how lavish her life had been.

"At the time of our wedding, he'd been constructing a home on Fifth Avenue. Its construction had fallen behind, until it seemed that none of the carpenters showed anymore. But after we were married, the house was rapidly completed. I didn't question him about it. That was the Christmas my mother took ill and died.

"There were many financial dealings that Hugh was involved in, mine as well. As was the norm of marriages, my affairs were now handled by my husband. I knew I had a considerable dowry, but the exact amount was unknown to me. Through investments my father made on my behalf, I had an income of my own which was to be used as I wished. I also had a household account, but money never crossed my hands. I had no idea how much I was allowed, but it never seemed to exceed my limit at the shops."

J.D. had credit at Klauffman's, but he paid it off each season. He always knew what his running bill was and only bought what he needed. Not what he wanted. There were a great many things he wanted, but they were too precious to spend hard-earned money on.

He was beginning to see that Josephine could never be happy with him. He'd been dreaming when he thought she could. She'd been raised for finer things. All he could give her was simplicity.

"During the first two years of our marriage, Hugh was never with me. We went to parties, but he never stayed by my side. He had his clique of friends, and I had mine. There was never any chance for us to . . ." Her voice faded. "We never had children.

"For my twenty-first birthday, he threw a grand party, and I had thought . . . hoped . . . Hugh loved me . . . a little. He didn't. He never did."

How could the man not love her? J.D. wondered. How could he live with her and not see that she was worthy of affection?

Despair laced her words as she continued. "The only reason he gave me for the party was to celebrate his own success. On the day I turned twenty-one, my trust fund was given to me. I didn't know it at the time, but it was four million dollars—"

"Good God," J.D. blurted before he could stop himself. He'd never imagined that amount.

Josephine seemed oddly embarrassed by the sum. "I should have gone to my father sooner and asked him. But I didn't." A tear fell from the curve of her cheek to spot the front of her shirt. "I was being dutiful to my husband. My whole life was a chain of dutiful obligations I neither questioned nor disobeyed. My thoughts stayed within me, and the passions I idolized"—her voice broke into a whisper—"from the Beadle's were kept in the secrecy of my room."

J.D. couldn't believe that she was speaking about the Jo he knew. The Josephine Whittaker who had hired on as a cook wasn't subservient. She had her own thoughts and ideals, and he'd heard her vocalize them. On more than one occasion.

"Everything came crumbling in when the stock market crashed. I went to see my father immediately. He looked in poor health with his unshaven face and disheveled hair. He had remained unmarried, and our house at Madison Square lacked loving arms to embrace him." Her gaze grew distant. "At that moment, I forgave him for not loving me the way I had hoped. He, like the rest of us, was a victim of society, brought up within its tight walls of decorum where showing emotion meant weakness.

"But I felt he did love me that day. He put his head on his desk and mumbled his regrets . . . his apologies. At the time, I didn't understand why he kept saying he was sorry. But then I learned. Only it was too late.

"His death . . . it hit me hard." Fresh tears fell.

J.D. sensed there was more to the circumstances surrounding her father's death, but he remained quiet.

"I went through the motions of the funeral, numb and empty. Hugh didn't even have the decency to show up. Something inside me gave way." A wistfulness filled her tone. "I could never gain my freedom honorably, but I could gain a degree of independence through financial security.

"I sought my father's attorney and asked him the conditions of my funds and assets. It was then I found out that Hugh had gone through the entire four million on our—*his*—estate. My income from my father was gone the moment the market crashed.

"When I confronted Hugh about his duplicity, he said that life was made up of compromises and that he was no longer going to compromise himself. I didn't know what he meant until the following morning when I was delivered a term of divorce sent by his solicitor. The grounds were adultery. A lie."

She stopped crying, her face stoic. "Though I had not found passion in my husband's bed, I had *not* sought it elsewhere."

Her admission wasn't spoken to him, rather to herself. For she didn't look at him when she talked. "There were names. Not just *a* name listed. But *names* in the suit against me. I didn't know a single one of them. They had to have been made up. But nobody would question Hugh's accusation. He was a man. I was a woman. I was human property at his disposal. He used me. He took away my virtue and my self-worth." Her tone grew bitter. "I'll never forgive him for that."

The handkerchief in her fingers was wadded into a ball, then twisted. "I confronted him on his falsities. He was so cruel, it pains me to recollect his hateful words. He said he'd only married me for my money and that I was useless to him. I had never given him an heir, and I had no more income."

"What did you do?" J.D. hadn't been able to ask her anything until now. Now his anger at this man Hugh surfaced and simmered at his waning self-control. Had Hugh Whittaker been in this room, J.D. would have taken a whip to his hide until he bled the injustices that Josephine had endured under his roof.

"I moved into an apartment with a friend. The divorce decree was granted two months ago. At first, I retreated from everything and everyone. Even my own anger. But after weeks of solitude, I came to the conclusion that my divorce was a source of self-revelation. I was free of social pressures and prejudices. I was at last my own self.

"There was a party at the Beauchamps'. I'd thought it would be a fitting place to show my newly found independence. But I was shunned. I was so humiliated that I left rather quickly and made a blind decision to come out West.

"Actually, it wasn't blind. I'd been thinking about it for a while. Only I hadn't had the courage to actually come. I had no money. What clothing and jewelry I had taken from my home I sold for train fare." She undid the handkerchief and wiped her nose. "I don't need the confines to dictate to me. I can survive on my own."

J.D. admired her mettle, but by the same token her resolve left him out in the cold. "So you don't need a husband because you can take care of yourself."

She shook her head. "I didn't mean that. I would like a husband . . . perhaps . . . one day. But now I can't. I've been a daughter and a wife. I've never been a woman until I met you. I'm afraid . . . I'm afraid if I marry you, I won't keep what I've gained. I can't risk losing the distance I've come." Her gaze searched his. "Can you understand that?"

J.D. slowly pushed away from the door, weighed down with a heaviness on his chest. He had no right to make her feel worse than she did, but he went ahead and said what was on his mind anyway. He guessed it was because he was still a son-of-a-bitch after all. "About all I understand is, you don't love me enough, or at all, to trust me not to crush you, Jo."

With that, he turned. He had to leave. He couldn't stay and face her anymore. Not when the only things left to say were the raw stings of an aching heart.

CHAPTER

→ 22 ←

Josephine stood next to the corral where Freckles was kept. The calf trotted to her and vocally complained about Josephine not bringing a bottle.

She rubbed the calf's head between her ears, staring through eyes clouded with tears.

She'd been worthless at breakfast, scorching the bottom of the cornmeal mush pot until the mixture lumped together like a clump of half-cooked beans, and the salt pork had been fried to the tenderness of rawhide.

Her concentration had constantly strayed from the kitchen and had fallen on J.D. She hadn't seen him this morning. He'd gotten up earlier than she, and she hadn't heard him in the kitchen. She didn't think he'd eaten anything or had a cup of the coffee that the cowboys lived for.

His chair at the table had been empty, but she didn't dare question his whereabouts with Boots's gaze blazing on her at every move she made.

Boots hadn't come into the kitchen to give her his usual tidbits of advice. The first she'd seen him was at the breakfast table, and his eyes had never left her as she made her rounds with the coffeepot. His constant staring had been unnerving. It was like he knew what had happened between her and J.D.

After J.D. left her room, she put away her cards and left the ticket on her washstand. There was no sense hiding it. Although she'd bought it because of a misunderstanding, that didn't mean she didn't intend to use it this Thursday. She had made her intentions clear, and there was no going back.

Freckles nudged Josephine's hand when she quit stroking her fingers across the wiry hair on the calf's head.

"Y'all are spoiling that cow," came Boots's crotchety commentary from behind her. "When I eat her, she's going to taste like sugar and not beef."

Josephine turned her head but didn't cease her swirling scratches on Freckles's ear. "You aren't going to eat Freckles."

"The hell I ain't. I can eat any cow on this place if I take a mind to. Give me an ax, and I'll kill every last one of them. They aren't pets." The fringe on Boots's buckskin shirt dangled as he put an arm over the railing and tweaked Freckles's fuzzy ear. The calf bawled and went scampering away.

"I wish you wouldn't do that."

"Do what?"

"Be so mean."

"Y'all have never seen me mean."

She gave him a sideways glance, wanting to differ with him but remaining silent.

"How come you turned J.D. down?" Boots asked with a thread of harsh accusation.

Momentarily startled by his words, Josephine didn't say anything. Why had J.D. discussed what had happened between them last night with Boots? Inasmuch as she wanted them to mend their rift, she was dazed with dread over Boots's confrontation.

"J.D. told you?" she gasped, still in disbelief.

"He didn't have to tell me anything. I heard y'all say no to him." His eyes pierced the space between them. "I came into the house to get my cigars on the mantel when I heard y'all in the kitchen. I stood behind the door and listened. Then y'all ran off into your bedroom, and I couldn't hear anymore."

She had no time to be appalled, as Boots continued without a breath.

"But what I overheard . . ." He ruefully shook his head. "I have never heard J.D. talk to someone the way he talked to y'all. He got things out in the open, which is a lot more than I can say for me and him. He's not good at expressing his feelings, just like me. I guess that's why we don't know each other." Boots's scratchy voice sounded old. "I didn't think he had it in him to talk that way. I reckon I've misjudged him. I wasn't exactly what he needed when he was growing up . . ."

His fingers, bent and scarred and with craggy nails, rubbed the underside of his nose. He sniffed, as if he were capable of crying. "So why did y'all turn him down? He loves you."

Josephine was sick with the struggle within her. She didn't want to have to go into her past with Boots. If all he'd heard was her refusal, then none of that was necessary. But how could she make him understand by generalizations? Boots, in spite of his expandable moods, was a detail person. He picked up on anything that needed attention.

And obviously, he felt that what had transpired between her and J.D. needed his attention.

"My reasons are private," Josephine finally offered on her behalf.

"Bullshit," Boots snorted, making her flinch. "Y'all are in love with him. Have been since y'all got back from Bircher. I noticed right off. Y'all were moon-eyed over him."

She couldn't deny that. "I do care for your son," she said, pushing her hat farther back on her head. "But I'm going to San Francisco."

"What for?"

"To start my life over."

"What for?" he badgered.

Frustrated, Josephine balled her hand into a fist. "Because I can't return to where I came from."

"Everybody has something they look back on with bitterness and regret. It doesn't have to ruin your life. Life marches on, or so it should." He pointed a finger at her. "I suggest y'all get on with it. Right here. With J.D."

"I can't."

"Y'all can, but don't want to."

The wind picked up the brim of her Stetson—a leftover article of her men's clothing that she couldn't part with because J.D. had given it to her—and blew the crown high, right into Freckles's corral. Rather than stay and argue with Boots, Josephine lifted the latch and let herself inside to retrieve the tumbling Stetson. In her haste, she didn't close the gate. The hat swirled and tripped toward Freckles; the calf caught a glimpse of it and raised its tail before running through the open gateway.

"Freckles!" Josephine called to the retreating calf.

Boots made a lunge for Freckles, but he missed her and fell onto his knees. "Good gawd," he moaned as he swayed to get back on his feet. His hands pushed at the ground, but he could barely get up.

Josephine dashed to his side to help him, putting her hands beneath his arms. "Are you hurt?"

"Of course I'm hurt! Y'all'd be hurt, too, if your bones were nearly sixty years old. But gawddammit, my mind is not gone yet, and I'm tired of everyone treating me like I was an invalid."

Once on his feet, he shrugged away from Josephine as if she pained him even worse by her concerned touch.

"I'll get Hazel to ride after her," Josephine said, then ran toward the barn.

One-Eyed Hazel had been trenching pasture irrigation that morning. His saddled paint horse stood tethered to a tree branch outside the barn while he rummaged around inside for the tools he needed.

Josephine came up to the wide-open double doors just as the horse behind her nickered. She wouldn't have paid it any mind if not for the sound of Boots's voice.

"Stand still, you bonehead."

Whirling around, Josephine stared in horror as Boots stood on the porch steps where he'd maneuvered the horse. He wasn't capable of mounting on flat ground, but at this level he could swing his leg over the saddle and take a seat.

"Boots!" she called. "What do you think you're doing?" Then she yelled, "Hazel!"

"To hell with Hazel. I'm not sitting on my duff around here anymore. If I can't ride, then y'all tell Hazel to get his shotgun and shoot me in the head."

With that, Boots kicked his blunt heels into the horse's flanks and took off in a lope down the drive of the ranch.

Josephine put her hand to her mouth, then rushed into the barn and yelled again. "Hazel! Hazel! Come quick!"

He came out from a shed area in the back, a shovel in his hand. "What?"

"Boots is riding your horse. I didn't close the gate, and—he's gone to get Freckles."

Hazel threw the shovel down and was instantly by her side. Rounding the corner of the barn, Josephine shaded her gaze with a cupped hand. "There he is!" She motioned to the horse and rider in the fore pasture.

Boots had slipped the coiled lariat free of the saddle and was attempting to lasso the calf. With amazing dexterity, he managed what he'd set out to do; but just as he caught Freckles by the neck, the horse hit a hole and fell. Boots toppled over the paint's neck and landed like a rag doll on the short grass.

Josephine and Hazel ran. They reached Boots, and Josephine collapsed onto her knees by his side.

Boots lay on his right hip and ribs, his right arm above his head. A swath of steel-gray hair covered his scratched forehead; blood trickled from his nose. His eyes were closed.

Her hand touched the sleeve of his shirt, the skin beneath the fabric warm. She and Hazel gently rolled him over.

Gazing into Boots's battered face, Josephine cried, "Oh, Hazel! Find J.D." Her voice broke with a sob. "Hurry . . ."

Boots's room was neat and orderly. The framed tintypes on his bureau individually displayed his sons in their Confederate uniforms. A single reproduction of Eugenia McCall had been set off to the side on a crocheted doily.

Furnishings were old and worn yet comfortable. A reading chair was upholstered with tufted burgundy leather, the seat indented in the middle. Blue-checked linen made up the coverlet, as well as the pillows on the bed. The curtains had been drawn, and a lantern glowed softly on the bedside table.

J.D. sat next to Boots. He held his father's hand; the skin was as dry as the riverbanks, and the bones in his fingers seemed to be as fragile as those of a sparrow.

Having been doctor to both cattle and people out of necessity, J.D. had assessed Boots's condition before he and the boys had moved his unconscious body inside.

Boots had some broken ribs, the lower two or three on the right. J.D. had wrapped them, but not so snug as to constrict Boots's breathing. J.D. couldn't be sure about the hip until Boots regained consciousness. He'd cut up his cheek, and the blood had spread to make that damage look worse than it was. He hadn't required stitches, but the gash at the cheekbone still lightly oozed blood.

J.D. picked up a damp cloth and wiped it across skin the texture of parchment. He paused at the temple, stroking his thumb over the band of skin that stayed white from the brim of his hat.

The trickle of water squeezing out of the cloth and into the washbowl was the only sound in the room, empty of anyone but Boots and J.D. He'd sent everyone away. He hadn't even allowed Josephine, who wept quietly in the shadows, to remain. J.D. was on edge with the hovering presence of the others. It was as if they were waiting for Boots to expire.

Not that J.D. really believed that. Nobody on the place wanted Boots dead, in spite of how they felt about him at times.

J.D. combed the silvery hair from Boots's creased brow, his fingertips passing over closed eyes to tenderly stroke and make peace. How long had it been since he'd touched Boots as if it meant something? Had he ever? He didn't know . . . he didn't think so.

It was a hell of a thing, to have an accident make J.D. recognize the need for a relationship with his father before it was too late.

But deep down, he was afraid of Boots. Afraid Boots would reject the idea of being father and son.

What had he been thinking, taking off on Hazel's horse like that? The fool. No damn calf was worth it. He was too old to ride. And he knew that. When Hazel had charged up to him and told him what had happened, J.D. had been gripped by a fear so potent and primitive, he swore he'd make amends with Boots if he was given another chance.

Boots stirred, his mouth tightened, and a moan slipped past his parched lips.

"Boots?" J.D. whispered, dropping the cloth into the bowl once more and retaking his father's hand. "Boots . . . how do you feel?"

"Like I'm dying," came the choked reply.

J.D. sucked in a breath, then calmed down enough to say, "You're not going to die. You just took a bad fall. You'll be all right."

No reply came. Boots had slipped away again.

Josephine found J.D. in the barn. Dust motes hung in the slants of sunlight that poked between the rafters. The day was nearly gone, and J.D. had spent its entirety in Boots's room. A little while ago, she'd heard the creak of the screen door as J.D. let himself outside.

She'd stayed in the dining room, letting him have his space for a moment longer. But she couldn't stay away anymore. She hurt for him. She wanted to help. Guilt stabbed at her. If she hadn't left the gate open on Freckles's corral, the calf wouldn't have gotten out, and Boots wouldn't have ridden that horse.

Hazel told her he'd given J.D. sketchy details, but Josephine wanted to tell J.D. herself. She wanted to explain that she hadn't meant to be so careless. But he'd shut her out. Just like he'd shut everyone else out of Boots's room.

And there he'd been for half the day, refusing dinner and not answering her when she'd knocked an hour ago. She'd gone away and left him with his father. But now that she'd watched him go into the yard, she had to follow him.

J.D. hadn't closed the doors to the barn, and she quietly walked in. She saw him at the tall workbench where a high stool had been pushed out. He sank onto the seat, stared into space, then shuddered.

She was about to go to him, when he put his face in his hands and broke down. He hunched over, a single tear breaking through the dam of his fingers, winding its way down his wrist to catch on his sleeve.

The heavy door creaked behind her and caused J.D. to look up and discover her. Wordlessly, she went to him. She opened her arms and took him in her embrace. He held on to her. For a change, it was her giving herself to him to lean on for support.

J.D. closed down his emotions, for she didn't feel his sorrow next to her heart. After a while, he pulled back and looked into her eyes. She felt she needed to say something to give him hope.

"I never told you about how my father died," she began, unable to resist smoothing a lock of his hair from his brow, but sorry for it afterward because the gesture was too intimate. The wall that had come between them was too tall for soft touches these days. "He lost everything in that stock market crash, and rather than face the facts that he was ruined and start over . . . he chose to die." She braced herself for his reaction, taking in a heavy breath of air. "He put a gun to his head and shot himself."

"Jo . . ."

She shook her head, not wanting his comfort or his pity. That wasn't why she was telling him. "Boots, he's a fighter. That's why he got on that horse. He'd rather fail at trying than not try at all. There was nothing you could have done to stop him, even though . . ." She couldn't finish the thought. She couldn't tell him that the accident had been her fault. That the guilt was tearing her up. Maybe Boots would have done something daring sooner or later, but he'd done it because she'd given him the chance. For that, she couldn't forgive herself.

"You can be his son still. I know you want to," she said quietly.

"I do," J.D. replied in a whisper. "I just wonder if we let things go too long."

"It's never too late as long as you're both together. You have the chance that I never took. I'm envious of you in that regard. I only wish . . ." She shook off the thought. This wasn't about her. This was about J.D. and Boots. "Just be patient with him. And have faith."

J.D. didn't say anything, and Josephine suddenly felt awkward. The reality of their situation hit her. Although they'd been lovers, at this moment they seemed like strangers. He was wary of her intentions, and she couldn't blame him. She was no less confused herself.

Suddenly feeling like an intruder, she slipped away from him. "I've got to check on supper," she lied, needing an excuse to leave.

Boots drifted in and out of coherency for the next several days. J.D. was the only one who tended him, and he reported very little the few times he sat and ate with the rest of them.

The meals were badly prepared, Josephine reverting back to her old habits of not fully reading the recipes. She omitted ingredients, or she put too much in. None of the boys complained, for their appetites had dwindled in the wake of Boots's accident.

Though nobody said anything directly to her, Josephine feared they thought the worst of her. She wasn't sure; perhaps it was just the unsettling guilt that she couldn't shake. But the atmosphere in the house was like that of a tomb.

Everybody spoke in a low voice, politeness was to the extreme, and rather than playing cards in the front room at night, early departures were made for the bunkhouse.

Thursday came and went, the train to California having departed without her. Josephine couldn't leave without knowing if Boots would pull through.

Friday, Josephine couldn't stand the solitude any longer. Around two o'clock, she got out a can of corn and attempted to make creamed corn on toast. It smelled a little peculiar compared to the kind Boots made, but it looked the same.

She arranged the bread on a plate and scooped a portion of the corn mixture on top. Then she went out the back door and picked a red tulip as decoration. After folding a napkin precisely, she grabbed a spoon and headed for Boots's room.

The door was closed, as usual. She knocked, but this time she didn't wait for J.D. to send her away. After their talk in the barn, they'd walked on eggshells around each other. But the strain was wearing J.D. down. He was snappish with the hands, and he could be short with her.

She let herself into the room as if she had been invited.

J.D. sat beside the bed in the oversized wing chair. His head snapped up upon her entrance, as if he'd been dozing. She made no mention of it as she crossed the room and set the plate on the bedside table.

"I made Boots some creamed corn on toast."

J.D. frowned. "He won't eat it. He's barely touched the soup I made him."

"Well, maybe he doesn't like soup."

"I know what he likes and what he doesn't."

Josephine refused to be put off. She dragged the wooden chair that was tucked beneath a writing desk over to the bed. Sitting, she folded her hands in her trousered lap.

"How is he today?" she asked firmly, looking J.D. directly in the eyes.

His eyes were bloodshot, and his chin prickled with three days' worth of beard. He looked horrible.

"He's better," J.D. replied, his voice edged with dryness from disuse. "He had a slight fever the past two days, but it's gone now."

Hope welled in her. "That's encouraging." She gazed at Boots, who lay still as the sheets. His complexion seemed just as white. The sour lines that normally marked his mouth had relaxed in his sleep. His breathing was even, his chest rising and falling softly.

"He woke up a while ago, when I gave him some of

the soup. He looked at me . . . like he was looking at me for the first time."

Josephine nodded her understanding.

Boots shifted his legs, then winced. His eyes fluttered open, and he stared for a long moment at Josephine. "Where the hell've y'all been?"

A smile trembled over her lips. "Here."

"I thought y'all were going to San Francisco . . ."

"Not today."

Managing no more than a hoarse whisper, he said, "Tomorrow?"

"Not tomorrow, either."

His nose twitched. "What stinks in here?"

"Your supper," Josephine admitted.

"I'm not eating anything that smells like dirty socks." He closed his cornflower-blue eyes and exhaled. "Where's that damn tabby cat?"

Josephine and J.D. traded looks, then J.D. replied, "In the barn, most likely."

"Go find him for me. I'm tired of y'all leaning over me like I'm a gawddamn corpse."

He let out a sigh, then the muscles in his face relaxed as he slept once more.

Boots's recovery was slow but steady. The next few days, J.D. sat in the room, allowing visitors to pay their respects. Boots gained some strength, but he slept a lot. J.D. had checked the rest of his joints, and nothing else had been broken or cracked as far as he could tell. Boots had asked for and had been given very small doses of laudanum to help with the pain in his ribs. But other than bed rest, there wasn't a whole lot that could be done. Time was the best medicine.

This morning, Boots had eaten a bowl of cornmeal mush with molasses. Afterward, J.D. had shaved him. Boots had put up a big stink about it, saying he could do it himself. But he could barely sit up when J.D. challenged him. In defeat, he'd fallen back into the pillows and had grumbled his consent.

Convinced Boots was on the mend, J.D. had been outside for a time today. He'd ridden in the close proximity of the house, to check on the irrigation trenches Hazel was working on and the lot fences that needed repairing.

Sitting in the broad chair by the bed, J.D. fought off the sleep that threatened to claim him. Normally, he could adjust to minimal shuteye, but that was when he was physically tired. The past week had drained him emotionally. He hadn't made any strong effort to put to rights the trouble between himself and Boots, as he should have done before. But the time had come when neither of them could afford to chase away the other. They were all they had.

He wasn't sure how Boots would react to his efforts, or if he should even come right out and say that it was time for them to put an end to their arguing. He had nobody to confide in . . . well, there was Jo. He would have talked to her about it, but he was unable to open himself up to her again.

Though the Thursday train had come and gone and she was still here, that train came through every Thursday. Her ticket was still good, and as soon as Boots was up, she'd eventually use it.

The sleeping cat curled up next to Boots's side stirred, causing Boots to rouse. His head turned in the direction of the chair as he opened his eyes. "Y'all're still here," he said, spoken more as a fact than a question.

"I reckon I am."

"Y'all've got better things to do than sit around with me."

"Not especially."

"That's bullshit, and y'all know it." Boots lifted his hand slightly in a gesture of disgust. "Y'all've always been mule-headed."

"Runs in the family."

"I expect it does." He gazed into space, his look one of vague amusement. "I remember when y'all were thirteen and thought you were dead tough. Y'all never listened to me." Struggling to lie higher on his pillows, Boots winced as he moved but glared off J.D.'s help as he resettled himself. "Y'all got your first six-shooter about then. Some idiot gave it to you."

"Lucas Strickland."

"He was a no-account."

"I liked him."

"He gave you a gun with the cylinder burnt out. Y'all told me he made you promise not to load it, to just pretend to shoot it." He frowned in exasperation. "What kind of a bonehead did you think I was? Nobody gives a boy a gun and then expects him not to load it."

J.D. brought his left calf to his right knee and sank deeper into the comfortable chair. "Lucas told me to just use caps with it. Caps and balls."

"Then how come William nearly blew his hand off?"

"Because he took it from my room and loaded it for real. I told you that. You didn't listen to me."

"I heard you. I didn't believe you."

"Sounds like you," J.D. said, then instantly regretted his sarcastic words. "You took an ax to that gun."

"I remember. But y'all got yourself another one."

"Of course I did."

Boots gazed at him with directness. "Back when I was a boy, I waited until my father gave me a percussion rifle."

"I didn't know they had them back then."

"What do y'all think I used?" he scoffed. "A flintlock?"

"I don't know. You never told me."

"I never told you a lot of things."

A silence gathered around them, a long and wistful pause filled with memories that were as solid as the furnishings in the room.

Quietly, J.D. asked, "Do you think William and Lewis are in heaven?"

Boots's face was expressionless a moment, then softened. "Eugenia does. I guess I believe it, too."

"Yeah . . . so do I."

Fingering the edge of his blanket, Boots said, "I wasn't fair to y'all after they died. I was missing them so much, I neglected the son I had left."

"I wasn't much help in making it easier on any of us. I ran away from the problems and came out here."

"And y'all did a fine job of turning into a man on your own." Boots's eyes grew cloudy. "I never told you, but I'm damn proud of all you've done. Even though I've never said it."

J.D. pulled in a slow breath, then said, "It's because we've been mad at each other for a long time."

"Have we?" Boots's white brows arched. "I thought we just didn't like each other."

"I like you enough, Boots."

"Is that right?"

"Well, dammit, you sure make it hard for me to like you."

"I don't need anybody to like me."

J.D. sat straighter. "Now who's full of bullshit?" He combed his hair away from his forehead. "You get a kick out of the boys joshing with you. If they didn't like you some, they wouldn't do it."

Boots grumbled. "Y'all have been inside too long. The sun can't soak through your head and warm your brain up to snuff. Y'all're not thinking." His hooded eyes narrowed down on J.D. "If you were, y'all'd be trying to win your sweetheart back instead of wasting time with me."

J.D. hadn't realized Boots knew anything about him and Josephine. Had she told him? When?

"I went and got my hopes up for y'all. I thought that by next spring, I could be taking my grandson into Walkingbars and opening up an account for him," Boots said matter-of-factly.

"How'd you know about me and Jo?"

"I live here," he muttered dryly. "I don't always

hear, but I can see. I've got two eyes that can look right through that knothole in y'all's head."

How Boots had figured out his relationship with Josephine didn't really matter. There was nothing to be done. He'd asked. She'd said no.

"She's got plans," J.D. remarked, lowering his leg and tenting his fingertips together over his chest.

"Her brains don't weigh an ounce of that two-ton idea. San Francisco isn't going to make her happy if y'all're not there with her." A frown set into Boots's features but ebbed away to a secret smile as he dug his fingers into the fur on the cat's belly for a slow scratch. "She's in love with you."

"She told you that?" J.D. shot back, damning the glimmer of hope that caught him.

"Didn't have to. I can tell."

J.D.'s optimism fell; cynicism took over in its wake. "Since when are you an expert on love?"

"Good gawd, but y'all're going to make me lay you across my knee," Boots retorted. "I know what love is. I love Eugenia."

"I didn't know that."

"I've always loved Eugenia. From the moment I first saw her. It's just that her and me, we can't live together. Doesn't mean I love her any less," Boots simply declared. "She wasn't happy here. She likes Boston, and that's fine with me as long as I don't have to live there, too."

J.D. stared wordlessly at him. He'd never have figured Boots to admit such a thing. All these years, he never thought his father loved his mother. But he had cared; that's why he let her go.

"Now, Josephine, she's not like Eugenia," Boots continued. "She doesn't need any fancy city to make her happy. She likes it here all right. She just doesn't know how much."

"I can't force her to stay." J.D. locked his hands on the chair's arm rests.

"I don't think y'all can afford to watch her go."

Their eyes locked. J.D. admitted to himself that Boots was right. He couldn't tell him he was right, but his gaze probably said as much.

J.D. was the first to look away. Disconcerted, he folded his arms across his chest. This was the longest, most honest conversation he and Boots had had in more years than J.D. could remember. He was at a loss over how to proceed.

Luckily, a knock sounded on the door as it opened. Josephine's head peeked around the corner.

"I just wanted to see how he's doing," she whispered to J.D. before looking at the bed.

"He's not pushing up daisies," Boots answered cryptically, causing Josephine's head to turn in his direction. "This room is about as placid as a duck pond. Something better liven it up, or I'm liable to expire from the boredom." Motioning to J.D., he said, "Get a deck of cards. We'll show the cookie here how to play twenty-one."

"I don't want to intrude," Josephine said.

"You're not," Boots assured her.

J.D. got up from the chair and went toward the door. Josephine stayed still, and J.D. couldn't go around her. "The cards are on the mantel," he explained.

She stepped out of his way, and he left.

Josephine knit her fingers together and waited. She had been in the kitchen most of the morning making peach pies. Alone with Boots, she was at a loss over how to say what had to be said, even though she'd had plenty of time to gather her thoughts properly.

She'd visited Boots in tiny intervals this past week, never staying overly long when J.D. was in the room; and never when he wasn't. She didn't know how to broach the subject, but she had to, so she came out and said, "I'm sorry you got hurt. It was my fault."

Boots shot her a withering glare. "Good gawd, but y'all can be greener than manure. You think because you left the gate open and that cow got out, that I just up and went loco?"

The tabby cat stood up, arched its back in a stretch, then recurled itself by Boots's side.

"I was going to get around to riding a horse sooner or later to see if I still knew how. And by gawd, I did. It's just that the horse caught his foot in a go-down. How is that paint, by the way?"

"He's okay. He had a little scrape. Hazel saw to him."

Boots's face displayed an uncanny awareness that said he saw clear through her. "A person ought to say they've made a mistake rather than go through with what they were intending just for pride's sake. I ought to know."

Before she could reply, J.D. returned with the cards. He brought the extra chair to the bed, then sat down himself.

Josephine hesitantly took a seat. She wavered, trying to decide whether or not she wanted to play cards. It wasn't the game itself that made her indecisive, rather her own emotions that reeled inside her. Her mind was unsettled with confusion. She had fought against believing what her heart had been telling her. And that was: stay and be J.D.'s wife.

But it was like Boots said, she'd made her decision and she felt she had to live with it because she was convinced leaving was the right thing to do. But whenever she thought ahead, her future looked vague and shadowy when she tried to imagine what life would be like in San Francisco.

"I must be worse off than I thought," Boots said with a lift of his nose, "because I smell peach pie."

"You do," Josephine replied. "I took four out of the oven a little while ago."

J.D. shuffled the cards. "I'll deal," he said stiffly, then tossed out three cards facedown in a circle on the blue coverlet.

Josephine had seen the cowboys play this game

before, but she hadn't ever sat close enough to determine its object.

Once the red-backed card was in front of her, she reached out for it but stopped short with a jump when Boots exploded, "Good gawd, y'all don't touch your card before the deal is done."

She mumbled her apologies, not particularly in the mood to be the brunt of Boots's sour temperament at the moment. There were times when she thought him the dearest man, and others when she just wanted to scream at him. She didn't think he'd ever change, but she'd hoped that the accident would have humbled him a little.

J.D. went around again, this time leaving cards faceup. She remained still, not moving a muscle.

"Well, go ahead and look at your bottom card now," Boots advised. "Just don't show anybody."

She did, feeling J.D.'s gaze on her. It was hard to be in the same room with him, feeling as if they were closed off and yet so far apart.

"Now, what you have to do is get twenty-one. That means your cards need to add up to that amount. Jacks, queens, and kings are ten. An ace is either eleven or one."

Josephine didn't utter a word. She was somewhat confused, her concentration just not targeted on the two of clubs that was exposed or the eight of hearts that wasn't. "I'm supposed to add these two numbers together?" she asked in a general question.

J.D. replied with a soft drawl that skimmed across her skin and made her tingle. "You take the two that's faceup, and you add it with the number of the card beneath it. You want the total to be twenty-one."

"All right."

Boots took his faceup card in his hand and flicked it abruptly across the spread. "Hit me."

J.D. tossed him another card, then looked at Josephine. "Do you want another card?"

She nodded.

He dealt her the ace of diamonds.

"Ho!" Boots declared. "Could be she's got twenty-one."

Josephine couldn't remember what the exact rule was about the ace card. Had Boots said it was worth one point or eleven points?

Boots flopped his cards to the center. "I'm busted."

J.D. took another card. "I'm out, too."

Wordlessly, she exposed her eight card. "I think I have twenty-one."

"Don't think it," Boots muttered, then began gathering up the messy pile of cards. "Y'all win."

"Oh . . ." But her heart just wasn't in the victory. J.D. sat to her right, the tension in his body visible from the tight set of his jaw. This wasn't any easier on her. How could she make him see that she had to go? But then again, how could he accept her departure, when she herself was having a hard time accepting it?

J.D. dealt another hand, and while he made the second pass with the faceup cards, Boots commented, "They've got a lot of gambling houses in San Francisco. And a lot of whores. It's not the kind of city y'all're used to, Josie girl. What are y'all going to do there?"

Josephine gazed at her cards but peered right through them as she replied, "I don't know . . . I haven't figured that out yet."

"Y'all've got to figure it out before you go. Y'all can do passably well with cooking, but is your calling to be a grub cook in a café?"

"I don't think so."

"Then what else can y'all do?"

Josephine thoughtfully bit her lip. "I can arrange a nice table setting."

"Is that all?"

"No," she countered, somewhat miffed. "I'm an excellent hostess."

"The only hostesses in San Francisco work at the bordellos." Boots flicked his cards, and J.D. shot him another one. "How do y'all look in your underwear?"

"What the hell kind of a question is that?" J.D. demanded, tossing what remained of the deck onto a ripple in the coverlet.

"A factual one," Boots barked back. "Y'all know as well as I, them hostess girlies greet the customers wearing nothing but a lacy shawl—if that—and silk underwear."

J.D. jerked to his feet. "Goddammit, I'm not playing cards anymore. Not when you're going to shoot your mouth off about ladies' underwear in front of Jo."

"I'm just stating a fact." Boots scooted a few inches higher on the pillows and swore as he did so. "She ought to know the kind of town she's headed for."

"What do you know about it?" J.D. shot back. "You've never been there."

"I know about it anyway."

"You know about everything. You're never wrong."

"The hell I'm not. I've been wrong about a lot of things, only I just don't admit it."

Their quarrel came to an abrupt halt when they apparently remembered Josephine was present, but its aftermath crackled through the room with the same electricity as lightning.

Josephine stared at her cards on the coverlet, then lifted her gaze. "I'd better go so you two can . . ." *Can what?* Finish yelling at each other? She felt she was being intrusive. She'd rather they work things out, but J.D. was halfway out the door.

She stammered, "Boots, J.D. is leaving."

"Good. Good-bye."

When she turned to leave as well, Boots called out, "No, Josephine, y'all stay on a minute. I need to talk to you."

Boots's tone softened to such a degree she was compelled to oblige him. She drew up to the bed. He fished something from beneath the covers and shoved it into her hand.

Looking down, she saw that it was a palm-sized wood carving of a cat. "Why, Boots . . . you made this."

"Whittling gives me something to do."

"Thank you." Tender emotions filled her.

"Yeah, well, never mind about that. I need y'all to ride out to the northeast line house and get my Bible," he said. "I'd ask J.D. to get it, but he doesn't put any faith in the Good Book. He wouldn't waste his time going out there."

"How far a ride is it?"

"Just follow the fence line that runs parallel to the house. The first shack y'all come to with a small corral in back, that's it."

"Oh. But I'm certain I don't have to go that far. One of the boys probably has a Bible that they'd—"

"I want my own." He trifled with the bed coverings, inching them toward his chin. "Have y'all ever read Psalm Twenty-three?"

"The Psalm of David . . . yes. But I've forgotten exactly how it goes."

"Well, y'all ought to refresh yourself. Y'all might have to use it on me. I didn't want to say anything to J.D., but I'm feeling poorly."

"You are?" she said in a fearful rush. "You have to let me tell him."

"No!" Boots snapped so loudly the tabby jumped off the mattress and hid beneath the bed. "Don't let J.D. know y'all're going out there. Y'all keep it quiet. Sneak out to Hazel, and watch for J.D."

"But . . ."

"Good gawd, I thought I could count on y'all to do this for me."

Josephine helplessly acquiesced. "All right, Boots. I'll get your Bible for you. It may take me a while."

"Take your time."

* * *

"I need y'all to ride out to the northeast line house and get my Bible." Boots licked his dry lips, and J.D. offered him the glass of water on the bedside table. J.D. had been gone from the room for half an hour when Boots hollered through the house for him. "I'd ask Josephine to get it so that y'all could stay with me, but she doesn't know a horse's ass from its head. She's liable to get lost."

J.D.'s eyes narrowed skeptically. "Don't start in on Jo again, and since when do you read the Bible?"

"Since I say I've got a notion to," he snapped.

"What'd you leave it out there for?"

"In case I ever got bit by a rattler when I was all alone checking the fences." He coughed and held his side with a grimace. "I figured I could give myself my own eulogy. There ought to be something in that book that applies to me." Glaring at J.D., he asked, "Now, are y'all going to get it or not?"

J.D. shoved his hands in his pockets, not relishing the idea of the two-hour ride with the steel-gray clouds that had been forming. "Looks like a storm coming in."

Boots didn't let up. "Are y'all or not?"

"Good God," J.D. countered, "I'll get it. But it may take me a while if the rain comes."

With a half-smile, Boots replied, "Take your time."

CHAPTER

➤ 23 ◄

Josephine had been riding Peaches for more than a good hour, and she still hadn't seen any signs of the line shack Boots had told her about. All she'd seen was miles of short-grass pasture and cattle. There weren't nearly as many of them as there had been on the drive. But every now and then, a small group of the brown-and-white-faced cows stood chewing their cuds by a stand of scrub brush.

Red-winged blackbirds soared in a heavy sky that threatened a downpour. Although she didn't want to be caught in a storm, she hoped it would rain. They needed a torrent of it to fill up the creek that meandered through the property.

Josephine mentally chided herself. She wasn't part of the *they*, as in Josephine and J.D. She was an outsider. A hired hand. A cook.

But she could have been more. If she had let herself.

She hated leaving without J.D. understanding her reasons for turning him down. But how could she make him understand when she herself was having a hard time coming to terms with her decision?

She wanted desperately to salvage their relationship. To remain his friend. No . . . that wasn't the truth. She wanted to be more than his friend. She wanted . . .

Peaches's ears prickled. In the distance came the rumble of thunder. Josephine shuddered. It had taken all of the courage she possessed just to get back on the horse after having been thrown off. All this way, Josephine had been gripping the saddle horn with one hand and the reins with the other. If Peaches spooked, Josephine would be stranded out here by herself.

The rumbling came again, only this time it didn't sound like the growl of thunder, rather the pounding of hooves. Fear prickled the back of her neck. Hazel had protested her riding out here alone. But her insistence, her mentioning that Boots had asked her to get his Bible because he was feeling so poorly, had made Hazel relent. After saddling Peaches and giving her a leg up, he'd cautioned her against the two bulls that roamed the land and could be grazing anywhere.

The image of the bulky animal with its pointed horns made her throat go dry. Maybe one of them was charging in on her to—

"Josephine!"

She swung her head to the right with a thump of her heart.

"What are you doing out here?" J.D. asked, reining his horse alongside hers.

The thought of being discovered hadn't crossed her mind. Hazel had said that with the foul weather coming in, the boys would be staying close to the main pastures. She hadn't thought up a reasonable excuse for why she *was* so far from the house on a horse.

"I . . . I felt like going for a ride." She could never lie very well to J.D. He'd known from the start she wasn't a cook, and he'd know right now that she wasn't telling him the truth.

"Who saddled that horse for you?"

"Hazel."

"Did he put you up to this?"

"No."

"Somebody did."

Josephine worried the inside of her lip. It was no use. If she had to be honest, she'd be vaguely honest and not admit to the graveness of the situation. "Boots wanted me to get his Bible."

"Oh, hell." J.D.'s brows shot down in a frown. "He told you that?"

"Yes."

"Damn him."

"J.D., I don't think—"

"He told me the same thing."

Josephine grew puzzled. "He did? He asked you to get his Bible, too?"

"He probably doesn't even have a Bible in that shack."

Clouds rolled on top of one another along the horizon. The wind picked up, ruffling the end of Josephine's braid that rested across her shoulder on her breast.

"We can't turn back now," J.D. said. "There's no telling what this weather's going to do."

"How far do we have to go?"

"Not that much farther."

They rode in a brittle silence, Josephine not knowing what she should say. She periodically glanced at J.D. from the corners of her eyes, noticing how his hands held the reins. He'd tucked his gloves into the band of his pants, and his bare fingers gripped the strips of leather.

His hands were slightly swollen, cut in places by the barbed wire that fenced off his prideful possession: the land. Though she couldn't see his gaze directly as he stared ahead, she felt it. His eyes reflected a strong spirit that mirrored a good heart.

She had never known a man like him. So rugged yet tender.

Against her will, a tear slipped from her eye, and she quickly dashed it away.

"Keep a watch for cattle," he said. "They might run if a stab of lightning comes down."

She nodded, unable to speak.

The fence line seemed endless, yet it wasn't long enough. This might be the last time she'd ride with J.D., and she wanted to remember the details. But she couldn't keep a clear head.

She felt J.D. occasionally watching her as the wind kicked up the curls that had formed at her temples from the dampness in the air. He couldn't be finding her attractive in the Stetson and men's clothes she wore. At length, she asked, "Why do you keep looking at me?"

"I'm thinking you ride like you've been riding on a ranch all your life."

Those words got to her, and it was all she could do not to break down and cry. All the agonized endurance she'd had to go through in the kitchen and on the drive was suddenly justified by this man's simple faith. It was more than she'd ever been given her entire marriage . . . and it was what she wanted were she to marry again.

Too soon, the line house came into view. J.D. led her horse into the corral, helped her dismount, then closed the gate on Peaches and Tequila. He opened the door to the shack and let her enter ahead of him.

The building was small and plainly furnished. There was no shade on the window, and what little glare of sunlight was beyond the clouds outside came filtering in with a soft gray tint. A wrought bedstead butted against the north wall, along with a crate that was used as a stand for the kerosene lamp. She didn't see a Bible on it, or any other place in the room. The only other thing was a potbelly stove.

"Where do you suppose the Bible is?" Josephine asked.

"There is no Bible," J.D. replied as he swung the door closed. "Boots sent us out here on a blind chase."

"What do you mean?"

"I mean, he thought he could bring us together." J.D. checked the stove for kindling. "Frankly, I didn't think he had it in him to be so damn clever."

"I didn't think he did, either."

After closing the stove's door, J.D. removed his hat and ran his hands through his hair. "We'll head back as soon as the storm passes over."

She nodded, then sat on the bed's edge. There was no other place in the room to relax, so J.D. joined her. They both sat with the tips of their boots facing the stove; they both stared ahead.

It was J.D. who broke the silence. "I know of a cattle buyer in San Francisco. He's got a nice wife. I've met her once. I think you'd like her." J.D. rested his elbows on his knees and examined the scars on his hands. "I'll telegraph him and let him know you're coming. They could put you up for a while until you get settled."

Josephine was speechless. She managed to say, "You'd do that for me?"

J.D. turned his head toward her. "Of course I'd do that for you."

She was unable to contain her tears, and they fell freely. "I thought you'd forget about me . . ."

His thumb reached out and touched her chin, gently rubbing. "Now, how could I forget you, Jo?" His voice dropped in tone. "Every time I see the forget-me-nots on the banks, I'll remember that blue hat of yours."

She lowered her chin to her chest, and suddenly she felt very ashamed and selfish. She'd hadn't given J.D. a chance. He wasn't like Hugh. She knew that. She'd known it all along.

"I'm sorry, J.D.," she cried. "I didn't mean to hurt you. It's just that . . . for all the time I was married, I never once did anything outside of convention. I did what was expected of me, and I was miserable in silence. So when I left New York, I told myself that from now on, I would be my own woman and go my own way. I'd do things for the fun of it." She gazed at him. "I'd be my own woman."

"You are that, Jo. I never tried to make you feel anything but."

"I know that. But before I came to realize it, I'd set my mind on going to San Francisco and being independent. I wanted to have my own home and do what I wanted in it."

"And so you should," he offered quietly. "You could have had my home, Jo. I would have given it to you."

She brushed at her tears. "That's so sweet . . ."

He caught her by the waist with his strong arm and brought her to his chest. His hand cradled her cheek, and he forced her to look at him. "I wasn't doing it to be sweet, so quit thinking I'm trying to impress you. I don't have a lot of money, and I never will be as rich as the men you've known. But I love you, Jo. And what I have is yours. I've got no use for it alone. Hell, it means nothing without you." His thumb caressed her cheek. "I'm not saying I like your decision, but I understand it, I suppose. You need to prove to yourself you can do it. But, Jo, you have to look at where you've been. Here. With me and the boys. When you came, you didn't know squat about ranching . . . or cooking," he said with a soft smile. "But you tried. And you learned. And you got better. You proved more to yourself here than you ever will in a city full of strangers."

His thumb caught a tear before it fell beyond his fingers. "Just so you'll know, I'm proud of you, Jo."

She couldn't meet his eyes any longer. It hurt too much. Burying her head in his shoulder, she spoke against the warm fabric of his collar. "Boots said a person should say they've made a mistake rather than go through with what they were intending just for pride's sake."

"He said that?"

"Yes." Her tears wet the material.

"Have you made a mistake, Jo?"

She heard the hope, yet fear, in his voice. She felt the same things in her heart, only they weren't the same hopes and fears. She hoped he could still love her; she feared that it was too late.

J.D. held her at arm's length and gazed into her eyes. "Do you still want me to take you to Sienna?"

"Sometimes . . ." she said in a shaky voice. "For more flour and sugar . . . beans and coffee when there's the need. Maybe some butterscotch candies, and a pattern and material . . . for a wedding dress. But I have to warn you, I can't sew as well as I can embroider."

J.D.'s hopeful smile was lost on her lips as he kissed her soundly. She kissed him back, dozens of small, loving touches of her mouth on his.

"I love you, J.D.," she whispered as he held her close.

"I love you, too, Jo."

Rain began to patter on the window, softly at first, then like splatters of pebbles as the sky opened up wide to a long-awaited spring shower.

A droplet fell on Josephine's nose, and she tilted her head. "There's a leak in the roof."

"Probably more than one. Nothing's ever fixed around here. There's always something that's broken."

She smiled into the curve of his shoulder. "I can help you fix things."

J.D. leaned back and pressed a quick kiss to her lips. "I can't think of anything more important that needs fixing right now than this." His mouth covered hers in a slow, arousing kiss as he laid her back on the cot.

Josephine was lost in the hazy world of desire. Everything inside her was in disorder. She felt hot, as if she were blushing across every part of her skin. Her blood raced through her veins, and her heart hammered. The heat seared a path to the pit of her stomach, and she wanted more than anything to surrender to the man she loved when she remembered Boots. He may have lied about the Bible, but . . .

"We can't stay," she murmured against J.D.'s lips. He put his weight on his elbows. "It's Boots. He told me not to tell you, but he said he wasn't feeling very well. I don't think he was lying."

J.D. shifted and sat up, lifting Josephine with him. "How do you figure he wasn't lying?"

"He wants me to reread Psalm Twenty-three. It's the one about greener pastures." Her brow furrowed. "The one they say at funerals."

"Boots is always going on about dying."

"But what if he really is in great pain? I think he might be."

J.D. pushed his hat back, gazed out the window at the steady flow of rain, then at Josephine. "All right. We better get back, then."

An eerie kind of silver fog rolled in, the likes of which J.D. had never seen. All of a sudden, there it was. A thick blanket of it, so dense he could barely see five feet in front of him. If the fence hadn't been there to direct them back, he would have lost his bearings.

But as quickly as that fog came, it evaporated, leaving in its stead a sound rainfall to drench him and Josephine as they came upon the outbuildings of the ranch.

Toby raced out to greet them, tail wagging. As they rounded the corner of the bunkhouse, the front yard came into view. Boots sat outside in his oversized wing chair, hat on his head, a saucer heaped with a wedge of pie in his hand. He hadn't dressed; his striped nightshirt was plastered to his chest and only came to his pale calves; but his feet were covered with a pair of high stockings and boots.

He brought a spoon to his mouth, and the pie on it

was dappled with rain before he got to chew the peaches and crust.

"What the hell are you doing?" J.D. hollered at him as they rode up, disbelieving what he saw yet knowing that with Boots anything was possible.

Boots laughed. A deep and earthy timbre, a rich, full-hearted sound. "Eating peach pie."

J.D. cocked his head and blazed, "Are you drunk?"

"I'm drunk on rainwater." Boots ate another bite of pie.

"You're going to catch your death." Josephine dismounted from Peaches and handed the reins to Hazel, who had come down off the porch where he'd been standing. "Hazel, how could you let him sit out here like this?"

Hazel gazed at her with his one eye, then shrugged. "If a body knows what's good for him, he doesn't argue with Boots."

J.D. swung his leg over Tequila and stalked to Boots. "Jo said you were ailing badly, but you didn't want to tell me."

"I'm not sick. Just a few broken ribs."

"Then why'd you send us out to that line shack for a Bible that wasn't even there?"

"If I'd've told y'all to go out there and get me a box of cigars, y'all wouldn't have gone."

"You're sure as hell right."

Boots ignored J.D. and gazed at Josephine. "This is some mighty fine pie, Josie girl. Will I be able to eat more of them until the day they put me six feet under?"

Josephine put her hands on her hips. "You tricked me."

"Will y'all be staying, Josie?"

He ignored her indignance, but she couldn't stay mad. A smile inched the corners of her mouth upward. "I reckon I will be."

"Hey, J.D., she talks like us now." Boots enjoyed another spoonful of pie.

J.D. wasn't amused. Although he and Josephine had settled things—and he was damn glad they'd gotten the chance before it was too late—the fact still remained, Boots had sent them on a wild chase in a storm that could have proved to be dangerous. For himself, he'd brave it, but he would never have forgiven Boots if something had happened to Josephine. "You sent us out there for nothing, you crazy son-of-a-bitch."

"That's Dad to you," Boots cautioned sternly.

J.D. stared, complete surprise taking hold of him and anchoring him to the spot. An unexpected warmth surged through his body, and he startled himself by replying, "You aim to sit out here for a while, Dad?"

"I expect I will until I finish my pie."

There was a slight tinge of wonder to J.D.'s voice when he turned to Josephine. "Would you mind bringing out a piece of that pie for me, Jo?"

She was already making her way up the front steps. J.D. moved toward Boots, taking the rawhide chair that Hazel brought down from the porch and angling it next to his father's. He took a seat, shaking his head at the absurdity of the moment.

Rain sputtered downward, dripping off the brim of J.D.'s hat and landing in his soaked lap as he crossed his legs.

"How long y'all reckon it's going to rain?" Boots asked, drops of water dotting his chin.

"I couldn't say."

Josephine returned with the pie but left before J.D. could thank her. He turned around, only to see Hazel and Josephine retreating into the house. Facing front, J.D. took a bite of the pie. Its crust was buttery the first bite, a little soggy the next, but he didn't mind.

He was sitting with his father for the first time, and nothing else mattered.

→ Epilogue ←

For her wedding present, J.D. gave Josephine the one-hundred-sixty-acre parcel of land that fit like a puzzle piece into the McCall Cattle Company range. It was the very spot he'd shown her that spring day when they'd gone out riding after returning home from Bircher.

It had taken most of the summer to fence it off and include it with the rest of the land, but J.D. kept the line of barbed fencing up that kept her property separate from his. He'd told her it was so that she could feel she had something of her own.

J.D.'s thoughtfulness had filled Josephine with more love for him than she ever thought possible. But it wasn't separateness she wanted out of this marriage. It was togetherness.

So on a fall day, just days before they would set out on the roundup, J.D. and Josephine had ridden out to cut the wire and knock down the fence posts. Birdie, Gus, Jidge, and Print had come along to help. As did Hazel with the wagon, with Boots sitting on the bench seat to watch.

Freckles, who'd grown incredibly big, stood on the opposite side of the fence, ears pricked.

"I never heard of anyone thinking a cow was

lonely," J.D. said as he took the wire cutters to the barbs and snipped the two-row string between the posts.

"Freckles wants to be with the rest of her kind." Josephine walked around him with a shovel and loosened the dirt at the base of the split rail.

J.D. kicked the post over; several other posts down the line fell as the boys clipped their segments free. Soon the space was wide open.

Boots did a little tip of his hat from his seat in the wagon. Josephine smiled at him. He'd given her away at their small, but nonetheless inspiring, sunset wedding on the top of the Tepee Range. She and Boots had prepared the wedding feast themselves.

Josephine gazed at the band of gold on her finger, the sunlight glinting off the precious circle. She cherished it more than anything she'd ever owned.

The wind ruffled her skirt, beneath which she wore trousers. It was easier to ride with the pants, but she liked the femininity the skirt had to offer. In a couple of months, she wouldn't be able to fit the pants on at all. She hadn't told J.D. yet, but she planned to once they were at the spring range. If he knew her condition now, he probably wouldn't let her go. And where would a chuck wagon be without the cook?

J.D. had hired Matt Sellars after all. He'd taken up the kitchen duties and would go along for the drive, but Josephine wanted to do the pie baking for the boys.

Freckles came trotting over, tail swishing and looking to Josephine before running off toward a patch of sagebrush where the calf's cousins lay with lazy eyes.

J.D. drew up to her and put his arm around her waist. "Just because the fence isn't there doesn't mean this land isn't yours. It is, and it always will be."

She nodded with a knowing smile. "I just don't like fences, is all. I like the wide open."

Winking at her, J.D. headed down the line toward the boys.

Josephine watched him go, her heart so swelled with love she thought she'd die of happiness.

Seasons for her had always meant changing fashions and parties. They now represented a greater importance. Here, seasons dictated a way of life. Birthing and regrowth. An anxious earth, waiting for its pleasure, and so grateful in return by giving back the grass and greenery. It was a life cycle in which the simple things mattered.

An hour later, when the fence had been cleared away and the pieces loaded into the back of the buckboard, everyone headed home. J.D. and Josephine straggled behind.

Tequila and Peaches probably thought it an entirely silly proceeding, but they reluctantly allowed themselves to be persuaded closer together, and then Josephine took her pleasure in another range technique.

A kiss while in the saddle could be very satisfactory.

Dear Readers:

Thanks to Barbara Ankrum and Rachel Gibson for their helpful critiques of this novel. Most especially to Sue Rich, who was extremely insightful. And without a doubt to Caroline Tolley, whose patience and understanding is what every writer dreams of in an editor. Without the library of Rose Gonzales at my disposal, in all likelihood this story would have taken on a different twist. Reading diaries and nonfiction accounts of women in the West unglorified my predisposed opinion that Wyoming in the mid-1800s would have been a cool place to live.

Although I'm a skilled chef in my own modern kitchen, I'd like to think that I could have done as capable a job as Josephine did on the trail drive over her fire pits; but when it comes to "camping," I'm a wimp. Unless there's a hot shower and a flushing toilet available, it's not for me. Oh, and insect repellent is a must.

To appease my family's yearly insistence that I go on a camping trip with them, I just bought an eleven-by-eleven-foot dome tent, two queen-size air mattresses, four cushy sleeping bags, a propane stove, a propane lantern, and some flashlights. I figure if I have to go along, we're going to do it with as little "roughing it" as possible.

I hope you enjoyed J.D. and Josephine's story. Let me know what you thought of *Forget Me Not*. As always, a self-addressed stamped envelope is helpful in speeding my reply.

Happy Trails,

Stef Ann Holm

Stef Ann Holm
P.O. Box 121
Meridian, ID 83680-0121

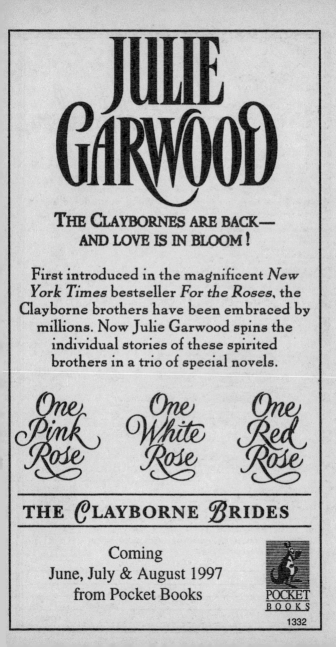

JULIE GARWOOD

THE CLAYBORNES ARE BACK—
AND LOVE IS IN BLOOM !

First introduced in the magnificent *New York Times* bestseller *For the Roses*, the Clayborne brothers have been embraced by millions. Now Julie Garwood spins the individual stories of these spirited brothers in a trio of special novels.

One Pink Rose   *One White Rose*   *One Red Rose*

THE *C*LAYBORNE *B*RIDES

Coming
June, July & August 1997
from Pocket Books

POCKET
B O O K S

**POCKET BOOKS
PROUDLY PRESENTS**

**Book One in the
"Brides for All Seasons"
Series**

HARMONY

STEF ANN HOLM

**Coming Soon
from Pocket Books**

**The following is a preview of
Harmony. . . .**

MURPHY MAGEE WAS KNOWN for his humorous antics when he was three sheets to the wind—which was each evening from around six o'clock until whenever Lynell Pickering, the bartender at the Blue Flame Saloon, cut him off.

When the hour neared midnight, Lynell told Murphy it was time to button up and be off to bed. Swilling down the last dram of whiskey from his tumbler, the wobbly Murphy allowed himself to be suited up for the elements by the barkeep.

Nudged through the door, Murphy stood on the boardwalk and recoiled as the wind blustered his face. The gusts whistled through tree boughs, stirred up foliage, and ruffled the storefront awnings on Main.

Warding off a shiver, Murphy set out on a path down the middle of the street. He had the niggling feeling that he had done something twice, but he couldn't recall exactly what.

It had rained while he was in the Blue Flame, the air now smelling like worms and musty wood. Large round puddles lay scattered before him like silver mirrors. He approached a shimmering pool, peered over scuffed boot toes, and gazed at his reflection. A fat white face rested on his shoulder.

Murphy quickly swung around, staggered, then searched the nearby shadows for a trace of the chap who was following him. No one stepped out to reveal himself. With a wry snort, Murphy meandered along until the next puddle, and that very same milky face hovered at his ear. As he turned around this time, he stepped backward. The wet splash at his feet caused him to look down once more.

In the rippling water, not only were his features distorted, but so was the man's face, which was as plump as pudding.

"Aye . . ." Murphy slurred with a broad grin at the reflection of the full moon that hung high in a dark sky. "I know who you be now, Mr. Man in the Moon. So you think to follow me, hey?" Then he purposefully jumped double-footed into the puddle with an uneven laugh. He wavered as he watched his face and the moon above him settle on the surface once more.

Giving the moon a crude gesture with his middle finger, Murphy moved on. He tried to remember the people he'd spoken with today. . . . Lynell Pickering's voice was the most prominent, but a few others came to the surface.

A lopsided smile hitched the corner of his mouth. There had been that Miss Edwina Huntington. A pretty lady, but too prissy to suit his fancy. She'd been nice to him, though. She'd given him five hundred dollars. *Why . . . ?* He couldn't readily recollect. Then he believed he'd traded words with Tom Wolcott. Tom he liked. The man was as red-blooded as they came.

For some reason, Murphy thought that his business with Miss Huntington in some way connected with Tom . . . but nothing came to mind.

Another puddle loomed, and Murphy hopped square into it, taking pleasure in the spray he sent onto the pavers. The road was torn up a bit here and there to make way for the sewers Harmony's Department of Public Roads had taken it into their fool brains the town needed.

Murphy ambled toward home with that great albino face in the sky floating after him. At every puddle, he took a leap dead center. It became a game of sorts as he met with each one. He paid no heed to the crude fence and its sign of dim words that faded into the night. All he could see was the circumference of the biggest of all puddles—just behind the slats of wood.

Disregarding the barrier, Murphy leaped skyward. Only he didn't connect with the ground. His feet sliced into a giant void.

"Sweet Jay-sus!" His lament echoed in his ears, yet was lost on the wind.

As Murphy plunged to a sure death, an ill-timed revelation sobered his brain. It was the queerest of moments to remember. But remember he did.

He knew now why Miss Huntington had given him five hundred dollars, and why Tom Wolcott had sought him out this evening at the Blue Flame.

Sweet Jesus. If the fall didn't kill him, surely the pair of them would once they found out what he'd done.

As Tom Wolcott rode his piebald into Harmony, a party of six exhausted but satisfied men fell in behind him on plodding horses. Their duckcloth hunting suits, spanking new a week ago, now bore smatterings of mud, dung, and blood. But they'd gotten their great outdoors thrill in Montana, having bagged between them two elk, a cougar, and a half dozen hares.

Cutting across Main Street toward Hess's livery, Tom spied Shay Dufresne lounging in the sunlit double-wide doorway. Seeing his old friend and new partner, Tom sat taller in the saddle, and his mood lightened. From now on, Shay would be in charge of the expeditions while Tom got his arms-and-tackle store off the ground.

"Hey, partner," Tom greeted, reining in and dismounting. He held on to the bridle leathers in one gloved hand while gripping the hand of his friend in the other. "When'd you get in?"

"Three days ago." Shay gave him a warm smile, laugh lines etching creases at the corners of his eyes.

Tom spoke around the cigarette in his mouth. "Max put you up?"

"As best he could." Shay withdrew his hand. "With all the crates and boxes you have stacked to the rafters, there's barely a free inch left to put up a cot."

Aside from stabling over two dozen riding and pack horses with Max Hess, Tom had been using the livery as his warehouse and temporary business quarters.

"It'll all be moved out tomorrow." Over his piebald's rump, Tom called to the grin-happy city slickers. "Gentlemen, unhitch your gear and trophies. There's a butcher on Hackberry Way who'll dress the meat, and if you want those horns mounted, I'm the man to see."

"By jinks, I want the whole head and neck on a lacquered wall plaque," came a jovial reply from the Bostonian banker.

"I can do that." Just as Tom tethered his horse on the branch of the only tree in front of the livery, a droopy-looking bloodhound came trotting up. The dog shook off and shot his owner with Evergreen Creek water. "Dammit, Barkly, you could have done that elsewhere."

Barkly sat on his haunches; wet, loose skin hung in folds about his head and neck. His nose lifted toward Tom, and he made a grunting noise through his black nostrils.

"Don't tell me anything I don't know," Tom said offhandedly to the canine. With a flick of his wrist, Tom tossed his smoke on the ground and crushed the butt with the instep of his boot. "I need to make myself feel human again."

Tired and dirty, Tom longed to shed the navy lace-up-at-the-throat sweater that hugged his shoulders. Dust-coated Levi's and chaps encased his long legs. His knee-high boots bore the nicks of twigs and pine needles. The stubble phase of a beard had lapsed into grubby; and he smelled like campfire smoke, game, and wet dog. He wanted nothing more than to soak in a hot sudsy tub, shave, then slip into a fresh set of clothes.

"Making yourself human will have to wait. A lawyer

came by twice while you were gone." Shay slipped his hand into his pocket, produced a calling card, and read, "Alastair Stykem. You know him?"

"I've never met him, but I know he's got an office on Birch Avenue."

"He's real anxious to talk to you."

"About what?"

Handing Tom the card, Shay shrugged. "Hell if I know. I told him you were expected back today. He pressed me for a time, so I gave him one. You've got a two o'clock appointment at his office."

Tom swore beneath his breath. "What time is it now?"

Shay fingered a watch out of his vest pocket. "Two-ten." Gazing up at Tom, he said, "I figured you'd be in by noon."

"We got that cougar just before lunch, and we had to pack it."

"You better get on over there. I'll handle things here."

To the dog, Tom instructed, "Wait," then to Shay, "Whatever this is, it better not take long."

Leaving the livery behind, Tom walked down Main for a block, giving cursory glances to the post office, Savage Feed and Fuel, and Buskala's Boarding House. He'd rather have been going in the opposite direction so that he could take a look at the warehouse on Old Oak Road. A vacant lot away from the blacksmith's stood the building he'd bought from Murphy Magee. The interior measured a good size: comfortable to stock his merchandise and display his trophies with plenty of aisle room. For the past few months, he'd spent nearly all his income on sporting goods to fill his store. Tom had been taking men on hunting trips for the better part of a year. The trial period was over. His advertisements in eastern papers had proved successful in attracting suit-and-collar types out West for camping adventures.

Grasping the handle of a door, Tom let himself inside a vestibule that housed the faint scent of ink. He crossed the granite floor tiles to a narrow stairwell on his right. He reached the top, where a single hall featured two doors. In gold lettering, the first had ALASTAIR STYKEM,

ATTORNEY AT LAW spelled out. Tom walked into the office.

A young woman in a high-buttoned blouse sat behind a receiving desk with one finger plucking at keys of a typewriter. On his intrusion, she looked up and down, then up again; then left and right as if she planned on fleeing. A pair of wire bow spectacles perched on her thin nose. Black ink smudged her forehead and chin.

"M-May I h-help you?" she stammered, not meeting his gaze while pushing her glasses farther up her nose. She left an ink smear across the freckled bridge.

"I have a two o'clock appointment."

"M-Mr. W-Wolcott?"

His nod went ignored because she refused to lift her head. He had to resort to saying, "Yes."

"T-They've been waiting for you."

They?

The woman stood, kept her gaze pinned to the carpet's cabbage rose pattern, and took a few steps to the paneled door. Knocking, she stuck her head through the crack she'd opened. "Mr. Wolcott is here," she announced in a clear, smooth voice.

"Good. Send him in." An exasperated breath punctuated the man's next words. "Crescencia, wipe that typewriter ink off your face."

"Yes, Papa."

Crescencia withdrew, then backed toward the desk so Tom couldn't see her face—as if he hadn't already. Mumbling into the hankie she'd produced from a fold in her skirt, she said, "Y-You may go in, M-Mr. W-Wolcott."

Tom slipped by the desk and with his shoulder nudged the interior door the rest of the way open.

Alastair Stykem sat with his back to the window, sheer curtains deflecting the intensity of afternoon sun. Upon Tom's entrance, the lawyer rose from behind a massive oak desk and extended his hand. Tom had to step further into the room to grasp it. After the formality, he felt a presence to his right and looked down at the occupant in the chair. A pair of pale, mint-colored eyes leveled on him. The woman had rich mahogany hair swept away from her oval face.

Huge bows ran around the band of her hat, sprouting a large blue chrysanthemum.

The lawyer's voice pulled Tom's gaze away. "Mr. Wolcott."

"Stykem," Tom acknowledged.

"You know Miss Huntington?"

Tom's glance once again landed on the seated woman. "I've seen her around." But he had never inquired after her. An old-maidish air surrounded the way she carried herself. Tom would have guessed her ten years older than him. But up this close, he could see he'd been mistaken. He had to have had her by at least five.

"Well then, please sit down, Mr. Wolcott."

Tom lowered himself into one of the plump leather chairs, but he didn't feel at ease in the cushioned depths. Anxiousness made him reach for the half-pack of Richmonds in his front pants pocket, but he stopped himself midway when he saw the disapproval on Miss Huntington's face.

"I see no reason for preamble," Alastair continued. "Miss Huntington has known about the situation for a week, so I'll come right to the point." The lawyer steepled pudgy fingers against his paunch. "Murphy Magee is dead. He fell into a sewer hole last Monday night and sustained fatal injuries."

Tom regarded Alastair quizzically for a moment. Some sixth sense made him proceed with care. "I'm sorry to hear that. Murphy was a regular guy."

"Be that as it may, in light of his death a problem has arisen that only Mr. Magee could have settled. Since he's not with us, the case has been brought to my attention by the county recorder's office in the hope that I can mediate a peaceful conclusion to this unfortunate situation."

The words *county recorder's office* cautioned Tom into silence. Resting his foot on a dusty knee, he pressed his back into the chair and depicted a comfort he didn't feel. Before he'd left Tuesday morning, he'd slipped the receipt Murphy had given him beneath the door to the county recorder's office so that he could pick up the deed when he got back into town. Obviously something had gone wrong. Maybe the clerk needed more information. Maybe Murphy hadn't written out the bill of sale correctly. The man had been drunk when they'd made the transaction at the Blue Flame. Even if Murphy had messed up, why was Miss Huntington sitting primly in the chair next to him?

Alastair opened a folder before him and produced two identical documents. He held them out for Tom to see. "As you can read, the warehouse at 47 Old Oak Road is deeded to both you and Miss Huntington. The clerk had recorded Miss Huntington's title on a Monday afternoon and yours on a Tuesday morning. For legality's sake, it doesn't really matter whose was recorded first or last. Both are binding. If Mr. Magee was here with us, he could explain how he happened to sell both of you his warehouse. By him taking money twice, he's committed fraud"—the lawyer gave a slight shrug—"but who can prosecute a dead man?"

Tom saw no humor in that. Accentuating the annoyance he felt with Stykem, Murphy, and Miss Huntington, who had begun to rummage through her purse, Tom brought his foot down hard on the floor and leaned forward. "What are you trying to tell me, Stykem?"

"You and Miss Huntington are both the legal owners of the parcel known as lot four, block two."

A cold knot formed in Tom's gut. Muscles on his forearms bunched as he took hold of the chair's arms and gripped the padded leather. If Murphy Magee wasn't dead already, he'd go for the man's throat. He should have known better than to do business with a man basted with whiskey. But Tom hadn't wanted to leave for the week without having secured the warehouse, so the transaction had taken place in the saloon.

He heard a dainty cough and sniff, then glared at Miss Huntington. "What do you have to say about this?"

Miss Huntington had brought out a hunk of lacy stuff and lifted the edge to her nostrils. "Mr. Stykem, I find I'm feeling a little lightheaded. Could you please open the window for ventilation?"

"Open the window?" Tom echoed. "You've known about this for a week. If anyone is sick, it's me."

She kept her eyes forward. Curved lashes caught his attention; they were softly fringed and the exact shade of her hair. His gaze lowered. A kind of feathery blue fabric gently outlined her figure, cutting in at her narrow, sashed waist. He knew enough about ladies' fashions to appreciate the fact that she wore pleats, bows, and trims in all the right places. Lingering on the controlled rise and fall of her breasts as she breathed into her handkerchief, he became aware of what he was doing. With a silent curse, he instantly stopped his appraisal of her.

Tom laid his palms on his thighs. "What now?"

The curtains fell back into place after Alastair unlatched the window lock and lifted the sash. He took his seat and pointedly gazed at the two of them. "Mr. Magee died on the installment plan—meaning, he owed people money." A shuffle of papers, and Stykem came up with a long list, from which he began to read. "Eight dollars and forty-two cents to one Madame Beauchaine of Tut Tut, Louisiana, for astrological readings, one dollar and ninety-one cents to Zipp's barbershop for a dozen goatees and a bottle of Imperial hair glue, three hundred and twenty-two dollars and four cents to the Blue Flame for a bar bill." Alastair waved his hand over the paper and set it down. "Et cetera, et cetera. Frankly, I don't know why he held on to the warehouse as long as he did. He could have used the revenue."

"What are you getting at?" Tom questioned.

"Murphy Magee's estate can't give a refund to either of you. After debtors get a hold of what he has left of the money you gave him, there'll barely be enough to cover my fees." Stykem bent his fingers and cracked the knuckles in succession from pinkie to thumb. "I didn't want to suggest this without you being together. But one of you could buy the other out. Of course that will mean you're paying twice for the property. You have to ask yourself, how badly do you want it?" Wiry brows arched as he waited for their reaction. Neither of them moved, so the lawyer continued. "Miss Huntington, you pay Mr. Wolcott five hundred dollars, and the warehouse is yours. Or, Mr. Wolcott, you pay Miss

Huntington four hundred and fifty dollars, and the warehouse goes to you."

"Four hundred and fifty?" came an indignant female squeak. "Mr. Stykem, I paid Mr. Magee five hundred dollars for the property."

"Yes, my dear, that is true. But the deal Mr. Wolcott worked out with Mr. Magee allowed him to buy the property for fifty dollars less than you paid."

Miss Huntington's rose-colored mouth thinned, and a blush crept up the ivory column of her neck. She was either highly embarrassed or angered to the boiling point. Tom couldn't tell for sure. He didn't really care. All he knew was he didn't have four hundred and fifty dollars with which to buy her out. Nor would he allow her to pay him five hundred for the right of ownership.

The warehouse on Old Oak Road was tailor-made for his needs, tucked away from the populace of the town in a semi-wooded area. A vacant lot sat on either side and to the rear of the building. He'd planned on setting up a target practice area out back, along with extension traps. He couldn't have that luxury in another building within Harmony's town limits.

"Well, hell," Tom exhaled at length. "That buy-out idea doesn't work for me."

"Miss Huntington?" Alastair queried.

"My business adviser would advise me against it. My funds are tied up and cannot be released to buy the building a second time." The piece of lace had been lowered onto her lap. She wound a corner of the handkerchief around her slender forefinger, then unwound it. Wind; unwind. Wind; unwind.

"Then we'll have to proceed the only other way." Stykem went to yet another folder and produced a bid form. "I've taken the liberty of having Mr. Trussel look at the property. For a moderate fee, he can construct a wall that will evenly divide the building. And he can frame in another entry door on the east side. You both would have your own entrances; however, he advised me that the storage room in the rear that runs the length of the building cannot be altered. Several of its posts are main supports to the roof, and tampering with them could be detrimental to the building's soundness. You would each have your own access to the area, only it wouldn't be sectioned in two like the main interior."

Tom mulled over the possibilities. He'd have to make everything fit in half the space. If he had to overload the walkways, where would he put his grizz? The bear had weighed six hundred pounds before he'd stuffed it. There had to be room for his mammoth eight-point bull elk, and the lynx he'd gotten last winter. He had an endless number of taxidermic fowl and small rodents that required counter space. Hunters liked to see trophies on display. And Tom had a shitload of them.

Massaging his temple, he fought against the idea of sharing the building with a woman who had a flower on her hat bigger than a moose's butt. He didn't like the thought of having to compromise with her. But it seemed the only choice.

"Forgive my saying so, Mr. Stykem, but I shouldn't have to pay half."

Tom gave the lawyer no opportunity to respond. "Sure you'll pay half."

Her gaze landed on his. "I shouldn't have to yield another cent." The tuft of lace resumed residency at her nostrils, and she spoke through the weblike pattern. "Already you've gotten your part of the building for fifty dollars less than me."

Alastair cut in. "I'm sorry, Miss Huntington, but the fact of the matter is, it doesn't matter if he paid one penny and you paid one thousand for the place. You both own separate deeds that have nothing to do with one another—except that they're for the same property."

She straightened. "Then my side should be at least a foot wider than his."

"There again, Miss Huntington, you can't measure against the original cost of the building. Both halves will have to be equivalent." A gold signet ring reflected light as Alastair twirled it on his finger. "So, are we all in agreement?"

"I'm afraid you leave us no other choice." Miss Huntington took the words right out of Tom's mouth.

"Mr. Wolcott?"

"It's like the lady said."

"Good, then everything is settled." Stykem tidied the documents on his desk. "I'll speak with Mr. Trussel and have him get started with the renovation right away."

Standing, Miss Huntington walked stiffly around the back of her chair to the umbrella stand and retrieved a folded parasol. "Good day, Mr. Stykem."

She'd gone out the door when Tom got to his feet and shoved his left hand in his pocket. "Stykem. I can't say it's been a pleasure."

The lawyer laughed. "I hear that a lot."

Tom stepped into the receiving office, where Miss Huntington and Crescencia were exchanging words. As soon as he came into the room, they shut up. He went past them, Crescencia saying, "G-Good day, M-Mr. W-Wolcott."

"Yeah, same to you." He let himself out, thinking he heard Miss Huntington say something like, *"Don't you fret about it, dear. You shall overcome, I assure you."* Whatever that meant.

Once down on the street level, Tom reached for his cigarettes and lit one while he stood on the boardwalk. As he waved out a match, Miss Huntington exited the building. She gave him a quick gaze, then proceeded. He had to go in her direction, so he trailed her. At the corner, they were forced to wait before crossing while the Harmony fire department backed its No. 1 engine into the firehouse.

He stood behind her. Tom was at least ten inches taller than Miss Huntington, so he had a view of the top of her hat. The air was as fresh as it could get out here, yet she started up with the handkerchief routine again. Then the reason hit him, dragging his pride down a notch. She thought he stunk. Hell, he knew he did. No wonder she'd had Stykem open the window.

On the proper heels of her shoes, Miss Huntington inched her way toward the curb. What did she think he was? A pig? He didn't like to be this in need of a bath, but when had there been time to put on his coattails before delivering himself in her presence?

Now realizing she was bothered by him, he cut the distance between them. His chest nearly pressed against her shoulder blades. He would have gone in even further if his jaw hadn't been in jeopardy of being run through by the lethal pin sticking out of her hat.

When she moved again, she went a bit too far and teetered. He grabbed her by the elbow before she could fall into the street.

"What's the matter, Miss Huntington?"

"Nothing." She'd swung her body halfway around so that she could gaze at his face. Exotic green eyes held on to him as physically as his hand held on to her arm. It was a damn shame such pretty eyes belonged to a guardian of morality.

The silkiness of her dress felt good beneath his fingertips, so he didn't readily release her. Because he'd been so bogged down in his business, it had been a while since he'd held a woman and explored the delights of perfumed skin. He wouldn't have guessed that by touching her elbow he could become aroused. But damn if he wasn't.

What had started out as teasing her was now teasing him.

Abruptly, he let her go, then took a deep pull on his cigarette.

"What are you going to do with your side?"

Her voice intruded in his head. Regaining a sense of indifference, he replied, "Sell sporting goods."

Speculation filled her gaze. "Oh . . ."

He felt obligated—not that he wasn't curious—to ask, "What are you going to do with your side?"

"Open a finishing school for ladies."

"What for?"

"To educate them in the rules, usages, and ceremonies of good society."

"You mean make them like you."

Her chin lifted, and for a minute he thought she might jab him with the point of her unopened parasol. "I should hope."

The boardwalk traffic began to move, but Miss Huntington stayed. "By the way, I hope you aren't *allergic*." She said the word as if she wished he was. "I'll be bringing my cat."

After giving her an uneven smile, he crossed the street and called over his shoulder, "No problem. I have a dog who *loves* cats."

Look for
HARMONY
**Wherever Paperback Books
Are Sold
Coming Soon from
Pocket Books**